Hour of the Wolves

A Novel by

Stephane Daimlen-Völs

illustrations by

Constantine Gedal

Printed in Canada

For information address:
Durban House Publishing Company, Inc.
7502 Greenville Avenue, Suite 500, Dallas, Texas 75231
214.890.4050

Library of Congress Cataloging-in-Publication Data
Daimlen-Völs, Stephane, 1951

Hour of the Wolves / by Stephane Daimlen-Völs

Library of Congress Catalog Card Number: 00-2001090316

p. cm.

ISBN 1-930754-08-6

First Edition

10 9 8 7 6 5 4 3 2 1

Visit our Web site at
http://www.durbanhouse.com

Book design by:
B[u]y-the-Book Design—Madeline Höfer & Jennifer Steinberg

In loving memory of
Emiliano Zabala Deheza

For
Werner Friedrich Höfer,
Sophie & Siggie

Hour of the Wolves

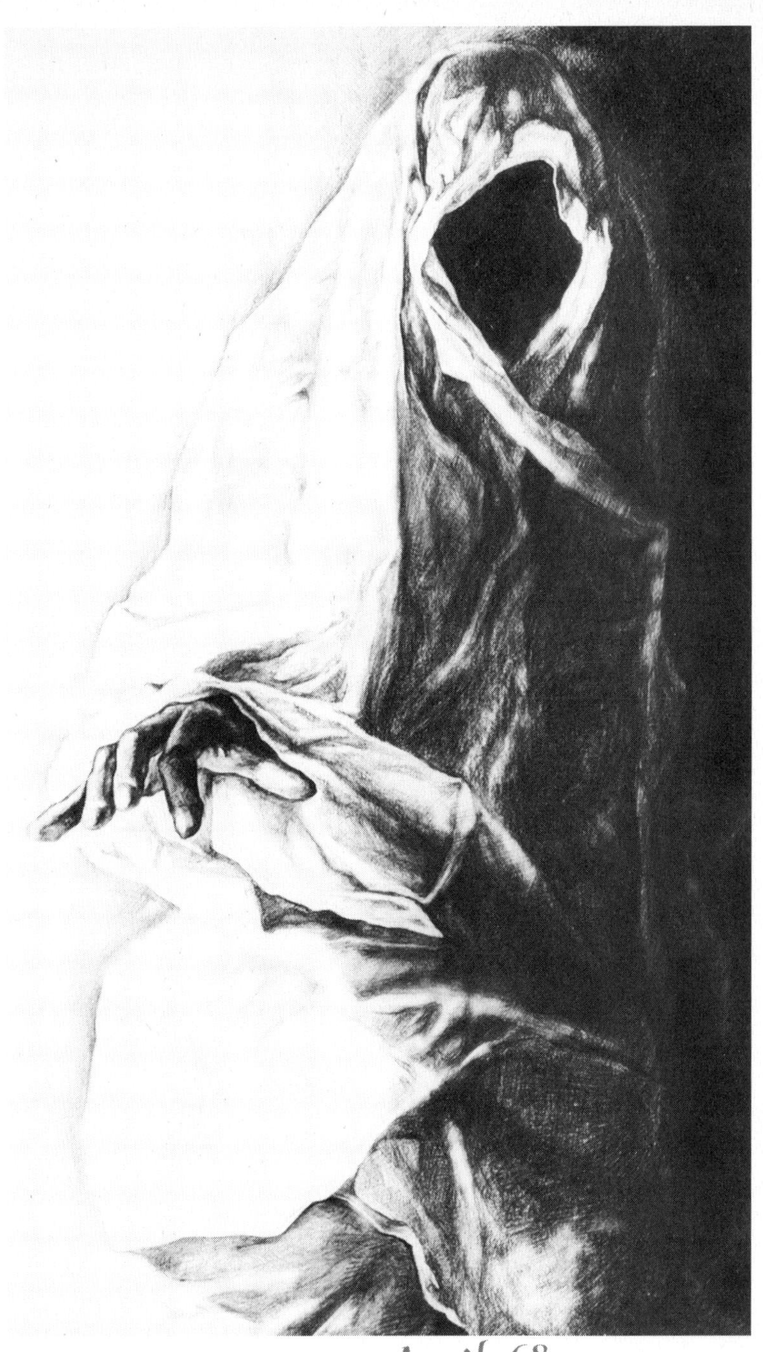

29 April 1682
Feast of Saint Catherine of Siena

White Paternoster: a prayer at twilight for Paradise lost

"Matthew, Mark, Luke and John, bless the bed that I lie on. Four corners to my bed, four angels 'round my head; one to watch and one to pray and two to bear my soul away."

No Act of Contrition? Have you forgotten prayer, Jean-Jacques-Armand Desgrez? This nightspell won't protect you from all evils lurking after sunset. Stand here, eclipsed in a seraphic nimbus casting its long shadow over you, and within this comfort look into my face. See, I am not the Son of Man.

Armand sang. "Hide me from the day's garish eye, for I never expected You would be so beautiful."

A thousand aeons past I was gloriously bright, thence after has been as nothing. Once I wore them all, the angels, as a garment transcending all in glory and knowledge. All of them together were not as beautiful as I. I was the brightest. Child of Light and resplendence itself. I am Son of the Morning fallen from Heaven to become Evening Star.

Armand sang. "Venus, the evening star, is on the horizon. It's twilight. I'm not afraid."

Hour of the wolf. Penumbra of the day when most births and deaths occur. Foreshadow and after-shadow of night. In the night, then you'll be afraid. For there's nothing man fears more than the touch of the unknown in the darkness.

Armand sang. "Venus, the morning star, is on the horizon. It's twilight. I'm not afraid."

Be you afraid, for I am with you always from every waking moment till dreaming sleep becomes dreamless death. I am the Touch in darkness. I am the Voice in temptation. I am the Kiss in life's final moment. I am Rex Mundi.

A son's fetish—A father's love

Friday—22 July 1667—Feast of Saint Mary Magdalene
A Carmelite Monastery—Aix-en-Provence

Yahweh's woman was made from a rib; Hephaestus worked in clay; a famed king of Cyprus preferred ivory. Beauty is in the gaze and every man fancies himself an artist or a necromancer, but to conjure the inanimate to life is a prerogative of gods.

Francois Galaup de Chasteuil was a man of overpowering willfulness for whom no woman was ever beautiful enough. His first concern was chestnut-colored hair. He liked it thick and with the sort of gloss particular to a well-groomed horse, a glow of robust health and vitality that comes from a suspension of sweat and body oils. He liked big-breasted women with small waists, nicely curved hips and milky white skin. Once impregnated with his masterly touch, he chiseled at his women till their skin was splotched black and blue, soured a sickly yellow and permanent bracelets of ruptured blood vessels and raw flesh encircled their ankles and wrists.

A hollow sound echoed in the chapel as pick ax slammed into floor. Hammer and anvil. Its cadence was of a smithy and not the rhythm of a cloister. With each punishing blow, stone gave a little until the mortar surrounding it cracked and larvae writhed up from the earth as workmen pulled away several slabs.

Armand Galaup de Chasteuil, attorney general of Aix-en-Provence, and his son-in-law, Georges Desgrez, pressed scented handkerchiefs over their mouths and nostrils. A foulness of spoiled meat and rancid fat cried out to heaven until Georges was overcome and vomited.

Chasteuil addressed the monks, "The prior and his secretary have disappeared?"

They nodded.

"When?"

"Several days ago. We've all been complaining about this smell for weeks. Especially in this heat. It's been impossible to hear Mass or say prayers."

"Can any of you recognize what's left?"

Several monks looked into the pit. A maggoty head smiled back, her crowning glory tarnished into a rat's nest matted with dirt and crusted blood. "The hair, Monsieur de Chasteuil. His mistress had a particularly thick head of hair, a very rich color of chestnut. He seemed to favor women with that sort of hair. Yes, it's she."

The corpse was pulled onto the floor, and as Chasteuil noticed familiar remains of some medieval contraption which still too tightly encased the pubes, Desgrez looked past the woman's bridled pelvis into her abdomen. He remembered, voiced an anguished cry and fled.

Go off and weep. Pathetic weakling. Hide away in the cathedral at Aix and beat your breast. Pester your confessor. Make the confession you've made a hundred times before. Which of your sins is so unbearable? Sins of omission aren't worth repenting. Where's the crime in being unable to prevent the unknowable? Why spend the rest of your life blaming yourself for something you didn't do? Chasteuil will only take advantage of your overly zealous conscience and go home to your wife in your absence.

Marie-Julie was beautiful, with long, thick hair the color of a roan horse. She had a nice curve to her hip and a small waist which had never been bloated or ruined by pregnancy. If Chasteuil had known she was barren, he'd never have bothered with the precaution of a husband for her.

Look into her eyes as she lies beneath you and think yourself fortunate to have such a lovingly compliant woman to share your bed. A model of every feminine virtue.

"Are you finished with me? May I get dressed now?"

Ignore her and that unpleasant tone in her voice. Why does she always have to ruin things with such a hard sound so at odds with all her physical softness?

He watched her mouth open again.

She doesn't know when to stop, when to leave things alone.

"Papa, you unearthed a woman's body in the monastery today."

"I thought Georges went to the cathedral."

"He's never coming back. Told me as he was leaving. Said she was cut up like Jeanne, Francoise and Marie-Jacqueline. The way they had been."

"Sisters, nieces, cousins. All in the same breath. You accuse your brother by naming them."

"Who else would remove a womb with a child in it? Did you let him escape again?"

Ignore her. Put some distance between you and her whining voice. Go to the adjoining room.

As he went, he wept. "O my son Francois, Francois my son: would to God that I might die for thee, O Francois my son, my son Francois."

"Oh, papa. Why don't you love me that much?"

Marie-Julie, weep tears of a child swallowed in a crowd by a parent's lapse of vigilance. Make a necklace of those bed curtain's ropes, and after securing it around a finial in the wooden canopy, let this partner swing you high into the air. Dance while it holds you more tenderly than your father's loving arms.

She found a secure footing when her toes dangled a few inches above the hardwood floor.

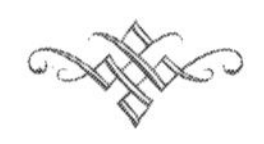

The Italian vice

Saturday—15 March 1670—Ferial Day of the Third Week in Lent
Von Fugger Bank—Rome

Good valets are not crows or ravens or magpies. They are faithful dogs and industrious bees and modest snakes. They see every little thing when they're not looking and hear every single word when they're not listening. They know all and tell nothing. They have their master's wholehearted confidence. They maneuver backstage to create a flawless mise-en-scene. They are omnipresent, omnipotent and omniscient. There is nothing so dangerous—no potential enemy more powerful—as a devoted servant.

You see it all, don't you, Jakob? Philippe Chevalier de Lorraine has taken so much extra care to dress himself properly, but he's been accustomed to being dressed by others his entire life, so he can't get all those subtle but important details. If he had a valet, that scorch mark wouldn't be on his cravat which is very nicely starched and pressed, nonetheless, there it is, a stain the color of burnt parchment, and no amount of folding can hide it. Herr Graf will notice, for one of his little conceits is his understanding of the mundane chemistry of scorching and scorch marks.

Remember his enforced stay in the country several years ago with His Holiness the Pope, Benedetto Cardinal Pamphilj and Dona Olimpia Doria Pamphilj Landi? Bored to tears as Herr Graf usually is by bucolic pleasures, one sunny day, he watched with vague amusement as you exposed to the sun's bleaching rays all of his linens, and in that moment when genius flashes, your master extrapolated the connection between sun and whiteness as all evidence of an inept laundress's ironing faded as if by white magic. For Herr Graf, it had been a singularly memorable event to witness concerns and matters of importance in the life of a caste positioned a squillion strata below his own.

Let's get back to Chevalier de Lorraine and his poorly ironed cravat. What are they doing here? The merchant banking house of von Fugger is three hundred years old. Herr Graf's family is banker to the Holy Roman Emperor and the Pope. It deals in higher stakes than fourth sons. What do you think about this young man with his good looks and rapacious aura? Is he a Trojan horse? Time's up, Jakob. No more debating.

After a pointedly haughty glance at the blemished lace, Jakob left Philippe Chevalier de Lorraine—this fourth son of the illustrious Comte de Harcourt and Monsieur de France's exiled lover—hat in hand, waiting in the vestibule.

"Herr Graf."

Jakob, settle your smile somewhere between a fox's and a weasel's. Let a bit of irritation creep in. Wait the beat of a hare's breath. Now, continue.

"There's an exceedingly beautiful, young man who insists on seeing you. Don't know him. He's never been here before, and is making a nuisance of himself. Refused to leave unless I showed you his letter of introduction."

A pause.

"If he wasn't so handsome…"

A breath.

"…and I didn't think him to your taste, I'd have had him thrown out. But—"

A pause to take a breath.

"—then I thought, what if you found out I'd turned away such an exceedingly beautiful, young man?"

Andreas Graf von Fugger, fondle Lorraine's letter in the way women are always trying to grapple and pet you. Look at the name. Read it out loud. Say it to the air, and this includes your valet.

"Philippe de Guise-Lorraine, Chevalier de Lorraine-Armagnac."

Are you in a bad mood today?

"Show him in. Be polite. Be obsequious. Then, make yourself scarce."

Jakob squared his impeccably garbed shoulders and exited. A prima donna snubbed by an unappreciative audience takes her revenge elsewhere. Valets are no different.

Lorraine, do try and be the height of grace and charm. Do try not to let Andreas Graf von Fugger see your narcissistic discomfort.

"Monsieur de Lorraine, you look terribly upset." Andreas crossed his arms, and pretending ingenuousness, waited with his typically ironic, yet gracious smile.

Lorraine's inferior birthright refused to genuflect before this tall, slim German who carried himself with the refinement and confidence of a man whose name, money and titles had the patina of a fine antique. "You're much older than I expected. Forty? At least forty."

"When you're forty, Monsieur de Lorraine, you won't think it's so old. Why are you here?"

"What's a famous German banker like you doing in Rome?"

"Monsieur de Lorraine, money goes where money is." Andreas motioned for his guest to sit down. "This can't be the case with you. How old are you?"

"Twenty-eight. Went to Mass this morning. Had nothing else to do."

Andreas shook his head. "Interesting amusement. My sweetheart's seventeen, so I have plenty to keep me from getting bored."

"The epistle was about Susanna putting her trust in God, and the gospel about an adulteress who was to be stoned, when Jesus said—"

"You're nothing but the fourth son of a minor French aristocrat, Monsieur de Lorraine. And you have no money. Of what service could I be to you?"

"Herr Graf von Fugger, today is also Ides of March."

Andreas's smile was radiant. "Monsieur de Lorraine, Gaius Julius Caesar died today."

"A day of ill omen. Of assassinations."

"Assassinations have, even before Caesar's time, cost a great deal of money. As I said before, you haven't any."

"I'm very underrated." His entire body spoke with emphasis.

Andreas surveyed him below the neck.

"I assure you, Herr Graf, Monsieur de France would be most grateful. His gratitude could very well express itself as his influence with the King of France on your behalf."

"You're acting as Monsieur's agent?" Andreas watched hesitation form around Lorraine's aura. "Monsieur wouldn't be disappointed if Madame joined her ancestors, but he's no murderer."

Andreas, he's an exceedingly beautiful young man. A shameless slut too.

"Madame de France. Interesting commission. How to make it appear a demise of natural causes. A challenge, actually. Still, there would be expenses."

"I'm very talented."

"No doubt. Be honest. Exile hasn't been kind or financially advantageous, Monsieur de Lorraine, has it?"

"I prefer women. Most of the time. Give up the ladies, that's asking an awful lot."

"Not if you want me to poison the only sister-in-law of the King of France for you, so you can get back into her husband's bed. Even if she were to die tomorrow, you can't expect amnesty for several years at least. Rome's an amusing city. But only if you have the right friends."

"How long before that miserable bitch succumbs?"

Andreas slouched more comfortably into his chair. "I'm curious. Don't you and Monsieur de France get confused, you know, having the same first name?"

"No. I'm Philippe and he's Monsieur."

"I thought you were on the most intimate of terms."

"He's still the king's brother. Worst snob in the world. Won't let anyone call him anything except 'Monsieur.' Not his mother, not his wife. The king calls him 'my brother' just to annoy him, but the king may call Monsieur anything he pleases."

Andreas was bored. "Your deliverance is at hand. Show some gratitude. Mustn't waste your meager resources paying for a Mass of thanksgiving when private prayer costs nothing. Don't you think, Philippe, you ought get on your knees? Offer a prayer of thanks for the impending demise of your nemesis."

Genuflect before your new liege lord, Lorraine. Be a good vassal, reverently bow your head and pray with a fervor befitting your youth, virility and desperation.

After a few minutes, Andreas looked heavenward and ejaculated a little prayer of his own.

Carnal indifference

Sunday—29 June 1670—Feast of Saints Peter & Paul
Chateau Saint-Cloud

Philippe Duc d'Orleans, the one the only Monsieur, little good it does you as you peer into your empty teacup, the fine crazing in the glaze no different from lines of fate on your left palm. Bite your lip, Monsieur, look to your past and search desperately for a brighter future. Where's your reward for doing your duty by this wife you'd been in love with for precisely two weeks? You repressed your sexuality enough times to give her at least eight pregnancies in a decade, but with miscarriages and still births and enfeebled infants who failed to cling to life, you've been robbed of almost every reward for your struggles. Only two small daughters remain. You have no son.

Your beloved wife is a creature of relentless habit. For ten years every day it's been the same damned thing: hot chicory water at six o'clock in the evening. She's always been too thin, as if her bones would break to the touch, and pallid. Tonight she looks cadaverous. Perhaps, she'll drop dead. What a pleasant thought. Your beloved brother will want you to marry again, but in exchange, maybe, Lorraine could come home to the Court. Problem is Minette's never going to die. Delicate women with semi-invalid constitutions have an unfailingly tenacious grip on life always managing to outlive their husbands. And that voice of hers. Everyone finds it light and gay and full of laughter. She never has any of that particular voice left over for you.

"Go to Paris, Monsieur. Dress up with your boys. Be the pretty little girl they like. I don't care what you do." Minette took another sip of her chicory water.

"Dear Minette, you don't look or sound well tonight."

"Why should I be? You've done nothing but make me miserable since my return from England. Everything to humiliate me. I'm going to write Charles about it."

Oh, Monsieur. Her big brother, the King of England, will quarrel with your big brother, the King of France. Instead of a family tiff, it'll be politics. You couldn't care less. Could you? All you know is after the inevitable scolding your allowance will be cut. You can't afford this. It's expensive keeping up appearances of wealth. Your lifestyle is a noticeable enough percentage of the national budget to merit an expense line. Your income is totally dependent on your brother's mood swings. It would behoove you to make nice to Minette.

"Maybe, if I was wasn't so unhappy, I could be kinder to you."

"While I live, your loathsome sodomite will never set foot in France, and by law you may never leave. You're never going to see him again. Get used to the idea."

Oh my, Monsieur. Swirl those imaginary contents of your empty cup. Lorraine is no sodomite. Everybody knows it. You are. Everybody knows this too. Pour some chicory water into your cup and force it down. It's a draught of wormwood, a penance. You're only thirty and she's twenty-six. How are you going to face another thirty, or maybe even forty, years with this woman? How will you ever make her understand you also need someone to love? Haven't you been generous enough to ignore her affair with your brother? Why can't she ignore your forbidden love?

"I'd better go now or I'll be late for the opera. You'll excuse me, Madame, until tomorrow."

"What a cramp in my side. What a pain." Minette clawed at her side and shrieked. "I've been poisoned."

Oh my, Monsieur. Every gaze in the room is riveted on you. Why is she moaning and screeching? It's so loud they'll hear it in the hallway. It's so loud your brother might hear it all the way at the other side of the palace. It's the end of the month. How will you get through July if you only receive half the allowance you expected?

"Madame de La Fayette, get the doctors for Madame."

Be nice, Monsieur.

"Minette, shall I stay with you? I won't go to the opera if it makes you feel better."

"Monsieur, you haven't loved me for a very long time. It isn't fair. I've never been unfaithful to you." She clutched his hand. "They've poisoned me."

"I drank the chicory water too. You haven't been poisoned. Just an attack of nerves or indigestion. Your stomach's always been very poor. When the doctors come, they'll bleed you. You'll feel much better."

Oh Monsieur, you need to prove she hasn't been poisoned, but nobody loves you enough to drink anything more out of the teapot, so have a maid-of-honor feed the rest to your wife's adorable English dog. It's as important as every other courtier present. Then pray her dog survives.

Minette's dog lived to a very old age for a dog. The doctors' consensus was Minette had been poisoned. Monsieur agreed to every remedy they suggested. Milk, oil, powder of viper, purging, bleeding. Nothing worked.

At midnight priests came to administer Extreme Unction. By one o'clock, the king and most of the Court had arrived to pay their respects and console Monsieur who was in a fit of grief and hysteria; by two o'clock, husband and wife were reconciled, exchanging tender words of love; and at three o'clock, nine hours after Minette's symptoms started, Monsieur was a widower.

1676–1678

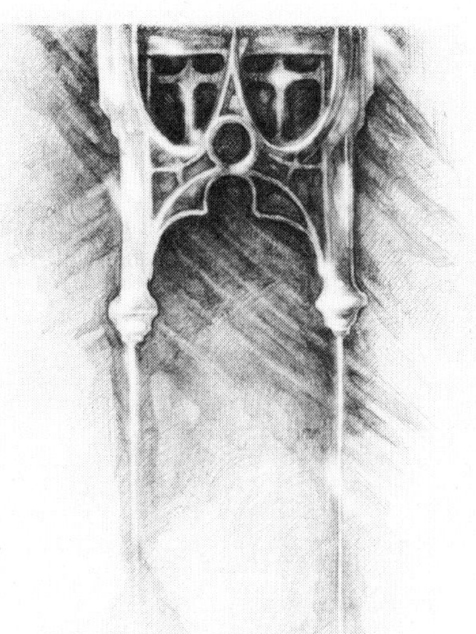

A poisoned teacup—A poisoned lover

Friday—10 June 1676—Feast of Saint Felicitas
Chateau Saint-Cloud

Most beloved Highness R_,

My Excellency is obliged to correct certain misapprehensions Your Highness has formed as it is a falsehood I changed my name. I may only be addressed as Madame, for my husband as brother of the king bears the title of Monsieur, and I as his wife may not bear any other title than that of Madame. And that is that.

Here is what is said concerning Minette's death, for you say throughout Europe she was celebrated for her youth, beauty and agreeableness, whereas the French say she was not handsome at all, only she had such grace everything became her. I know the true story of her death from Monsieur le Duc.

I leave it to Your Highness, if as a good and loyal English subject, you wish to tell His English Majesty what I have learned, for even though he is my cousin too I am by marriage constrained to ally myself to French interests even if it is not my natural inclination, so what I say now is without any political alliance as one good German to another.

They say Monsieur had many motives for killing her. He was in love with Sodomite Lorraine and out of spite Minette schemed to have this lover exiled, also she had a thinly veiled love affair of her own with the king, she filched Monsieur's young men from his bed, and most unforgivable of all she was always borrowing jewels from Monsieur's jewelry box without asking his permission.

Sodomite Lorraine sent poison from Italy by way of a gentleman who was afterward made chief maitre d'hotel of Saint-Cloud as a reward for his services. It is true Minette was poisoned, but I think it was without Monsieur's knowledge, for when those scoundrels held counsel to determine how they would poison her, they discussed whether or not they should warn Monsieur.

One said, "No, do not let us tell him, for he cannot hold his tongue. If he does not speak of it in the first year, he will get us hanged ten years later." Another persisted Monsieur ought to be told, and reasoned if Monsieur knew, he would be as guilty as they and thus constrained to protect them. It is known yet another of the wretches added, "Be careful not to let Monsieur know of it. He will not take our part. He will tell the king and this would hang us." They made Monsieur believe the Dutch gave her a slow poison in chocolate, and that was well imagined, for it is known the Dutch believe Minette tried to turn His English Majesty away from his other sister, Princesse d'Orange.

Here is the truth of the clever way they accomplished the deed, for they did not poison the chicory water, but poisoned the cup and that was also well imagined because no one drinks from our cups but ourselves. On the day she was poisoned, when she asked for her cup at breakfast, they said it was mislaid, and while Monsieur and she were at Mass, a valet discovered one of the poisoners in the buffet rubbing her cup with some paper. The valet said, "What are you doing in our closet and why are you touching Madame's cup?" The poisoner answered, "I am dying of thirst, and as the cup was dirty, I cleaned it with paper." The valet took the cup from the poisoner's hand and said, "Go away from here at once or I shall tell Monsieur of your knavery. A person such as you to dare drink from the cup of Her Royal Highness. Unthinkable."

That same evening Minette called for her chicory water and as soon as she drank it cried out she was poisoned. Those who were there drank the same water but not from her cup, so they were not taken ill, for everyone drank from his own cup as is the custom. They put her to bed and she grew worse and worse and died three hours after midnight in a frightful suffering. Monsieur never troubled her about her love affair with the king, and when he related to me himself the whole of her life, passed this matter over in silence which he would not have done had he believed it true, so I think in this circumstance the world has been unjust to her. They say her death broke His English Majesty's heart and he still refers to her as Minette though she is dead all this time. Is this so?

I have a most amazing scandal to tell Your Highness concerning Madeleine Marquise de Brinvilliers. She is a great poisoner. She was married while still virtually a child into a family of textile manufacturers surnamed Gobelin, and as with most marriages it was an alliance of families and fortunes, so husband and wife did their duty by their ancestors, produced legitimate descendants, and having secured survival of family name and money, each went his own way, for here in France love is an activity which seldom involves one's spouse.

Madeleine came under the spell of an unscrupulous lover. Neither could she bear the thought of life without him nor could she stand being parted from him or the stolen moments, for time with him disappeared through her clenched fist, while away from him she could not shake it free from her parted fingers, but mostly she could not bear thoughts of other women he wiled whiling away his time when not with her, so she contrived at the impractical and absurd, to become his wife. To her relief, her lover's passion to become her husband was equal to her own.

There were problems. Not that they were insurmountable. The lover was unencumbered with a wife but burdened by debt, and being that despised faction of society known as a younger son, had no hope or prospects of future wealth. That he might have earned a living was out of the question, for he was a gentleman and even more than a gentleman, he was a minor aristocrat. Madeleine had plenty money but it was not hers as it belonged to her husband. She had children. They were minors. If she could be rid of her husband, she could squander her children's inheritance on her lover until her eldest son reached his majority which was at least a decade away. Divorce was possible, for Frenchmen have cleverly named it a separation of domicile, but this would in no way free her to remarry and her husband would keep all property, money and children, so another method of divorcing had to be found.

How does one divorce one's husband and avoid getting caught? Well may you ask. In this country one poisons him over a series of months, makes it appear a mysterious disease while lovingly nursing him till he draws his last breath, and one does not ever attempt it again on any other acquaintance. A simple plan.

The lover knew the art, having learned it from a master perfumer-poisoner who succumbed to a wasting illness and tender ministrations, for it is true we are usually punished in this world by our own sins. The lover then taught Madeleine the art. She was a good student and successfully poisoned her father, then a brother, then another brother, then an older sister, then one of her own children, then a younger sister, then her husband's younger brother, then one of her lover's mistresses, then another of his mistresses. Madeleine's enthusiasm became too keen. Her lover was so in love he did not notice this weakness in his beloved, but then Madeleine probably accidently poisoned him, so he denounced her to the authorities just before he died. They say she experimented on patients in charity hospitals and *Le Mercure Galant* reports official opinion is that hundreds died during those years she took to perfect her art.

I am sending Your Highness one those Gobelin tapestries you like so very much. I designed it myself. Various scenes show Madeleine being tortured at Bastille, her repentance at Notre-Dame and her burning at the stake. When I made my request of soon-to-be-widowed Marquis de Brinvilliers, he seemed hesitant and it made no favorable impression on him the tapestry was to be a gift for Your Highness, so I complained to Monsieur asking him to speak with that lazy, good-for-nothing textile manufacturer. Monsieur was delighted to assist saying it was an amusing business, though I cannot understand how it is Monsieur finds tapestry weaving a funny occupation.

You know, in the days of Louvois Elder they read all letters as they do now, but at least they sent them on in decent time, whereas that fawning toad of a son (a toad, a donkey, a fox and an utter dolt) directs the postal service and letters are delayed for an interminable length of time. As Toad Louvois cannot read German he must have Monsieur de La Reynie translate my letters, and I do not thank either gentleman for his attentions.

I have never known a heat such as this. Leaves on trees are shriveled as if a fire had gone over them, but there are prophesies rain will begin to fall by next Friday. God grant it. Until it rains no one shall see me in Paris. We think it is hot here, but everyone who comes from Paris exclaims, "Oh. How cool Saint-Cloud is."

Paris is horrible, hot and stinking. There is such a shocking smell one cannot endure it as the extreme heat makes meat and fish rot which joined with piss and crap from crowds of people who relieve themselves in public makes an odor so detestable it cannot be borne.

I must stop now, for the heat is extraordinary and I am sweating in a terrible way. It is months since a drop of rain has fallen and leaves are frying on trees. There is the news.

Lovingly,
Liselotte

A gosling among a bevy of swans

Tuesday–14 July 1676–feast of Saint Bonaventure
Chateau Saint-Cloud

My darling A_-E_,

My husband is Monsieur. Plain and simple. It is a title of respect exalted by its directness of address and by the fact it is uncomplicated by modifiers of any sort (neither surname nor appanage) to distinguish Monsieur This from Monsieur That. There was but one Monsieur and he is the reigning king's brother, for it is a booby prize awarded second sons the moment first sons ascend the throne, and as always third and fourth sons count for nothing, the French being ungrateful wretches who take for granted any surfeit gifts from God.

Titles become more complicated and prestige diminishes in direct correlation to degree of distance from the pinnacle where the king sits alone, and at the pyramid's base names and titles are so long it is comical with the likes of Monsieur This-That-and-the-Other-from-Here-There-and-Everywhere who is in truth Monsieur Nobody-of-No-Account, so to be Monsieur is to be third most important man in the realm after the dauphin, heir to the throne. The dauphin is addressed in similarly exalted form as Monseigneur. The king is addressed as Sire. At the king's death Monsieur must relinquish his title to the incumbent's brother and become merely Monsieur This-of-That.

I am Madame, as in the wife of Monsieur. I am Monsieur's second Madame. In truth I have a host of names and titles as I may refer to myself as Elisabeth-Charlotte von der Pfalz, Princesse Palatine, Elisabeth-Charlotte d'Orleans, Duchesse d'Orleans, Madame de France, Liselotte, Lotte, etc., etc. and behind my back courtiers call me every imaginable thing, but to my face they dare only call me Madame.

I am no fool as the French think me and know my one outstanding feature (my renowned superlative) is my ugliness, for I am undeniably the ugliest princess in Europe and it was this only which won for me a most coveted of royal marriages. My bear-cat-monkey face, as His Highness my Papa is so fond of calling me, has brought me into the Court of France (they think it the most splendid in the world) and within this holy of holies I have precedence over every noble in the kingdom except the king, the queen, the dauphin and Monsieur. When the dauphin finally marries, the dauphine will stand in line ahead of Monsieur and me, but this is all and everyone else must get in line behind My Excellency. Only my precedence makes bearable all their name calling, cruel words, practical jokes, snubs, disrespect and hatred of Germans.

I so very much miss our German ways at the Court in Heidelberg where they do not know about precedence. I explained to Monsieur all German princes are equal, but he did not understand my meaning, so I explained to him as I would to a child. I said, "At official Court functions and on public occasions German princes behave themselves as a crowd of onlookers at a parade, for they push and shove their way to be first, to be in front for the best view, and having established themselves in certain positions, they remain there until someone comes along who pushes and shoves better, but the French do not like things so jolly and pell-mell. They are the parade itself. First is Sire, then Sa Majeste, then Monseigneur, then you, Monsieur, then My Excellency, then etc. and etc., until Messieurs

This-That-and-the-Other-from-Here-There-and-Everywhere arrive, and as with all parades these dung sweepers signal the spectacle is at an end." Monsieur did not understand my meaning, so I drew pictures for him and even took my daughter's dolls and my son's soldiers and showed him, but Monsieur is being very French about it and refuses to make any effort to be logical or enlightened. I fear if my children inherit Monsieur's brain they will be dunces.

How did this ugly German gosling become loose among a bevy of French swans? And well may you wonder, for in spite of being eldest daughter I had every disadvantage, especially after His Highness my Papa's scandalous divorce from Her Highness my Maman and his marriage to that scheming slut of a maid-of-honor which makes me want to burst out of my skin. I shall say nothing more about Morganatic Wife-Whore, and it is no comfort she is so afraid of His Highness my Papa he can bully her day and night with that disgusting business of making children, though little good all those little bastards do him, for they are all morganatic and cannot inherit, so are no more useful than if they were in truth real bastards. But that is about morganatic whores and bastards and not about my marriage to Monsieur and how I came to live here.

King of France had several problems for which I was a solution, for his queen is a Spanish Habsburg infanta and living proof centuries of constant inbreeding lead to mishaps, his infatuation with his sister-in-law and their incestuous affair had been an open secret (never tell this to His Highness R_) and he had to parry gossip that Monsieur had poisoned Madame by quickly replacing her. His Most Christian Majesty's decision to form a royal alliance between France and the Palatinate was a stroke of politic genius as he revenged himself on his brother, he can never again be accused of being overly fond of his brother's wife, and if the queen cannot be attractive, she may at least seem less ugly compared with My Excellency.

At present I am anxious about my debts which the great of the Earth are not apt to be, for I am never easy unless I have secured their payment and I am forever forestalling demands, sometimes wishes and always impatience or complaints, but my plight is not of my own making as you have been unjustly told.

Monsieur received much property with me which I was obliged to give up to him as all my jewels, furniture, pictures, in short, all that came from my family was taken from me, so I have no means to live according to my rank and maintain my household which is considerable, and that I have been ill-used in this respect is rather the fault of Morganatic Wife-Whore who allowed my marriage contract to be ill-drawn. I live on a paltry allowance from Monsieur and am reduced to a state no better than a beggar.

It is very expensive to live in this country and you are ill informed concerning frugality of the French, for it is true they are stingy, but stinginess and frugality are two different animals, so Frenchmen will not hesitate to be stingy with others, whereas they will never be frugal with themselves. More households are on verge of bankruptcy than anyone dare speak of aloud and even princely establishments with princely incomes are strained to breaking point as everyone lives by the rule that one must live and dress to impress even if on credit. Necessities of an average establishment are like nothing to be found in the Palatinate or any of the German States.

They are very complicated in how they live here. All households are a complication of servants and horses, and the measure of one's exalted-ness is in numbers of each that one possesses. Every man is worth forty servants and forty horses. A wife being of lesser value is worth but twenty servants and twenty horses. Each child has five servants, a nurse and three horses. There are servants who have servants and horses who have servants, but there are no servants with horses, for a good horse is more costly to replace than a servant, so in short, servants walk.

In the hierarchy of servants there are servants who only give orders and who must have servants of their own, but of all these servants and horses perhaps only two-thirds actually do any work. You will ask why having a child requires acquiring three horses, and well you might, for I have asked this very same question myself. "This is how things are done" is the only answer Monsieur gave when I complained of this extravagance at the birth of our three children, but it is not reversed when a child dies, for after my first son's death all accompanying servants and horses continue to burden me till this very day.

Monsieur's household costs the king nearly two million louis d'or a year to maintain, yet Monsieur is forever whining and complaining it is not enough, so the king is forever paying another half million a year to keep creditors at bay, but if Monsieur would rid himself of a few of his sodomite boys, he might be better able to balance his ledger books which is unlikely to happen, so my children will be reduced to being beggars no better off than I.

I am alone and despised by all. Everyone in this country, young and old, runs after favor and it is well known I am without influence, so I consort with no one except my own people. I am as polite as I can be to everyone but contract no intimate relations with anyone. I live alone. I go to walk. I go to drive. From two o'clock to half past nine I never see a human face. I read, I write or I amuse myself by making baskets like the one I sent Her Highness S_ von B_-L_, but I would rather be alone than have to give myself any trouble of finding something to say, for the French think it bad if you ignore them and they go away discontented. You are lucky to still live in the Palatinate where good sense rules common man and clergy alike.

Her Highness S_ von B_-L_ sent me two fine dachshunde from Anhalt-Dessau. I named them Gabriel and Minette. They are little babies and it brings me much happiness to have a fond reminder of my fatherland and family.

I must go to play with my little dogs.

Your loving,
Liselotte

Celibacy: cleanliness is next to godliness

Thursday–8 September 1678–Feast of the Nativity of the Virgin
Chateau Marly

My dearest Highness S_ von B_-L_,

I am as the French proverb says a donkey betwixt two meadows and cannot decide my mind, for there is so much to tell it is difficult to know where to begin.

It is true Paris and Heidelberg have the same latitude and also the same ascendent of Virgo, but the air in Paris stinks. The air in Heidelberg, above all, I remember it best about the palace where my apartments were. Nothing better could ever be found. My God. How many times I ate cherries on that mountain with a good bit of bread at five in the morning.

Streets in Paris are like nothing to be imagined, for being French and neither German nor Swiss or Dutch, or Swedes, or perhaps even Danes, in short, Frenchmen know nothing of cleanliness. Paris is the most densely populated city in Europe with five hundred thousand dirty French souls and each morning perhaps half of those five hundred thousand souls greet the dawn by emptying chamber pots onto the streets. Day in. Day out. Year in. Year out. Your Highness can well imagine at least one millard of chamber pots has been emptied onto Parisian streets since my arrival in this country.

Bad odors in Paris are a direct result of a bad political system. Long ago, Paris had been divided into seigneuries, each governed by a seigneur who was a law unto himself, but most disappeared during the reign of Late King, though many remained until recently when Lieutenant General of Police of Paris cleverly made them disappear completely. But that is not about politics and stinky odors.

In truth the seigneur was not an individual but rather guilds or ecclesiastical orders, and as committees of men do not know how to live in peace or cleanliness, they became nothing more than marauding gangs cloaked with the respectability of authority, for as their territorial boundaries ran down the center of the streets, they fought one another to keep the crap on the streets from being removed, otherwise there would be no reason to argue as the truth would be clearly exposed.

Once a bad example is set by those in authority and by the clergy, everyone else becomes lazy also, so all Parisians became indifferent to cleaning the streets and in truth became so lazy all dirt, trash, waste, filth, in short, all disgusting things were disposed of at one's front door. Paris became one large network of troughs for pigs and fowls and rats to forage, for water in the gutters mixed with ordure to make a tasty stew. Until Monsieur de La Reynie's ascendancy, many a clever foreigner saw the whole of Paris (and avoided getting lost) by following a foraging pig from one end of town to another until it returned home at night.

Little more than a decade ago, king and seigneuries reached a stalemate. The king began a new game with a new set of rules by vesting an impressive morsel of his absolute power to a newly created appointment, Lieutenant General of Police of Paris, and they say Nicolas-Gabriel de La Reynie mortgaged his birthright, his soul, and as eldest son his entire clan's posterity to buy this post with its mandate to "Establish law and order in our good city of Paris."

I like Monsieur de La Reynie, for even though he is French, he is not Parisian (being from an unknown corner of the Earth known as Limousin) and thinks so much like a good German one would mistake him as such. He combated the seigneuries with his own marauding brigades, cloaked with a more modern approach to authority, and now there are street cleaners (they collect garbage with regularity), uniformed constables (everywhere and with routine patrols) and municipal firemen (this last usurped from Capuchin monks).

Monsieur de La Reynie is an innovative man and is having all streets paved with cobblestones (a very nice pattern with stones fanning outward in a clever way so as to hide any irregularities) and is doing away with gutters which are nothing more than pigs' troughs, and though Paris is still very stinky, it is much less so than before. The pavers also dig small wells on every street corner, connecting street level to sewers, so Parisians may empty their chamber pots (men use the wells as pissoirs). There are nearly five thousand street lights (very pretty at night) which is a unique sight in all the world, for there is nothing of its like in the Palatinate or any of the German States, and His Highness R_ agrees it does not exist in London, and Her Highness H_ and His Highness S_-A_-A_ have written they have nothing like it in Transylvania, and no other of our family anywhere has seen the likes of it, but Your Highness will agree it would be too long a list to name them all, so in short, street lights at night exist but in Paris.

Monsieur de La Reynie is also a moral man who believes in ethics and good behavior. He supervises prostitution and gambling, licenses butchers and fishmongers during Lent, censors the press, censors the mail (for which I do not thank him), issues permits for public gatherings, prohibits hissing in theaters, defines highs and lows of a woman's decolletage in public, fines the use of white bone-handled fish knives instead of black ones during Lent, etc. No detail of the public good escapes him. There are times when good men (even those trying to comport themselves with good German traits) can be most annoying.

Your Highness will be pleased to know I am now celibate, for it is true celibacy is the best condition and the best of men is not worth the Devil. Love in marriage is no longer fashionable here, is thought ridiculous and though Catholics say in their catechism marriage is a sacrament, they live with their wives as if it was no sacrament at all, for nothing is more approved than to see men have affairs and desert their wives.

Monsieur is worst of all as his love affairs are never with women. In public he wears too much rouge, too many jewels, too much perfume and his red heels are so high he is in constant danger of losing his balance and walks as if he will topple forward at any moment. Whenever he is alone with his favorites, he dresses in women's clothes, though who can blame him as he cuts a much finer figure than I, and it is a great scandal and a wonder I have any children, but somehow Monsieur managed to stick the babies in.

I am glad now as Monsieur has taken a bed to himself and I never liked the business of making children. When he made me this proposal, I said, "Yes, with all my heart. I shall be glad of it provided you do not hate me and continue to be a little kind to me." He promised me and we are now always well satisfied with each other, for in truth it was annoying to sleep with him as he could not endure anyone disturbing his sleep, and if my big toe as much as touched him, he would wake me in order to scold me viciously for an hour, so I was obliged to keep myself on the edge of the bed and sometimes I fell out like a sack. I was therefore extremely pleased when Monsieur, in good friendship and without bitterness, proposed we should sleep in separate rooms.

These days I neither fret myself about being scolded in the small hours of the morning nor tumbling from the bed and it is a comfort, but not as much a comfort as not having to endure marriage, for I am like His Highness R_ and cannot imagine why anyone would marry. There is but one motive I can conceive which is dying of hunger and getting one's bread in this way.

Monsieur de La Reynie has told me interesting news. Your Highness will recall a story I told of Morel's death last springtime and of an awful Friday 13th with so many servants dropping dead like flies. Three weeks ago Monsieur told me a curious piece of gossip as it seems Morel was not himself, and when they went through his things, they found documents proving his true identity was Francois Galaup de Chasteuil. I told this to Monsieur de La Reynie who promised to uncover this fellow's history. But that is about three weeks ago and is not news.

A year ago Jesuits from rue Saint-Antoine and priests of Notre-Dame warned of a plot to poison the king and the dauphin, and it also seems Parisians are poisoning one another with abandon. But that is another story. Next day, the Paris police arrested a galley captain, his mistress and his valet. They also arrested a banker, a lawyer, a dubious nobleman and one of the king's secretaries at Paris Royal Mint, whereas a physician who was known to this gang escaped to England and has installed himself comfortably at His English Majesty's Court of St. James.

No one knows for certain what these men were plotting, but Toad Louvois is convinced they were in league with bankers of Holy Roman Emperor and King of Spain to debase French currency, whereas Monsieur de La Reynie believes it is an international poisoning ring dabbling in counterfeiting to generate extra profit, and as he is infinitely more clever than Toad Louvois could ever hope to be, what more is to be said?

This confederation of poisoners is exceedingly well organized, therefore able to accept commission and payment in any given city for any other country, so Sodomite Lorraine used this service to poison Minette, for as payments and arrangements were made in Rome it gave the appearance he was conspicuously beyond reproach. The entire business is simple and flawless. Such acumen impresses me greatly and one would think them good German merchants.

When they tortured the galley captain, he claimed La Chatte Comtesse (the king's former whore) had employed him on occasion but refused to say how or why, then said the king's Official Whore had also used his services, then recanted everything, but at a second questioning denounced Francois Galaup de Chasteuil as a horrible fiend who knows a great many important secrets, but it is too late for Chasteuil is dead.

Monsieur de La Reynie toys with the idea of warning English Secretary of State about the physician who escaped to England, but as he has no idea of what to warn the English about he is afraid he will appear foolish, and being very French about it, feels whatever happens to His English Majesty is England's problem and not France's. Does Your Highness think we ought not to advise His Highness R_?

Your Highness must always keep yourself well and happy.

Liselotte

A loving brother's gift

Wednesday–14 September 1678–Feast of the Exaltation of the Cross
Chateau Fontainebleau

L_-M_-A_, my dear,

Who told you such silly lies concerning my marriage to Monsieur? I was married by proxy at Metz, for a French prince may not marry on foreign soil and a princess of any land may not leave her country unmarried without being considered a slut, so they baptized, confirmed and married me in the Roman religion all at once. What a lot of sacraments in a single day.

I did not see Monsieur till we met on the road between Chalons and Bellay, and he was not pleased with me, for upon first laying eyes on me he exclaimed with an audible groan, "Oh, how shall I ever be able to sleep with her?" It is true I cried so much I made myself sick over it and did nothing but howl with tears all that first night long, but after those first uncomfortable days much to everyone's surprise (our own especially), our early years of marriage were completely happy.

Monsieur was the best man in the world and we got on very well together as our life was full of laughter with a handsome little family of our three children and my stepdaughters, but the king recalled Sodomite Lorraine from exile and ruined it all. Here is the truth of it. His Majesty said to Monsieur, "Do you still think of Chevalier de Lorraine? Do you love him? Shall I return him to you?" Monsieur replied, "It would give me the greatest joy." "You must remember to be grateful always if I give you this gift," the king said. Whereupon Monsieur threw himself at the king's feet, embraced his knees and kissed his hands which seemed to please him, and from that moment no child has ever been born who is more blindly obedient to his parents than Monsieur is to his brother.

When Sodomite Lorraine returned six years ago, Monsieur was happy for it but paid little attention to him, so he amused himself with women, but then as the king excluded Monsieur from important matters, stripped him of any useful duties and forced him into an idle and meaningless existence, he came more and more under the influence of Sodomite Lorraine, till I am now in a bedroom of my own while he sleeps in my place next to Monsieur. You may wonder why I do not complain, but what would I gain from it? Monsieur will do what he pleases, and as long as he continues to be kind to me, why should I begrudge him this small happiness? Certainly, the king is not concerned whether Monsieur is happy or not.

Valets of competence and repute are most certainly more useful members of society than younger sons of titled men, especially those of mediocre intellect and talent who are in truth no better than beggars as they pander among elegantly elitist men. Fortune smiled down on Sodomite Lorraine, for he leeched himself onto Monsieur, but he is only a younger son of Comte de Harcourt and any military genius (or other prodigious gifts) which had made the father a most celebrated man is decidedly lacking in this fourth son who is but a turkey disguised as a peacock.

As Sodomite Lorraine reasons with his testa and never his caput, whenever it is capable of speech it declares it possesses such intangible gifts from Almighty God as an ancient and noble lineage, beauty of face and form, a modicum of intelligence, good manners, a nice family, in short, everything but financial self-sufficiency. Is this to be held against it? Is it doomed forever to fall short of its potential due to a misfortune of having been born the fourth son? I shall say no more, for it makes me want to burst my skin and I am becoming cranky as a bedbug from it.

My solace in this detestable country is my good and loyal companion Die Rotzenhäuserin. Hers was a sad life filled with many tribulations and sorrows. She had idolized her father all his life and he had adored her with equal intensity, for they had each other only which made their bond profound despite frequent separations brought about by his careers as adventurer and soldier. Whenever Lenor's father went to sea as a pirate or was on a battlefield serving whoever had bought his services, she was relegated to the care of a Dominican nun who was abbess of a convent.

In July 1666, Baron von Ratsamhausen was killed fighting for the Dutch against the English at the St. James Day Battle. Lenor was but fifteen, and as her inheritance amounted to nothing more than her father's empty title and a small trunk filled with his possessions, she was left at the mercy and guardianship of the abbess who browbeat a formidable education into her for five years with unflagging attempts to convert her. Lenor studied with diligence but remained a staunch Lutheran to honor her father.

As Lenor refused to enter the convent, the abbess prevailed upon Her Highness A_ de M_ to secure a position as one of my maids-of-honor, so after the prerequisite formality of converting to the Roman religion, Lenor became part of the German entourage accompanying My Excellency.

They say as she packed to leave she heard for the first time a rumor that the abbess was her mother, something everyone else had known for years, but Lenor kept silent, buried the past, and armed with her father's cunning and resourcefulness (and his dreadful eyesight which had finally managed to get him killed) as well as an impressive wit honed by an education denied most women, turned her face into the future which is the reason she is here with me now.

No, there are no brothers in the world as different as the king and Monsieur, yet they love each other very much. The king is tall with fair hair or rather a light brown, has a manly air and an extremely fine face, whereas Monsieur is not disagreeable in appearance, but he is small with hair black as jet, eyebrows thick and brown, large dark eyes, a long and narrow face, a big nose, a small mouth and shockingly villainous teeth.

Monsieur has the manner of a woman rather than of a man and likes neither horses nor hunting. Soldiers say of him, "He is more afraid of sun and dust than he is of guns," which is very true and he cares for nothing but cards, holding court, good eating, dancing and dressing himself, in a word, he takes pleasure in all things women like. The king loves hunting, music and theatre, whereas Monsieur likes nothing but great assemblies and masked balls, and whereas the king likes having love affairs with women, I do not believe Monsieur has ever been in love with anyone but Sodomite Lorraine.

Monsieur is most fond of the sound of bells and declares it gives him great pleasure, but he has enough good sense to laugh at himself about this crap and silliness, yet I must always spend All Saints Night in Paris with him just expressly to hear bells ringing all night long.

I wish you could see my son, for he is old enough to be more human and sensible in appearance, and as it will not be much longer before he gives up wearing his skirts to wear breeches and a doublet, he will surely be a very smart looking little fellow, but he resembles me so he will not be handsome in the end. Though his sister is two years younger she is stronger and taller for her age. My daughter is the funniest child you could ever meet, chatters like a magpie about everything that comes into her head, has wit and is full of mischief, but she is also pretty and I cannot imagine where she gets it from. She has had her ondoiement but is too young to be christened, whereas my son shall be christened soon so he finally has a name.

His Highness R_ tells me there is no custom of ondoiement in England, and certainly it does not exist in the Palatinate or any other of the German States (all being more sensible than France) and His Highness S_-A_-A_ says there is no such silliness in Transylvania. How this custom began or why I cannot tell and the reason Frenchmen think it a singular mark of distinction is something they cannot explain to anyone's satisfaction including their own.

The king did not receive his name until he was five and Grande Mademoiselle remained nameless until she was ten (I think this was much too long) while a brother of Late King died nameless at four. It is not a practical or useful custom, for if a child goes to Heaven without a name, I am sure angels will have as difficult a time getting his attention there as we had getting my first son's attention here while he was alive.

Monsieur claims, his reasoning being singularly French and singularly royal, there is no point to naming a child till one is sure one is going to keep it, for once a child has a name it is like a real person and one becomes attached to it. Perhaps this is the reason he was less grieved at losing our first son than I (that quack of a royal doctor killed him as surely as if he had shot him through the head), and perhaps also had I not been so hasty and insisted we at least give him his appanage at such a young age, it would not have broken my heart so when he died. But that is ancient history. The boy was Duc de Valois, but as it is unlucky (everyone given this appanage dies before his time), Monsieur forbad to let my second son bear it which is the reason he will be Philippe Duc de Chartres.

This is enough gossip for you. I hope I have not taxed your brain with too many serious matters which will put you to thinking too hard, for there are doctors here who say that if one overworks the brain beyond its capacity, blood will rush to it too quickly and cause it to explode inside the skull which is the reason people die of apoplectic fits and I would not wish for your brain to hurt itself on my account.

Most tenderly and lovingly,
Liselotte

La Chatte Comtesse: an amorous mouser

Saturday–29 October 1678–Feast of Bede the Venerable
Chateau Saint-Germain

Good and dear L_-H_,

You will forgive me not writing these many weeks, for I had a weakness in my arm which prevented me from doing anything for myself and Die Rotzenhäuserin had even to feed me, but all this is over and I am myself again. Everyday from six to eight o'clock I drive out with Monsieur and my ladies. Three times a week, whenever Monsieur and I are in residence elsewhere, I go to Paris and every day I write my friends who live there. I hunt twice a week. This is how I pass my time.

With each day that passes my life becomes more tolerable as His Majesty shows me his singular regard and favor, and in this country wherever the king rests his gaze, the Court flocks to pay homage. It is akin to the custom of adoring saints. Priests say Almighty God hears one's supplications through the intercession of saints, but the trick lies in choosing, for if one has the misfortune of praying to a saint who is out of favor or if one's enemy's saint is more powerful, then God will hear an enemy's prayer over one's own. It is exactly as this in the Court of France.

I am in His Majesty's good offices, for he finds my frankness and open nature agreeable and thinks me amusing, so now whenever the king dislikes saying anything directly to anyone, he addresses his speech to me, and as no one believes I am likely to fall from grace, I am besieged by admirers who care little how I behave or how I treat them. Good or bad, whatever I do is in fashion and greatly admired by all. I started a new fashion called a palatine in my honor when I took out my old sable to keep my neck warm in this cold weather, and in less than a fortnight, everyone at Court was wearing sable made in a same pattern as my own. It makes me laugh. Five years ago these same fashionables mocked my unfashionable German sable so viciously I wore it with great shame. If the king was His Highness my Papa, I could not love him more.

Monsieur is popular in Paris, for he loves the city and always makes a great show of his love, whereas the king shows no love is lost between him and Paris and thus is less popular. I like Parisians but I dislike living in their town. I am well at Saint-Cloud and whenever I am there I am tranquil and happy, whereas in Paris I am never allowed an instance of peace, for one person brings me a petition, another requests me to interest myself on his behalf, another solicits an audience, another demands an answer to letters he has written, and so forth until I cannot bear it any longer. In this world great people have their troubles as well as little people which is unsurprising, but it is most annoying to be always surrounded by a crowd, so one cannot hide one's griefs or indulge them in solitude.

I have a little gossip. Persian Ambassador made his entry into Paris several weeks ago and is the oddest looking fellow with a soothsayer who rules his life. La Chatte Comtesse lends Persian Ambassador use of her body in exchange for use of his soothsayer, and it is so she can divine her future with Captain Desgrez and his constant companion, Chevalier de Rais, who they say is an older exact likeness, but this man can be neither father nor brother as Captain Desgrez is an orphan whose only younger brother died as a babe.

The king says of me, "Madame cannot endure misalliances. She is always mocking them." This is very true, for great ladies who contract such misalliances are well rewarded as they are usually unhappy and ill-treated by men who are their inferiors, and this is indeed the case with La Chatte Comtesse who has taken Captain Desgrez and his friend as her lovers. She finds herself badly off but I have no pity for her. She deserves it. "Like meets like," as Devil said to coal heaver. I cannot help laughing when I think how I forewarned her of what would happen.

She was with me at the opera and wanted with all her might to have those wretches sit behind us. I said, "For love of God, madame, keep quiet and do not worry yourself so. You know how they are in this country. When people show such anxiety about persons who are no better than their servants, it is always supposed they are in love with them." "Cannot persons feel an interest in those who are good and loyal servants of the State," she asked. I said, "Yes, and they may take them to the opera, but there is no need to have them sit close behind us." I was unaware I had guessed true and she was indeed in love with those men which is a horrible thing for her to declare in face of the world that she is as amorous as a cat who has jumped out of her husband's bed to catch a few mice.

La Chatte Comtesse is beautiful, has much grace and many engaging ways, for she is good company, always gay, makes the liveliest sallies, is insinuating, in all her life has never been out of temper, and when she wants to please, she can take all shapes, but if she is false as she truly is, there never was anyone more agreeable. Wit sparkles in her eyes but also malice. She knows how to adapt herself to everyone's humor, and one would think she has a genuine sympathy for those to whom she shows it, but one must distrust her. I always say she is like a pretty cat that lets you feel her claws even while she plays.

It is not surprising Monsieur le Duc is in love with his duchesse and there exists no greater attachment of a husband for a wife, for she has much intelligence, can be very agreeable when she chooses and is always gay, whereas he is devout and rather melancholy in temperament, so her cheery ways serve to animate him and disperse his gloom, and as he has a strong liking for women (humpbacked persons always have) but is so pious he thinks he commits a sin by looking at any woman other than his wife, it is very simple he is much in love with her. She can make him believe anything she likes, and whenever she looks favorably at him, he goes into an ecstasy and is quite beside himself.

I have seen Monsieur le Duc squint to make himself ugly when a woman complimented him that he had fine eyes though it was not necessary, for the good soul is ugly enough without endeavoring to be more so as he has a shocking mouth and sickly skin, is very short, humpbacked and deformed. His wife lives very well with him but does not love him, for she sees him as others do, yet I think she is touched by the passion he has for her and by his many good qualities. Monsieur le Duc is very charitable and helps great numbers of the poor but does so in secret, so the courtiers will not ridicule his good works.

I know fine story of saints and heard it only this morning. At a Jesuit school in Paris was a boy full of mischief who ran about all night and did not sleep in his room. The priests threatened if he was caught out of his room another time, they would beat him, so this boy went to a painter to have Saint-Ignace de Loyola put on the right cheek and Saint-Francois de Xavier on the left, and with this done he returned to school to make all sorts of trouble that same night. When they went to beat him, he prayed, "O Saint-Ignace, O Saint-Xavier, have pity and perform a miracle to prove my innocence."

When the Jesuits pulled down his breeches, seeing the two saints, they exclaimed, "A miracle. The boy is a saint." They fell to their knees, kissed the images and called every student to come in procession to kiss the holy ass which they all did, but when the Jesuit superior heard of it, he expelled the boy, then warned the father his son would need more than the intercession of saints to keep from going to the Devil. So, here is a fine lesson for censors in the postal service who have enough wit to understand my meaning.

Nothing else is new under the sun.

Kisses for you,
Liselotte

Esclavage: an iron head

Wednesday–2 November 1678–Feast of All Souls'
Palais-Royal

Dear and beloved Highness R_,

Your Highness must think me dead. It has been almost three weeks since I received your letter of 30th September, but it has remained unanswered as I was in no state to write and Die Rotzenhäuserin spells so badly I do not care to dictate to her.

With each day that passes, one is not like the other as the French proverb goes and this is true, for some days are jolly, others boring, some good and others bad. Once a month I go with Monseigneur, the dauphin, to hunt a wolf which is always a boring day, for he insists I sit in his coach to keep him company, but as he is terrified to have anyone know what he is thinking, he says not one word and moreover I cannot sleep, for he complains constantly why no wolf is to be found. This makes him disagreeable company.

As the dauphin will not betake himself to make conversation I always carry a book to read. Other than three or four pages I read when I sit on the pot, morning and night, it is the only time I set aside for reading romances and I am sure Your Highness will agree in this way romances stay amusing and become neither fatiguing nor boring.

On All Hallows Eve, while Monsieur and I were out for a drive, I made acquaintance of Maurice de La Mer when our carriage turned onto rue Sainte-Croix de La Bretonnierie and Sodomite Lorraine pointed out a giant of a fellow who was carrying a red sack.

Monsieur de La Mer is a proud man who hates torturing and executing, but it is his livelihood as ten generations ago one of his ancestors had misfortune of becoming an executioner and this profession is passed from father to son as an enforced inheritance sanctified by God in that He has put in the family's way no means of escape.

When Monsieur was curious enough to inquire about the vocation of torture and execution, Monsieur de La Mer explained it with dignity and a bit of immodesty as one would discuss baking or gardening or sewing, gentle arts, domestic concerns, for he is a sensitive soul with a genuinely tender heart, though it seems he is well suited to his vocation despite his disliking of it, for he is Virgo with Virgo rising and has taken great care to learn his science well. He has even studied with some comedians, so he may do a better job of showing the instruments (a special art) and has developed a secret method of performing procedures and degrees of torture (first degree and second degree) in such a manner as to produce great discomfort without harming prisoners too much.

He is especially proud of his four heating chairs and has more than anyone else, except for Dominican inquisitors in Spain but Dominicans are especially cruel-minded. How does he use all his fabulous instruments of torture? According to their purpose. But this is about torture and Dominicans and not about our torturer's visit.

That devil Sodomite Lorraine had our coach stopped and engaged Monsieur de La Mer in a conversation which he ought not have done, for it is not correct etiquette, but as Monsieur enjoys talking with Parisians, the fellow joined us in our coach and proceeded to torture us with descriptions of how he tortures those placed in his care. All the while he had his sack at his feet. Your Highness can guess I wished to break off our pleasant chat and have him immediately ejected from our coach, but Sodomite Lorraine would have none of it, and as Monsieur can deny his darling nothing, I was forced to hear the rest.

After an interminable length of time he did the strangest thing, and putting the sack which had been at his feet on his lap, he said, "May I show Monsieur, Madame, Monsieur de Lorraine my head?" This is when I became ill which did not seem to perturb him, so he must not be unaccustomed to people becoming sick listening to his stories, but Monsieur has been cross with me for these past several days as I ruined his new suit.

Yesterday, Monsieur de La Reynie came with news of Morel and Chasteuil who robbed and pillaged me till the day he died when death came upon him so suddenly he had no time to repent even had he wished to repent which he did not, for he had the cleverness of the Devil so I am sure he is burning terribly in the other world.

"Madame," he said, "Morel was Francois Galaup de Chasteuil. Only one man died." "I know," I said, "I told you that, Monsieur de La Reynie. The two are the same man, but you are wrong, for three men died that night." He seemed confused. But that is about his confusion and not about Morel.

This wretch Chasteuil was a gentleman and a murderer (he is guilty of Minette's death) with a valet who went by the name of Esclavage. Is it not odd what some people will allow themselves to be called in the name of friendship? Chasteuil was from a noble family of Provence and had been condemned to seven years in the galleys, but Monsieur de La Reynie refused to give details of his crime. Esclavage, being a most loyal valet, went to the galleys with Chasteuil.

Yesterday, my children came to see me before dinner and I gave them an entertainment suited to their years of a triumphal car drawn by a cat named Castille in which was a bitch named Andrienne with a pigeon as coachman and two others were pages while a dog named Picard was footman and sat behind until Lady Andrienne alighted from her carriage when Picard let down the steps. Picard also allows himself to be saddled, so we put a doll on his back and he does everything a circus horse would do. These animals belong to Die Rotzenhäuserin who has cleverly trained them to perform these little tricks. She also has a bitch whom we call Badine who knows the cards and will bring whichever we tell her.

Please do me a kindness, Your Highness, by sending some bolts of your good English wool in bright colors and do have it all embroidered in gold and silver threads as I need a few warm dresses. The rooms are damp and great drafts whistle through the galleries, yet the French insist on wearing silks even in the meanest weather, so about half the time a Court lady's bosom pops out of her bodice and her nipples are erect it is from the cold.

Toad Louvois will have the kindness to forward my letter to Your Highness with haste, so you are not made to suffer over my well-being longer than absolutely necessary, and Monsieur de La Reynie had better get to his work quickly as he has become my good friend over the years, for he reads every thought I have and has come to know me better than even His Highness my Papa.

Monsieur and I came to Paris to hear the ringing of bells on All Saints. What a commotion there was throughout town from midnight until dawn, and if one believed in such superstitions, I would say many witches fell out of the sky, for it is said the sound of church bells makes a witch's broom cease to fly and fall to the ground.

I must go now. Lenor calls me to Mass for All Souls'.

I love you with all my heart,
Liselotte

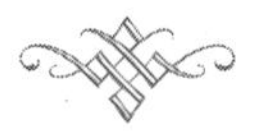

Sainte-Genevieve's guard dog

Wednesday–1 July 1676–Feast of the Precious Blood
Bastille

Nicolas-Gabriel de La Reynie looked at his watch.

Madeleine is the same age as your younger sister, but at forty-six this woman still oozes a fascinating childlike innocence for you. It's three-quarters past the hour. With another minute's passing, time will match her age.

"Let's start again, madame. You poisoned your father, then your two brothers. This much is clear. Now you say they had sex with you. What acts did you have to perform as a child? It's no reason for murdering them."

Madeleine stared into some distant imaginary landscape.

"Last month you said it was to help your lover revenge himself on your father. Last week you said it was to inherit everything for your children. But you tried to poison your husband and your children also. Was it all for yourself? Or for your lover?"

"He's with God and holy angels now."

"I don't think so."

"Monsieur de La Reynie, I want to go to Heaven too. I can't if you won't let me pray."

"Maurice, please undo Madame de Brinvilliers hands, and we'll all sit quietly for a few moments, while she says her prayers."

A giant's hands gently removed manacles from her diminutive wrists. Madeleine lunged for an iron poker. With violent force she stabbed herself. Gabriel pulled out the rod and pressed her skirt between her legs in a vain attempt to stop the bleeding. His right hand went bloody, then the lace of his sleeve, then his white silk stockings. By the time a red lukewarm wetness had slipped into his shoes, he'd pulled her so tightly against his body it could have been mistaken for an act of sex.

"Chatelet."

Your companion said something else, but you weren't listening, Gabriel. You're too busy staring at the blood on your hands. Paris stinks. It stinks less now than it did nine years ago, nevertheless it still stinks. Has anything really changed? What have you done to better the life of the citizens of this city you love more than your own life? What have you done with your authority? Have you only enjoyed the privileges and prestige, while avoiding the responsibilities?

"Monsieur General, she's going to live. When word gets out where she stabbed herself, there won't be a man in Paris who won't come to lick her wound like wolves after a bitch in heat."

Most days Gabriel didn't like Francois-Michel de Visscher very much, but this young lawyer was brilliant and always around at the appropriate moment. "You have an uncanny sixth sense, de Visscher. It's annoying."

Michel opened his book and started reading.

"How old are you?" Gabriel reached over and closed the book. "What's changed in your lifetime?"

"When I was a boy there weren't any street lights. Now there's thousands. It's a pretty sight, and it's useful for seeing in the dark."

"Like Marshal Turenne and his soup bowl."

"But that's the sort of thing history remembers. Your innovations are no different from Turenne's new fashion when he stole the Brandenburgers overcoats."

"Now every Frenchman wears a German brandenburg, and thinks warms thoughts about Marshal Turenne. You're very shallow, de Visscher."

"You want to make men moral. You can't." He removed Gabriel's hand from the book. "Monsieur General's leaving bloody fingerprints all over my expensive book. And I haven't the money to replace it."

Michel opened his book again. Gabriel stared at his bloody hands.

"Sainte-Genevieve is keeping an eye on her city, Monsieur General. She found you in Limousin. She must have been desperate to look for a watch dog there."

Gabriel, the bubbling sludge fermenting in the gutters is nothing more than a physical expression of the moral state of these people you govern. Madeleine is just an outstanding example of those doomed souls under your care. She'll survive her attempted suicide. She'll stand trial, be tortured some more and then publicly executed. She'll be dragged through so much rotting shit in the streets. Crowds will pelt her with more of it before Maurice de La Mer and his assistants dismember and burn her. Probably, the last taste in her mouth will be Parisian stink.

A good neighbor

Thursday–2 July 1676–Feast of the Visitation
La Villeneuve-sur-Gravois

Past Porte Saint-Denis, in Faubourg Saint-Denis, on rue Beauregard, Catherine Montvoisin lived the life of a prosperous bourgeois. Her property, La Villeneuve-sur-Gravois, was large with an expanse of lawn, vegetable patches, flower gardens and a coppice of shade trees. Sturdy, well-kept buildings with a history going back a dozen generations had a permanence more deeply rooted than those centuries-old forests cohabiting with a rapidly expanding suburbanization of the countryside.

Catherine Montvoisin was more commonly known as La Voisin. She was a very good neighbor and helped people in distress, but wasn't indiscriminate, inclining her sympathetic nature toward women of social position and even more so to women of means. To keep a nice home and good property for generations in the same family cost money. Charity wasn't going to secure her children's future. La Voisin did a little of this and a little of that to earn a living—the kind of things women can only seek from one another and will pay for handsomely, which is the reason La Voisin was the prosperous bourgeois she was.

Today was one of those days when La Voisin's husband would be away and her lover would keep her warm instead. She shouldn't have booked any clients, but this one had insisted with fistsful of money. A few misshapen, bloody clots dumped into a hole in the ground, and magically, golden coins would sprout in her palm. A couple of thoughtless kicks at a small mound of soil and another woman's secret would compost into fertilizer for a thriving lawn and lush flora. Much easier than spinning straw into gold.

La Voisin caught up with her patient in the courtyard. "The pain will be gone soon." Her eyes narrowed till they were sneering lips. "Madame should be used to it by now."

"It's no worse than childbirth. And hurts less than a beating." At the sight of a man sauntering into the courtyard, the patient hurriedly masked her face and ordered her coach to pull away.

The jaunty man wore a rusty wig and too much rouge on his cheeks and lips which gave a menacing absurdity to the grin slashed across his face and the mocking fond farewell he waved. "Why, Catherine, my darling, you've been keeping her a secret."

"Sweetums, my Carrot Top, keep your grubby hands off my customers. You poach another one out from under me—"

"Kitty, dear, I'd say she's been coming here a long time. On such friendly terms she doesn't even bother wearing a mask. Trusts you that much?"

"You can't give her what she wants, Pumpkin Head, so don't try stealing her."

"My sweetheart, my Kitten, do confess, my aphrodisiacs are much better than yours."

"That's not what she needs, my Little Cabbage." La Voisin pinched her lover's cheek through his breeches.

"Another Brinvilliers? What a scandal if the lieutenant general suddenly keels over."

"You cabbage head, she doesn't come for that."

"Big Fat Pussy, my sugar, this gorgeous, young wife of his comes to get rid of the babies? What a dreadful bitch. All Paris knows almighty La Reynie has no son. What a mortal sin for a woman to make a man think that after all his hard efforts, God's not answering his prayers. She'll go to Hell for it."

41

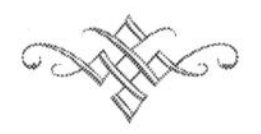

The German & the werewolf

Thursday—2 July 1676—Feast of the Visitation
Chateau Saint-Cloud

Liselotte rifled through the mess on her writing table, flinging sheets of paper into the air. They swirled to the floor with the grace of autumn leaves while she picked at a pimple on her chin until it burst. "There you are. How naughty of you to hide from me. You see, Minette, how God rewards perseverance." She waved a dozen pages under a dachshund's nose. "Here is the other half of her letter. Now, what do you say? Perfectly correct. I must not confuse what I write to one with that of another. Some are too educated for idle gossip while others have no sense at all for serious and important matters."

"Woof."

"Correct again. What a tragedy it would be to send news intended for one to the other."

Liselotte spoke to the knock at the door. "What do you want?"

A footman entered and announced the valet of Monsieur le Duc.

Her face pinched tightly. "Well, Monsieur-le-Valet-who-belongs-to-Monsieur-le-Duc, what do you want?"

"Madame. Monsieur le Duc pays his respects and wishes to make a short visit with Madame de France."

"Really. And what is Monsieur le Duc today?" Liselotte waved her finger at the valet. "For if he is a shiny cockroach, or a slithering octopus, or a slimy giant larvae, My Excellency is in no mood to be nauseated, and Monsieur le Duc may betake himself directly back to Saint-Germain, where he may burden the king with his attentions."

"Monsieur le Duc is a *canis lupus*—"

"Is that so? But which kind? For he could be a rabid *lupus lupus* or one of those disgustingly small and ugly King Charles *lupus familiaris*, and My Excellency has no desire to entertain either."

"Madame. Monsieur le Duc is a medium-sized *familiaris* of no particular distinction."

"Is he on a leash?"

"Most assuredly. And well mannered also. I'll get him and just perch him here on the sofa."

"Monsieur le Duc." Liselotte sudden turned to the valet. "You are dismissed. Your master and I are able to woof at each other perfectly well without fear of a misunderstanding."

"But Madame knows Monsieur le Duc never goes anywhere without me."

Liselotte, be nice. Try to ignore his benign insanity, if you can. He is a Prince of the Blood, ranking above all other nobles in France, his family second in importance only to immediate relations of the king. Monsieur le Duc's a poor fool who never hurts a soul, yet everyone at Court singles him out as a target of cruel practical jokes. But that's what fools are for, aren't they?

"Well, Monsieur le Duc, we have fine weather, though it is quite warm. Do you not agree? Have you heard about the incident between Maddening Politeness and Monsieur? No? He was invited to a dinner given by Monsieur for his sodomite darling, and hounded them with an unceasing rhetoric of compliments. So that sly Sodomite Lorraine tricked Maddening Politeness into an empty closet and locked him in. Hours later, when they finally let him out, he continued uninterrupted and unabated. So, Sodomite Lorraine had some of the other boys hold down Maddening Politeness while Monsieur and he fled the scene. But just as Monsieur was getting into his coach, Maddening Politeness appeared in the courtyard, so he could keep thanking Monsieur for a marvelous evening of hospitality. No, no, Monsieur le Duc. Obviously, the boys had let go of him too soon. Monsieur was in such a hurry to escape he left his darling behind in the courtyard with Maddening Politeness. Fortunately, when he jumped from a second floor window to the courtyard, he landed on Sodomite Lorraine, thus breaking his fall, which is the reason poor Maddening Politeness only dislocated his thumb. No. There is more. You know how much His Majesty detests Sodomite Lorraine. The king felt a little sympathy for Maddening Politeness, so had his own surgeon reset the thumb. The surgeon had to do the thing twice, for Maddening Politeness dislocated his thumb a second time, when he and the surgeon argued as to who should open the door and let the other go through it first. His Majesty feared some harm might come to his surgeon from too much politeness, so he ordered Maddening Politeness to stay put while the surgeon left the room. Of course, His Majesty could leave the room whenever it pleased him to do so, which he did, and left Maddening Politeness all alone to be polite to himself only."

Monsieur le Duc scurried on all fours over to a casement window, undid his breeches, lifted his leg and aimed at a large potted plant.

"Monsieur le Duc." Liselotte was on her feet and pulling at his leash. "That is most unhealthy for plants and brocade drapes. Stop it at once."

The valet offered a profusion of apologies as he dragged his master from the room.

Liselotte went back to her writing table. The dachshund uncurled from her nap and presented her belly to be rubbed. "Ahhh, Minette. God may reward perseverance, but He needs to understand forbearance is not its own reward."

Gabriel's curse

Tuesday–4 August 1676–Feast of Saint Dominic
Hotel de Ville

Armand and his sister, Marie-Julie, began life with every privilege, but then the Fates became capricious. Their mother died. Their father departed with their baby brother and abandoned them to a loving aunt. A few years later, when she died suddenly, they became the responsibility of a grandfather. His indifference marooned them on an obscure chateau governed by a drunken uncle who comforted his own failures and disappointments through regular beatings of his wards.

Nicolas-Gabriel de La Reynie was in his thirties when he stumbled onto Marie-Julie and Armand during a visit to one of his younger sisters in a nearby convent. Having just lost a wife and two children to measles, he was particularly susceptible to Marie-Julie's nubile charm, while the old drunkard was charmed by Gabriel's wealth.

Long negotiations ensued, a great deal of money exchanged hands, and Gabriel married his ravishing child bride without a dowry but with her younger brother as an encumbrance. Gabriel didn't care. He was besotted with his new wife and his passion enabled him to tolerate Armand, just barely, despite a mutual hatred at first meeting.

Armand was rakishly handsome, even as a boy. He was a charmer. Women panted after him. Girls swooned. He knew just the right words or actions to get whatever he desired from anyone and became an insufferable spoiled brat. Whenever Armand couldn't get what he wanted from Gabriel, which was all the time, he used his sister to get it for him.

With the arrival of manhood, everything good and bad in Armand increased a hundredfold. Marie-Julie charmed Gabriel into appointing Armand Captain of Police of Paris, the lieutenant general's second in command. Armand became rich, traveled in the right social circles, made some powerful friends, chased every pretty thing in skirts and pursued some good looking things who wore breeches. He had the means and the mind to be independent, to be master in his own household, but chose instead to live under Gabriel's roof like a poor relation.

Women from every district of Paris swarmed into and around Place de Greve. Two stories above this public square, Jean-Jacques-Armand Desgrez gazed in the window at his own reflection, and then at the pattern of his vest.

Last year's fashion. The Comtesse will notice. Damned your brother-in-law for rushing you. Look, not bad, third one from the left on the scaffolding. Get his name from Maurice de La Mer.

Armand's eyes pounced next on an auburn-haired beauty on the steps of the Hotel de Ville. She was sleek as a race horse. He had to leave in half an hour to change his vest, but women with reddish hair should never wear bright pink anything, so the Comtesse might have to wait while he taught the auburn beauty a thing or two about fashion.

Ten more minutes. Those men in black leather will hack apart and burn two unlucky women. Odd the curious forms entertainment can take. Public executions are nothing more than spectator sport with methods of torture as imaginative as any the Romans devised and calling for at least as much emotional audience participation. Bread and circus. Keep the citizens satiated and docile.

Gabriel's put aside his translation of Liselotte's letter and has been staring at you for a long time. Look at the window instead of through it. See the reflection of his eyes boring into your back? What's going on in his head? Same misery as always? Your sister's made him endure you for a score of years. Older men can be such stupid sots over beautiful younger wives. Well, one has to pay the price to enjoy the privilege.

Armand turned around and grinned. "Stale gossip in Madame's love letters?"

"Some old. Some new."

"How long before this one succumbs to Lorraine's fatal charms?"

"I don't think so." Gabriel walked over to the window. "Lorraine's little clique can't afford to have lightning strike twice. Madame will probably die in her bed of old age."

Armand fixed his gaze on the executioner's handsome assistant again. "I don't think I like the stench of burning flesh."

"Not your preferred sport? They'll do the same to Brinvilliers. How do you feel about it?"

"You'd be lost without her letters. She's indiscreet and writes whatever comes into her head. But she rambles on without rhyme or reason. Don't you find it annoying?"

Gabriel glanced down at the roasting corpses and then scrutinized Armand. "Look at the crowd. Every mother in Paris must be there. We've quieted a mob by torturing and burning two witches. Why the riots? Why the attacks on midwives? And the abortionists? What's behind the talk of sacrilege? Babies bought for as little as one ecu on the open market. What's going on?"

"Gabriel, you fret too much. I have an appointment." Armand turned to leave.

"Weren't you sixteen the first time you faced down a vindictive husband in a duel?"

"What's your point?"

He looked Armand straight in the eye. "Your luck can't hold forever."

"You're jealous."

"You're right. I worry too much."

Armand, his eyes are stabbing you in the back again. Is he getting a queasy feeling in his stomach? It'll gnaw at him till it turns into genuine pain. It's the same thing whenever he sees Marie-Julie with you. How perverse for a man to be jealous of his wife and her brother.

Gabriel watched Armand's retreating figure, and whispered, "You over-active prick. I hope you catch the Spanish curse."

An Act of Contrition

Rex Mundi's shadow faded from midnight to dawn.

Whether Armand thought or yelled or whispered, to his ear, it was all the same. "Bless me, father, for I have sinned. It has been—"

Armand, listen to what they're saying about you.

"Does he want a priest?"

"Of course, he wants a priest."

"Doesn't deserve one."

"In the end even the Devil deserves one. I won't have his damned spirit bound to my home now that I'm going to be free of him at last. Get him a priest."

Armand, feel those luxurious chestnut curls you loved so much come looming down to clutch you. Eyes of burning coals embedded in a stone face sear your cheek. The curls wrap themselves around your head and begin to tighten, slithering, hissing, flicking forked tongues on your skin.

Listen. Listen to what they're saying about you, Armand.

"Why's he screaming?"

"Make him stop."

"He's in pain."

"You think so? I say it's his conscience."

Armand, you really don't want a priest, do you?

47

Inviolate sanctity of Confession

Tuesday–21 September 1677–Feast of Saint Matthew
Notre-Dame Cathedral

"Bless me, father, for I have sinned. It's been—"

"Monsieur de La Reynie, is that you?"

"Yes, Father Jean."

"I have something to tell you. Come closer." Gabriel inclined his ear toward the screen till his confessor's words filtered through this membrane as a whisper. "Last few months, I've heard a lot of confessions about poisonings. Seems it's the easiest way to divorce a spouse. I was disturbed by it, so I told the bishop. Thought I was alone, but all the priests are hearing the same thing. Bishop told me to keep silent."

"So, why are you confessing to me?"

"If all our parishioners poison one another, where would it leave us priests? And perhaps, a little pocket money. Vow of poverty can be so trying. Bishop needn't know."

"No, he needn't, but it's not the sort of information that's worth anything."

"Well, I'm sure this is. Someone's going to poison the king and the dauphin. A man who's a distant cousin by marriage to the attorney general of Aix-en-Provence knows all the details. Used to be captain of a galley, but now he's an alchemist-poisoner."

"Old news is worthless. I already know. Jesuits from rue Saint-Antoine told me. Someone dropped a letter into their confessional box this morning."

"Huh. Damned Jesuits. Should have gone to Chatelet yesterday and told you."

"But I don't have any names, Father Jean."

"You know I can't do that. I heard it in Confession."

"Give me a name. Any name you heard not connected to a sin of any kind."

The priest's memory scrambled through thousands of confessions. "Andreas von Fugger."

"And how did you hear his name, Father Jean?"

"From a banker. Travels to Rome a lot. I asked him to bring me back a holy relic next time he goes. Said he knew a German nobleman with a lot of influence and important connections who could get the Pope to bless it for me."

"Andreas Graf von Fugger."

The priest nodded. "Monsieur de La Reynie, there's something else. The banker knows one of the king's secretaries who has an important position at Paris Royal Mint, and the king's secretary knows a lawyer in Parlement who holds a large number of royal distillery licenses. And all of them know the galley captain turned alchemist-poisoner, Vanens, who lives on rue de Nevers."

"Vanens on rue de Nevers?"

"Monsieur de La Reynie. Did I let it slip?"

The priest held out a hand. Gabriel dropped large gold coins into it. They counted to ten together. As the palm shut tightly, lines of fate creased into a modest smile.

A poisoned Communion wafer: dinner at midnight for the Pope & an opera singer

Thursday–20 January 1678–Feast of Saint Sebastian
Von Fugger Bank–Rome

Andreas Graf von Fugger sat at the head of a huge table contemplating late afternoon sunlight, for as days were getting longer with each sunset that brought the vernal equinox closer, light was changing from a golden amber to the color of pirates' gold. With a family fortune in excess of eighty million florins he could afford to enjoy the simple pleasures of life, while lesser men such as those several dozen in the room cut one another's throats to hold on to their hides and their pathetically small fortunes. Occasionally, Andreas glimpsed their chaos with detached bemusement.

Sheep are stupid animals. They panic at the mere thought of a wolf in their vicinity. These men in your office, all of them arguing, simultaneously yelling at one another, aren't any better. Desperation can be so undignified.

Listen, Andreas. Use your gift for understanding the real meanings behind words. More importantly, don't throw away your trumps early in the game. Hold them till the very last second. How much longer should you let them sweat? Another half hour, an hour? Look at the clock. You have plenty of time. Listen to their pathetic wailing.

"He's inherited a spy network from two previous Cardinal Prime Ministers. It's the envy of every State Department in Europe. It's perfection."

"Marquis de Louvois? That idiot? If he had it written out in front of him, in a book, he couldn't figure it out."

"Forget him and his spies. You should be worried about the Lieutenant General of Police of Paris and his constables. La Reynie has gotten almost all of them. The banker, that fake nobleman, our man at Paris Royal Mint."

"The lawyer with the royal distillery licenses too?"

"They have the galley captain, his mistress and his valet. Everybody but the doctor who escaped to England. The doctor denounced them. Sold out for a king's ransom."

"The French police confiscated all alchemic equipment, counterfeit silver and poisons. They found purchase authorizations on the banker. They know Paris Royal Mint was buying counterfeit silver for the sterling price."

"They'll figure it out once they realize poison is the key."

"La Reynie will torture it out of the woman. He knows about the plot to poison the French king and the dauphin."

"Jesuits are unethical and can't be trusted. Heard they broke the seal of Confession to tell La Reynie about the assassination scheme."

"My people in Madrid, Rotterdam and Vienna report Louvois's spies are crawling all over their banks. And every other bank in every major commercial city. They've made the connection between this

Parisian gang and all the great banking houses on the Continent. Now, this is the real problem we have to deal with."

"No one in Bruges or Antwerp has had any problems."

"Yet. That fool Louvois has a conspiratorial mania which is all consuming. And he likes easy answers. Feed his spies information that he's dealing with a ring of counterfeiters. Make them believe there's some political machination afoot to debase French currency. He'll more than happily swallow it."

"What about the Paris police? It doesn't explain distillery licenses, alchemic laboratories, the physician, perfumes or poisons. La Reynie will never buy a currency-debasing story."

Jakob saw Andreas was bored, so he leaned over and whispered into his master's ear. "Herr Graf. I've heard a story." Andreas's eyes lit up. "Your young French sweetheart and that travestied castrato, the one he's been pursuing with his unwanted attentions."

Andreas whispered back. "Zambinella's a shameless flirt. Poor Jean-Baptiste is being led on. But, he'll come back. When Zambinella gets tired of him. And her protector finds the whole affair amusing. You know how it is with these cardinals. One has to humor them once in a while."

"I'm afraid not. Appears no one could convince him Zambinella wasn't a woman. Cardinal Cicognara couldn't stand it anymore. Had Jean-Baptiste put out of his misery this morning. Poisoned the Communion wafer they gave him at Mass. Cicognara locked Zambinella in her room. She's been in tears all day."

Andreas rose from his chair. "Gentlemen, festivities are over. Go home."

"But Herr Graf. What are we going to do?"

"I'm going to a dinner party. Good evening, gentlemen."

Jakob had the room cleared of its unwanted guests, and as the last of the men left, thought it prudent to depart also.

"Where are you going? Get Balthasar and come back with him." Andreas wrote two invitations while he waited for Jakob to return with one of his best agents. "Balthasar, you're going to Paris for a few years. Shut down all operations there. Get rid of anyone who's a problem. Keep an eye on Philippe Chevalier de Lorraine and there's a woman he's been blackmailing. Governess to the king's bastards." Andreas gestured toward Jakob.

Jakob said, "Marquise de Maintenon."

"Keep an eye on her too." Andreas waved at Balthasar to disappear, then hesitated. "Wait. You've been carrying on a correspondence with Monsieur de Visscher."

"Herr Graf. I didn't mean any harm by it."

"You did well. It won't seem suspicious when you strike up your acquaintance again. He's been independent a bit too long now. Every spare moment you have, follow him. I want a weekly report of every detail of every moment of his life. Get him away from Philippe and keep him away. Most importantly, find out the exact nature of his relationship with Monsieur de La Reynie."

Balthasar bowed deeply, then departed.

Andreas handed Jakob two letters. "Dinner for four at midnight. And musicians. Tell cook that the meal had better be extraordinary. Have the servants set up in the library. His Holiness fancies himself an intellectual. Best of everything."

"Which invitation do I deliver first?"

"Go first to Cardinal Cicognara. Wait for an answer. Make sure he agrees to bring Zambinella."

"If he demurs, Herr Graf? Cicognara's very jealous of Zambinella."

"Tell him the Pope is the only other guest tonight and expects a private, and an intimate, performance. Then, go to the Vatican and tell His Holiness that Zambinella's dying to sing for him, in whatever way he wants."

Jakob grinned with the delight of a child. "Herr Graf, Cicognara will be most unhappy."

"Double-dealing doppelganger. Who does he think he is? When His Holiness is finished with Zambinella, poison her."

A night at the opera

Friday–13 May 1678–Feast of Saint Euthymius the Enlightener
Chateau Saint-Cloud

"It's Friday the thirteenth. I won't go. It's twilight. That's when she sits by the fountain. It's cursed and the day's unlucky."

"Her Royal Highness isn't getting out of her comfortable grave for the sake of frightening a useless sot like you. You do what I say or I'll beat the living crap out of you."

"She'll snatch my soul and give it to the Devil. Get it yourself." The lackey threw a bucket at Morel's head and ran away.

Morel yelled after him. "Tomorrow. When I get my hands on you, you'll wish you had gone to the Devil." Morel threw the bucket at another lackey. "You go get it."

The man walked away quickly and faded into twilight. He had to pass the fountain to get to the well. There was no other way to go. Minette always sat within the fountain's cool mist whenever the weather was warm, so after she died rumors spread of peasants and villagers in the district seeing her there. She seemed to be smiling at everybody who saw her, then the sightings stopped, but in the last few years people were seeing her again, only now, Minette wasn't smiling. They said she was looking for revenge.

The lackey made it safely to the well and was making his way back. "Matthew, Mark, Luke and John, bless me, bless me, bless me," he prayed.

A few more yards. That's all. Your heart's pounding. Your chest hurts. There she is all white and shimmery in the moonlight sitting on the other side of the fountain. If you're very quiet, maybe you can slip past her. But she'll hear your heart's beating, it's so loud.

A phantom within a mist rose up, doubled its height, then turned toward him. Was there a face half way up? Such a hideous face. A wrinkled skull with moist red eyes, thick nose and huge mouth. A devil's laugh rang in the lackey's ears and chased him all the way back to the chateau.

"I've seen the late Madame," he screamed over and over. Morel grabbed the lackey and shook him. Suddenly, the man turned very red in the face. In the throws of a fit, he foamed at the mouth and swallowed his tongue. A doctor pronounced him dead of suffocation.

Morel grabbed a stick and went to the fountain. "Show yourself, damn you. We killed you once, I'll kill you again if I have to."

"Have pity. Monsieur Morel, don't hurt me. It's only poor Philippinette."

Morel hauled Philippinette to the chateau and proceeded to beat her, but the spunky crone fought back and raised such a commotion that Monsieur and Madame intervened.

Morel protested. "Monsieur. She deserves to be put in prison. She murdered the lackey. Frightened him to death."

Philippinette said, "It was only a joke."

Liselotte assumed the attitude of a Hun. "Monsieur, do not do it. She is but an old woman."

Monsieur stroked Liselotte's hand. "Morel, I can't see what justice will be served by jailing Philippinette. She's very very old. She'll die soon anyway, and the lackey won't come back to life no matter who's punished. Let her go. You may go also, Morel."

Morel bowed and started to leave, dragging the old woman with him.

"No, no. Leave her here. I wish to speak with her."

Monsieur spoke to Liselotte as if Philippinette was deaf or too stupid to understand. "Don't let her touch anything. She's very stinky, and it'll get into the fabric. Philippe and I are going to Paris for the night. To the opera. I'll see you tomorrow." He kissed the top of her head and left.

All hunched over, Philippinette stood, weeping. "Many thanks, Madame." She kissed Liselotte's hands. "I would kneel before Madame, but I wouldn't be able to get up."

Liselotte helped her onto a chair. "Never tell that I permitted you to sit in my presence. It is not done, you know. They would imprison you for such disrespect and I could not save you. Now, I want to know. What possessed you to play ghost instead of staying in your bed?"

"I regret nothing. I'm old and don't sleep much. My whole life I carry faggots on my back to make my living. Every hour the sun is up. I still do it. I need something to keep up my spirits. When I was a girl, I always played mean tricks on people. Everybody said I'd die young because of it. I'm eighty. Playing ghost is the most fun I've ever had. If they aren't afraid of the sheet, they're afraid of my face. I always have a good laugh before I go to bed."

"How do you make yourself so tall?"

"With a pole. A long slim pole, half as tall as me again. I move it up over my head when I want to make the sheet go high in the air."

"A clever trick. I shall have to remember it."

Liselotte, it's time to go to the nursery for your customary visit before your children go to bed. You still haven't learned not to fawn tenderly over them like a bourgeoise. If Monsieur catches you, and he will find out because the servants will tell him, he'll have a fit. Why can't you be more like Monsieur? He's highly accessible to his children, yet his behavior isn't in the least bit undignified or un-aristocratic. He kisses and hugs them, plays with them or stuffs them with bon bons and cakes at every opportune moment, but he never lets the servants see him. A bit of hypocrisy never hurt anyone.

A valet entered the nursery and bowed. "Madame."

Liselotte handed her daughter to a nurse. "What is it now? Cannot you see I am playing?"

"Madame, Morel is dying. Immediately after the business with the ghost, he took to his bed in a spasm of hot fever. A doctor's with him now. Morel needs to speak with you."

"I do not like Morel and would be of no comfort. He does not need me. He needs a priest."

"Said he had something he wanted to confess. Said to tell you it was most useful gossip about the death of the late Madame."

"Let us hurry. Come with me." Liselotte waddled as quickly as she could to the other end of Saint-Cloud to swoop down on Morel. "Where is that evil wretch who robbed and pillaged me all these years?"

In a hushed, respectful voice, the doctor said, "Madame, Monsieur Morel is dying."

"I know." Liselotte plopped onto a chair the valet placed at Morel's bedside. "Do you want a priest, Monsieur Morel?"

"Madame. I don't believe in God. Let this carcass alone. It's no good for anything anymore. I only wanted to tell you, it was Chevalier de Lorraine who had us poison the late Madame."

"Bah! This is no news. Monsieur Morel, you have been living under a rock these many years. You made My Excellency stop playing and had me come all this way to the other side of my chateau, where My Excellency has never bothered myself to come before now, just to hear this? What are you dying from?"

The doctor said, "Poisoned, Madame."

She waved an admonishing finger. "You always had the cleverness of the Devil."

Morel wheezed and turned his head away from Liselotte. With his last breath a sarcastic smile froze onto his lips.

"Monsieur Morel, if we examine things well, we always see the justice of God. People are usually punished in this world by their own sins. Monsieur Morel? Are you listening to me you lazy, good-for-nothing, thieving maitre d'hotel?" A too quiet moment passed. Liselotte bent over Morel's body and looked into his face. "Well, then. My Excellency was of some comfort to the poor wretch. He died happy."

Once the doctor was left alone with Morel's body, he locked the door and let someone in through the window. Together, they destroyed every shred of Morel's identity and replaced it with another man's.

Liselotte went to sleep directly after leaving Morel's deathbed, but the valet didn't let her rest in peace for long. "Come in if you must, but stop that cannon fire. You will wake the dead."

The valet entered and bowed. "Madame."

A look on his face told her everything. "You are a harbinger of death. Who is it now?"

"Madame, the doctor's dead. Poisoned."

"What a busy day it has been. It is not even midnight yet. Oh, Monsieur, where are you when you are needed? At the opera with a sodomite. Such a lot of poison in one day."

"Odd thing, Madame. I was standing close by the priest, while the doctor was making his last confession. He confessed he's the one who poisoned Morel."

A giant shadow sat by the fountain keeping Minette's Shade company.

Smile gently into the night at that splotch of black iridescence ogling you. Tonight's work was an unparalleled success. This unkind raven congratulates you. "Bravo." Another shadow half your bulk has arrived. Look. Minette's ghost is dissolving into a mist of moonlight.

Mortified metamorphosis

Monday—15 August 1678—Feast of the Assumption
Chateau Saint-Cloud

Nicolas-Gabriel de La Reynie closed his eyes and prayed he was asleep.

"Night before last, Princesse Slut was supposed to entertain the king. His valet hid her in a secret passage and waited with her till dawn, but the king never kept their appointment. Her other lover had a jealous fit, locked the king's door from the outside, then threw the key into a privy. In the morning they had to break down the door, or His Majesty would have had to go, you know where, all by himself. And this is something he is unaccustomed to doing. Princesse Potrag was more fortunate."

Gabriel said, "Dull-witted prank. The duc's going to get himself exiled. And poor princesse is in complete disfavor now."

"You are listening, Monsieur de La Reynie. I thought you had fallen asleep. Which would be a very clever trick when one has been standing as long as you have been. Is there something wrong with your eyes?"

"No, Madame. I was just trying to form a mental picture of Madame's amusing story. Is there yet another?"

"I did not know you liked my little gossips so very much. Well, yes, Monsieur de La Reynie. As I was saying, Princesse Potrag was more fortunate. When the king's valet went to fetch her for the night, her husband had the good sense to continue snoring. Very loudly. So loudly, his snores were heard in the corridor. With Princesse Slut's sad aftermath before him to serve as a lesson, he closed his eyes and ears, but not his mouth, to his wife's romantic interlude with the king."

"He'll be Court fool." Gabriel laughed quietly. "What does he care? Soon, he'll be an extremely wealthy cuckold. His Majesty will shower him with riches."

"But jealously breeds contempt, and the more he is given, the crueler they will be to him. Now, My Excellency has entertained you enough. You must tell us a droll tale."

Gabriel, open your eyes. Survey your nightmare one more time. Your patroness sits before you, a mountain of lard decorated by a konditormeister gone mad with a set of novelty pastry tubes and an endless supply of buttercream in a rainbow of colors.

Monsieur le Duc suspiciously eyes six dachshunds crammed between him and Liselotte, while Monsieur-le-Valet-who-belongs-to-Monsieur-le-Duc stands behind them, struggling with another two dogs. Several chew on a tightly rolled sheaf of papers. Is their chew bone a vital piece of evidence? Notice how none of the dogs averts a nervous gaze from Monsieur le Duc. Two hours have crept from morning to afternoon. If you finally tell them a story, Gabriel, they might set you free.

Monsieur le Duc took out his snuff box. "Grrr."

"Monsieur le Duc, that is most unhealthy. It makes noses horrible and spreads a fetid odor." Liselotte waved her finger under his nose, but his attention was still completely focused on the dachshunds. "Like goats. Very stinky. Noses besmeared with snuff make their owners look as if they had tumbled into a latrine."

"They call it the magic herb, Madame." He snorted a large pinch of powdered tobacco and flicked another generous pinch onto the dogs which began sneezing.

"Well, you are yourself today, Monsieur le Duc."

The valet said, "No, Madame. Monsieur le Duc is *canis lupus lupus* today."

"No one addressed you Monsieur-le-Valet-who-belongs-to-Monsieur-le-Duc, but this is most useful information, nonetheless, and My Excellency thanks you."

The valet bowed his head while Liselotte addressed Monsieur le Duc. "I hope, Your Highness the *Canis Lupus,* is not a hungry *lupus lupus,* for My Excellency is in no mood to be chewed upon." Liselotte peered into his face, then gave his hand a sharp smack. "And stop regarding my little babies with such a hungry eye."

"I am no *canis lupus lycaon.* I am *lykos anthropos,* for I may have the appearance of a *lykos,* but I have the intelligence of an *anthropos.*"

"Well, then tell me this, Monsieur le Loup-garou. Why does Monsieur jingle jangle at night?"

Gabriel returned from his daydream. "Pardon, Madame?"

"Monsieur jingle jangles at night. After he gets into bed and is kind enough to let me sleep and not do any disgusting business of making children, he jingle janlges. Monsieur takes his rosary to bed and holds it all through the night so as to be protected from the Devil. It has all sorts of medals on it and it dances and makes jingle jangle noises right here." Liselotte gestured with both hands toward her own groin. "For a long time before Monsieur finally goes to sleep. The noise is most annoying."

Gabriel stared in disbelief. "Is this a riddle, Madame?"

Monsieur le Duc looked down at his own groin with smirking eyes. "Can't imagine what Monsieur might be doing with himself. But as to the other story, I think I'm confused. What was it we were going to tell Monsieur de La Reynie?"

"Yes, Madame, why am I here?"

"About so many of my servants dropping dead like flies."

Monsieur le Duc laughed. "Why would anyone care about your dead servants?"

"Because, Monsieur de La Reynie, must solve the mystery of Francois Galaup de Chasteuil. See here. I have his papers." The dachshunds surrendered their chew bone of documents to Liselotte who waved this limp, soggy baton with authority of a field marshal.

Monsieur le Duc said, "But, Madame, you said he was Morel. What's the mystery?"

"Morel was not himself. He was Francois Galaup de Chasteuil."

Gabriel said, "Yes, Madame. But for whom am I searching, Morel or Chasteuil?"

"You need not seek Morel, for he is dead."

Monsieur le Duc said, "But, I thought it's Chasteuil who died."

"He is dead too."

"But, it's only one man who's dead."

"I know what I said, Monsieur de La Reynie. The two men are the same. But you are wrong, for on that night three men died."

Monsieur le Duc looked as if he was about to have a tantrum. Instead, he metamorphosed.

Liselotte turned a sympathetic face toward him. "This is enough crap and gossip for you, Monsieur le Duc. You must not tax yourself with too many serious thoughts. I would never forgive myself if your brain hurt itself on account of My Excellency."

Gabriel bowed to his hosts. "May I be excused, Madame? Monsieur le Duc?"

"Quack, quack."

Bedtime prayers

Wednesday–24 August 1678–Feast of Saint Bartholomew
Chateau Saint-Cloud

What kind of fool does Monsieur take you for? You certainly know jingling and jangling when you hear it. If he thinks he can make you believe, with his absolutely insistent and insulting attitude, you're hearing things, well, he's very wrong.

Liselotte balanced a slab of gooey cheese atop a jagged hunk she had ripped from a German rye bread. At the same time she kept a careful watch on Monsieur as he knelt at the foot of the bed, saying his bedtime prayers.

"Monsieur."

"Shhh."

"When Monsieur is finished praying, I have a question." She filled her mouth with the midnight snack which forced her jaws completely open.

Monsieur got into bed and helped her lubricate her jaws with beer. "I'm afraid Lotte you've put too much food in your mouth." He reached in, pulled out half the cheese, then pushed her mouth shut. "That's better. Can you chew now?"

She swallowed. "Thank you, Monsieur."

"You must learn to eat smaller pieces."

"It did not look very large."

"Never put anything into your mouth larger than your fist."

"Monsieur, must we do any disgusting business of making children tonight?"

"Not if you don't want to, Lotte."

Liselotte shook her head, stuffed her mouth with the rest of the cheese and sputtered bits of her meal as she spoke. "Thank you, Monsieur."

"Only, do keep your food, your dogs and your big toes on your side of the bed."

"Is Monsieur going to jingle jangle again tonight?"

"Madame. I told you, you're imagining things."

She pointed to his rosary with its dozens of holy medals. "Your medals were dancing a long time last night. God forgive me for saying it this way, but I suspect you were marching the Virgin into territory quite foreign to her."

"You don't know what you're talking about. Now, be quiet and go to sleep."

Liselotte, place the candle on your side, so it lights up the entire bed. Pretended to go to sleep. Feel his breath? He's leaned over to see if your eyes are closed. Lie very still. He'd better not take too long or you really will fall asleep. There it is. Jingle, jangle. Jingle, jangle. You'll have to be fast. Now. Shoot out your arm under the covers. Grab his hand.

She choked with laughter. "Caught in the act, Monsieur."

He laughed too. "It's a miracle, Lotte. You grew up Protestant and don't understand these things. Holy relics bring success to everything they touch."

"Monsieur. You will never convince me, Monsieur, the Virgin would be happy to bring success to those parts made to destroy her virginity."

"Don't tell a soul. Please, Lotte."

The Devil's departed Elysium for France

Monday–31 October 1678–All Hallows Eve
Chatelet Courts

Francois-Michel de Visscher was beautiful as an angel. His beauty was beyond that which plucks canniness from a wary eye. His was a beauty that caused a longing of distinct intensity, which ever so tenuously put out invisible fingers to caress his aura, being no different from an actual touch, and forced him to acknowledge its staring hunger with a look into nervously averted eyes. Michel accepted it as naturally as he did his lean, six-foot frame, dark sandy hair and hazel eyes which refracted from green to deep plum. It's how he'd been treated in Rome, but in Paris this gaze was tinged with an envy which wanted to slap and hit until the fist became an openhanded strangle.

What are you doing here? Your law degrees are from Bologna, oldest university and finest school of jurisprudence in Europe. Your academic record was impressive. Your patron opened with ease any and all doors of opportunity. Your life was touched by magic. Exalted families vied for you, and one of the most venerated, Doria Pamphilj Landi, employed you as personal secretary to Benedetto Cardinal Pamphilj, nephew of the late, inordinately powerful Pope Innocent X. For one bright moment, your future prospects held unlimited promise. Not anymore.

You're a foreigner in Paris and it doesn't matter if your French ancestry is considerably less diluted than the king's. The French hold your Italian education against you. Graduates of the Sorbonne with decidedly less ability advance quickly through the bureaucratic system while you're still doing research in the archives. Two years of demeaning, menial labor. What do you have to show for it? Nothing but an exquisite wardrobe from your days in Italy that's slowly turning shabby. If you'd been able to get your hands on even a small portion of your money, it would've made a difference. Starting over wouldn't be such a struggle. But money was a noose around your neck no one thought you had enough character to remove. You surprised everybody by leaving it behind.

Running away is a family trait. Isn't it? Remember your father's decision to avoid the executioner's block? Besides, there was nothing left after the Crown attained your family's titles and properties. Do you think Monsieur le Duc will ever recall it's your father who murdered a jealous husband in a duel who happened to be a distant cousin of his? Are you any different, Michel? Now you're finally back in Paris. Do you meditate often, ruefully, at how your father dragged you into a glorious exile?

Michel assessed the constable who'd been sent to fetch him. The man's boots were scuffed and unpolished, his face a ruddy color from broken capillaries, and he smelled of unwashed laundry. He was probably in his mid-thirties, only a few years older than himself. At twenty the freshness of youth would have made him appear good-looking to lower class girls, especially with the cocky arrogance of a schoolyard bully he still carried. But a hard life on the streets, and spending what few leisure hours he might have soaked in liquor, had turned him hopelessly vulgar and men of his class usually hadn't the intelligence to rise above their birth. A hard existence stales life prematurely.

"Hurry up, Maitre de Visscher." Michel heard but didn't listen. "You haven't got all day. Stop fooling with those god-damned papers, and get upstairs. Now. Monsieur General doesn't like to be kept waiting."

Even a constable, sent like a lowly messenger, feels entitled to address you with contempt and authority. Gather up your armful of documents, Michel. Make your way from your miserable cubbyhole of an office in an obscure corner of the building, through a maze of corridors and stairs, to the second floor. You're on the landing. Decide now. Make the right turn? Deliberately make a wrong turn. There's an empty courtroom. Go in and throw everything on the floor. If you could have anything in the world at this very moment, what would it be? Laugh at yourself. To be in bed with the love of your life? Sit down and weep, overwhelmed with heartache. Let La Reynie wait.

Gabriel smiled at the beautiful angel of a man who entered his office. He couldn't help himself.

"Monsieur General."

"De Visscher, I sent for you an hour ago."

"I know." Michel threw the documents on Gabriel's desk. "Do you want me to tell you or do you want to read it for yourself?"

Gabriel got up and pushed a chair underneath Michel. "Sit down." He poured a couple glasses of wine and offered him one. "Why don't you go back to Rome? You had impressive credentials there. And important friends. Are your enemies so powerful?"

Michel sipped his wine, looked sadly vulnerable and kept quiet, a trick he'd learned from Cardinal Pamphilj.

"De Visscher, I don't know why I don't like you. I've really thought about it. There's nothing to dislike. And I trust you with things like this that I don't want anyone else to know about. You're hardworking. Sober. Refined. Not a hint of scandal in your life. You're too brilliant for this menial work. A lackey wouldn't do it, and you never complain. What am I going to do with you?"

Michel's face was a cipher. "Francois Galaup de Chasteuil was condemned to seven years in the galleys for the rape-murder of his two nieces. Officially, it was the most decent crime they could accuse him of. There was talk about a young boy being involved, probably his son, but it was kept out of official court records."

"How did you find this out?"

"I have my ways. Chasteuil's father is attorney general of Aix-en-Provence, so he wasn't hanged. The father is obviously an indulgent type, because a number of years before the incident with his nieces, Chasteuil did the same to a sister. And the father hushed it all up."

"And Chasteuil's wife?"

"Had his son by the sister he murdered. There was also a valet, an inciseur by training, named Esclavage. He and Chasteuil met in the late 1640's, on a tour of military duty in Algeria."

"And Esclavage?"

"Went to the galleys with Chasteuil. After two years their ship, Elysium, had a new captain, Vanens, whose cousin german married Chasteuil's cousin german once removed."

"God. Practically blood kin."

"Exactly. That's why, after Barbary pirates attacked the galley fleet off the coast of North Africa, Vanens reported Chasteuil and Esclavage as drowned."

Gabriel refilled Michel's empty glass. "So, Vanens let them escape. Where'd they go?"

"To Aix-en-Provence. Chasteuil's father hid him in a Carmelite monastery half way between Marseilles and Aix. Bought his son the priorship, so Chasteuil and Esclavage went there as the new prior and his secretary. There were scandals involving some local women who disappeared, but generally, they went unnoticed for a few years."

"Then, he was up to his old tricks again?"

"Last woman who disappeared, Chasteuil got careless, or lazy. Buried her under the floor of the monastery's chapel. Autopsy disclosed she'd been horribly, bizarrely tortured, and she'd been pregnant, but the fetus was missing. Chasteuil's father helped him escape again, with Vanens's help."

"And then, they ended up at Saint-Cloud. Chasteuil as Morel. But, what about Esclavage's identity? Who's he?"

"Not quite. They traveled from Marseilles to Nice to Turin. Along the way they picked up a lawyer, a physician, a banker and a nobleman of dubious authenticity. Vanens got himself a valet and a mistress, whom everyone shared."

"The valet was awfully busy."

"No, the mistress." Michel looked up from his wine glass. Gabriel laughed at him. Then, Michel laughed too. "Chasteuil was in Italy, till the mysterious death of his employer."

"Who was?"

"Duc de Savoie."

"Jesus Christ. And Chasteuil got away again?"

"Vanished into thin air. All of them."

"Then, Chasteuil and Esclavage ended up at Saint-Cloud and the rest of the gang in Paris."

Michel sipped his wine. "Is that what you believe?"

"What does it tell you, de Visscher?" Gabriel stared into the fireplace for a moment. "You don't get it, do you? Have you ever heard of Andreas Graf von Fugger?"

"Anyone who's ever set foot in Rome has heard of him."

"Heard a rumor, a few years ago. When Chevalier de Lorraine went into exile, he ended up in Rome and met von Fugger. Then the first Madame died suddenly. Italians practically invented the art of assassination by poison."

"No, they just refined it into an art. And, von Fugger's a German name, not Italian."

"Point is this. To murder the sovereign of a country, like the Duc de Savoie, and not get caught means someone awfully powerful is behind it. As a matter of courtesy, sovereigns don't assassinate one another. They go to war when they're having a difference of opinion or a conflict of personalities, or even a familial falling out. Assassination is a tool of powerful men behind the scenes. Von Fugger fits the profile well."

Michel turned so Gabriel couldn't see his cunning smile. "You want me to go to Rome and learn what I can for you from the people I know, Monsieur General?"

"Not just yet. First, I need to figure out what I need to know. In the meantime, you need a better attitude." Gabriel pulled a stack of files from a shelf and dropped them on Michel's lap. "You've been a clerk too long. It's time you were a lawyer again. Third door down the hall on your left. It's big, you don't have to share it with anybody, and it comes with a secretary. You're my second in command now."

"Thank you. But what about Captain Desgrez? I thought he was your second in command?"

"My brother-in-law? He doesn't do anything except make a pain in the ass out of himself. But, family's always an obligation. Well, will you take it? Or do I offer it to someone less talented?"

"You don't like me."

"You kept me waiting an hour. Anybody else would've come running like a dog. You're brilliant and you have backbone." Gabriel finished his wine and shrugged his shoulders, bewildered at himself. "And, I trust you."

An inspiration from angels

Monday—31 October 1678—All Hallows Eve
rue Sainte-Croix de La Bretonnierie

Monsieur loved talking to the average Parisian. Rubbing elbows with commoners threw an adventurous slant on his dreary life, so every time Monsieur was in town for an extended stay, he played this game at least once a week, the objective being to spot somebody who looked interesting and engage him in a short conversation. It filled a void, and living vicariously through this brief encounter, reassured Monsieur he wasn't missing out on anything life had to offer.

As his coach rolled along at a fast clip on its trip to nowhere in particular, he sat contentedly with Liselotte on his left and Chevalier de Lorraine on his right. Liselotte buried her nose in a book and ignored Lorraine who stared glumly out the window.

Lorraine looked over at her. "Aren't you going to play with us, Madame?"

"Monsieur de Lorraine, I am too old for childish games."

Monsieur dug deep in his pockets and pulled bon bons from every conceivable hiding place. "Want a cookie, Lotte?" She shook her head. He stuffed her mouth and laughed. "You'll like it. It's really sausage and sauerkraut disguised as chocolate."

"I want to go home."

"All the way to Heidelberg," Lorraine grumbled under his breath.

"I heard you, Philippe. Be kind to Lotte, you know I don't like it when you're mean to her."

"Pardon, Monsieur." Lorraine poked his head out of the carriage. "There. Stop the coach. Let's talk to him." Lorraine yelled, "You, come here. Monsieur wishes to speak with you."

A giant burly man dressed in black leather and carrying a blood red sack under his arm approached the carriage.

Lorraine and Monsieur whispered back and forth. "He's got a head in the sack."

"No he doesn't, Philippe. You just don't walk around the streets with a head in a sack. You'd put it in a box or something."

"I'll bet fifty ecus he does. Look, the thing's round, like a large ball."

"Then, it is more likely it is a large ball, Monsieur de Lorraine," Liselotte said.

"Will Madame wager me fifty ecus?"

"I am too poor, Monsieur de Lorraine, to squander my meager allowance gambling."

Lorraine addressed the man standing patiently beside the coach. "What's your name and what's your living?"

"Maurice de La Mer. Master Torturer and Chief Executioner of Paris."

With a wicked smile, Lorraine swung open the door. "Do join us, Monsieur de La Mer."

Maurice was so large he took up most of the space on the seat opposite the trio. Liselotte began fidgeting, so to punish her, Monsieur crammed her next to Maurice and ordered her to keep silent. Maurice placed his red sack at his feet. After swallowing a chocolate-covered biscuit, Monsieur began his interrogation.

"Monsieur de La Mer, why did you choose your vocation?"

"It was chosen for me. My family's passed down its profession from one to another for over two hundred years. We La Mers have executed some very important people in our time."

Lorraine said, "How do you torture a prisoner? Do you make it up as you go along?"

Monsieur poised a chocolate at his lips. "What's 'showing the instruments'?"

Lorraine said, "'First degree' consists of what?" He watched Liselotte slowly turning green. "Interesting. And, what about 'second degree'?"

"Monsieur de La Mer, and what fee do you receive," Monsieur said.

"I'm bored," Lorraine said. "How do you inspire fear with 'showing the instruments'?"

"After 'first degree' of torture, the doctor's always impressed with my work. My prisoner's pulse is always strong. I produce maximum discomfort with minimum damage."

"That wasn't the question, Monsieur de La Mer."

"No, it wasn't, but I didn't explain this before and thought you'd want to know."

Monsieur popped a chocolate into his mouth. "Tell us how you inspire fear."

Maurice, now's the time to put all those expensive acting lessons to good effect. Use your hands to act out your words. Snarl. Growl. Explain how you use pincers to pull eyeballs from their sockets and lay those little devils on a prisoner's cheeks—how you leave them dangling from their cords of blood which keep them attached to one's head. Cackle. Now, continue your litany of gadgets and their functions. Liselotte's face is bright green. Monsieur is stuffing chocolates in his mouth. Lorraine is humming music for your performance. Remember that one, Maurice. Try it on your next prisoner. Have a quartet play scary music in the background while you cook your prisoner's ham hocks on a roasting chair.

"May I show Monsieur, Madame, Monsieur de Lorraine my iron head?"

Monsieur and Lorraine nodded. Liselotte shook her head. Maurice put on his lap the sack which had been at his feet. He pulled out a contraption similar to a medieval steel helmet with slits for eyes and nose, a hinged jaw, and where it fit snugly at the base of the neck, a locking mechanism. He moved its iron jaw up-and-down to coordinate with his own mouth's movements.

"Isn't it beautiful? My father invented it, but had no idea what to do with it. Came to me in a dream. Like an inspiration from angels. We can torture people with it."

Liselotte vomited. Maurice sat in embarrassed silence and pretended not to notice.

"Madame." Monsieur was in tears. "You've ruined my new suit."

69

The Comtesse's pussy

Friday—11 November 1678—Feast of Saint Martin of Tours
17 quai d'Anjou

The Comtesse was a handsome woman, even at thirty-nine, and in advanced middle-age, she was a wonder to behold. As a girl she'd half bewitched the king with her soft and yielding body which she still used to beguile all men at every opportunity. She hadn't, however, tried her black magic on Nicolas-Gabriel de La Reynie.

Here you are, Gabriel, all alone in this dining room, spying on her as she prowls among her other guests in an adjoining salon. Your eyes narrow. Your jaw tightens. She's ambushing Francois-Michel de Visscher, rescuing him from a pleasing giant who's been monopolizing his company. Notice how the giant bows with open contempt and withdraws.

The Comtesse is too animated and vivacious. Watch her closely. She looks up into Michel's eyes, then demurely lowers them at precisely the right moment; she beams the smile of an ingenue; she nervously opens and closes her fan with the skill of a professional virgin. Gabriel, you're getting an erection. Michel seems captivated. A little closer and the young fool will spring her mousetrap onto his neck, and she's going to strangle him with her thighs. Lucky man.

"Bitch-whore, cheap slut," you think as you walk up and down the length of an immense dining room table. It's draped to the floor in damask linen as etiquette prescribes, but there's too much gold, too much silver and crystal, too many rare pieces of oriental porcelain. Ostentatious. In bad taste. Don't you think so? Too bad. Tonight, you'll have to settle for eating and drinking yourself sick, like everybody else, and go home with mal de Saint-Martin instead of a sore cock.

A small crowd of guests ambled into the dining room. The Comtesse was among them. "What a surprise, Monsieur de La Reynie. I thought you didn't like me."

"Madame la Comtesse. Who told you such a vicious lie?"

"Who hasn't told me? And Madame de La Reynie?"

"She's tending Monsieur Desgrez. He's been seriously ill with the grippe for the past week."

"I'm sure she is. And, I'm sure he is. Enjoy yourself."

Gabriel reached out to squeeze her hand just as her eyes fixed on a moving target. She lunged for the man in her sights so quickly Gabriel never actually saw her leave. He couldn't miss, however, that she had left to pursue the man who had pursued Michel the entire evening.

Michel who had observed everything walked up behind Gabriel. "Over there, Monsieur General. You can see almost everything from there. Even into the next room."

Gabriel turned around to see Michel pointing toward the other end of the table. "Are you trying to impress me?" Michel bowed politely while Gabriel speculated his entire outfit cost less than the lace on Michel's shirt. "You're not a man of modest desires."

"No, I'm not. I want an appointment at Court. Given the chance, maybe I could earn myself a title. Will you help me?"

"Let's sit down. I'll trust your judgement on the seating arrangements." Gabriel paused for a moment before he took his place. He was calm and quiet, and seemed distracted. "What would be in it for me?"

"My gratitude and my loyalty, Monsieur General."

"I already have those. The Comtesse seems willing. Ask her."

"Don't be so sure." Michel knew Gabriel didn't catch his double entendre. "Anyway, I'll bet she's too much hard work."

"I wouldn't know."

From the first selection of appetizers, Michel chose smoked sturgeon and mussels grilled with sweet herbs. Gabriel held up a raw oyster.

Several rounds of appetizers, soup and two fish courses later, a succession of entrees started appearing, and with each dish, the appropriate wine. Michel decided to enjoy his meal in silence. There was no point making small talk with Gabriel who was paying attention to anybody and everything but him. Golden rissoles of pork on skewers, capon demi-deuil, roasted venison, tongue roasted with Rhenish wine, lamb with rosemary, duck with turnips, roasted brace of rabbits, brain fritters in orange sauce, foie gras and stalks of sweet fennel. Michel began feeling the wine.

Gabriel ignored Michel's departure to another room and finished his meal with a plate of assorted cheeses, skipping French puffs with green herbs, pears in wine syrup, apple Florentine, crystallized sweets, musk pastilles and amber-scented sugar. He preferred armagnac to wines of Champagne and thought the toothpicks in rose water were an elegant touch. He'd have to remember it for his dinner parties.

"Come on, I want you to see something." Michel grabbed Gabriel's arm and pulled him into the next room. "She's Catherine Montvoisin, but everybody calls her La Voisin. Claims the king's official mistress is a client of hers."

"De Visscher, you're very drunk. Don't joke like this, or you'll end up dead." Gabriel took an immediate disliking to La Voisin who was squat, pox-marked and smelled of overripe Brie. "She's just a fortune-teller. A charlatan."

"Do you think so?" Michel cornered her and pushed Gabriel's palm in her face. "Madame La Voisin, my friend here has a troublesome brother-in-law. Can you see how soon he'll be rid of his pest?"

La Voisin ignored the hand pressed up underneath her nose and looked Gabriel in the eyes. "Not long. If monsieur puts his mind to it."

"He can will him to death?"

"I doubt your friend's will is as strong as mine."

Gabriel gave her a knowing look. "How much?"

"How soon?"

Michel said, "Yesterday wouldn't be soon enough."

La Voisin appraised the value of Gabriel's diamond buttons. "A hundred louis d'or."

"And, where does my friend find you?"

"La Villeneuve-sur-Gravois, on rue Beauregard." She kept her eyes on Gabriel as she cocked her head in Michel's direction. "Send your footman here for an appointment."

"Business so good? Or are your clients so exalted they like to guard their privacy?"

"I never see anybody without an appointment. Excuse me, gentlemen."

"What did I tell you, La Reynie?"

"About what? What have I agreed to pay for?"

"To get rid of Desgrez."

"She's said nothing. She's going to 'will' him to death."

"Not going to arrest her?"

"She said Madame de Montespan's name? Do what you're good at. Be discreet. I'll get around to arresting her at the right time. And, don't think being drunk is any excuse to get familiar with me. I'm not 'La Reynie' to you yet, nor is there any chance of it. Monsieur General to you."

"Monsieur de La Reynie." The Comtesse had appeared out of nowhere and locked her fingers in his. She could feel his hand getting sweaty and his fingers tighten. Just where she wanted him. "Cackling like a hen with Maitre de Visscher. Excuse us. I need the lieutenant general's opinion on a matter." She led him from the salon down a narrow hallway to a back staircase.

"Where are we going?"

"Upstairs. My problem's upstairs. I saw you and Maitre de Visscher in a clutch with my fortune-teller. She's very good. Hasn't given me a wrong prediction for at least a year. If it isn't a secret, what did she tell you?"

"Asked for an appointment."

"Oh?"

"A potion."

"Oh!"

"A boy. I have two daughters. Who's the giant I saw earlier this evening?"

She laughed. "Jealous? It's down the hall there. Come along."

Gabriel, look at those hips, rolling side-to-side, like the keel of an English frigate rounding Cape Horn. Now, there's something which isn't happening for you at home lately. Push her against the wall with your body. A little higher. You want her feet dangling off the ground. Grope your hands up her dress. Put your mouth all over her breasts.

She laughed louder than before. "I'm not the one to give you a son, monsieur."

Put your fingers where they'll get her attention. It's what she wants. And, don't look her in the eyes. No need to be intimidating. You're not trying to wrangle a confession. Whisper something romantic. A tender word so she knows your depth of feeling.

"A little pleasure. That's all."

"Then do it right." She kissed him violently. "I like it comfortable. In a bed."

"What about your guests? They'll notice if we're gone too long."

"Who's going to miss you? La Voisin's reading everybody's cards tonight."

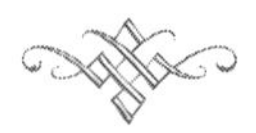

Charms for love: nearly fourteen, ripe and naked

Friday—11 November 1678—Feast of Saint Martin of Tours
Hotel Reynie

Why so cautious, Armand? Because it's nearly midnight? If you slammed the door to her bedroom, you'd disturb only mice. Gabriel is still at the Comtesse's party. Your nieces sleep in another wing of the mansion. The servants are all dead drunk. Of course, you don't know this, but you'll discover it presently when you try to rouse them.

Your stomach growls. You need a midnight snack after all your physical exertions. Make your half dozen unsuccessful attempts to wake the servants. A kick or a punch usually suffices, but not tonight. You'll have to get your own meal. Damn Saint-Martin and his damned cloak. And damn naked beggars.

After your brief detour through the servants' quarters, you'll go down the backstairs leading to the kitchen. When you turn that last corner in the pantry, a frigid blast of air will extinguish your candle. Pull your robe closer and curse the damned fool who's left open a window. You decide to find the guilty party, so you may have the pleasure of giving him a good beating. But you're about to get a surprise, Armand. And the last thing you'd dream of doing is putting a violent hand on this culprit. At least for now. While she's still an innocent.

At the kitchen entrance Armand stopped and stared in silence. Moonlight glistened off the snow to cast a ghostly pallor throughout the room. His younger niece and goddaughter stood with her back toward him. She was nearly fourteen, ripe and naked. A pentagram was carefully chalked across the entire length and breadth of the floor. Herbs were scattered everywhere. Jeanne-Jacqueline raised her arms to beckon a full moon through an open window, softly chanting unintelligible words.

"What are you doing?"

"Uncle Armand." Her entire body flushed red. She quickly pulled on her chemise and robe.

He shut the window, pulled a chair up to the fireplace and rekindled the embers. "What are you doing? Light some candles."

"A charm. How long have you been here?"

"You'll let the Devil into your father's home with your sinister business. Get me some chicken out of the cupboard, and a glass of wine. Please."

"No, I won't. It's a love charm, and I pray to angels."

He took the things from her arms and put them on the floor. "Come here." She sat on his lap. "You're too young to be in love."

"No, I'm not." She put her hand to her head to stop him playing with her hair.

"Who is it?"

"I can't say, or it won't work." She reached down for a piece of chicken. "You've ruined this charm. I wasn't finished."

"I'll buy you another. If you give me a kiss."

She stuffed chicken into his mouth, then kissed his cheek and laughed. "Promise?"

"How much?"

"Fifty pistoles."

"What? Highway robbery."

"She's no robber."

"Because she doesn't hold a pistol to your head? Your charm peddler's a thief."

"I was doing it myself to save money. Costs a great deal more to have a powerful diviner do a charm for you. Of course, it may not work if I do it."

"Why should it? Physical charm's more practical, and it works."

"Father's told Anne-Sophie a man won't buy a cow when the milk's free. Take me there tomorrow?"

"I'll bet. They're so alike those two." He wrapped his arms around her tightly and kissed her neck. "You look more like your mother every day."

75

A potion to make an amiable man amenable

Saturday—12 November 1678—feast of Saint Martin I
Hotel Reynie

Venus, the morning star, was on the horizon as servants crept down from their fourth-floor roost. With their descent came life. Heat of bodies moving through rooms turned into the warmth of rekindled hearths. Smells traveled upward from giant kitchen fireplaces below ground in the belly of the house. A yawn of hushed voices stretched building timbers awake while shutters opened and windowpanes blinked at the sunrise. But today, the pulse in the house was sluggish with a hangover. The servants were each and all recuperating from mal de Saint-Martin.

Armand was up with the servants, while the rest of the family was asleep, but wasn't yet dressed when he entered Jeanne-Jacqueline's room to stroke her into wakefulness. She felt his cool hand on her neck. Her shoulders tightened. She felt his breath in her ear and could hear a smile in his voice. She smiled too.

"Get dressed, meet me in the vestibule. We'll sneak out for breakfast. And a little bit of magic."

Together they raced down the street, giggling, until they ran out of breath. Jeanne-Jacqueline blew puffs of frosty air into Armand's face. She complained it was too early and nothing was open yet. He swung her into the air. He'd just have to take her to the bakery. They linked arms and trudged playfully through the snow toward Notre-Dame. After breakfast they stopped at a merciere's shop, and from among the fans, masks, lace, buttons and handkerchiefs, he bought her an excessively expensive pair of scented kidskin gloves.

Armand took Jeanne-Jacqueline in his arms. "Where's your charm peddler?"

"Rue d'Enfer. May I have money for two charms?"

"Jeanne-Jacqueline, are you a slut? In love with two men at the same time?"

"It's not nice to talk to me that way." She slapped his arm. "I'll tell you a secret, Uncle Armand. Anne-Sophie's desperately in love with somebody father would never approve of. I thought I'd get a charm to help her."

"I don't believe it. Who?"

"Don't know." Jeanne-Jacqueline smiled mischievously. "She sneaks out the garden gate to meet him. In the middle of the night. She wouldn't do that if he was respectable."

"You need a potion to make your father amenable. That's impossible."

"Father's perfectly amiable."

"That's not what I said. Tell your charm peddler you want a potion to make a stubborn man compliant."

Jeanne-Jacqueline frowned.

"I'll wait for you inside." He pointed to the main gate of Luxembourg gardens which ran parallel to rue d'Enfer. "Don't take forever, I'm not interested in freezing to death."

"I need money."

Armand handed her a leather pouch with twenty louis d'or.

Jeanne-Jacqueline gasped. "I'm buying a charm not a horse."

"Remember. A potion to make a stubborn man compliant. It's very expensive."

"How would you know? I thought you don't believe in charms."

"I guess I do." He caressed her cheek. "It'll be our secret, like Anne-Sophie's lover."

An hour passed. What the devil was she doing? Should he get a man from Chatelet and rush the house or do nothing? La Reynie would be a real pain in the ass if anything happened to her. Armand hailed a constable on patrol, but as they approached the house, Jeanne-Jacqueline appeared at the door.

She showed Armand a pale-green bottle. "Here. One drop everyday into either food or drink, while the moon is waxing, till the moon turns full. Then stop. Wait until the new moon. Give whatever remains in one large dose. The man will do whatever he's told."

"You'll have to wait. The moon begins to wane the day after tomorrow. Give it to me."

"It's for Anne-Sophie, so she can get married."

"I'll give it back, I promise."

Armand went to an apothecary at La Villeneuve-sur-Gravois on rue Beauregard in Faubourg Saint-Denis. The bottle contained wolfsbane. He kept his promise and returned it, unadulterated, to his niece.

Revenge: the blood of Able

Saturday–31 December 1678–New Year's Eve
Palais Tuileries

Genius. Divine spirit who endows a privileged few with creativity. Guardian muse who brings down from Olympian heights artistic temperament and with it divine madness, paradoxical gift and curse of the gods. Melancholia—brooding genius—the black bile of those born under the sign of Saturn.

Philippe Chevalier de Lorraine stood in the limelight, center stage of the ballroom, within a sacred circle formed by the courtiers in deference to his creative genius. It was marvelous honor afforded at the insistence of Monsieur's temper tantrum with the king.

Now, Lorraine was on the spot and had better present something worthy of the privilege he'd been given. He had sweated his heart's blood into this play. It was genius, but its audience was unworthy and he was sick at heart as he inspected the ridiculous tableaux of characters who would surround the actors.

Lorraine, regard your short king with arrogant contempt. Such hubris. You eclipse him only in height while he towers over everyone else in every other respect. Your point is well taken, however, with his extremely diminutive, homely queen and her rotted, black teeth. As usual, she's behaving herself like a child. The Moorish dwarf she pets is infinitely more dignified. And the son's not much better. Monseigneur, pudgy dauphin, has the look and air of a dullard which indeed he is. But what about the brother? Monsieur's dress has so much froufrou and he's wearing so much jewelry one could easily mistaken him for a nouveau riche. Aren't you embarrassed for him? You couldn't possibly be so much in love, could you? Perhaps, you ought to think about something else, Lorraine, otherwise you'll jump into some woman's bed to forget your woes. Then, Monsieur will throw one of his famous tantrums and cut your allowance.

Think petty thoughts instead about the king's surrogate family: the official whore, Madame de Montespan, and her legendary beauty, which is fading and gross from her insatiable appetites; and tall, slim, elegant Madame de Maintenon, dressed head-to-toe in black and putting on airs far too aristocratic for a bastards' governess. Savor the cruel joke you're about to play on Limping Bastard who leans into his father's embrace. That bright crimson mantel which trails on the floor and overwhelms the handsome boy with his insipid, sweet disposition is the prop for your cunning. But will you get away with it? You had better be a genius. Don't forget, the boy may be a bastard with a limp, but he's the king's favorite child.

As for the courtiers, Lorraine, what do you think? Nearly half of the several hundred who fill the ballroom are holding oranges. A ship of fools all of them.

Now, we come to your two favorite people in the whole world, Monsieur le Duc and Madame. Take in every detail of their appearance as they're an imaginative pair and will win prizes for best costumes. She's a tall lime green weed topped by an enormous shocking pink flower. He's an orange tree planted in an ornate silver tub that's been borrowed from the king's Orangeries. Monsieur-le-Valet-who-belongs-to-Monsieur-le-Duc is a gardener and carries a large vermeil watering can which he uses whenever his master droops. He's also been harvesting oranges and handing them out to whoever comes eavesdropping on Monsieur le Duc and Liselotte. At this moment, the valet is ladling water from the Orangeries tub back into the watering can, while Liselotte leans toward Monsieur le Duc to rest her weary flower against his fruit-laden branches. Something is up among those three musketeers.

You haven't time for them just now. A horde of footmen is coming your way with all your scenery and props. While they set up, push the courtiers up against the walls so your actors have room to perform. Liselotte refuses to yield on principle and Monsieur le Duc is rooted to the spot. What to do? Now is not the time, Lorraine, to quarrel with your lover's wife over artistic integrity. Put your genius to good use. Just incorporate your nemesis and her sidekick into the stage set, and get on with the show.

Liselotte and Monsieur le Duc were in a fantasy of their own.

"The world is topsy-turvy, Monsieur le Duc, when a king may fawn in public over his Limping Bastard. Her Majesty and Monseigneur make crabby faces, as well they should."

"Monsieur's dress is very nice. And he has the biggest jewels of all the ladies."

"Not so, Monsieur le Duc. His jewels are not so big as the ones he is wearing."

"But, Monsieur does make a pretty woman standing next to Monsieur de Lorraine's very masculine outfit. Do you think they planned it?"

"That sodomite devil."

"Well, I don't like Madame de Maintenon's swan. It's all black. Swans are white. Hasn't she ever seen a swan?"

"Bastards' Governess is a black widow. They say she poisoned her husband."

"A spider? No, Madame. You're wrong. She's most definitely a swan."

"Official Whore is no swan. His Majesty has turned her into a breeding cow, but the milk she spills is all curds and whey."

"What cow? Madame de Montespan's dressed as Diana. Not a cow."

"All her children are curds and whey. Horribly ugly cripples. Melonhead. Limping Bastard. Humpbacked, uh pardon, Monsieur le Duc. Club Foot. Withered Arm."

"The new baby hasn't curdled."

"It will, never fear."

"His Majesty's confessor said the king is still amorous several times a day. If he wasn't working constantly on the queen, Madame de Montespan and several others, he would explode from having to keep it all bottled up inside."

"Similar to brain explosions."

"Madame, look at the ugly face Madame de Montespan's making at Madame de Maintenon. And the nasty face she in turn is making at Monsieur de Lorraine."

"Official Whore is jealous of Bastards' Governess, who knows in her heart Sodomite Lorraine is about to play some evil trick on Limping Bastard."

"But Monsieur de Lorraine named his play after Limping Bastard's character."

"Monsieur le Duc. You are out of touch with Court politics again. Official Whore tried to lay a trap for Sodomite Lorraine."

"But Monsieur de Lorraine's very talented. I like his play."

"Indeed. He has spent all his allowance from Monsieur and creditors are beating down his door. This is the muse who inspires his talent."

The play was about to end. Cain had hacked Able to death with an ax. Limping Bastard limped with innocent dignity to center stage. He pulled the voluminous cloak close to his body, lay down and rolled across the floor. At the top of his lungs he shouted, "Revenge. Revenge. Revenge."

The king was seized with a laughing fit. The queen and the dauphin wore cruel smiles. Madame de Maintenon rushed to set the boy free from the twisted cloak which swaddled him. After a stunned hesitation, the courtiers applauded politely. Lorraine almost tripped over the struggling bundle of boy and fabric as he dashed to take center stage 'a la prima donna.' He bowed, he smiled, with both hands he blew kisses to his appreciative audience. Madame de Montespan walked up to Lorraine and all applause died abruptly.

"You humiliate me, Monsieur de Lorraine. I'll make you pay."

"I? Humiliate you, madame? Certainly not. Your son has the title role. Wrote the part especially for him. Something I didn't do for anyone else." Lorraine gestured toward the king who was stilling laughing. "His Majesty seems to appreciate all my hard work and efforts, even if you don't. As long as the king's pleased, it's all that matters."

Montespan stormed out as Lorraine bowed deeply to the king. The applause began again. Maintenon had finally gotten Limping Bastard on his feet. She knelt in front of him, removed the cloak and whispered praise which made him beam with happiness. They exchanged tender hugs and kisses. The boy smiled sweetly and contentedly at everyone as his governess's shadow loomed protectively over him. She stared viciously at the courtiers. Liselotte suddenly lowered her pink flower and clobbered Maintenon on the head.

"Now, I have your attention. Why such a sour face before you skulk away? One would think you had eaten a whole lemon, which is a most unhealthy diet for a bastards' governess. It makes for a bitter heart."

Monsieur le Duc smiled broadly and bounced up-and-down in his planter, splashing water onto the floor. He smacked Liselotte's flower with one of his branches. "Madame. Madame. That's why the play's called *The Blood of Able.*"

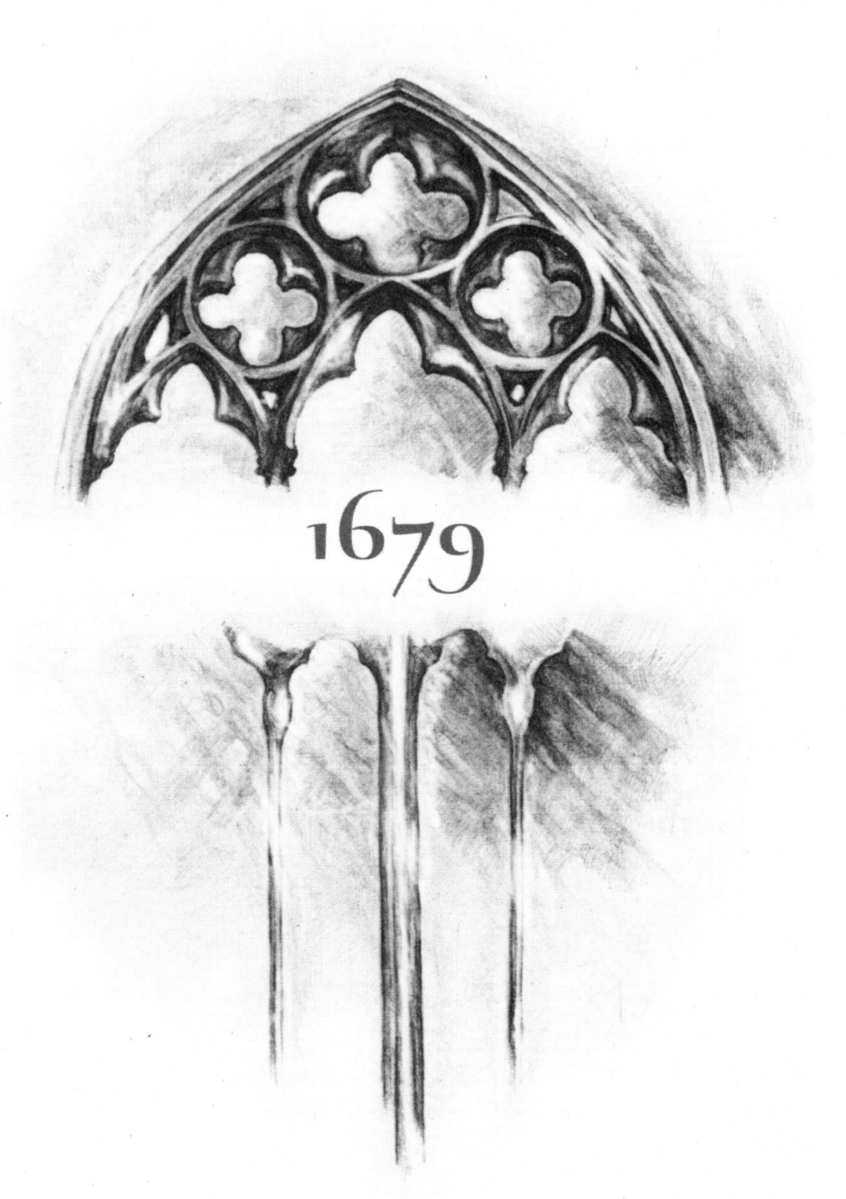

1679

Lycanthropy: a pussy catches a werewolf

Sunday—1 January 1679—Feast of the Circumcision
Palais-Royal

Dearest English Majesty,

In dul**ci ju**bilo-lo-lo sing, Christians, a**n**d rejoy-oy-oyce,
Our hearts' del**i-i-i**ght lies in praesepio-io-io,
A**n**d sparkles like the su-u-un **matris** in g**rem**io-io-io,
Alpha exedo-o-o, Alpha **exe**do-o-**o**.

If Your English Majesty has not yet sung this today, I am honored to be the first to sing it for you though trumpeters and kettle drummers may have already played it, wherefore I pray God grant every felicity and gladness Your English Majesty may favor and hope for yourself, and as I know the English are among those with the old calendar who celebrate Epiphany after My Excellency, so it is still but 21st December of last year in England, Your English Majesty had better have gotten this on time as I especially allowed extra days to account for those who open the letters and the slow post, or I shall be forced to complain to the king.

La Chatte Comtesse had sunk her claws into my poor simple friend, Monsieur le Duc, by very cleverly convincing him she was an alley cat to his tomcat, so as he was not himself and besotted with her, he was spending a fortune to gratify her every whim with jewels and clothes and perfumes and every other sort of crap and silliness, but in truth he was spending two fortunes, another being for spies who reported her every move. I said to him in all my lifetime I never had heard of catching an alley cat with diamonds and he was offering her the wrong sort of jewels, but at this he became so disconcerted and ran off weeping to his confessor I had not the heart to burden his good conscience any more than I already had.

Thanks to God My Excellency has some imagination, and suddenly finding a means to put an end to La Chatte Comtesse's pillage of my friend, I hunted him down at his confessor and explained that if in truth he wished to catch her, he must become a dog, for it is the natural order of things and the nature of dogs to catch cats, so as this seemed to please the priest, it pleased Monsieur le Duc also, but it did not please that alley cat who quickly tired of this new little game.

One cannot blame Monsieur le Duc his enchantment for La Chatte Comtesse, for she is still one of the most celebrated women in France. At Court or in the salons of Paris she glitters like a diamond and all the best and brightest people frequent her soirees as she is quite a patroness of the arts. I must confess her taste is impeccable, she has intelligence also, has managed to keep her beauty in spite of her age and has the longest, finest, thickest hair in the world for which she is renowned. The late Cardinal Prime Minister was her uncle.

Cardinal Prime Minister was the power behind the throne and acting stepfather to the king during His Majesty's minority and rumor has it he secretly married Queen Mother which would have been possible as he had never been an ordained priest. In those days they wrote horrible books against him and he appeared much irritated, sending for all copies as if intending to burn them up, but when he had got them, being a clever Italian, sold them secretly and made ten thousand livres out of them, then laughed and said, "The French are pretty fellows. As long as I let them sing and write, they will let me do as I choose."

Your English Majesty will see how blood imitates its own, for La Chatte Comtesse has the same Italian nature as her uncle, so this is the reason she was able to take advantage of Monsieur le Duc who is as mad as all his ancestors, and they being of a like disposition as himself, it follows most logically he inherited this weakness from them, for he believes himself to be a werewolf, but in truth has this delusion only sometimes as most of the time he is a dog and is always barking at the king. During Christmas week he was a bat and poor fool became all black-and-blue from flying into walls and doors. Last week his valet was compelled to water him everyday, for he was a drooping plant, but the day before yesterday at Luxembourg gardens was the worst in a very long time. Monsieur le Duc was a rabbit in earnest while his lackeys were hounds chasing him about. What a gay time they were having at the expense of their master's dignity. It was a disgrace.

Mind you, no one speaks of it openly for lycanthropy is considered the most abominable of sins against God, more so even than witchcraft and the law is by far and away most ruthless with this than any other demonology, but as long as Monsieur Le Duc confines himself to benign animals, the king turns a blind eye and of course everyone follows suit.

Never in my lifetime have I known such a gloomy period and Your English Majesty is mistaken if you think no lamentations are heard here. Night and day we hear of nothing else. People are dying like flies. Wolves go about in bands of eight and ten attacking travelers as the extreme severity of the cold is driving these poor wretched animals mad with hunger. Mills have stopped and this has forced many people to starve to death. If one leaves one's house, one is followed by a crowd of pathetic creatures who cry for food, and famine is so great children have eaten each other. Everything one sees and hears is dreadful. We are living in a fatal epoch.

Yesterday, they told me a sorrowful story of a woman who stole a loaf of bread from a baker's shop in Paris. The baker had the police arrest her. She said, weeping, "If you knew my misery, you would permit me to keep the loaf. I have three children. All naked. They ask me for bread. I cannot bear it, so I stole the loaf."

Maitre de Visscher (they took her before him) went to her home where he found three little children huddled in a corner under a heap of rags, trembling with cold as if they had ague. "Where is your father," he asked the eldest. The child answered, "Behind the door." He looked to see why their father was hiding and recoiled with horror, for the man had hanged himself in despair. Out of pity, Maitre de Visscher has given the woman and her children a small pension from his own pocket, and as they say he has not much money of his own, he is a good man like Saint-Martin de Tours who gave half his cloak to a naked beggar who was Christ in disguise.

I do believe Her Highness S_ von B_-L_ loves me better than His Highness R_, for she sent me a fine quantity of smoked sausage, a barrel of sauerkraut and six hogshead of beer. I know I am short a number of sausages as I was told by a reliable source they filched a box at customs and gobbled them up. But that is another complaint.

Your English Majesty must scold His Highness R_ for My Excellency, for he has sent me ten bolts of wool in seven colors. Ten bolts are fine but seven colors are not. Ten colors would give me ten different dresses. Seven colors will give me four different dresses and three pair of similar dresses. If I give away the duplicate colors, I shall have seven different dresses, but someone else would have three dresses similar to three of my own, and this would leave me with but four unique dresses. This will not do.

The solution is to return three bolts of fabric in duplicate colors. In this manner I shall have seven unique dresses. This will be satisfactory for the time. I shall not worry myself if someone in England has three dresses similar to three of my own as no one at Court here would have occasion to see me and someone in England wearing the same dress at the same time.

His Highness R_ may make up the difference of what he owes me by sending one of those large wolfhounds from Ireland. It must be a male dog. Gabrielle (the little dog had to be renamed) needs a companion as she is lonely since Minette went to live with Monsieur de La Reynie.

All during the day I keep going to the window to watch people sliding about on skates. I have seen some clever somersaults, but I cannot imagine how they manage not to break their necks.

I must go now. My Excellency has no other little gossips to tell.

Your English Majesty's most humble,
Madame de France

Masks & masques

Friday–6 January 1679–Feast of the Epiphany
Chateau Fontainebleau

Dearest K_ von P_,

You will be delighted by my Christmas gossip and will find it very funny, and I take time to announce this, for while I know you are perfectly able to read the words, you are not always very clever at stringing them together into a meaningful thought, so if your brain should fail you once again, then do have one of my old retainers explain to you the amusing parts.

Master of the King's Wardrobe can ill afford to be a laughing stock at Court, but this is exactly his current state, for his wife has brought disgrace upon his family name by playing prostitute in a brothel her husband frequents. A rebuffed suitor denounced Madame-la-Wardrobe to her husband who flew into a rage at this cuckold, and deciding to confirm the matter for himself, bought his wife's services for an evening, whereupon satisfied with his proof, he sought a legal separation of domicile from his wife by identifying every detail of her body for the judges, but it was insufficient to convince them and they threw the case out of court, for he had no way of identifying her face. She was wearing a mask.

Monsieur-le-Wardrobe was further humiliated when the magistrates reprimanded him for attempting to deceive and entrap his wife, for he too was wearing a mask, and though Maitre de Visscher of Chatelet Courts had been retained to argue the complaint (he is a noted and gifted lawyer), the suit failed as it is difficult to argue against simple logic, and frankly Monsieur-le-Wardrobe ought to cease his laments and whining and be grateful his wife has some talent, for if she has any other talents, she has been keeping them secret.

The other mask incident involved the king. Almost all the courtiers sent their servants to attend His Majesty at Midnight Mass, and as everyone was very well-behaved, the king suspected something was amiss, so with his own hands he ripped the masks from the servants' faces. They were chagrined but their masters will pay the price, for the king was infuriated, and sending forthwith for Monsieur de La Reynie, issued a decree that anyone caught wearing a mask in church will be thrown into Bastille. No one may claim privilege to be exempt, not even My Excellency.

During the Christmas gala I rebuked a pompous duc as he was placing himself at the His Majesty's table above a Prince of the Blood. I said loudly, "How comes monsieur to be pressing up so close? Does the duc want the prince to take one of his sons as a page?" Everyone laughed, so the duc had to go away. In France ducs and lords have such excessive pride they think themselves above everybody, and if allowed to have their way, they would consider themselves superior to Princes of the Blood.

Many of them are man-made nobles as I told Archbishop of Reims who is first Duc and Peer of France. He said, "Madame is not as impressed with us as she is with German princes." "That is true," I answered dryly. "Why is that," he asked. "Because you are like Turks," said I. "How so," said he. I said, "Grand Turk makes his lords what they are, so they have dignities but no birth to go with them, just as the king does in France. German princes are made solely by God and by their parents. Moreover, German princes are free, whereas in France nobles are subjects." I thought the archbishop would burst out of his skin.

On New Year's Eve there was a grand Masque Ball in the Great Salon. Everyone wore the most beautiful costumes and a splendid time was had by all trying to guess who was hidden behind each disguise. I have not a lot of money, as you well know, to waste on useless finery, but God has been kind enough to bless me with some little imagination.

I had my maids-of-honor gather a great length of green silk taffeta His Highness R_ had kindly sent me, and folding it in half, they seamed together the selvages, so it formed a long tube some two times my own height, then into this tube I had a long pole inserted which was anchored in place by a monstrously large pink rosette on the outside with the result that the whole looked like a pink in full bloom with a long stem. As my costume made His Majesty burst out laughing the prize for best costume was given to me, and I am pleased, for it was ten thousand louis d'or which I shall use to buy an important collection of antique Roman medals that recently came on the market and is to be sold for weight, but the best is the seams can be undone on the green taffeta and I shall have a dress made.

Monsieur's darling sodomite wrote a comedy, *The Blood of Able,* purportedly to provide entertainment for the festivities, but in truth in order to sell the roles, for he is badly in debt again and creditors are beating at his door. All the courtiers paid handsomely to outperform one another before the king and after their triumphs upon the stage congratulated themselves into extreme drunkenness. Sodomite Lorraine became so drunk he was confused and walked about with a chamber pot as a mask complaining to everyone, "This mask has no eyes and it stinks like an old woman's ass."

Here is a marvel of French bureaucratic logic to fascinate that very clever legal mind your husband possesses. Galeriens are officially considered dead thus deprived of citizenship, without citizenship they have no lawful status, without lawful status they are obviously outside normal course of the law, but also there is the economics of flogging a dead man which costs the government nothing whereas executing one does. If an average disgruntled citizen harbors any doubts, it is forcefully pointed out that even though galeriens are dead men, they are still living fuel for the galleys, and this fuel being the king's property may be flogged only when it commits a crime of such enormity the galley captain must appease living citizens.

Thanks to God, German princes are much too sensible to waste the good German logic God gave them on such foolishness as the French do to whom God in His wisdom gave no logic at all and what little logic Frenchmen do possess they waste on the Devil in any event.

I thank you for the silver coin you sent. It comes extremely apropos, is most agreeable and a fine addition to my collection. I have also the Doctor Luther in gold and silver. I am convinced Luther would have done much better not to make a separate Church but to have confined himself to opposing abuses of the papacy. More good would have come from it.

On New Year's morning as I was washing my hands, His Majesty came into my room and made me a fine New Year's present of seventeen antique gold coins for my collection as fresh as if they had come out of the mint. They were found near Modena and the king had them secretly carried to Rome asking Monsieur de La Reynie to ask Maitre de Visscher to write his former patrons in Rome to do the thing just expressly for me, and this attention on the part of His Majesty gave me the greatest pleasure not so much for the value of the present as for the attention.

Monsieur de La Reynie also has my heartfelt thanks and I am sure he will not fail to express my gratitude to Maitre de Visscher, for if he does not I shall be most disappointed in his thoughtless bad manners.

My love to you,
Lotte

Holy Trinity: old whore, new whore & dark horse

Friday–17 February 1679–Feast of the Flight into Egypt
Chateau Fontainebleau

Dear dear Highness-es S_-A_-A_ & H_,

I heard a most curious lie. They say Monsieur de La Reynie has taken the lease of Hotel Bordes at 17 quai d'Anjou on Ile-Saint-Louis. Why would a man of good sense and logic act like a dolt and do such a thing for that alley cat La Chatte Comtesse? Although I wonder when he reads this if he will not ask himself the same, I would say as the lease is for a fraction of its real value, the Bordes scheme at something and it will be no surprise when they approach him for some small benevolence. This Bordes family is well settled not only on Ile-Saint-Louis but also on Ile-de-la-Cite as for nearly two hundred years they have owned a cabaret, La Pomme de Pin, on rue de la Juiverie which is famed for its clientele who are the smart people in society and the latest creative darlings of these fashionables.

Concerning my Lenten duties, I am at a loss as to what to do, for I cannot endure fish or fasting and am quite convinced we can do better works than spoiling our stomachs. The day before yesterday they smeared me with ashes upon the brow to remind me I am mortal and made of dust, but as I can see for myself the fleetingness of being in and out of favor at Court, I am always mindful of my mortality, and as to being made of dust I must disagree, for dust is light and I am a heavy bundle being more like mud.

I must confess to my shame I know of nothing more wearisome than a sermon and opium could not make me sleep more soundly. I was never scolded for sleeping in church and acquired a habit of it which I cannot get rid of. Mornings I can keep my eyes open but afternoons I cannot go to church, for I fall asleep at once and snore loudly which makes people laugh and the preacher himself is always disconcerted. Evenings it is the same as afternoons. After dinner it is impossible for me to keep awake in church. I never sleep at the theatre but do so often at the opera. I believe the Devil cares little whether I sleep or not in church, for sleep is not a sin but the result of human weakness.

Official Whore has had that distinction for eleven years and like the collar of a shirt worn too many times is frayed at the edges. The years have been unkind as she is gross, has had too many children, eats too much, drinks too much, is as fat as I and at thirty-eight her great beauty has deserted her, but her greatest flaw is a hubris which is without restraints. His Majesty is becoming disenchanted and it is her own fault.

Last summer on one of our pique-niques she grabbed an innocent young thing, then pulling down the girl's bodice in front of the king, fondled her breasts and offered her to him as she was playing sophisticate pandering to His Majesty's lust which lost no time in taking up the offer. Dumb Beauty is now the new whore and a duchesse, whereas Official Whore is still but a marquise, but then again she is encumbered with a spouse whom the king detests, and

His Majesty balks at making the husband a duc for her sake which leaves Official Whore in a most uncomfortable position in the matter of precedence at Court, for Dumb Beauty being a duchesse comes first.

On New Year's Day His Majesty gave his new whore a magnificent coach-and-eight and pearls, both much bigger and better than anything Official Whore has, and if this is not enough to make her burst with spite, she is constrained to assist in Dumb Beauty's toilette, but it is no more than what she made her predecessor endure, for as Scripture warns us all, "Whatsoever a man soweth that shall he also reap," and so Official Whore is now the old whore, and if she is not careful, she will soon join that sisterhood of the king's former whores.

Official Whore is so unnerved her rages and jealousy are causing talk even in the gazettes. She throws temper tantrums, gambles at hoca for huge stakes and has lost hundreds of thousands of livres at gaming tables. His Majesty was annoyed and called her to task. What was her reply? "At least I do not stink to high heaven as you do." In truth His Majesty is very stinky, for he bathes only on written prescription from his doctors, and they being a lazy lot of quacks will only prescribe but once a year.

Dumb Beauty is a good girl and had been one of my maids-of-honor. Handsome from head to foot, but she has no judgement and lacks a brain so she chatters like a betiding magpie, incessantly and without purpose, for her head is so empty one can hear her eyeballs rolling about in her skull. During Mardi Gras dinner I was forced to suffer three hours of her worthless blabbering in my ear. Dumb Beauty is but seventeen and I am afraid she will live forever.

One must keep a hawk's eye on Francoise Marquise de Maintenon who is not the king's mistress but something much higher. She is governess to Official Whore's bastards and from this has gotten a footing in the salons but will go much further, because she cares for the king's bastards by Official Whore as if they were her own darlings and as His Majesty is fond of his little bastards, there is no better way to ingratiate oneself to him. Bastards' Governess lives by the code, "Nothing is more clever than to behave beyond reproach," and to this end turns the king away from her bed frustrated, but he never leaves despairing.

Bastards' Governess keeps herself completely retired to the royal nursery, and in this way no one can say she meddles in the slightest thing, but it is precisely this which makes me think she has some project in her head, though I cannot imagine what it can be as she appears to have no designs on becoming the king's maitresse en titre, but I shall tell Your Highness-es the reason I see dark ambition in this woman.

Bastards' Governess has often reproached me saying it is a shame I have no ambition and never take part in anything. One day I answered, "If a person had intrigued a great deal to become Madame, might she not be permitted to enjoy that title in tranquility? Imagine this to be my case and leave me in peace." She said, "You are very obstinate." I answered, "No, madame, but I like my peace and regard your ambition as pure vanity." I thought she would burst her skin she was so angry. She said, "Make the attempt. You will be aided." "No, madame," I replied. "When I think that you, who have a hundredfold more cleverness than I, have not been able to maintain yourself at Court as you wished, what would happen to me, a poor foreigner who knows nothing of intrigues and dislikes them?" She was angry and said, "Fie. You are good for nothing."

The Irish dog arrived from His Highness R_ and is wonderfully big like a small horse. I was unaware dogs could grow so large and as he pleases me greatly he has been christened Sigismund-Amadeus-Augustus in your honor. Yet another gaggle of dachshunde properly mixed up for breeding has also arrived, and again, I see the word 'matching' has not caused a confusion for Her Highness S_ von B_-L_ as when she sent me two females at my first request for a matched pair of German dogs.

Her Highness loves me very much, for the Wopkes of Anhalt-Dessau (father and son who are foresters to the Elector) wrote to say how Elector J_-G_ commanded them at her request to pick out the best and send them to me. I am thankful for these kind considerations, but I must say they are odd looking little dogs for dachshunde, for they have long wavy coats and this I have never seen or heard of before in my lifetime.

I must go now. My kind felicitations to His Highness R_'s bastard children whom they say are burdening Your Highness-es with their attentions. Your Highness-es have become very liberal in their old age to welcome bastards into their Court with honors even if they are Your Highness H_'s brother's bastards, or is this an accepted custom among citizens of Transylvania? In any event, Your Highness-es are remote enough so hopefully not too many may hear of this scandal.

I hug you both with all my heart,
Liselotte

Rivals for a booby prize

Sunday–26 March 1679–Palm Sunday
Chateau Saint-Germain

Beloved Highness R_,

Your Highness must remember little of me if you do not rank me among ugly ones as I have always been so and am more so now on account of smallpox. I am square as a cube. My skin is red mottled with yellow, my nose is honeycombed with smallpox as are my cheeks, my mouth is large, my teeth are bad and there is a portrait of my pretty bear-cat-monkey face as His Highness my Papa was always fond of calling me.

So Your Highness may know how much I love you I am sending a fine portrait of myself. Just to please you I sat an entire afternoon to have my face painted. It was no pleasure, but one must sometimes do things for one's loved ones that one would not otherwise do. Do not be disappointed or frightened by what you see, for it does not matter whether one is handsome or not as a fine face soon changes, but a good conscience is always good.

Dumb Beauty is out of sight but not out of mind, for His Majesty finds illness an inconvenient business and she is ill which is a mortal sin, whereas being stupid is but a venial one. All the talk is of a bastard's birth and death that is being kept a great secret as it was poisoned. Dumb Beauty is hemorrhaging from a bad childbirth (wounded on the battlefield like a good musketeer at the front lines) and demands bodyguards, for she thinks someone wants to poison her as well. Who would waste so much time and effort? The old German proverb is true that mouse droppings always want to mix with peppercorns. The king can be such a sop. His own royal bodyguards watch over her day and night as if she was some pearl of great price which only proves it is very true that when men become of a certain age they make fools of themselves over beautiful younger women who are often hardly worth such trouble.

Official Whore bolted from Saint-Germain like a flash of lightning and was off to Paris on Wednesday 15th March. No word of explanation to anyone not even to the king, but I say she went to Paris as her favorite clairvoyant, La Voisin, was arrested and in this Official Whore is like La Chatte Comtesse, for she is wild about the fortune-tellers but tries to keep it secret.

La Chatte Comtesse is also gone from Court as she is humiliated and cannot show her face in public. First in a long line of royal concubines, she might have become Queen of France had Cardinal Prime Minister permitted it, but he thought it a better political strategy for the king to marry a cousin german in the Spanish infanta. After the king was married and had supplanted La Chatte Comtesse with another mistress, he compensated her with royal posts as Head of the Queen's Council and Superintendent of the Queen's Household, so she could gain a stupendous royal pension and privileges of a duchesse and undisputed precedence at Court. It was an excellent booby prize for one who had aspired to be Queen of France but a booby prize nonetheless.

Now, the king has browbeaten her into giving up her positions in the queen's council and household, and though she has been paid handsomely for her sacrifice, no money can make amends for aspersions to her honor. What has His Majesty done with these grand and wondrous treasures? He has bestowed them on Official Whore who like La Chatte Comtesse before her is thrilled to death with her new status, for she now has precedence at Court over her rival, Dumb Beauty, and no longer must assist in that beautiful imbecile's toilette.

Is it not amazing how the king managed to subdue two of the most conniving women in France with the same booby prize? Neither La Chatte Comtesse nor Official Whore could see past a pretty box to this gift's heart (a way to yank them gracefully from center stage), for a scorned woman engrossed in a struggle to destroy a rival often has difficulty seeing her former lover stabbing her in the back. When the king stabs someone in the back, he behaves so politely one never feels him put the knife in or take it out which is a great art. Here is a lesson to be learned. The higher one's position in life the more polite one ought to be in order to set a good example to others. It is impossible to be more polite than His Majesty.

Monsieur de La Reynie has arrested the most fashionable clairvoyant in Paris, La Voisin. The Court is in an uproar and never have I seen such fear and trepidation as there is fantastic talk of possible suicides over the affair. Meanwhile, Chatelet Courts put up for sale a costume belonging to her. They say it will be very expensive to imprison, torture and execute her, therefore she must sell as much as she can, for costs of all these responsibilities are her own, but of course the court officials will pocket any profits after expenses, so they will make every effort to secure as much as possible for her possessions and will spend as little as possible to condemn her. But none of this talk is concerning her garment.

La Voisin's regalia (it is indeed quite a regal thing) is crimson velvet with a skirt of green silk, the whole of it trimmed with finest gold Alencon lace and more than two hundred double-headed eagles of pure gold thread embroidered on the cloak. It is valued at over ten thousand livres. Monsieur bought this gaudy thing and his tailor is remaking it into a coat and breeches for him.

I have determined the one useful French food that exists. Sigi is quite fond of sausage, and as I am reluctant to share with him my good German sausage from Her Highness S_ von B_-L_, saucisson is a good substitute. Because of its wondrous effects on his digestion, I was able to discover Sigi's special talent which is most rewarding.

First to be honored with my discovery was that gorgon and harpy Bastards' Governess. I waited until all Saint-Germain was asleep, took Sigi to her door where he laid a great pile, then he and I returned to my rooms. Your Highness cannot imagine how stinky it was. Bastards' Governess had to wait till morning for someone to clean the floor as no servant was willing to leave his bed to accommodate her.

Next day everyone put on scented gloves which they held to their noses whenever they had to pass through the gallery by her apartments, and as Bastards' Governess was livid, I retreated to my own apartments and locked my door tightly as I was sure the king would be unamused. His Majesty holds her in such great esteem and never turns a deaf ear in the direction of that lady, for His Majesty's radiance shines on Bastards' Governess and Dumb Beauty with equal warmth, just as snow falls as easily on a cow plop as on a rose petal.

Concerning your children, who told Your Highness such a lie? Is it my fault they are bastards? I cannot see why Your Highness has suddenly chosen to take such offense at my referring to them as such after all these years. Your Highness never married their mother and this is the reason they are bastards now. That I call them bastards is merely and logically a statement of fact. What should I call them? I cannot call them cousin for being bastards they are no blood kin of mine, but as Your Highness is old and I like to please you, I shall refrain in future from calling your bastards by that word until you have thought of something for me to call them other than bastards.

As for your complaint I do not seal my letters, there is no use in sealing letters with wax, for the censors have a species of composition made of quicksilver and other substances that lifts wax, and when letters have been opened, read and copied, they are sealed up adroitly, so no one can perceive they were ever opened. Die Rotzenhäuserin is clever and knows how to manufacture the composition. It is called gama.

I must go now. My fingers are cramped from writing. My son is riding Sigi like an ass and wishes me to salute him with blessed palms we received from the bishop this morning.

Your most loving,
Lotte

97

A fly on the wall—A conversation of princes

Saturday—1 April 1679—Paschal Vigil
Palais-Royal

Dear Highness A_ de M_,

Her Highness S_ von B_-L_ may be too devout to go to the theatre on Sunday, but I think visiting is more dangerous as it is difficult during a visit to avoid saying harm of your neighbor which is a much worse sin than seeing a comedy, but Your Highness's point is well taken and I would never approve of going to the theatre instead of church, although I cannot see any harm in going to a comedy after performing one's duty to God.

There have been strange doings at Chatelet Courts since Laetare Sunday when that witch La Voisin was arrested, for the next day Monsieur le Duc paid a visit and was present at an argument between Monsieur de La Reynie and Maitre de Visscher, all fault seeming to lie with the latter. There were a great many papers to be signed and all were signed, but with the last the lawyer became quite agitated and began to argue that the lieutenant general must read this particular document carefully unlike all the others, for he himself had taken great care in the writing of it.

After a long and tense silence the lieutenant general began to shout unpleasantly, so Monsieur le Duc thought it best to become a fly and immediately attached himself onto the nearest wall while the lawyer retaliated, and there ensued many vicious words and summoning of policemen who testified about the most awful things, then everyone was dismissed (except Monsieur le Duc who was quietly buzzing in a corner) and the lieutenant general sat at his desk a long time weeping. Then he vomited. Then he drank half a bottle of armagnac. Then he pulled Monsieur le Duc off the wall and together they went to see the king.

His Majesty granted Monsieur de La Reynie a private audience, but as private means a half dozen of the king's trusted counselors are present with twelve eager ears that will become six gossiping mouths, the lieutenant general requested to walk in the gardens. This was cleverly imagined, for a large entourage lined up in order of precedence, and as it had to keep a discreet distance, a lot of feet tramping on gravel paths mingled with bored conversations of empty-headed courtiers vying for amorous conquests among ladies, which kept eavesdropping to a minimum. Within this crowd Monsieur le Duc wore the perfect disguise in his role as spy, for he is the village idiot and no one cares where he insinuates himself, so this is the reason I know all that I do now.

The king had read but a few words of Maitre de Visscher's document when he stopped and turned to face the mob following him with the result that a wave of people collided onto itself like a caterpillar with arms and legs tangled and flailing as its head slammed into the invisible barrier of another beast's dominance, then with a magical outward wave of his arm, the king segmented the monster into pieces which scattered throughout the gardens.

The king paid the lieutenant general the supreme compliment of reading the document carefully and taking it seriously. "Is this true? Is that true," asked the king. Monsieur de La Reynie lied, "Yes, Sire. Every detail is true, Sire." He answered with conviction and sincerity and without a single image in his head to confirm the truth of what he attested as being true, for Monsieur le Duc heard him utter a prayer that God forgive him for trusting in a sly lawyer's veracity which he swore to the king (God's divinely appointed) was his own.

Finally, the lieutenant general wept openly. The king thought aloud of all his headaches, and though Official Whore has always been his most expensive and most annoying, she is mother to seven of his children, but now there are other witches besides her who may have potentially disastrous consequences on the kingdom. His Majesty was openly disturbed and created a new appointment for Monsieur de La Reynie, ordering him to uncover the truth of the matter in the document, but also warning him of absolute discretion and secrecy.

Several weeks have passed and Monsieur de La Reynie has not spoken a single word to Maitre de Visscher in all this time, for the lawyer is in exile and everyday must go to La Villeneuve-sur-Gravois, rue Beauregard, Faubourg Saint-Denis, where he supervises police who dig in shifts day and night without ceasing, and when no more volunteers are to be had, they say he threatens the men with imprisonment to get the work done. Good men of good conscience and good sense do not wish to go to that place as they say the Devil walks the Earth there and will steal their souls, and this is very true, for even Maitre de Visscher has admitted openly he senses it as he watches the unearthing of embryos and newborns and children below the age of reason. Most have been eviscerated. All had their throats slit and their tongues cut out. At his insistence they rise up prematurely from their small graves, but there is no Second Coming to greet this Children's Crusade. He is no archangel but only a Pied Piper. More than a thousand children have been found and there is no end in sight to the horror.

How is Monsieur de La Reynie occupying his time? He has assembled twelve judges, a solicitor-general and a court clerk. All are men as discreet as himself, but none are as discreet as his formerly beloved Maitre de Visscher, and all these men are holding clandestine hearings in a courtroom at Paris Royal Arsenal, its ceiling and walls draped in heavy black silk as a means to intimidate the accused with this last being Maurice de La Mer's stroke of genius, for he brags of it to everyone. Daily, they move prisoners to and fro and in great secret between Bastille and Paris Royal Arsenal.

Why? Well may you ask. The Lieutenant General of Police of Paris is now also Rapporteur-Commissaire and this bestows on him unlimited authority answerable only to the king which can mean but one thing, there is to be a witch hunt. It will take years. Inquisitions usually do, do they not? He will have a stranglehold over France and everything (investigations, accusations, arrests, interrogations, imprisonments, executions, exiles, disappearances) will be solely at his discretion and only he will report daily to the king on the proceedings and its findings.

Monsieur de La Reynie is now a man to be feared. A hushed awe pervades the halls of Chatelet Courts and for weeks everyone has tiptoed around him with a newfound respect.

They told me the other day of an old man who imparted his spirit to his excessively young wife. As he lay dying, he made her place her mouth upon his own, breathed into it, and said, "I bequeath you my spirit." Then he turned away and died. Although the young widow firmly believes her husband's spirit is within her, she would much prefer it was with him in the next world. It seems to me if thoughts are any indication, our spirit is lodged in our head, so it is better to hold out an ear than a mouth when receiving a spirit, for when a spirit goes into a mouth, its only logical destination is a stomach, and from there one is likely to expel it in a fart where it may end up in a latrine rather than staying put in the body.

While I think on it, as regards my son, it is false he has a smelly head. My son's ears do smell a bit like rotten cheese, but I trust by the time he is old enough to marry he will have gotten over it. This afternoon I sat down to table with my son and Monsieur. Getting up from table, we sat, the three of us, in the drawing room in a long silence, for Monsieur was in one of his moods when he does not think us good enough company to talk to us. Then he made a great fart, and turning to me, demanded, "What was that, Lotte?" Addressing him with my backside, I played him the same music, and said, "That is what, Monsieur." Saying, "I can do as well as Madame and Monsieur," my son then let out a great one. We laughed and then left the room.

If anyone be curious, I offer this princely crap as a gift to the first person who may open this letter before Your Highness.

I have no other gossip, for everyone is otherwise subdued with fear. I must go.

Many kisses,
Liselotte

Royal weddings: mischiefs on account of one's jewels

Friday–25 August 1679–Feast of Saint Louis IX
Chateau Saint-Cloud

My dear A_-E_,

I have been sad and as you know my being sad always makes me sick, for when I fret my spleen swells, and being swollen, I get vapors and this makes me sad which then makes me ill, so while everyone hunted daily with the king and went twice a week to the theatre, my poor health deprived me of those things which was a considerable privation, but as my health is now perfect, to keep it so, I go out as much as I can. I go often on foot a good three miles in the forest to disperse melancholy that would otherwise make me as annoying and irritating as a bedbug.

This was the month of royal marriages in France, for upon Monsieur's and my return from Montargis his eldest daughter by Minette was married by proxy to her Habsburg cousin, King of Spain, and we were also fortunate to marry off the dullard dauphin. His Majesty was anxious as Monseigneur is his sole heir, and seeing as the young man never puts his head to good use, it is time he used some other part of his body to profit the nation. They found him an equally torpid companion in M_-A_-C_ of Bavaria, a minor German princesse who was given the spot originally promised to my godchild, S_-C_, Her Highness S_ von B_-L_'s daughter, and my blood boils over at this slight, but on reconsidering the matter the old German proverb is true that a clever thief in the smokehouse will throw away a sausage for a side of bacon.

Monseigneur's wedding was very grand, but a marriage which begins with laughter is not necessarily the happiest one, and the cause of it beginning as a comedy was the fault of Monsieur's darling, Sodomite Lorraine. Monsieur was embattled for a time with his cousin german, Grande Mademoiselle, over a necklace (pearls so large and fine as to be unique in all the world) which had originally belonged to the late Queen Mother and was a gift to her from Duc de Buckingham, sent by the hands of d'Artagnan who had gone to fetch the diamond tags, but it is also true perhaps it was Cardinal Prime Minister who gave her the necklace. Nonetheless, the king declined any association with such a scandalous gift, so when she died, the pearls came into Monsieur's possession.

Another story is told that Queen Mother, needing a great deal of money, sold the necklace to Previous Monsieur (Grande Mademoiselle's father) and at his death through some mistake of the lawyers the necklace was returned, but this is unconvincing, for everyone knows Cain and Able hated each other less than did wife and brother of Late King.

Here is the irony, for the necklace does indeed belong to Grande Mademoiselle as several years ago Monsieur exchanged it for an enormous diamond of hers which he promptly gave to Sodomite Lorraine. Recently, Sodomite Lorraine decided he wanted the pearls also, so Monsieur demanded their return claiming they had been given on loan, but when Grande Mademoiselle tried to exact a million livres for the diamond, Monsieur refused to pay.

To vex and humiliate Monsieur, she wore the coveted pearls to my stepdaughter's wedding, and as the affront was pointed, none of the Court could refrain from whispering and twittering throughout the ceremony, so at the wedding breakfast Monsieur displayed such tantrums and tears the king was finally forced to intervene in the dispute on the side of Grande Mademoiselle. The quarrel was fine entertainment and kept everyone in good spirits.

At the dauphin's wedding Grande Mademoiselle pressed her luck and wore the necklace again. When it came time to unite bride and bridegroom, we took our appropriate places on the steps of the altar with Grande Mademoiselle standing on the highest step. As she is more than six foot tall and towers above everyone she need not have twisted every which way for all to see, but this is exactly what she did and so her foot slipped, although I rather think Monsieur who was standing next to her pushed her, but in any event the result would have been the same and she fell on the cardinal as his hand was raised to bless the couple, so in falling forward, he smacked Monseigneur and the bride on the face while they in turn toppled over onto the king, who in trying to reach out and catch them ended at the bottom of the pile.

Like a deck of cards they fell over. I would have been part of the deck had I not realized Grand Mademoiselle was about to fall on me, so I bounced out of the way taking four steps at once and this is the reason she fell onto the cardinal. Everyone nearly died of laughter, except His Majesty who disliked being at the bottom of the pile with his peruke askew, and as Grande Mademoiselle was on top of the pile he blames her for his humiliation.

She relinquished the necklace to Monsieur at last, for they say the king threatened her, and at this very moment Sodomite Lorraine is wearing pearls and diamond. You can well see for yourself what problems are caused by owning too many garments, for the more clothes one has the more jewelry one needs for one's clothes, and if one is a miserable sodomite beggar, then all sorts of mischiefs result on account of one's jewels.

There have been few queens in France who have been perfectly happy, for though a crown shines with great beauty it is a heavy hat and causes headaches. It is not long from French memory the story of their queen who died in exile, Queen Mother was miserable as long as her husband lived and our own queen says that from the very day she became queen she has never had but one day of true contentment.

Her Majesty is excessively silly but the best most virtuous woman on Earth. She has grandeur and knows well how to hold a Court, but believes everything (good and bad) the king tells her, is clumsy and short, has white skin and her teeth are black (decayed too) which comes from eating chocolate. When she neither dances nor walks, she looks taller than she is. She eats frequently and is very long about it, for it is always in little scraps as if for a canary. Never has she forgotten her native land, so many of her ways are still Spanish and her accoutrements are ridiculous. She also eats a great deal of garlic and in this she is like Sigi, for the result is the same and she goes about farting all the time which makes her very stinky. She loves cards beyond measure and plays at bassette, reversi and ombre, sometimes at petit prime but never wins, for like all Habsburgs she is too feeble-minded to learn to play well.

Her Majesty has such a passion for the king she tries to read in his eyes what would please him. Provided he looks at her kindly, she is gay all day and is glad when the king passes the night with her, for being a true Spanish woman she likes the business, so whenever it happens she is so gay everybody knows of it. She likes to be joked about it and laughs, winks her eyes and rubs her little hands. It is to her credit there is never anything at Court but modesty and dignity, and those who are licentious in secret must affect propriety in public, so God forbid any evil thing befall her, for Official Whore would govern and introduce her bastards among the royal family, then everything will go topsy-turvy.

Concerning curious things, His Highness R_ sent me several well-made microscopes which have already given me wonderful hours of pleasure. It is the most perfect of gifts bringing delight and knowledge also. I find such amusing things to enlarge under the lenses which make a louse look so big compared with the magnifying glass Herr Leibniz gave me last year, but one has no need of a microscope to see the doings of the lousy French.

I must go. Die Rotzenhäuserin is going to visit His Highness R_ and I must write him to announce her arrival.

Much love,
Lotte

four & twenty blackbirds baked in a pie

Tuesday–29 August 1679–Feast of the Beheading of John the Baptist
Chateau Marly

Precious Highness R_,

I did not write Your Highness more often, because Monsieur and I went to Montargis where I had to endure the squandering of my inheritance on his boys, and then we returned to Saint-Cloud, whereupon we found a courier who brought us dispensations for my stepdaughter's marriage to her Habsburg cousin, King of Spain. My stepdaughter who is the image of our late cousin Minette was seventeen this month and is two inches taller than I.

With dispensations from Rome in hand the marriage took place by proxy. On the morning of the wedding I started out at seven o'clock with Die Rotzenhäuserin. Bastards' Governess had herself bled expressly to be too feeble to come, but it was a waste for her to do such a thing, for I would have forbidden her to come anyway, and besides her extreme laziness would prevent her from getting up early.

Spanish Ambassador says King of Spain is deformed from rickets and is scrofulous, cannot see a foot in front of his nose, suffers from fits of distemper, his teeth are black and rotted and turn inward, his hair is falling out, it is impossible to keep him from soiling himself and is monstrous to look at. He will be but eighteen in November.

Speaking of the Devil, one hears some curious tidings from Paris. Bastille is full of witches cawing like magpies with so many denunciations being made that Monsieur de La Reynie has finally solved the mystery of those 1676 riots against midwives and abortionists. Also, he has discovered the link between witches and all hysterical talk of sacrilege and child sacrifice. There is wholesale slaughter of children in France, so a certain privileged few may offer up child sacrifices at Black Masses in order to buy their desires from the Devil, and it seems the noble classes and the Court are also killing the unborn with abortions to make magic potions and aphrodisiacs. Midwives are happy for the business as they collect a fee for performing abortions and make a profit by selling fetuses to witches.

All witches point accusing fingers in one direction, claiming that from the very day Official Whore was presented at Court in 1662 she had been a client of La Voisin who is the blackest witch of all, for what they say of her arts is so horrible as to be beyond believing, but what is said is still below the truth. More than two thousand five hundred children were found buried on her property, but she is said to have performed over ten thousand abortions and the police found a pavilion in which she baked the unborn into 'petites pâtes.' All this was done to aid her clients with love potions, poisons, Black Masses and child sacrifices.

Official Whore's original desires to obtain and keep the king's love has degenerated with time and pregnancies into assassination plots. The king's mistake was legitimizing his bastards by her, for if the queen dies, Official Whore will find a way of becoming a widow, and if the dauphin dies, she will be sure the king marries her, so her sons can inherit the throne. Well, one cannot ask a boon of the Devil without paying a price as downing La Voisin's potions all these years has adversely affected her offspring, for the first was born with a head the size of a melon and the rest are deformed or crippled. She may have dominated the king's bed for twelve years, but God's displeasure is written all over her bastards.

Monsieur de La Reynie was fortunate when he arrested La Voisin earlier this year, for on Saturday 11th March she went to Saint-Germain in a royal coach to assassinate the king, but that attempt failed and a second, foolproof attempt was postponed as it was Laetare Sunday. The king's life was saved by a holy day.

Maitre de Visscher was sorting through records of the witchcraft purge from twelve years ago and found disturbingly similar accusations made against Official Whore at that time. Why all this fuss now and not then? Then, she was immensely powerful and no one listened to ravings of second class citizens, least of all the newly appointed Lieutenant General of Police of Paris. The king was besotted with her, then. He is not now.

I fear My Excellency may have cast too much gloomy news over Your Highness, so for more cheerful gossip there is talk of two aristocratic cases brought before Chambre Ardente. In the past stories have been of witches and goblins and commoners and Official Whore. For the first time word has gotten abroad concerning two women of nobility who have been involved in some unsavory business, and what they say is most unkind and probably true, for you know all women in this country are sluts and potrags.

First is a young woman with an aged husband and a handsome lover with expensive tastes. She needed large sums of money to keep her lover interested, but as her husband is niggardly she pawned and sold his property right down to the family plate. When the old man put a stop to her pillage, she hired professional assassins to run him through, but they failed, so she went to a witch to obtain poison. This last makes no sense, for here in France as in Italy one goes to a perfumer for poison. But that is about witches and perfumes and not about poison. In any event she acquired arsenic enemas and arsenic-treated chemises with which to torment her husband.

An anonymous letter saved the old man from certain death. Armed with this letter, he secured a lettre de cachet against his wayward wife, and bringing her into Chatelet Courts for punishment, he had to show his private parts in court (front and back) to validate damage to his person, for his parts are said to look as if he had the French curse. Chambre Ardente heard of the affair and took an interest, so the wife was brought before the tribunal. The solicitor-general demanded the death penalty, but the young woman's wit saved her, for she gratified five judges with her talented mouth. The lover abandoned her at the first signs of trouble and fled.

The second woman's case is simpler. Her husband is a member of Parlement and a special aide in the Department of Justice. He discovered his wife was another Madeleine Marquise de Brinvilliers only much worse, for her lover denounced her as it seems her addiction to poison was uncontrollable, and fearing for his own life, decided to join forces with the husband even if it meant saving his life in the bargain. Husband and lover brought charges against the woman. Two Chambre Ardente judges are related to her by blood which is the reason she was merely reprimanded before her release. Her penance is to pay a fine of five hundred livres to charity and she is under house arrest at her husband's discretion. They say Captain Desgrez is involved in both these affairs but no one can say how.

His Majesty has taken too keen an interest in Die Rotzenhäuserin who is exactly like My Excellency, only slim and handsome which is not as great a shortcoming in her as it is with most women. Your Highness will like her as she is clever, well read and can discuss many and diverse things. She will be amusing and not bore you too much, for she knows a good deal of ships and sailing from her father who was a pirate just the same as you were in your youth. She has a helpful temperament but cannot spell one wit, so do not have her write anything for you.

Your Highness will please advise if you will do this kindness and accept her company for a while as I am anxious for her to be away. I shall send her without an allowance, for I am too poor to manage this added expense, whereas Your Highness is alone, has a fine pension from His English Majesty and Lenor eats like a bird, so it will cost you very little to keep her for a few months.

I must go. Die Rotzenhäuserin is chasing Sigi and screaming frantically, for I see he has conceived the odd notion my dachshunde are mobile sausages and is trying to catch and eat one of them. I shall put an end to that. Lenor has no time for silly and childish games when she ought to be packing for her journey.

I love you very much,
Lotte

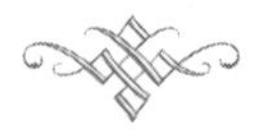

Iron maiden

Friday–6 January 1679–Feast of the Epiphany
Hotel Reynie

Gabriel named Anne-Sophie after his mother for the pleasure of saying such a beautiful name aloud. He'd forgotten its music which had a different sound in the mind. It was a melody imagined and not heard. He only remembered his mother being addressed as Madame de La Reynie or referred to as Iron Maiden, the diminutive everyone called her, but never to her face, though it wasn't a pejorative said with a sneer or a chuckle.

Gabriel's daughter grew to be the image of her namesake. By the age of fifteen, Anne-Sophie was a presence who lorded over the entire household staff, including the maitre d'hotel. When other girls her age were still in convent school, learning the niceties of being a young lady and having romantic thoughts about gallant suitors, Anne-Sophie was already chatelaine of her father's large establishment in

Paris and of his country estates. Despite Gabriel's concern over her youth and immaturity, and despite his shame at the impropriety that his daughter and not his wife was chatelaine, Anne-Sophie assumed this role of authority. Now, at seventeen Anne-Sophie was three years older than her sister, Jeanne-Jacqueline, and decades more mature than her own mother whose life was devoted to dressmakers, perfumers, an endless round of society parties and fortune-tellers.

Anne-Sophie looked into one of the silvered glass tiles which mirrored the fireplace wall. In the foreground she saw herself, and in the far background she saw what she'd never let herself become. How reassuring to see La Reynie and not Desgrez features reflected back. She had her father's temperament, his intellect and his reticence. Like him also, something was always quietly gestating behind the fixed smile masking her thoughts. The luxurious thick auburn curls were her mother's and so were the large blue eyes, but how she used those eyes to perceive the world had nothing in common with her maternal genes.

Maybe you have your mother's skin and her figure. Perhaps there's also something in the shape of your nose and your sensual pouting lips. But you're every inch your father's daughter. Thank goodness.

She refocused her gaze to the middle ground. The salle-a-manger, an oval room which easily accommodated a hundred fifty at a formal sitting, and all the other rooms on the mansion's rez-de-chaussee were being readied by a legion of servants. Anne-Sophie's critical eye supervised everything. She wanted it all perfect for her father's party. Epiphany was one of his favorite holidays. She looked again at her mother in the far background.

Look away again. Look back again. How can she behave like this in front of the servants? Does she really believe they're deaf, dumb, blind and thoroughly stupid beasts? She isn't any different from most women of her class. You know better. Don't you, Anne-Sophie? You've overheard what servants say to one another. They have an amazingly simple and direct astuteness about people and life. Don't they? Look away again from your mother to another part of the room. See those repressed smiles and downcast eyes? What is it the servants intuit which you refuse to perceive? Look again.

The reflection of her mother at the far end of the connecting room was still there. Uncle Armand had his arms around her again. He always had his arms around her. It wasn't the way he kissed her, but how long it lasted, always a second too long.

Anne-Sophie, they're coming toward you. Relax. Your lips are taut. Your jaw is clenched. There's a grimace on your lovely face. You don't want that. Smile. Sweetly. Pretend to search through the armful of papers you're holding. Wait until their footsteps are very close. Now, turn and face them. Smile. Sweetly. Mask your shock at your uncle's sudden, outrageous impropriety. Right in front of you. Do they think you're too young to understand? You're not. Your mother smiles at her brother. She gives you a bored look.

"I'm done now, maman. I'll go see if father wants anything else."

"Don't bother him. He's hiding in his study, again. The jeweler hasn't sent my pearls. I want my pearls for tonight. Send someone to get them."

"Yes, maman." Anne-Sophie kissed her mother's hands, then bowed her head and departed.

Armand, it's your turn to look. And look away. And look again. Watch your niece's quiet, modest retreat. You don't believe for a moment she's what she portrays, an obedient, loving daughter. Do you? It makes you uneasy to look at her. Nervous. Giddy. Her aura conjures another's. You see in her too much of your father. Don't you? You neither love nor respect him. You don't feel this way from any contempt or hatred. If only you could. You hate and fear him, because it's what he's taught you. It's the only form of veneration he wants, and as he's the kind of man who could make even the Iron Maiden shudder, you duly adore him in the manner he prefers. You can't help thinking of him as you speak about your niece.

"Don't like her. Don't like the way she looks at me. Like she's thinking something wicked."

"I think I'm pregnant."

Armand slapped Marie-Julie. "Don't talk to Anne-Sophie in that offhanded way of yours. I don't like it."

Marie-Julie winced. "I have to go to La Voisin again."

Armand smiled. "You'll end up in Hell."

Anne-Sophie ran upstairs to her father's grand-cabinet to his haven where he often secluded himself. Gabriel jealously guarded this room and his privacy within it. Whenever he wasn't in the house, he kept it locked. Armand had never set foot in it. Marie-Julie avoided it. Gabriel was the only person who was ever in it alone and it was Anne-Sophie's favorite place to be alone with him. Here, his graceful decorum and polished manners relaxed into an informality which made him accessible, and here, she could share all her secrets with him, except for one, the man with whom she was in love.

Gabriel's grand-cabinet was atypical of such private reception salons. Architects had created it by joining the three largest rooms on the second floor contiguous to his bedroom. Over ten thousand books neatly filled shelves built into three walls. Every tome lined up with the precision of an accountant's ledger columns. His favorite paintings and his collection of regimental flags were displayed above these bookcases. The floor was pristine: only fine oriental rugs and furniture took up any space, with seating arrangements and tables placed throughout to form intimate groups.

A telescope and two large floor globes, one of the Earth and the other of constellations, were the room's focal points. Gabriel's desk top was immaculate with a few well-placed accessories. Every surface was free of clutter. Silver shone; brass twinkled; glass sparkled; woodwork glowed; floorboards gleamed. The room was white-glove clean. Everything had a place with everything in its place.

Minette was curled up on the hearth. Gabriel was stretched out on a daybed in front of the casement windows, wrapped in a sealskin blanket, with the latest issue of *Le Mercure Galant.* He sipped his armagnac. He loved reading society gossip sheets.

Anne-Sophie scratched at the door, then opened it. "Father, may I come in?" Without waiting for an answer, she crossed the room and sat down on the daybed.

"What's the matter?"

"Can't we be rid of him?"

"What's your uncle done now?"

"It's disgusting. A thirty-two year old man who hasn't his own household. He can afford it. He's filthy rich. You've let him steal enough as your captain of police. And his weasel of a valet. I'm sure he's stealing you blind."

"What's really bothering you? He bought Jeanne-Jacqueline a pearl and sapphire ring for New Year's. And a very expensive pair of scented gloves a while ago. He never buys you anything. Jealous?"

She rested her head on his chest. "He's an arrogant, spoiled brat. His being here is breaking your heart. I hate him for this most of all."

He hugged her. "Let's you and I hatch a plot. We'll find him a wife."

Anne-Sophie finally smiled. "Who'd want him?"

"It's that or we'll have to kill him." He kissed her forehead. "But I want to talk about you. It's time I found you a husband. Best dowry I could afford is a marquis."

"If it's what you really want, Father."

"Don't you?"

She leaned down to pick up Minette. "Madame must think highly of you to give you one of her little babies."

"She's a good protectress to have."

"Do Germans really use this dog for hunting badgers and foxes? It looks like a saucisson. I say we kill him. It'll be much easier."

Ashes:
encouragement toward a correct Lenten attitude

Wednesday–15 February 1679–Ash Wednesday
Chatelet Courts

Gabriel, the frost is the thickness of a copper engraving plate. Let the beauty of icy crystals seduce you. Succumb to your creative impulse. It's an irresistible force in man. Genius impels you. Scratch exquisite geometric patterns with your letter opener. Now, ink your design. Just a dot of black on the tip of your quill. It's all you dare risk. Touch a bare spot of glass. Ink runs through these channels you made, then bleeds into surrounding frozen dew. It's perfect for a fraction of a blink, collapsing into ruin as ink coalesces with frost, their disparate temperatures and states meeting at some reciprocal point of warmth and wetness to become a single fluid mass. All that remains is a smear.

Look at this ugly blackish smear, Gabriel. What sort of mark did God place on Cain to protect him from men's vengeance? Was it a protection spell? Was it a smudge like the one which marks your own forehead today? Or was it this ox blood stain running down the windowpane onto the sill? What do you care about Cain's exile, east of Eden in the land of Nod, or about the penitential season of Lent? What about the creative impulse sucked out of you to coalesce with warmth and wetness into life? Your Ice Queen miscarried another son. Think about this for a fraction of a blink. Now, bury it deeply into an eternal recess between two whole numbers.

Armand burst into the room and headed straight for the fireplace. "Jesus. It's cold." He lifted the coattails of his brandenburg and stood with his back to the fire. "Are you smiling at me?" Gabriel ignored him. "Do you have a mistress?"

"Don't unbutton your coat. Go to 17 quai d'Anjou. The Comtesse is making a devil of a fuss over a servant's dead bastard. She's sent for me and I don't feel like going. That's why I have you. Take care of it. Now, please."

Gabriel didn't hear the door slam shut or open again.

"Excuse me, Monsieur General, Madame is here."

Gabriel looked up at Michel's face which was riot with amusement. "Madame who?"

"Madame," Michel said again before he disappeared.

"Madame," she said in her heavy German accent. "There is but one Madame in France. As in the wife of Monsieur."

"Madame." Gabriel stood to greet Liselotte.

She waddled up to the fireplace. "Monsieur de La Reynie, a chair if you please. You may remain standing."

"As I always do. How may I be of service to Madame?"

"Monsieur de La Reynie, do not you start behaving like a fawning Toad Louvois. Today is Ash Wednesday and I must begin my Lenten duties, but have a poor spirit for doing the thing right. Help me."

Liselotte crossed her eyes to get a better look at the ashes which had drifted from her forehead onto the bridge of her nose and tried to wipe it clean with the back of her hand, but instead, smeared soot. "I hate this custom of ashes. You know, when I was a Lutheran in

Heidelberg, we never did this thing with ashes. They promised me, when they made me Catholic, it would be easier. But it is not."

"Forgive me." Gabriel offered her his handkerchief. "But I can't help Madame with this."

"No, Monsieur de La Reynie. His Majesty and Monsieur tell me, if I wipe them off, I shall burn in Hell. Not that I believe them, but everyone else does, so it would cause a scandal. You misunderstand. I need a torture chamber. Priests do not have one of those."

"That, Madame, is a matter of opinion. Some think a confessional is."

Liselotte crossed and uncrossed her eyes hoping with the next look, miraculously, the ashes would be gone, but they were embedded in the pox marks cratering her nose and cheeks. With her big face, round as a plate, it gave her an appearance of the man in the moon with a dirty face. Her eyes were unscrewed as she rehearsed the exchange with Gabriel one more time. Had he or had he not? She decided that he had.

"You made a joke. Very witty. I am smiling, Monsieur de La Reynie. Now. Let us become serious again. Mine is a joyful nature, and I need inspiration to suffer for Lent. I thought a tour of torture chambers in Bastille might encourage me toward a correct Lenten attitude."

"No. Madame. I wasn't making a witticism and what you ask is impossible."

"Are you saying 'no' to me?"

"Yes, Madame."

"His Majesty will be so...disappointed—"

"Then His Majesty should take Madame to Bastille."

There was a long, a very long, silence while they locked stares and each waited for the other to relent.

"We are not pleased, Monsieur de La Reynie. You will read of it in all our letters. And as you are not very good or amusing company today, I shall betake My Excellency elsewhere."

Liselotte stomped out and slammed the door.

Gabriel whispered after her. "Lucky me, Madame. I already have my reason for suffering."

Horror vacui: an empty purse, bloodless & ashes

Wednesday–15 February 1679–Ash Wednesday
17 quai d'Anjou

Horror vacui. Fear of emptiness. To fill every square inch of empty space with meaningless, tiresome embellishment. What is fear of the void? Is it fear where there is no light darkness will reach out and touch us? Is darkness a place where God or His handiwork doesn't exist? Where God doesn't exist, is the converse true? Does the Devil reign supreme? Is this the reason man became afraid of the dark?

Why do men equate the dark with the void? Was it zero's intrusion into Arabic numerals which emerged it from man's dark unconscious? Were men's fears forever changed by a concept of nothingness? Did the dusky Moors scrawl their holy scriptures across their constructions of eight centuries defining Spain in order to fill a vacuum they created? Is the key to salvation to lock out Rex Mundi with the Word of God?

What of the penumbra between these Eternities? Do gods and devils wage battle in twilight? Do men detest wolves because they envy those who hunt in the foreshadow of immortality?

Armand's key was hidden away at home. He rang the bell and waited with a killing impatience.

Neither this nor a thousand previous visits has ever engaged your awareness of Hotel Bordes, its facade or the courtyard renowned throughout Paris as highly unconventional masterpieces of extreme simplicity. As if in reaction to this puritanical plainness, the interior's architect suffered an attack of horror vacui. What do you think, Armand? Did the architect believe that because beauty plucks canniness from a wary eye, an excess of it would mask simple evil? Perhaps, he cast a protection spell to lock out devils. Maybe, he just created a grandiose stage for an inconsequential death of a bastard? Did he have a premonition?

The footman's shock on opening the door of the porte-cochere quickly dissolved into brooding silence as his body shriveled and hunched over until he lost all semblance of being human and changed into a cowering dog. Armand followed him from the main gate, across the courtyard, through the main entrance to a reception salon on the second floor. He was a man on a hunt with his faithful hound, while the footman like an abused animal expecting to be hit, but powerless to disobey, led him to his prey.

The atmosphere at Hotel Bordes was different today as the servants weren't exhibiting their usual aloofness toward Armand. They were hostile and he knew the reason. They blamed him for this mishap, as they blamed him for all other misery pervading their lives in this grand house of secrets, but he had a more pressing worry. It would be at least an hour before the Comtesse deigned to make an appearance. Would she be wearing something new? She'd look expensive and be dressed in the height of fashion. It was her modus vivendi. She might even be ingratiating to better seduce the man she expected. Wouldn't she be surprised to see him instead of her latest sex toy?

Finally, the Comtesse arrived with a soft smile which congealed—just for him. She asked for La Reynie. He had sent Armand in his place. La Reynie sent peppercorns in place of caviar? How rude. Did she have a problem? A murder perhaps? That was one. He should take care of her other problem first.

Don't you think, Armand, you should finally get around to dealing with your own problem? Go to the kitchen. The servants are gathered there, but can't intuit their compulsion to form a crowd. They're waiting for the courage to riot. They want to cut your throat and haul your carcass across the floor and out onto the street. They want to leave a long, convoluted ribbon of your blood across the length and breath of Paris to tie their rage into a neat package. But that sort of defiance won't come in this lifetime. It won't come for at least another five generations. So, these servants whisper to one another in angry or fearful voices while they continue to toil. And, they fall silent and bow their heads when authority stands in their midst, because fortunately for you, man's history hasn't aged into enlightenment yet.

Ask them, Armand, where they've put the body. A maid's pointing to a bundle of linen on the servants' dinner table. A napkin makes a sad shroud for a newborn. Why bother unwrapping the boy? You already know his throat is slit, his tongue's cut out and he's disemboweled. All the blood's been drained from his body. Your friends were thorough. They created empty spaces to let in the Devil. They conjured magick. The only mess they left for you to clean up was the evidence. The corpse won't matter as long as you destroy any link between you and this baby.

How can you look at this newborn with indifference? How can you have more concern for such a tiny black purse? Untie it from his equally tiny wrist. Slip two fingers in, pickpocket. Does the silk feel as sensuous as those places your fingers were in this boy? It's not there, is it? Turn the pouch inside out, just to make sure. Nothing but ashes and a small ragged triangle of bloodstained parchment falls onto the table. Where is it? You've come too late. Your magick can't be undone and your empty spaces can't be refilled. You're no longer indifferent, Armand. Why is your expression as colorless as this bloodless baby?

Acheron, Cocytus, Phlegethon, Lethe, Styx

Open your mouth.

Armand obeyed. A large gold coin was shoved down his throat.

You'll vomit it up when you embark upon the River of Hate. There's a toll to pay.

"What do I need to know?"

A Quartet of mouths sang a chorus to him.

Four rivers before you come to a stream of hatred. Bitter waves where many souls sit wailing woefully. Where the unburied are doomed to wander lamenting a hundred years. Fierce waves of torrent fire inflamed with rage. A dusky vale where forgetfulness rolls to dip poetic souls and blunt the senses.

A Quartet of mouths, each in turn, sang a stanza.

Remember this. You'll know the fifth river, for it flows nine times around the infernal regions. Its waters are poison and its hate dissolves any and all who put upon it. You must place the coin in the ferryman's mouth. He'll ask you to take an oath. Refuse him. Whatever by the black infernal waters you swear, 'tis fixed. Go through this portal.

Armand obeyed. "I see nothing."

Once again, the Voice's mouths sang in unison.

Close the door behind you and you'll see what you're meant to see.

Armand obeyed.

Look, Armand, beyond the threshold. An eternal void cut by the dullness of an obsidian plane which gyrates with slow precision and absorbs all light until both its dimensions are more luminous than a mirror winking at the sun. In the distance a black and white Death's-head moth flutters within the halo of a dim flame. Walk toward it, Armand. The insect grows until its wings are black robes afloat in a gentle wind. An old man with hair as white as white wool is writing into glazed stone with a stylus of fire.

Armand peered over the old man's shoulder. "What are you doing?"

"I'm writing wisdom."

"You're writing the alphabet in capital and lower case letters."

"A child is a man in a small letter, yet the best copy of Adam before he tasted of Eve or the apple. A child is nature's fresh picture newly drawn, which time and much handling, dims and defaces. His soul is a white paper unscribbled with observations of the world, which at length becomes a blurred notebook. He is purely happy, because he knows no evil, nor by means of sin to be acquainted with misery. Nature and his parents alike dandle him, and entice him on with a bait of sugar to a draught of wormwood. The older he grows, he is a stair lower from God. His is the Christian's example, and the old man's fate. The one imitates his pureness, and the other falls into his simplicity. Could he put off his body with his little coat, he had got eternity without a burden, and exchanged one heaven for another."

The Voice spoke.

Have you learned anything?

Armand answered the Voice, "We live in an age when innocence is a fatal liability."

Gabriel looked into Armand's eyes. A vomit of blackish blood surged over a cold stone floor.

A girdle of chastity surrounding her heart

Sunday—12 March 1679—Laetare Sunday
Hotel Reynie

Marie-Julie possessed a delicate heart, chastely belted and padlocked, encased since childhood in an armor to harden the world and human sentiment against it. At puberty, she retreated further into narcissism. She learned to create more pleasing realities for herself and to mask tenderness with a coldness verging on arrogance. Her egotistical and unkind heart had been predestined by a rule of men. Father, uncle, brother and husband each in turn had exerted his control until she was incapable of open rebellion. At the beginning of January, another man was destined for her life. The astrologer had predicted a son. If she hadn't gotten rid of him, other males would have taught this child his right to force his will on her too. Subversion was the only expression of free will men had left her.

Your life is adrift in a vortex of clashing wills. Your days swept away by tides and winds of stronger resolution. Your thoughts whirl and plunge in a maelstrom. You struggle in vain for the breath of your life. Abandon yourself, Marie-Julie. Scavengers always leave the wreckage of ghost ships unmolested.

Another tumult overwhelmed her. Gabriel suddenly hated her. She felt his loathing from the manner in which he denied access to his bed. She lay on the floor of a small closet connecting her bedroom with his and peered over the threshold with the alertness of a mouse. She had lain there for hours. Waiting. Finally, at four o'clock in the morning, a faint light streamed in from Gabriel's bedroom. She rose up and pounded her fists on the locked door until a valet unbolted it.

"Stop it. You'll wake the servants." Gabriel's voice was even and quiet. He was rationally indifferent.

If he'd hit her with a clenched fist, it would've hurt less. She needed to rouse some passion in him, even a murderous rage. She needed to draw him in, to heat his emotions to match her own. With the shrewish tone of a harridan she attacked him, but the undercurrent was pathetic and begging.

"Where are you going?"

Gabriel turned his back to her. "Go to your room."

"You didn't come home last night."

"I'm getting dressed. Get out. Now."

She tore the cravat out of his hands, "Answer me," and ripped apart the lace until it was in the same state as her marriage. "Answer me."

"Get me another," he said to the valet.

She threw herself at him. He pushed her away and continued dressing. "Gabriel." She shrieked; she wept. She made small fits and beat her own face. She whimpered. "You barely look at me, never speak to me. Never sleep in my bed."

Gabriel's voice was almost a monotone. "Would you care to tell me what your business is with La Voisin? Before I pay her a visit."

"La Voisin? You've taken to humiliating me. With mistresses and whores. Everyone in Paris is laughing at me. And you want to know about my fortune-teller."

"Blame yourself. If you behaved as my wife more often, I'd go searching elsewhere less. I let you do what you please. You spend without restraint. I never complain. They laugh a thousand times more at me. Over how blindly I was in love with you all these years. What advantage you took of it to make a fool of me. It's finished."

"I think I'm pregnant again. La Voisin predicts a son. I'm going to give you a son after all these years."

"So soon? You lost my last son at the end of January. Are you going to miscarry again? Or is it your lover's?" Gabriel looked Marie-Julie straight in the eye. "I know you have a lover. I'm just not clever enough to catch you with him. But if it gives me peace, you sleep in whatever bed you want. And I do the same. But in my home, madame, you sleep in your bed alone. If I find out another man's been under my roof, your life won't be worth the price of a cheap whore's trick."

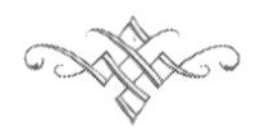

Diarrhea & vomiting: the noblest of the nobility

Sunday—12 March 1679—Laetare Sunday
La Villeneuve-sur-Gravois

Munin sat on Odin's shoulder whispering memories into his ear. The one's fate was to remember always and the other's always to remind. Forgetfulness was in neither's nature nor in the nature of their descendants. Psyches box memory in unlit chambers, but Subconscious perched over a doorway to all dark secrets caws remembrance.

Stephane Daimlen-Völs

Gabriel's soul remembered every detail, so for the next thirty years, he would become ill during the fourth week of Lent. In 1680, he was gripped suddenly by acutely painful stomach cramps. Everyone, especially Michel, was convinced he suffered a bout of poisoning, but then Gabriel succumbed to ague accompanied by diarrhea and vomiting. Doctors diagnosed 'change of seasons.' What did doctors know? They were all a bunch of quacks. Madame said so and so did Poquelin.

The following year, when the same happened, nobody paid attention; the year after, everyone commented on the odd coincidence; and the next, the servants laid wagers on when Gabriel would become sick, how ill he'd be and when he'd recover. Behind his back, they sneered at him 'Le Malade Imaginaire.'

What was it Gabriel had chosen to forget about Laetare Sunday 1679 which he kept reliving till he died? He remembered the journey from Paris to Faubourg Saint-Denis. He had taken a troop of police to arrest Catherine Montvoisin, her family and her lover, because Louvois's spies had discovered her plan to assassinate the king during Holy Week. He remembered also catching first sight of her property and thinking it was a nice cozy homestead, conveying comfort and security, but almost all recollection of the house itself was gone. Gabriel could see neither its contents nor a piece of human bone which prompted him to have his men dig up the grounds, though he could smell an odor of debris that had turned foul and eaten its way into every pore of the building's skin and bones. Even thirty years later it still had the power to make him gag.

Gabriel erased from memory almost every detail of La Voisin's studio, which the police found in a remote corner of the property, camouflaged by a thicket. It was small, windowless and filled to the rafters with witchcraft paraphernalia, yet remarkably clean. A large cupboard built into the fireplace wall masked an oven within, redolent of a smell: sickly sweet and more repulsive than the putrid odor in the main house.

Gather from formless mist into phantom an oven door and fine chalky dust filling your lungs from a thick coating of greasy ashes. Sift through charred remains. You still refuse to see what you've found. Look up, Gabriel. There's an angel looking at you with mild disgust. He shoves aside a weeping, frantic policeman who's in the doorway. He stands directly in front of you now. Have you ever seen such eyes? Their color undulates from stony beaches to pine forests to violet horizons at sunset. Do all angels have such beautiful eyes? He takes hold of your arm. Now, just when you wish, Gabriel, your memory fails you, you remember too much, too clearly.

"Come, Monsieur General. Come. Come, quickly."

Michel dragged Gabriel from the studio to the lawns. Some policemen wandered around aimlessly. Others dug into the ground with the repetitive, mindless action of a machine. Many simply sat on the ground and cried. A few opened small black silk bags.

Gabriel, look at the ground. Gaia in earth's disguise is dark and ugly, and smells worse than streets of Paris. Everywhere, holes pockmark richly verdant lawn. Mounds of deep black loam dot the landscape. The sky is a beautiful pale silvery blue now that the sun is high over the horizon. Cumulonimbus clouds of fantastical shapes sail leisurely on their voyage to nowhere. They're dense and puffy goose down and would make lovely pillows to rest one's weariness. They'll block the sun as they pass overhead. A giant shadow falls across your path. An unkindness of ravens pecks at the ground. You've seen this shadow's agreeable face before. Where?

Michel wandered among the policemen opening pouches, then thrust little pieces of dried lamb's membrane into Gabriel's hands. On each piece was written a name in blood:

Duc de Luxembourg, Madame de Poulaillon, Duchesse de Vivonne,
Princesse de Tingry, Duchesse de Bouillon, Marquis de Feuquieres,
Madame de Dreux, Vicomtesse de Polignac, Duchesse de Mazarin,
Marquis de Sainte-Croix, Marquise de Brinvilliers
Comtesse de Soissons, Mademoiselle des Oeillets
Marquise de Montespan

The names went on and on: the noblest of France's nobility.

The giant shadow clung to Michel's steely aura and wept. Michel watched impassively as Gabriel dropped small white parchments onto the ground and vomited.

The Devil has cleft hooves for hands

Saturday–1 April 1679–Paschal Vigil
La Pomme de Pin

Therese Rousseau was a woman of pleasure which was not the life destiny had originally planned for her. She'd been born to be an honest wife of a baker or printer or some other hardworking bourgeois. She might have aspired toward the middle or upper middle class for a minor civil servant or prosperous silk merchant. It wouldn't have been out of her reach: a very pretty girl with charming, precocious ways, whose family was respectable and popular in its town of Obernai. She should have been a genteel housewife with a yard full of children.

Hubris ruined her. She eloped with a young, handsome aristocrat and hopes of marriage planted firmly in her head. He used her till the novelty of her body bored him, passed her among his friends for their entertainment, then went on with his life and abandoned Therese to survive by her wits. If she'd managed to beguile an older man into becoming a protector, she might have become a successful demimondaine, but there hadn't been enough time and she wasn't cunning.

Therese's father was a gifted decorative painter with ambitions to be a portraitist. His clients were social climbers, poised on one rung of the bourgeoisie about to step up, with money to commemorate their grandness for their descendants, but not enough to engage an important portraitist. Fine muralist though Rousseau was, he was abominable at capturing his sitters' likenesses. Fortunately, he had an eye for talent and saw it in his daughter. His business improved dramatically after he apprenticed her to finish his commissions.

It was a particular skill, developed while helping her father at his portraits, which saved Therese from a life exclusively on the streets. Hands, feet and ears have no personality, so every artist learns to render a set particular to himself and gives the same ones to all sitters, but if one looks carefully, all hands, feet and ears are different. Therese liked looking at people's hands. This was how she remembered people and it was how she found herself employment at La Pomme de Pin on rue de la Juiverie.

When Gabriel first met Therese at La Pomme de Pin she was just shy of turning seventeen.

Therese cuddled up next to Gabriel, readjusting her position, to avoid a kink in her neck while she manipulated him. "Monsieur de La Reynie? You know, you look like Monsieur de La Reynie."

"Well, I'm not, and if you think I look like him, it's a pretty neat trick. You can see through my mask?"

"Of course not. It's your hands, you have Monsieur de La Reynie's hands. Seen them dozens of times. I'd recognize them anywhere."

Gabriel examined his hands, then looked into the girl's knowing eyes. "Do I know you? I don't recall ever seeing you before."

"Therese. You've seen me, you just never noticed. At Chatelet Courts. Police brought me in all the time when I was on my own. I saw you often, till Captain Desgrez took a liking to me and brought me here. He introduced me to Messieurs des Bordes. They like me. Use me for special customers. Now, the police never arrest me."

"What's this thing with hands?"

"A trick my papa showed me."

"Well, Therese, it's a clever talent you have along with your others. How old are you?"

"I'm very grown-up." She let go of his penis. "Monsieur de La Reynie, your life's in danger. Heard they have someone in your home who's trying to poison you. They've already tried and failed once."

"Who?"

"I don't know, but I do see and hear important things, I could tell you, if you'll help me leave here. I want to go home. You could get me a pension. I'd say it came from having once given service to the king. People would believe that and admire it. I'd have money for a large dowry. I could get married. Will you help me?"

Gabriel lay on his back and stared at the ceiling. "It depends on what you know."

"People think they're clever if they whisper they know La Pomme de Pin's real business. That it's where the Court comes for its wickedness. That Messieurs des Bordes sell the most unspeakable vices. But this place is more than people think. The Devil lives here."

"The Devil?"

She nodded. "There's a priest. They call him the Devil Incarnate of Paris. I think he lives below the basement."

"Here? In the basement?"

"No, below it. There's a passage in the basement, and at the end, a flight of stairs made of stone. With bloody footprints. Wednesday and Friday nights, Messieurs des Bordes go down there with all sorts of important people from Court. But I'm afraid to follow. The stairs are dark and it smells, like something rotting."

"Have you ever seen the Devil? He has cleft hooves for hands."

"You don't believe me."

"I think you're sincere, Therese, I just don't think you understand what you've seen."

"I know what I've seen. On Mardi Gras night, dozens from Court went down and never came up again. Not one of them. But, after I was at quai d'Anjou, the next morning, when I went to early morning Mass, the same ones who'd gone down the night before were already in Notre-Dame. I saw some of them come through the door from the church basement."

"You mean the crypt. What you've told me means nothing. It's not important." Gabriel pushed her down and got on top of her again.

"Listen." She pulled at his mask and struggled beneath him. "They still talk about that poisoner you executed three years ago, Marquise de Brinvilliers. They're afraid she might have told you about La Voisin and Esclavage."

"He's dead. What about La Voisin?"

"He's not dead. He has this trick. Painless abortions. He uses a potion to put the women into a deep sleep. When they wake, it's done. Fifty louis d'or he gets. What the women don't know is he molests them while they're asleep."

"Only the very wealthiest and most powerful women could afford that sum."

"All the noblewomen come here."

"Like the Comtesse? Have you ever seen her hands?"

"Hands? I've seen her face, hers and lots others. All the Court women. They don't bother masking in front of me, I'm just another woman. When they're here for their other business. But they wear masks when they use me for sex, like the Comtesse. They think they can fool me."

"What other business?"

"The other business in the basement. Sometimes I've seen them leave with bottles of potions. I'll tell you something I know about Madame de Montespan."

"Madame de Montespan?"

"Every woman wants to be the king's mistress. La Voisin's lover makes love potions. From disgusting things. Cock's testicles, bat blood, hanged-man's fat, semen. He does those potions best. Claims it's his work whenever the king seduces a new woman. Madame de Montespan has been his customer for years. When she first started with him, he bragged too much about her, so she had him sent to the galleys. She told the king he unjustly accused her doing witchcraft. Now, they're on good terms again. He says she must have gotten him a royal pardon, so he gives her his best potions and that's why she's still the king's main mistress. It's really La Voisin's doing. Now she's gone, so Madame de Montespan will surely fall."

"Why didn't you come to me sooner? At Chatelet?"

"If I'd gone to Chatelet, I'd be dead now. I have no reason to go there, except if I'm arrested. And, I'm never arrested anymore."

"What about when you sell your information?"

"The police come to me."

"Have you told anybody else about this? The police or your patron, Captain Desgrez?"

"Never. They're wolves and treat me like an animal. You're a just man, everybody says so."

"Isn't La Voisin an abortionist? What has she to do with love potions? Stop crying, Therese. Think about your pension."

"They made me do it. I confessed, but the priests won't forgive me, because they know I wasn't born Catholic. I should have stayed Huguenot, then God Himself would forgive me."

Gabriel slapped her. "Tell me."

"I had to help her make a love potion from a dead baby. They cut him up and took his blood. And his insides."

"You did this here?"

She shook her head. "In a great house on Ile-Saint-Louis. Midnight of Ash Wednesday. The Comtesse was there." She wiped her nose on the sheets. "They got careless and left it behind. The servants found it. The Comtesse came here at dawn and made a great fuss. She wanted to know what she should do. A few days later, Chevalier de Rais and Madame de Maintenon were screaming at La Voisin that she would to get everybody hanged."

"Madame de Montespan. Chevalier de Rais?"

"No, the governess, Madame de Maintenon."

"But the potion was for Montespan."

"I think so. She was still sending for potions until the very day La Voisin was arrested. Mostly through her two women."

"And, why did they make you help them?"

"They use me for sex during Black Masses. I do anything to please them, so they don't give me to the chevalier." She shuddered violently. "He tortures the women and children given to him. He does unspeakable things. One girl here had to watch him cut a baby out of its mother's womb. And do horrible things to a child. She told me before they gave her to him and she disappeared."

"Francois Galaup de Chasteuil? He's dead."

"No, Chevalier de Rais. Please help me."

"Chevalier de Rais? Are you sure?"

"Yes. I've prayed and prayed for you to come here someday. God's sent you."

"I don't think so." Gabriel gave her a kiss and caressed her till she was calm again. "Find out all you can. Help me a while longer and I'll get you back to the provinces, eventually. If you disappear now, they'll know you're up to something, and I won't be able to protect you."

"I'll learn lots to tell you, Monsieur de La Reynie."

"I shouldn't come back. They have a better chance of killing me here."

"You'll be safe here, if you're careful. Just don't make a habit of anything. Come on different days and don't tell anyone when you're coming. Ask for a boy or young man sometimes. And sometimes, change your mind at the last minute and leave. Most men get so lazy. They do the same thing every time. Pretty soon, everybody knows what you're going to do before you know it yourself." Therese wiggled herself underneath Gabriel and went back to work.

"So, how old are you? They said you'd just turned fourteen."

"I'll be seventeen in a few weeks. I know I'm small, but I'm not a little girl."

Gabriel laughed. "I've been cheated."

Divine intervention is witchcraft with a difference

Tuesday–25 April 1679–Feast of Saint Mark
Hotel Reynie

Why did you force Gabriel to read it? He never reads anything you put under his nose for signature. He trusts you implicitly. Do you realize what you've done, Michel? If you'd left things alone, if you'd let Gabriel toss off his signature, if you hadn't gotten angry, a thousand 'if's,' none of what will happen would ever have been. You're the catalyst. It doesn't matter to you, because after six weeks of penance, Gabriel's about to grant absolution. Why else would he invite you to his home? Why does he suddenly want to make up and be friends again?

As Michel followed the footman up the main staircase he thought of Palazzo Pamphilj and his privileged lifestyle within its household. For all the obvious wealth on display here, for all the evidence of refined tastes, this was not splendor. Gabriel was hardly a connoisseur or a great and powerful patron of the arts. God, how he missed Rome where he'd been indulged by men of importance. Life in Paris was a poor imitation. How was he ever going to get home to Italy again? How was he going to free himself? Did he want to? Could he accept the consequences and do his duty the rest of his life? Should he own up to Gabriel? He was praying for divine intervention when the footman announced, "Maitre de Visscher." Michel found himself deposited at the door of Gabriel's grand-cabinet. As always, Michel never said what he was thinking.

"What an exquisite, grand room. My compliments, Monsieur General."

"All right, de Visscher. I need another solicitor-general for a special investigation. If you do a good job, I could probably get you a title. A modest one, but chevalier is a start."

"And, an appointment at Court, Monsieur General?"

Gabriel launched into a description of the proposed duties. Michel listened carefully and looked for the meaning behind the words, a trick he'd learned in Rome.

"Call it Chambre Ardente."

"You're thinking up clever epithets. This is important."

"Can't be so important. First session of your inquisition sat on April 10th. So, why are you bringing me in on it now? Why not before, when you assembled the others?"

"De Visscher. That galley captain, Vanens, may be completely insane now, but all the prisoners are corroborating his crazed allegations. It's witchcraft. With a difference."

"May I have something to drink?"

Michel, keep your own counsel and let Gabriel play the gracious host. His monologue bores you. Snippets of it intrude on your thoughts of a beautiful girl's luscious curls and smiling blue eyes. She really is just a girl.

"Entrenched in Paris and most of France. Maybe all Europe. Insidious. Well concealed. Totally underground. Trafficking heavily in murder via poisons. And well paid for its services." Gabriel shook his head. "Everybody's going to the Devil, instead of the Church."

"Will there be another purge like the one in '68? Doesn't seem like anything new. Burn the witches and people will stop poisoning one another."

"Two witches I had executed in August '76 were trafficking in babies. So was La Voisin."

Gabriel doesn't have it quite right. Does he? He doesn't have any logical reason for making his assumptions. Michel, don't correct him, or you'll have to explain how you know the things you do. You can't do that. Sip your wine. Now, let the Devil take hold of your heart. With all this talk of witches and poisonings, find the moment to bring up Andreas Graf von Fugger. Gabriel will send you to Rome. Take the girl with her thick curls and smiling blue eyes. Marry her. She wouldn't be the first woman to die in childbed. Solve your problem. With any luck you'll be rewarded with a son. A son might just solve your other problem in Rome. You need to maneuver this conversation in another direction. Get up, Michel. Pour Gabriel a large armagnac and hovered over him until his skin blushes with warmth.

"Monsieur General. Montespan, the witches have named her. Haven't they? The others don't matter. You have to protect her, no matter how guilty she is. The rest are scapegoats. Caesar's wife, or in this case, Caesar's official mistress."

"If the people found out. England's Civil War is still a living memory. Members of Court, the king's mistress, murdering children like sacrificial goats. They'd say the king had to know. I know I wouldn't stop at murdering a witch or two. There'd be a bloodbath."

"Don't get carried away, Monsieur General. Regicide could never happen here. It happened in England, because the English are uncivilized. Who's running the baby trade now?"

"Don't know. Something else. La Voisin's lover and his royal pardon. Who got it for him?"

Wouldn't Gabriel like to know? Louvois's spies scrutinized every shred of official paper. There isn't any record. They'll never find out. You know who it is, Michel, but you aren't saying.

"Ask him."

"Says he thinks it was Montespan, but doesn't know for sure, and I believe him. Who's so powerful he could get a request for a royal pardon erased from every official record? Something else." Gabriel smiled warmly. "It's time you went to Rome for me."

It certainly is, Michel. There's divine intervention after all.

131

"As men die, so shall they arise:
if in faith, toward the south;
if in unbelief, toward the north."

Monday–1 May 1679–Feast of Saints Philip & James the Less
Notre-Dame Cathedral

Anne-Sophie lifted the half mask from her eyes, just as the Man in the Moon pulled a veiled mourning of leisurely gathering storm clouds across his face. What mischief in the moonlight was he attempting to conceal with a haunting sky? What Shades were his masked eyes overshadowing on the cathedral's north side?

Why had he asked her to wait on the north side where evildoers are traditionally buried. What if he didn't come? What if he didn't see her in the pitch blackness? He might be on the other side of the cathedral. Should she go look for him there? He'd told her the north side, but maybe he'd changed his mind. What if he'd come and gone? He'd said between eleven and midnight and she'd arrived at a quarter after eleven. He would have waited, but maybe he couldn't.

"Father, it's all your fault." Why had he made her play an extra round of nine men's morris? An idiotic game may have ruined her entire life. He must have come at eleven, waited, then couldn't wait anymore and she missed him. By how long? A minute? A second?

All the church bells in Paris were tolling midnight. What was she going to do? He forgot or decided to go without her. Maybe, she shouldn't have told him. Anne-Sophie leaned her head against the cold stone and wept. After the storm of pealing bells a stillness broke and a light spring rain cried for her too. A few minutes passed, days, years. Someone grabbed her shoulders.

"You came." She threw her arms around him. "You didn't forget me."

A thousand knots of necessity

Tuesday–30 May 1679–Feast of Saint Joan of Arc
Palazzo Pamphilj–Rome

Velazquez's portrait of Pope Innocent X was renowned as one of the most splendid in the world. Giacinto Gigi's verbal delineation, however, was less kind: tall, thin, choleric, splenetic, with a red face, bald in front with thick eyebrows revealing his severity and harshness, his face the most deformed ever born among men, the most repugnant of all the Fisherman's successors, insignificant, indeed vulgar, with an expression similar to a cunning lawyer. Benedetto Cardinal Pamphilj was like his uncle, Innocent, in every way, but now there were no painters in Rome with Velazquez's magical ability to make the cardinal a beautiful image for future ages.

In one respect, Benedetto wasn't quite like his uncle. Innocent had been thin. Benedetto wasn't fat. He wasn't roly-poly and didn't have a pregnant woman's belly hanging over the top of his breeches. In his cardinal's robes he cut an elegant figure except for his Punchinello's head, but naked he took on the appearance of those phallic-shaped balloons which have been twisted and knotted into three-dimensional stick figures to amuse children. With an erection, he was obscenely mutant: one large sausage stuffed to the breaking point sprouting another fat weiner with a frilly tip.

Power and wealth impart an immense beauty, so unless Benedetto was to suffer a fall from grace (unlikely as the Pamphilj ruled virtually sovereign in Rome), he would die a most pleasingly handsome man. He used his comeliness to satisfy his every carnal desire, knowing none of his favorites could resist his allure or avoid adoring his sausage casing for long, even when they deserted him for more vigorous flesh.

"Andreas, late as always. Missed the ceremony. Romantic. Bride's a sweet young girl." Benedetto smiled pathetically. "And very pregnant."

Andreas was bored. He looked beyond Benedetto's shoulder into the next room and gave the bride a cursory glance. "Is that the silly thing?"

Benedetto turned to scrutinize her also. "Take a closer look, Andreas."

Suddenly, Andreas caught his breath. "Jesus Christ. Luisa. That hair."

"Eyes too. Very large, very blue. Like the Mediterranean on a clear summer day."

"Stop trying to be poetic. Doesn't ring true from a hawk."

Benedetto took a few steps in several directions, looked down long vistas of rooms and corridors, then went back to Andreas with a puzzled expression. "Groom was here a moment ago. He's a Frenchman, Andreas. Very beautiful. Much more so than Chevalier de Lorraine. And younger. I know how much you like young Frenchmen, Andreas. You've been so lonely since Cicognara did away with poor Jean-Baptiste." Benedetto sadly poised his hands in an attitude of fervent prayer. "Everybody misses Zambinella."

Wily Italian.

"Benedetto, dear friend, I'm not chasing after some married French whore who likes his men discreetly on the side, so everyone in Rome can have a good laugh."

"That's not it at all. A friend of yours is here. Expressly asked to see you. He's in the upstairs gallery where that Spaniard's portrait of Uncle Innocent is. Excuse me while I join Olimpia and keep the bride occupied, until her husband returns."

Andreas, try not to choke at the thought of Dona Olimpia Doria Pamphilj Landi's blissful awareness of your hatred. Be polite. Benedetto is too important an ally to turn into a rabid enemy.

"My respects to your sister, Benedetto."

Andreas, you know exactly where Innocent X is hanging on the wall. He's to the left of Caravaggio's 'Rest during the Flight into Egypt.' Before a beautiful boy angel with luminous skin, an angel playing on his heavenly violin for the Holy Family, you met the love of your life next to Innocent's disapproving gaze. After more than a decade of perfect happiness, you lost your great love on that very same spot to a boy angel's temporal music, but Innocent was still frowning.

Look. Another beautiful angel with luminous skin, as if he'd put down his violin, and stepped out of this Caravaggio to converse with Balthasar. Be a romantic. Do what you did fifteen years ago. Steal up behind this young man, put your arms around the passion of your life and kiss him with great tenderness.

Balthasar bowed deeply and silently withdrew.

"Don't, Andreas, my wife might catch you."

"Michel. So, you're the bridegroom."

Bravo, Benedetto. You've played your cruel trick.

"How did you get a silly girl pregnant? Didn't think you had it in you."

"Neither did I."

"Who is she?"

"Older daughter of the Lieutenant General of Police of Paris."

"Ah, ha. Monsieur de La Reynie. Balthasar has nothing but complimentary things to say about him. Still, I don't think he'll be inclined to be your protector. You've used his heiress like a whore. He was planning a marquis for her. Fathers don't like it when their daughters elope with poor men who have no prospects."

"Don't start with me. I'm in no mood. The king has put La Reynie in charge of a tribunal to investigate your chaotic mess in France. He's afraid Montespan's involved up to her neck."

"Well, she is, but so is everyone else. I have everything under control. As always."

"When the king finds out, all hell will break loose. Andreas, listen to me for once. La Reynie sent me to spy on you. He's a bright man. He's beginning to put things together. Eventually, he'll figure it out."

"If he becomes a nuisance, we'll get rid of him. As for his daughter, she'll die in childbirth. If God's smiling on you, He might bless all the penance you've performed with a son. Don't deny it. I know it's what you want."

"No, it's not. Leave him alone. Please, leave her alone. I think I suddenly like her."

"Suddenly? You think? And when did this happen?"

"Tonight."

"A miracle. Sacrament of Matrimony has made a husband of you. Or it is your father-in-law you're in love with? Can't be your mother-in-law. Nobody loves a mother-in-law. That would be totally perverse." Andreas was bored. "There's your conscience again, Michel. It's why you'll never amount to anything without me. Ambition and a good conscience cancel each other out. Why did you marry her?"

"She reminds me a lot of you. Same intellect. Same ruthless nature."

"And, because she looks like Luisa? I'll never understand your taste for opera singers. Luisa's dead. Get over it."

"Benedetto's complaining these days that you're poisoning all the opera singers in Rome."

"Have you come back? I've forgiven you for Luisa. It's all forgotten."

"I haven't."

Andreas suddenly walked away and sat down on one of the sofas in the gallery.

Michel chased after him. "You're not listening to me. This game you like playing, you can't personally decide the fates of nations from the comfort of your bank."

"Why did you marry her, Michel? Are you still lusting after Luisa? Or did you think marrying La Reynie's daughter would make you a match for me? Did you really think his power and wealth would rub off on you? La Reynie's nothing."

"Andreas, Balthasar's concerned too. Everything in France has gotten out of hand. And Chasteuil's worst of all. He's completely out of control. Get rid of him."

"He's very useful. And resourceful."

"And insane. He's passing himself off as Chevalier de Rais and a dozen other aliases. I don't think he can keep them all straight anymore."

"Never gets caught."

"I wrote the report on La Voisin. Balthasar and I went there. Every day for six weeks. We examined hundreds of those bodies. To make sure it was his work. He's not cutting up just women anymore. Balthasar thinks Chasteuil sincerely believes he's the Devil Incarnate of Paris."

"Balthasar's not afraid of him."

"If Satan himself walked up to Balthasar, he'd spit in Satan's eye just to see if it would sizzle. Get rid of Chasteuil. He's become like that lamia, Gilles de Rais."

Andreas, so much talking. Take Michel by the arm and lead him down the gallery on a leisurely stroll while you needle him. Walk slower. You don't want to appear eager.

"Why did you marry her? I thought you'd gotten over Luisa. I gave you everything. You were just a boy and had nothing. Your education, your position in society, your career, everything. I put a crown on your head."

"What a deceit. A crown, a garland, a necklace. Underneath the gilding, they're all the same. A circle of unadorned chains."

"Always enough to keep you tethered, never enough to break away? You let yourself be dependent on me. You'll never be free, Michel, you still love me too much."

You raced to get here. A greyhound chasing a rabbit. He's not a virgin, Andreas. Well, open the door. Pray it's not locked. If it is, but it isn't. Lucky you. For more than a decade, you fettered him in a suffocating embrace. Bound him by a thousand knots of necessity. He's used to it by now. He'll succumb and let himself be seduced just as he has a thousand knots before. But, be generous. Tell him you love him before you throw him on the bed.

"It's your wedding night. How fair and pleasant you are, O love, for delights. Love of my life. Only love of my life."

Andreas waited for the longest minute of his life and was rewarded with Michel's passionate kiss.

Michel wept. "You also. The only love of my life. Till I die. Beyond death. Always."

Andreas watched his lover's retreat down the gallery. He'd heard the Paris police had a regimen of training and discipline equivalent to the military's. Michel's bad posture was gone. His back was ramrod straight.

Andreas, it must be from all that standing at attention.

Satyricon: deception in marriage leads to all kinds of unpleasantness

Tuesday–1 August 1679–Feast of Saint Peter's Chains
Palazzo Pamphilj–Rome

"Anne-Sophie. My poor little eggplant, left all alone to yourself by such a thoughtless husband." Benedetto Cardinal Pamphilj stood over her, a wide, reptilian grin on his face.

"Sorry, Your Eminence, I didn't see you." She smiled politely.

"Lost in happy thoughts, I'm sure." He helped her lopsided body onto its feet so she could genuflect and bow her head to kiss his ring, to humble herself properly before his eminence-ness. "Come. Dona Olimpia and I have a surprise for you."

Lamb and lion, they walked arm-in-arm from the library to a salon where Dona Olimpia held a plate groaning with a little bit of everything from an exquisite buffet set with a gourmand's delight of fruits, cheeses, pastries and sweets. Andreas von Fugger sipped white wine, behaved a gentleman if only for a nanosecond, stood, bowed and immediately fell back onto his chair as a servant startled Anne-Sophie by shoving in her face a plate laden with very little of anything.

Dona Olimpia spoke the first words in this farce. "Anne-Sophie. Our dear friend Andreas Graf von Fugger. Who is also a friend of our dear Michel."

"A pleasure, Graf von Fugger. I've seen you before, I think."

Andreas never shifted his gaze from his hosts. "Not likely. Dona Olimpia, you haven't given one of your evenings of music since the spring. You must definitely hostess another before Michel leaves. He'd enjoy it so much. Do you know this about your husband, Madame de Visscher? He loves opera. He loves a lot of drama."

"And opera singers." Benedetto wept crocodile tears. "It's not the same without Zambinella. What a voice she had. Last musical dinner we gave wasn't the same success as our others. Andreas, everyone blames you. Rome lost one it's finest singers, because you had a petty fit of jealousy. You owe it to everybody to find someone who can take Zambinella's place."

Anne-Sophie's gaze shifted slowly around the room. On every wall ancestral portraits bore exultant eyes and meaningful smiles.

"Our Michel was just a young boy." Dona Olimpia dabbed her eyes with a lace handkerchief so ethereal it was useless against anything except her nonexistent tears. "After his father died. We couldn't bear it. He was also our dear friend, so of course, we adopted his beautiful son. Michel wasn't here but a few months." She grinned at Andreas. "Dreadful man. Stole our Michel when we weren't looking. Swept him off his feet. A knight come to rescue a damsel. My dear, dear Anne-Sophie."

Here was Benedetto's cue to continue his sister's thoughts, as always. "Everything your husband is, he owes to Andreas. Paid for his education at the University of Bologna. Gave him everything his heart desired. Took Michel in hand and molded him." He feigned a search for just the right expression. "The way an older man delights in teaching a young innocent mistress everything he knows."

Andreas scrutinized Anne-Sophie's composed, vacuous look. Could she be so stupid?

"But, our dear Michel returned, didn't he, Benedetto."

His Eminence's mouth was full of Gorgonzola. It wasn't Delft porcelain he flashed for everyone's pleasure with an enthusiastic nod of his head.

"We begged. We made him my dear Benedetto's secretary. We gave him an outrageous pension. Of course, Andreas refused to let him live with us. So, we had to let him go home every night to sleep." Dona Olimpia, muttered a barely audible, "With Andreas."

Anne-Sophie put on her gambling face. The words lilted from her throat. "I remember now. Herr Graf. I saw you in the hallway, speaking with His Eminence, the night Michel and I were married. You're Michel's old lover."

Benedetto gagged on his mouthful of food. Dona Olimpia's eyes bulged as if her corset had been tightened several inches. Andreas saw beyond bulging eyes to confoundment and the confusion of defeat.

On the verge of an orgasm, he set aside his wine glass, then felt himself get sticky as the bitterness which fueled his enemy's life surfaced onto her face and curdled.

"And, did Michel tell you of his beautiful singer, Luisa? Madly in love, they were. They'd be together now, but she was poisoned." Dona Olimpia stared straight into Anne-Sophie's eyes. "You're her virtual twin. Hair. Eyes."

Anne-Sophie stood. Everyone waited for a counterattack. Each one's own anxiousness held himself mesmerized. With the skill of a conjurer she made them blink a flutter of time for vanishing.

Another nanosecond of politeness escaped Andreas as he fled his hosts. "Excuse me. I must chase after that charming little cunt. I'm afraid I've just fallen in love."

Michel, contemplate Anne-Sophie's progress. Be wary. She's a blur of precious silk unraveling down terrace steps, along garden paths and among the lilies—a delicate Shade in search of Orpheus to lead her out of Hades. Beyond the flower beds, fountains spit and retch at her approach—a Gorgon running the gauntlet of threatening gods she's petrified impotent. Watch, with a newlywed's mesmerized passion, your Medea, with her enchanting and terrifying ways, repose herself on a marble bench by a privet maze. This girl's bewitched you.

Isn't it a pleasure to have found another Medusa to lock horns with your enemy. Isn't it delightful sport watching two dominatrix circle each other in a mental wrestling match where neither has managed a headlock. If only your bride was a handsome boy, she'd ravish your heart.

Will you keep up this pretense of marriage the rest of your life? Do try to be good to her. Won't you? She's extremely likeable and young enough to be influenced. If you take control of her now, and mold her expectations to suit your needs, after a few children, she'll do what women always do and give her offspring precedence over her husband. Most men complain at being preempted by their children, but what a relief for you.

Michel appeared from nowhere. "You should be upstairs in bed. What are you reading?"

"Where are you going? You're all dressed to go out."

"I'm spending the day with friends. I'll be back by supper. Do you want anything?" Michel sat astride the bench, and from behind, took her in his arms. "I love your hair." He pressed his face into her mass of thick, soft curls, taking deep breaths, running his fingers through it. "I'll get combs with lots of diamonds, so your beautiful hair will sparkle. Are you happy? Do you like Rome?"

"You want to stay, don't you? Would the cardinal take you back as his secretary?"

"Probably."

"I want to see father and Jeanne-Jacqueline. I never said good-bye. I miss them." She felt his chin on her shoulder. "Father's letters have been very kind. He's excited about our baby. A few years? Could we go home for a few years?"

Michel turned her just enough to look at her smiling blue eyes. "We'll see." He gave her a quick kiss. "We get on so well. You're very easy to get along with. I enjoy talking with you. We like the same things. Have the same attitudes. I like doing things with you. Do you feel the same?"

She looked down at the book in her hands and nodded. "I love you, Michel."

"Later. When I get back, after supper, we'll go through the upstairs gallery. There's Caravaggio, Titian, Memling, Brueghel, lots more. A nice way to spend the next couple of evenings. Don't you think so?" He gave her another cheerful kiss.

"Yes." She watched as he walked back to the palace. At the steps to the terrace Benedetto took Michel in his arms and embraced him too intimately. "But, you don't love me, Michel."

How could he be so dishonest? Deception in marriage leads to all kinds of unpleasantness. What should she do? What a simple mistake of the Fates. It wasn't fair. Why should anyone have to wake up each morning to regret being in love for the next fifty or sixty years?

Jealousy and cynicism warred for Andreas's heart as he spied on Michel and Anne-Sophie. Their smiles were radiant. Their laughter was easy. Their bodies were familiar and comfortable with each other. They caressed. They petted. A thousand small intimacies passed between them. It was all a lie. It was as false as the Earth's flatness.

Michel must have thought about killing her. What was her hold over him? Could she possibly be disciplining him into goodness with birch and cane and leather? Anne-Sophie was indeed the image of Luisa.

Andreas emerged from hiding and sat beside Anne-Sophie, then grabbed the book from her hands. "Petronius Arbiter. How apropos. Satyricon isn't for women. Who taught you Latin?"

Anne-Sophie stared him down.

"Permit me to introduce myself properly."

"Yes, I know. You're the lover. But I'm the wife. I take precedence."

"Who told you?"

"Who hasn't? Even servants. They all hint. Broadly. Think I'm too stupid or naive to understand what the Italian vice is. When you first seduced Michel, had his voice changed yet? You corrupted a boy who didn't know his own mind. Didn't you?"

Andreas blushed and put his handkerchief in her hand. "Brava, you handle yourself magnificently. You may weep now."

Anne-Sophie laughed at him. "Why should I cry? Will it change the past? Will it make him different? Would you disappear?"

"No, but a woman's supposed to weep pathetically when she discovers her husband's vices."

"I don't cry. I hate. But I never cry. No one gets the better of me. Including you."

"What a monster you are. Give me the pleasure of introducing you into Vatican society and politics. By the time you're fifty, you and I, we'll have given the Pope and his Roman prelates thirty years worth of stomach ulcers and such heartache."

"What would be in it for me? Tell me something compelling and I'll think about it."

"Michel's shameless. He wants us both. He'll make us share. So, why fight over him? Besides, it's bad form to poison one's friends."

"I'm not your friend."

"I like you. Don't think I'm going to poison you after all. Be grateful and don't be difficult. I know your father's forgiven you for eloping with Michel, but if he discovered our menage a trois, he'd be very unhappy. Might disown you. Tell you to stay in Rome."

"You wouldn't risk it. You'd lose Michel again."

"Anne-Sophie, if you're a good girl, you'll be a marquise and wife of the French Ambassador to Rome and the Pope. Much better than anything your father could ever afford to buy as a husband for you. Whatever squealing brats you squeeze out of Michel is your affair. You got him to do the impossible at least once. I have every confidence you'll get him to manage it plenty more times."

"Like Monsieur and Madame? And Chevalier de Lorraine?"

"Not at all like them. Monsieur's too delicate to be a man and Madame's a Hunnish warrior. And how dare you compare me to that narcissistic twit, Philippe." Andreas offered his hand to Anne-Sophie. "Friends? A truce to start?"

"How powerful are you?"

"I'm the Pope's banker. Almost every Eminence and Excellency in the Vatican belongs to me. You weren't part of my plans, of course. Michel was to have taken Holy Orders. Become the Pope's secretary. I wanted the tiara on his head and the Fisherman's shoes on his feet." He shrugged his shoulders. "Oh, well. Were you different, I'd say there was still plenty of time. But you are what you are. More complicated than you can imagine. Someday, I'll tell you all about it. Maybe."

"How would any of this benefit me? Or my children?"

"Now, you're being a brainless, silly cunt. Like Philippe de Lorraine. Think about it. I hold God's purse strings. His ordained are my messenger boys. What could there possibly be in this world that I couldn't give you?"

"Anything I want?"

"Anything but the obvious. But that aside, the more ambitious you are, the more enjoyable for me. I do hope you have some imagination."

Anne-Sophie looked quietly into distant vistas of gardens. Andreas offered her his friendship once again. She turned a shark's dead, black eyes on him, looked at his outstretched hand with disdain, then leaned over and kissed his cheek. With the Siren's voice she beguiled him. "Andreas. What a wonderful godfather you'll make for all my children."

In the Palazzo Pamphilj, Dona Olimpia and Benedetto sat morose and silent, each with a spyglass trained on Andreas's captivated expression. "He's not bored," they said to each other.

Isaiah 34:14

Friday–29 September 1679–Feast of Michael the Archangel
Von Fugger Bank–Rome

Autumn. Days were getting shorter. Dark of winter was closing in to strangle Andreas with bitter heartache. He stared out the window contemplating a blood red sunset being pushed below the horizon by twilight. "Oh, Michel."

A month ago everything was perfect, though it hadn't been from late spring through summer with all those entertaining debates in the salons of Rome and the Vatican centered around who would ultimately dominate Michel: wife or lover. The second honeymoon to recapture the twelve happiest years of his life began in early August when Anne-Sophie insisted Andreas be honored as her firstborn's godfather. All Rome fell silent for one ambivalent moment while it reassessed and reformed its theories before reviving gossip with new vigor and delighted maliciousness. Bitchy tongues became permanently mute, however, when the Pope himself washed away Original Sin from Michel-Nicolas-Andreas to immortalize him beautiful as an angel who begat him who was beautiful as a luminous incarnation in a Caravaggio. "Oh, Michel."

Your beloved is gone and run away with Anne-Sophie to put his son into a father-in-law's loving, forgiving arms. They'll lie to La Reynie and say the boy's name is Michel-Nicolas. You're their dirty little secret. That silly cunt's just like Benedetto's sister who sent Michel running to France the first time. Well, not quite. Nonetheless, women are the scourge of the Earth and it would be a better world without them.

"Herr Graf has been despondent too many days." Jakob handed Andreas a handkerchief. "The lease on Hotel Beauvais, on rue Francois-Miron, is available. Only a few minutes walk to Hotel Reynie."

"I was so hoping this could all be managed from here. Do I really have to go to France? It's so uncivilized. There's no Pope in France."

"Balthasar desperately needs you in Paris, Herr Graf. Chasteuil's much worse than that French lamia, Gilles de Rais."

Andreas was roused from his torpor. He smiled at nightfall sucking life from a dying sun. *"Et occurent daemonia onocentauris, et pilosus clamabit alter ad alterum: ibi cubavit lamis, et invenit sibi requiem."*

"Bravo, Herr Graf. France is indeed a land of God's judgment on the wicked." Jakob was about to make a dramatic exit.

Andreas raised a finger. "We'll go via Isle Sainte-Marguerite. Let's pay a visit."

"To Monsieur de Saint-Mars?"

"Don't write. I want to catch him unawares."

"Monsieur de Saint-Mars?"

"No, my friend in the iron mask. Now. I've been kind enough to satisfy your curiosity. You may kneel and do the same for me."

Jakob frowned. "That is a duty beneath my dignity as Herr Graf's valet. I'll send in your secretary. It's what a secretary's for."

The prodigal son-in-law

Wednesday—18 October 1679—Feast of Saint Luke
Hotel Reynie

What is child sacrifice? Is it an offering to God or Devil or an effect of woman's body to entrap a man? Is it how Eve tamed Adam? Is this how Anne-Sophie caught you? Beyond one's own flesh and blood, Michel, it's in the spirit one secures a foothold to Paradise. What keeps you ensnared? Is she Andreas? When you turn her face down into the bed, mounting her from behind in darkness, making her submit to your every physical desire, is she Luisa? Is she Andreas and Luisa? Is twilight at sunrise disillusioning or are you a man who isn't ungrateful in glaring daylight?

Do you see in your firstborn's eyes your father's father and your grandson's sons? Do you see immortality from your own arbitrary point in time stretch through a two dimensional linear eternity of ancestors and descendants? Do you realize your primacy over Gabriel? Your father-in-law will be racked with grief and envy every moment of his life. Love of woman can't do as much for a man. Sons make the dominant male, Michel.

In the pit of Gabriel's stomach a washerwoman's laundry was readied for the clothesline, looped and drawn, inverted in on itself and wrung tightly. Hydrochloric acid seeped through mucus lining, ate his organ with a slow burn and traveled up his esophagus till he tasted bile, forcing involuntary, little burps along the way. He was Poisoned Fly: he could regurgitate hatred onto a son-in-law, dissolve him into a palatable mass, suck him into oblivion and make a hungry stomachache go away.

Gabriel, look at your son-in-law. Insufferable young man. Not a hint of arrogance. A prodigal son come home to weep in his father's arms, to beg forgiveness, to offer his prized olive branch—a grandson.

"You stole into my home. A thief through the back door. Into my daughter's bed. Without paying your respects to me. You don't love her."

"What man marries for love? You were arranging a title and wealth, not a love match. Get me a title, I have my own wealth again. She loves me. She'll have it all. What more could you want? You'll be such a good father in your daughter's eyes."

Gabriel, he's not your enemy.

"Gabriel, I'm not your enemy."

"Name your son my heir? Poison me and have control of his fortune till he comes of age."

"You're sick with fear and suspicion."

"You have no patrimony. Titles, property, all lost. Your family disgraced. You bought back your good name by hyphenating it with mine. Now, you scheme to buy me with my daughter's happiness. You're a cunning lawyer."

"If you want, I'll return to Rome, with my wife and my son. But I'm not your enemy."

He's a Borgia. He's Saint Francis of Assisi. He's an oxymoron this young man with his sadly vulnerable look and contemplative silence—confident, empathetic, omniscient. You trust him more than your own confessor.

Gabriel was exhausted. "Sit down, Michel. Someone's trying to poison me in my own home. I wouldn't be surprised if it's my wife."

Twilight is the hour of the wolf

Friday—8 December 1679—Feast of the Immaculate Conception
Chatelet Courts

Madame's epistles were accumulating. With an average of twenty letters per week, at least fifteen pages per letter and over two hundred words per page, the twelve dozen packets, squarely stacked in twelve neat piles, arranged three-by-four, monopolizing the top of Gabriel's desk represented nearly a half million German words to be translated.

"Michel, I say a little prayer every morning. 'Matthew, Mark, Luke and John, someone please break her arm.' Like I have nothing better to do with my life. Your German's all right, help me."

"God's not listening. Neither am I. You've read her letters, it's half the battle."

"I can't keep up. The woman's a god-damned printing press." Gabriel flopped onto his chair. "How the devil can she find time to do anything else?"

"Better translate a few and send them on, otherwise, she's coming for a visit." Michel did an elegant mimic of Liselotte's haughty waddle. "Like a great sea monster risen from the deep. Lumbering through the hallways with her booming German voice. Like a tone-deaf Siren she'll sing to you. 'Are your fingers broken, Monsieur de La Reynie, or what?'"

Gabriel put his feet on the window sill and crossed his legs. "Not funny."

"Yes, it is. So, what do her letters say about Limping Bastard? His mother wants to make him the king's heir? Hasn't got that right."

"King's legitimized all Montespan's bastards. Limping Bastard's his favorite. Why not?"

"Dullard Dauphin and Melonhead would have to drop dead before Limping Bastard could sit on the throne."

"Maybe, they will. There's a lot of poison being flung around at Court these days. But, it's not the point. In September of '77, there was a plot to murder the king and the dauphin. Holy Week it was a plot to murder the king. Everybody keeps saying Montespan. Montespan. Don't you get it? She's not the one."

"Yes, she is. Too many witnesses have placed her at Black Masses and sacrifices."

"That yes. But there's two different things going on here. Plots to murder the king and the dauphin have nothing to do with witchcraft. Why would Montespan murder the king? She gains from the dauphin's death, but not the king's. She needs the queen out of the way. Don't see anyone trying to kill her. It's someone else who wants the king dead. And, the business about Maintenon slipping love potions into the king's food and drink. What's the governess in this?"

"What's really bothering you? Right now, you could care less if the king was poisoned."

Gabriel looked at chipped paint on the windowsill, then at scratches on his gold shoe buckles. A flutter of time played a discordant note with the rhythm of his heart beat. When did he come to love this son-in-law so very much? With love comes trust, or was it the other way around? "My wife's been going to La Voisin for years. All her miscarriages…abortions." He showed Michel a pressed flower of white translucence veined oxblood which could have been some unfortunate child's lucky caul. "But she's been going to La Voisin for more."

Michel unfolded the parchment and read: 'Madame de La Reynie.' "Where did you get this? From the stack at La Voisin's?"

"From a prostitute at La Pomme de Pin who's been spying for me. Kept it hidden a long time. Thought I'd become angry, not give her a pension I promised. She's afraid all of a sudden. It's from a baby murdered at Hotel Bordes on Ash Wednesday. A piece is missing. Look."

Michel took a ragged, bloodstained triangle from Gabriel and matched it neatly against the missing corner of the larger parchment. "I don't get it."

"My brother-in-law gave me the pouch tied to that baby's wrist. This bloodied scrap was in it. Mustn't have thought it was important. Couldn't imagine I'd ever come across the parchment itself. Marie-Julie's going to Black Masses. Making packs with Satan. Desgrez has to be involved too."

"I know Cardinal Pamphilj. If you pay him enough, he'll have the Pope annul your marriage. Get a lettre de cachet for Desgrez and lock him up. Chateau d'If would be a good place."

"Michel, I can't. Can't afford a scandal like this right now. Truth is, it'd be easier and cleaner to poison them both. Can you believe the irony?"

Therese Rousseau followed a policeman through the corridors of Chatelet to Gabriel's office. Her appearance was cadaverous. She staggered a drunkard's dance which evoked indifference from the men on duty. None of them wanted to partner with a prostitute who was obviously suffering from the Spanish curse. At the lieutenant general's door, Therese pushed her way into the room. Gabriel eased her into an armchair, while Michel slammed the door shut on an indignant policeman left standing in the hallway.

"My pension, Monsieur de La Reynie, I've come for it." She wheezed. "You promised me your confessor would forgive me."

Gabriel waved his hand in front of her blank stare. Michel leaned over her and recited something in Latin.

Therese grabbed Michel's coat and pulled until his ear was at her lips. "Cernonnus. Cernonnus. Notre-Dame. Cernonnus. Notre-Dame." Her eyes rolled back into her head.

"She's been poisoned."

Gabriel sobbed quietly. "She called them wolves, Michel. It's the hour of the wolf."

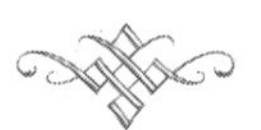

Incest: a fetish for love

Wednesday–27 December 1679–Feast of Saint John
Hotel Reynie

New moon, dark of the moon, dark of the night, night dark as blood, blood on the moon. Perfect for casting a spell.

Jeanne-Jacqueline, everything you need is scattered everywhere. Gather it all together and carefully arrange the ingredients on your down coverlet. Hurry up. Only a few minutes to go. This charm has to be started at the first stroke of midnight.

The bells of Saint-Gervais began tolling her cue. "With this ring I thee wed."

Open your prayer book to the Sacrament of Matrimony. Crack the spine a bit to make it lay flat. Center it on this large square of lace. Arrange on the pages each item in this order: a gold ring, an old key, a dried rose, sprigs of willow and of rosemary, a crust of bread, a small heart-shaped sweetmeat. Fan out a hand of the ace of spades, ace of diamonds, nine of hearts, ten of clubs. Place the cards on top. Tie up the corners, set the bundle by the headboard, squoosh your pillow before you cover your fetish. Now, climb into bed. Carefully. Rest your head. Gently. Let your head sink into the pillow, so magical images can percolate up through goose down directly into your brain. Pray for a divine benevolence.

"Luna, every woman's friend, to me thy goodness condescend, let this night in visions see emblems of my destiny. All hail to the moon, all hail to thee. I prithee, good moon, declare to me this night who my husband must be."

The door creaked open. "Father?"

"Shhh." Armand held his finger to his lips. Jeanne-Jacqueline giggled. He locked the door before creeping over to her. "Your neck looks cramped, let me fix your pillow."

"Don't touch it." She slapped his hand.

"You're not doing another one of those silly charms."

"I told you, they're not silly."

"Really. How does this one work?"

"If thou dream of storms at sea, troubles will come to thee. Of diamonds or snow-white swans in flight, love and marriage come this night. A willow or wood-elves bring, treachery and all hopes vanishing. And wild geese in winter months, marry will you more than once."

"And you believe this nonsense. My darling, men need a little help." He stretched out on the bed and started playing with her hair. "You're almost fifteen. Not like your mother was at that age. Too shy, so innocent." He blew out the candle. "You need to learn what a man likes."

She stiffened.

Armand rolled onto her and kissed her in the mouth. "I'll teach you everything I know. And charm you in every way I can."

Jeanne-Jacqueline, close your eyes and dream of graveyards.

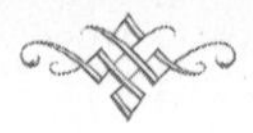

Knouts: a fetish for love

Thursday–28 December 1679–Feast of the Holy Innocents
Hotel Beauvais

Andreas, touch the hollow behind his knee, luminous as an angelic incarnation in a Caravaggio, radiant as a holy nimbus denied to any sacred head resting during a flight into Egypt. All the light of Heaven is in the hollow of that knee. Men without faith would be moved to believe, the sight is so glorious. Sightless men could sense where the painter's gaze had rested—consumed, aching, longing. You always spare the hollow behind the knee of your beloved angel. Knouts of pleasure never dim to a reddish glow the golden luminosity of his flesh in this place.

"Get up, dear, you've got to go now." Michel rolled onto his back. "Get up. Don't do that." Andreas rolled Michel onto his stomach to examine thin red stripes, marking the sheets in a predominately horizontal pattern, until they oxidized brown. "Jakob will be furious."

Michel spoke into the pillow. "Five more minutes."

"Look at this nasty mess you've made." Andreas crawled back into bed. "Where does La Reynie think you go three nights a week?"

"Don't start, Andreas." Michel sat on the edge of the bed, then turned and looked down at the sheets. "What's a little blood?"

"Blood doesn't was out so easily. He can't be happy you're being unfaithful to his daughter."

"He doesn't care."

"I suppose he doesn't. Certainly can't cast stones at you. Sleeps with the Comtesse and a few others. Frequents La Pomme de Pin, quite a bit. Such a paragon of virtue. What a slut. It's not fair, Michel. You haven't confided a thing about him. He must know everything about me by now."

"I've told him nothing."

"Of course. Sent you to Rome to spy on me. You returned and said, 'Forgive me, Monsieur General, I'm such a bad spy. Couldn't manage an introduction to Graf von Fugger. Benedetto Cardinal Pamphilj, who only sucked my cock hundreds of times when I was his secretary, was so very unhelpful. I'm such a failure, I decided to marry your daughter instead.'"

"Exactly."

Andreas slapped him.

Michel was still a few minutes. "It's all right to mock me, isn't it? You're entitled to anyone you want, but I belong exclusively to you. Let it go."

"Benedetto wasn't the problem. That was business. What you do to advance your career or your station in life, I can understand. It was that foul bitch Dona Olimpia's fault."

"Blame yourself. Ruined everything with your jealousy. Couldn't let me have something I wanted, could you?"

"Here we go with Luisa again. Hasn't your wife figured it out yet?"

"She's not at all like Luisa."

"Wouldn't say that. Luisa didn't have any testicles either. Made her thlibiae, after they discovered she could sing." Andreas smiled a radiant smile. "I take it back, your wife actually has balls. Incredibly sophisticated. You don't give her enough credit. Why don't you tell her? She's bound to find out sooner or later. Especially, after you return to Rome. Prelates are very bad at keeping secrets. How they love to gossip. Wouldn't it be better coming from you?"

"You're mad. Why don't they just poison her and be done with it?"

"The way they induced me to poison Luisa? And Zambinella? What's one travestied castrato singer more or less in Rome? Cardinals were only using them to annoy me. So, I annoyed them back. But they like to think they believe in the sanctity of their Sacrament of Marriage. They'll never do anything to your wife. She's giving them a good enough laugh as it is. Michel. Benedetto's wagering all over Rome you're going to father at least a half dozen children. You're the sport of the social season." Andreas grabbed Michel's hand and pulled him back. "Sorry. I won't meddle. Do what you want. But you should tell her. Deception's a nasty thing."

"Words from a master."

Andreas was bored. "You're really a fool."

Michel was quiet again. "What are you doing about Chasteuil?"

"Balthasar can't find him."

"You have limitless resources. Put some of them to work for you."

"Balthasar and a few of his men are looking. I'm not wasting anything more on Chasteuil. He's unimportant." Andreas sulked. "I didn't come here for him. I don't like Paris. It smells, and the weather in Rome is better. Food's better there too. Italians are much more cosmopolitan. France has very little to recommend it."

"Find Chasteuil and get rid of him."

"I'm trying, Michel. As God is my judge. Can't find him. He's like twilight. Elusive."

"Good morning, Andreas."

A devil's smile settled on Andreas's lips. "Kiss your guileless, charming Omphale good morning for me. And you know, even hanging linens in sunlight probably won't bleach out bloodstains."

1680

Listeners never hear any good said of themselves

Monday–5 February 1680–Feast of Saint Agatha
Chateau Versailles

Dearest L_-H_,

Feast of the Holy Innocents is an ill-omened day and here is a gossip proving this true. Captain Desgrez coveted a post because of its large annuity, but when it became available, he could not buy the appointment, for it cost so much no one but the king himself could afford to pay for it, so he asked Sodomite Lorraine to ask Monsieur to ask the king to purchase it for him and went away assured everything was well in hand.

On Feast of the Holy Innocents, the very day Sodomite Lorraine was to plead the request, Captain Desgrez seeking to ensure his case hid under Monsieur's bed. Did I not once tell you listeners never hear any good said of themselves? While Monsieur and his darling spoke together with their heads on the pillow, the captain heard himself ridiculed in the most vicious way, so later that same evening while the Court was at gaming tables, he asked if all was arranged. That sodomite gave his most gracious and beautiful smile, and furious at this double dealing, the captain enacted for all present the scene upon the bed and how he had been betrayed, whereupon Sodomite Lorraine shouted back at him he was a bitch and a whore and left in a fearful tantrum. Monsieur then ran weeping to the king.

Monsieur was determined upon revenge, so Sodomite Lorraine took to bed with La Chatte Comtesse, then gossiped to everyone she is a slut to be had by anyone, but most especially by lowborn wretches who are far beneath her rank and dignity such as policemen, and when Captain Desgrez heard of it, he became crazed with anger. On Epiphany La Chatte Comtesse was sitting on the floor with some other ladies when he happened by, and whether by design or by accident, he stepped on her hand and broke her little finger which should have been a happy ending to this little comedy, but Sodomite Lorraine would not hear of it, so next day when he came upon the captain (combing his peruke on his head before a foray on the ladies), he pushed him roughly, whereupon the captain hit his attacker in the face with his comb and that sodomite's peruke fell off. To save face, that stupid Sodomite Lorraine now runs about proclaiming he has purposely contracted the French curse so he may give it to La Chatte Comtesse in order that she may give it to Captain Desgrez.

The French lead the most reprehensible life. You think my life is spent in pleasure parties and amusements. That is a lie and here is the truth. I rise at nine o'clock. After my first fart of the day I choose a book (usually a romance) and go where, you can guess. Next, I say my prayers and read three chapters of the Bible. Then I dress myself and receive visits of many courtiers. At eleven, I return to my cabinet where I write and read for pleasure. At twelve, I go to church after which I dine alone. This amuses me little, for I think there is nothing as tiresome as to be alone at table surrounded by servants who look at everything one puts in one's mouth, and besides though I have been here nearly a decade, I am as yet unaccustomed to the detestable cooking of this country. After my dinner which is usually done by a quarter of two I return to my cabinet. I walk my room for half an hour for sake of digestion and play with my little animals. I have two parrots, a canary and eighteen little dogs to amuse me. Then I rest half an hour. After my rest I read and write till it is time for the king's supper.

Whenever letters arrive from Herr Gottfried Leibniz and Herr Franz Helmont (they write me often) I set this time aside for studying them. Both gentlemen are clever and most enlightening on many subjects, but being a mystic, Herr Helmont becomes confused albeit on a high level. Sometimes my ladies play ombre or brelan beside my table or sometimes my children come to see me between half past nine and ten. Sometimes Monsieur comes with Sodomite Lorraine, but this is not often, for Monsieur knows how much I detest his companion.

At a quarter to eleven, we go to supper and await the king who arrives at half-past the hour. We eat without saying a word, then pass into the king's room where we stay about the length of a Pater Noster. His Majesty makes a low bow and retires into his grand-cabinet. We follow him and he talks with us. At half-past twelve, he says good night and we retire to our own apartments. I go to bed. When there is a comedy I go to it at seven o'clock and thence to the king's supper. When there is hunting, it is at one o'clock, so I get up at eight and go to church at eleven.

There is a strange lot of noisemakers at my door. I must go and see to it. I am returned, for it was nothing of importance or interest, only Monsieur, Sodomite Lorraine, Monsieur le Duc and Monsieur-le-Valet-who-belongs-to-Monsieur-le-Duc, all of them playing at bumble bees and spitting honey at one another. Monsieur le Duc has conceived the oddest notion that Bastards' Governess is poisoning melons to which I explained this is not possible as it is not the season for melons and none is to be had, and even were melons plentiful it is a most foolish employment, more for the likes of Dumb Beauty than for one as sly as Bastards' Governess, but Monsieur le Duc insists. Poor fool. I fear we must endure him being a Persian melon for a short while.

His Highness S_-A_-A_ has been planting strange Transylvania ideas into Her Highness H_'s sensible German head, for she now believes in angels known as Masters of Howling. Each dawn, because these lords of shouting chant God's glory, He puts off the Last Judgement one more day, but when a day comes these angels no longer feel inclined to shout, it will mean the end of us. I shall put an end to this silliness. His Highness R_ and Her Highness S_ von B_-L_ must warn their brother-in-law to keep his unorthodox religious ideas to himself or before long their younger sister will become a howling fool herself, and I cannot imagine anything more undignified than that.

There all is the news I have to tell. It is late, so good night to you.

Many kisses,
Liselotte

Bloody ghosts & Bluebeard's sins

Wednesday–5 June 1680–Feast of Saint Boniface
Chateau Fontainebleau

Dear darling Highness S_ von B_-L_,

We have been at Fontainebleau for several weeks and of all places to which the Court roams it pleases me best. I often walk about at night in the gallery where they say King Francois's ghost appears, but that good man never does me the honor, for perhaps he thinks my prayers insufficiently efficacious to call him out of Purgatory and in this he may be justified.

Die Rotzenhäuserin always sees him and last time she was here imagined he tried to sleep with her as he was pulling on the bed linens, hovering and huffing by the bed, and would not leave her in peace till she pulled back the covers to let him in. Lenor also claims that whenever she sits down to do her toilette he stares in the mirror of her dressing table making faces at her. I tell her she sees what she wants to see. She says I annoy ghosts because I am skeptical which is the reason they hide themselves from me and this is very true, for I am of a scientific mind and nature, but I shall say in truth it is well known King Francois was very lecherous, and if I did believe his ghost was trying to get into Lenor's bed, it would prove men do not give up their old habits even after they are dead.

In the Great Salon on certain floors and walls are stains left by a bloody ghost. No matter how hard the servants scrub the blood remains. The king was in a good humor one day and explained how these stains came to be there. He told me stories concerning Queen of Sweden who came to France in 1656. A quarter century later we can still see blood left by her grand-equerry whom she caused to be murdered there, for she wanted all he knew about her to remain secret and was afraid certain things would surely be divulged as he had begun to tattle out of jealousy when another man had supplanted him in her good graces.

Concerning matters of licentious behavior, Maitre de Visscher imparted to me a most disgusting fable, so I shall impart it in turn to Your Highness. It is of Bluebeard who is called thus here in France on account of his bluish-black beard, but his name was Gilles de Rais and they say he murdered all his wives (supposedly very many of them), for the French think it a perfectly acceptable thing for a man to kill his wife, so the more wives one kills the better a thing they think it is. But that is a lie and here is the truth.

A Marechal de France and comrade-in-arms to Jeanne d'Arc, Gilles de Rais's sole weakness was an inability to manage his inheritance properly, so in spite of a vastness of fortune that beggared King of France by comparison, soon he was in desperate financial straits, but being a Frenchman, to curb his extravagance and become frugal with himself was tantamount to being stingy with others, and while the latter was perfectly acceptable the former was unthinkable. His only solution was to marry another vast fortune and to accomplish this he kidnapped Catherine de Thouars into marrying him, but she did not complain as Frenchwomen think it romantic when they are brutalized.

Gilles de Rais's schemes to dismantle his wife's birthright were thwarted by her family, and frustrated by this unexpected obstacle, he became too keenly enthused with alchemy. Charlatans from everywhere and nowhere found a new home at his Court and generous pensions for scientific experiments to acquire the Philosopher's Stone. In the course of this folly he came under the spell of a Paduan priest who convinced him that contracts to part with one's soul in the next world never induced the Devil to part with anything of value in this world, for only offerings of consequence would gain his attention and produce any worthwhile profits, in short, sacrifices of children.

When Gilles de Rais's sins came to light, they were monstrous crimes of stunning proportions. Arraigned before the ecclesiastical courts for witchcraft and summoning of demons, as an afterthought the civil courts also indicted him of lycanthropy, for he tortured, abused, butchered and dismembered children in the manner of werewolves. There were accusations of sodomy but also of necrophilia as he particularly enjoyed manipulating his own pleasure a multitude of times while the corpse was still warm. Eyewitnesses testified he would slit children's throats, sit holding their legs between his own while doing his pleasure on their stomachs, then drink their blood. They say no less than one hundred fifty and as many as nine hundred were murdered.

The Church courts burned him at the stake for apostasy and heresy. The civil courts condemned him for murder and lycanthropy after ecclesiastical justice had finished with him, but it hardly mattered, for beheading a pile of ashes would have been difficult. He was but thirty-six years old at the time of his execution. I would not believe such gruesome things possible by any human being even a Frenchman, but Maitre de Visscher showed me many original documents of the courts, so I cannot argue this story false.

"Why do you wish to know such horrible things," I asked Maitre de Visscher. "There is another Gilles de Rais among us now in Paris," said he. "That is not possible," I replied, "His Majesty would never allow such a horror, for God would punish him severely for being a poor shepherd to the flock He has given into the king's care." "But I speak the truth, Madame. This new Gilles de Rais's handiwork was among the children found at La Voisin's. Many hundreds had been murdered as if by a werewolf." Maitre de Visscher assured me all is being done to find and execute this wretched beast. God grant they do away with him very soon.

This morning Monsieur de La Reynie was present at His Majesty's lever which is an extraordinary honor for someone outside the Court. He was told that no investigation of Chambre Ardente is to extend into the Italian vice, for though the king is known to abhor the sin of sodomy, as Monsieur is the most uninhibited sodomite of all, it is better to avoid the matter completely.

Official Whore is sour grapes again because the king has three mistresses these days. She whines in a worse way than a spoiled child. I cannot see why. Dumb Beauty must lay on her back and do the work, Bastards' Governess must use her brains to provide the amusement, but Official Whore still holds the title. She has the glory without any of the travail. What more could she possibly want? I say she has the best of all worlds. Sometimes people are not clever enough to know when fortune is smiling down on them.

Seeing as Your Highness asks it, dueling is a capital offense carrying the death penalty and has been so since the early part of this century, for at that time blood feuds had reached epidemic proportions and Late King's first Cardinal Prime Minister's older brother had been a casualty. The law was a clever way of deterring nobles from pruning one another's family trees into extinction.

I am delighted His Highness R_ and Die Rotzenhäuserin are getting along well. I had promised she would be amusing which apparently she is, but do remind your brother not to let her write anything for him as she cannot spell one wit. Her stay has been much longer than I intended, but as long as the king still asks after her it is better she stay in London.

Does not Your Highness think it curious His Highness R_ has not written My Excellency a single word of his thoughts concerning Lenor? What could be the reason for this? Does he complain to you of the expense of keeping her?

This is all the news. I must go.

Much love and many kisses,
Liselotte

Lame ducks & simpleminded wasps

Saturday–10 August 1680–feast of Saint Lawrence of Rome
Chateau Versailles

Dear English Majesty,

If I could with propriety return to the Palatinate, one would see me there quickly, for I love my fatherland and think it more agreeable than all others as there is less of luxury that I do not care for and more of frankness and integrity which I seek. Be it said between us when I came to France it was purely in obedience to His Highness my Late Papa, Her Highness S_ von B_-L_, His Highness R_ and Your English Majesty. I was as Iphigenia sacrificed for a fair wind.

My inclination did in no way bring me here, and having been placed against my will, I must stay till I die. There is no likelihood we shall see each other again in this life and what will become of us afterward only God knows.

Were it not for my Bible, the theatre and the great hunts, this country would have driven me completely mad by now. Hunting does not make me quite as happy as the theatre, but more so than the Bible, and while it is true there are as many tragedies upon the stage as there are in Holy Scripture, one can avoid going to the theatre, whereas one cannot avoid reading the Bible.

Of all things tragical nothing is worse than Chambre Ardente. All last year Monsieur de La Reynie quickly overfilled the capacity of Vincennes and Bastille. As the tribunal had to constantly clear the jails to accommodate more prisoners, unfortunately for those being vacated, the sole place which can always board another tenant is the cemetery, so whenever prisons needed emptying, a multitude of executions were staged to entertain the public.

For a short time winter was a relief from the workings of Chambre Ardente. Perhaps, it was because blood is more noticeable juxtaposed against snow than camouflaged by the ordure typically found at Place de Greve, but with the first snowfall in late October arrests stopped, there were no more public executions, Monsieur de La Reynie's inquisitors found other means of occupying themselves, and though they are in France masters at dissembling and stalling, the world ambling along at an easy gait even when it is rushing, at this moment they are galloping away with themselves, for there is nothing quite like witch hunts to spur Frenchmen into action, so once again since the of coming of springtime, one hears of nothing but tragical events.

Chambre Ardente has called in eighteen women who killed their husbands. Last month a very grand duchesse stood before the tribunal, and having answered simply 'no' to each of seventy questions, impressed the judges with her sang-froid. She was fortunate and they let her go. Others have killed themselves to avoid scandal and punishment. Being a pragmatic man, Monsieur-le-Wardrobe packed his own bags for a change and fled, whereas one of the more popular vicomtes goes about whining his innocence to anyone who will listen which is quickly making him an unpopular bore. Everyday the list grows longer of those who must make answer for some charge before Chambre Ardente. Everyday another member of Court disappears into Bastille. No one sleeps well at night for fear of whose turn will be next. My Excellency sleeps the sleep of the dead, for my conscience is clear.

Some days ago while walking alone in the Orangeries at Versailles I was singing unconsciously Calvinist psalms or Lutheran canticles. I cannot say which, for I mix them up. Unknown to me, Monsieur Rousseau was at work on a scaffolding. He is a most excellent painter and has decorated many rooms at Versailles, Saint-Cloud and Marly, but all faces of all figures in his landscapes and decorations look the same, for all of them, men and women, have but one face which they say it is the image of his lost daughter, poor man, and it is fortunate he does not paint portraits for his living or he would starve, but in any event coming down hurriedly from his perch, he nearly scared me out of my wits. He looked crazed, so I asked him, "My goodness, monsieur, what troubles you?" Throwing himself at my feet, he said with tears and gratitude, "Is it possible, Madame, you still remember our Psalms? God bless you always for keeping your Faith true." It seems Monsieur Rousseau is a Reformer and next day he ran away, but no one knows where he has gone. It is a pity, for he paints walls nicely and wherever he is, I pray he is happy and employed as he is an agreeable man and his frescoes are beautiful.

After my encounter with the painter I walked to the parterres. I wish Your English Majesty could be with My Excellency to see how beautiful the gardens are. One ought to be able to walk about them with kind and agreeable people, and not with persons who hate and despise each other mutually, sentiments met with here more frequently than those of friendship. What is worse is that the French waddle like lame ducks. Except for His Majesty, Die Rotzenhäuserin and My Excellency, no one here can tread twoscore paces without sweating and puffing. But these things have nothing to do with my walk.

The flower beds are changed daily and I was curious to know the flower of the day. The gardeners had put out large tubs of tuberose which were stinkier than streets in Paris and it was most amusing to see the king and most of the Court as they fled the gardens, for they looked like ninepins bowled down, reeling and whirling before they toppled over, but then an even funnier thing happened as the gardens are plagued with wasps (mosquitoes too) and everyday someone is stung by one. While I stood watching, it seems one of these little fellows flew up La Chatte Comtesse's skirt, and stinging her where her legs join together, she pulled up her skirt and ran about crying, "Help me. Help me. Close your eyes and pull him out." Suddenly a half dozen men were chasing her to get their hands on the amorous wasp, but the more they chased her the faster she ran. Some time passed before the men were able to pile themselves on top and rescue her.

They disapprove here of that new Italian fashion of wearing underlinens, but it might be useful in protecting against wasps. It is a pity the little fellow did not choose to fly under Bastards' Governess's skirt, for I would have liked to see that decorous figure with her skirts over her head, but even a simpleminded creature like a wasp has the good sense not to want to be poisoned.

I thank Your English Majesty for news concerning Chevalier de Rais. As My Excellency only met the fellow once at the opera, when La Chatte Comtesse forced me to endure his company and that of Captain Desgrez, I would have thought the matter of no interest to anyone, but just to please you I did as you insisted and communicated this gossip to the king, but naturally not saying Your English Majesty was its source. His Majesty was much obliged and thanked me, but in the evening he said, laughing, "My ministers insist you are ill-informed. They say there is no word of truth in what was written to you." I answered, "Time will show who is better informed, your ministers or the person who wrote to me. My intentions were good, Sire."

Some days later after it was proved Chevalier de Rais had gone to England as Your English Majesty said His Highness R_ told you, Toad Louvois came to me and said I ought to have informed him of news I received. I replied, "You assured the king I received false news, so I ordered nothing more be written to me, for I dislike to spread false reports." He laughed as he usually does and said, "Your news is always good." I answered, "A great and able minister must have surer news than I, for he knows all things."

That same evening the king said to me, "You have been ridiculing my ministers." I replied, "I returned them what they gave." Sly Toad Louvois thought to browbeat me not only by himself but through His Majesty also. It failed as no one believes better than I the old proverb that he who dies from threats deserves to be buried with nothing more than a mule's farts.

There is the news. My Excellency must be off.

Your English Majesty's most humble,
Madame de France

Those who know the art do not betray the master's secrets

Sunday—15 September 1680—Feast of the Seven Sorrows of the Virgin
Chateau Saint-Germain

Darling Highness R_,

Had I not heard from Her Highness A_ de M_ of Your Highness going to Holland I would have been quite surprised at getting your last letter from The Hague. I remember The Hague perfectly and always thought it an agreeable city, but the air is not as good as it is in the Palatinate and everything is so very dear in Holland. As I am sure you will agree there is no air in the world better than the air in Heidelberg.

It is very true Paris and Heidelberg have the same latitude and also the same ascendent of Virgo, but the air in Paris is very stinky. My son's doctor, a German and learned logical gentleman, has discovered the reason. He was walking on one of Monsieur de La Reynie's newly paved streets, wondering why air in Heidelberg is healthy and air in Paris not, and as he passed some workmen laying cobblestones, he saw underneath was a layer of black sludge more than a foot thick, so wrapping some in paper, took it home, distilled it and found it to be niter and saltpeter, thus deducing the sun's heat draws this essence into the Parisian air making it harmful, whereas the niter comes from many thousands of Parisians who piss in public.

He is a clever fellow and performs many experiments with pleasing results, distilling a white crystal acid from borax and concocting a substance which sparks and ignites when it is scratched or struck which are clever things if he could find some use for them. They remind me very much of the cleverly useless things Your Highness invents.

Dumb Beauty is dead. They say Bastards' Governess poisoned her. I cannot feel any pity, for this foolish girl's death was her own fault. She had discovered proof of La Voisin and Bastards' Governess having been involved together for many years in some wickedness and in the poisoning of the latter's husband, so instead of showing the documents to His Majesty, Dumb Beauty threatened Bastards' Governess she would tell and now it is as if these papers never existed. Can there be any greater proof of that imbecile girl's empty skull?

Never in his lifetime will the king hear of this adventure, for as no one is inclined to be poisoned every tongue is respectful, and moreover the king has a passion for Bastards' Governess as he has had for none of his other mistresses, so to see them together is like nothing you can imagine. Even when he has spent an entire day in the nursery with his little bastards and her, he cannot stand having her out of his sight, so she is always sent for, she forthwith appears, and in less than a quarter of an hour he cannot bear it anymore and is whispering secrets in her ear. Now, Bastard's Governess is a sought-after and feared person at Court. There is high opinion of her intelligence, little esteem for her heart and no liking for her person.

Monsieur's favorites fear I shall tell His Majesty how they pillage Monsieur and how they trouble me with their profligate lives. They wished to get Bastards' Governess on their side, so to do this they told her they knew her life, and if she was against them, they would tell everything to the king, for all evil said of this diabolical woman is still below the truth. I know a union exists between Monsieur's favorites and her because Monsieur le Duc told me so.

Until this opportunity I was afraid to unburden my heart, for as you know they always read my letters. Even if that lazy, good-for-nothing secretary I send to Your Highness shows this letter to Monsieur de La Reynie, the lieutenant general owes me much and certainly is neither an ungrateful wretch nor a disloyal frog to reveal this confidence to anyone who might use it against My Excellency, for if he should, he could never again count upon my friendship and as they say there are many assassins who wish to be rid of him, he would find himself without any friends in this world to help and protect him. But that is about ingrates and not about the shocking conspiracy against me.

Sodomite Lorraine has promised Bastards' Governess he will persuade Monsieur to marry my son and my daughter to a daughter and a son of Official Whore's. Assuredly, one of those bastards will be Limping Bastard and this would suit the king perfectly, for as Monseigneur is his sole surviving child by the queen and has no sons of his own as of yet, marriage to my daughter would tie Limping Bastard closer to the throne. This would also suit Bastards' Governess, for it is she who persuaded His Majesty to legitimize Official Whore's bastards.

God will give me revenge. My son will come to be a dunce someday, for though he now begins to talk of learned things, I see plainly instead of giving him pleasure they bore him, and while I have often scolded him for this, he answers it is not his fault as he takes pleasure in learning all things, but as soon as he knows them he has no further pleasure in them, so if those devils manage to marry him to one of the king's mouse droppings by Official Whore, it will serve them right if he is easily bored by his wife.

In truth it is better this disgrace for my son than the honor done Monsieur by Cardinal Prime Minister and Queen Mother. For the twenty years she had no sons she suffered greatly at the hands of Previous Monsieur who was always a threat to Late King and to the throne, so to avoid such a thing happening again, Queen Mother and Cardinal Prime Minister turned Monsieur over at a very young age to sodomites who vitiated his will by spending all their time dressing him as a girl which is the reason he is a brainless chatterbox with his liking of beautiful clothes, expensive jewels, rare perfumes and fine cosmetics.

All the Court seeks Monsieur's advice in his expertise with fashion, jewelry, ceremony, etiquette, genealogy, decorating, in short, all things better suited to a woman than to a man, all of which pleases His Majesty greatly who says Monsieur must never have any home but the Court or any resource but the king's love, so Monsieur is a most obedient and loving brother.

Thanks to heaven Monsieur loathes Official Whore and has always resisted every overture to disgraceful misalliances, but these days I am afraid, for Monsieur cannot deny Sodomite Lorraine anything he asks, and neither do I know how to stop these wretched devils from ruining my children nor can I bear the thought of them married to horribly ugly cripples as all of Official Whore's offspring are lame and sickly and have bad natures, and whenever I see them it makes my blood boil, but worst of all they are bastards of a double adultery which is the reason it would be shameful for my children to be married to such base villains. Your Highness must never discuss this with anyone or write to me through the regular post concerning it, for if anyone at Court knew my true feelings, it would cause me no end of trouble with His Majesty.

Your Highness writes that Her Highness S_ von B_-L_ and Her Highness H_ think it strange I have no say in managing my inheritance. I think it strange also, for as you know this is not the way of things in the Palatinate, but it is the way things are here, for marriage contracts drawn in France are always for advantage of husband and never wife, so everything is the husband's property while he lives doing with it as he pleases, though all business involving his wife's property must be executed in her name. When a man dies, his estate belongs to his children, whereas the widow may claim but that portion of her property her husband has not squandered. This is the law and you must believe I am no dim-witted fool to let Monsieur waste my inheritance from the Palatinate on his boys were it not. I know Sodomite Lorraine is spending my money faster than it can be invested, but what can I do? It behooves one never to complain about these things.

Her Highness A_ de M_ wrote your stay in Holland was until middle of September, so when you return to England, this letter will have arrived as I am sending it by hand of one of my secretaries. For a change Toad Louvois will not get his hands on it first. I shall also entrust my secretary to bring those diamond buttons you requested of His Majesty. Monsieur was aflutter you ought to wear them properly upon your sleeves and vexed he cannot show you the correct way himself, so after much debate he had a paper pattern made which I am sending also. I cannot imagine what Your Highness wants with this useless crap, and if it were permitted, I would often say the like to Monsieur.

They say His English Majesty is Catholic in private and Protestant in public. It reminds me of an Englishman with whom Monsieur once discussed religion. "Are you Huguenot, monsieur," asked Monsieur. "No," replied the Englishman. "So you are Catholic," said Monsieur. "Even less," said he. "Ah, ha. Then you are Lutheran." "Not at all," answered the Englishman. "What the devil are you," asked Monsieur. The Englishman said, "I have a little religion all my own." To dissemble with such grace is more clever than the tricks they play upon the stage, and as conjurers are taught when they are apprentices, those who know the art do not betray the master's secrets.

That is the news. Be kind to my secretary and do not worry about him. His visit will not cost you much if you do not keep him overly long. He is to bring Die Rotzenhäuserin back to France, for His Majesty's attention is firmly fixed elsewhere, so any danger of losing another of my maids-of-honor is past.

My Excellency has no idea what Your Highness means concerning our neighbors the storks never failing to come back every year. We have none in France. I wish you would tell me if you see them in England, for it is said they never stay in any kingdom.

My most affectionate love,
Lotte

Nothing but crap & gossip

Thursday–24 October 1680–Feast of Raphael the Archangel
Palais-Royal

Beloved Highness S_ von B_-L_,

Monsieur, his sodomite darling and I are again in Paris to hear bells ringing for All Saints Night. Never before did I believe in witches, but now see they are everywhere in France and most particularly at Court, for Bastards' Governess is grandest witch of all, formerly an honor reserved for Official Whore who is now just oldest witch of all.

Monsieur le Duc was a wolf again for a longest while, howling at the moon every night for weeks which disturbed everyone's sleep except the king's (his snoring drowns out all other noises), so we were all forced to endure it, and moreover as Monsieur le Duc has been going about on all fours, this caused him a problem with Sigi who being much larger tried to mount him. As usual His Majesty pays no attention till Monsieur le Duc makes himself a bother as he did two days ago when he scurried up to Bastards' Governess, lifted his leg and relieved himself on her new dress, but I do not think he mistook her for a tree, poor fool, so the king ordered him to keep to his apartments till he became a bat or something else equally harmless. Yesterday, he began buzzing around the palace and his valet's duties now include chasing him with a fly swatter.

I have a droll story to tell Your Highness concerning Monsieur le Duc. Madame la Duchesse is notorious for running after men and there are too many of them at Court in her good graces who are indiscreet which is the reason one of my medals was able to play a practical joke on my poor friend when he asked to see my collection, for as he assumes to know much about medals, Baron von Pufendorf who is an honorable and learned man in charge of my collection but who is not the most discreet of men either and little informed as to what goes on at Court made a dissertation on one of my medals to prove against opinions of other savants that a head with horns which appears upon it is of Pan and not of Jupiter Ammon.

To prove his erudition, the worthy soul said, "Ah, Monsieur le Duc, here is one of the finest medals Madame has. It is the triumph of Cornificius. He has all sorts of horns. He has horns of Juno and of Faunus." "Go on," I said, "if you stop to talk about each medal, you will have no time to show them all." But full of his subject, he replied, "Oh, Madame, this one is worth all the rest. Cornificius is one of the rarest medals on earth. Consider it, Madame. Look at it. Here is Juno crowned with horns crowning this great general with horns almost has grand as her own horns." In spite of everything I did I was helpless to prevent him from harping on horns. "Monsieur le Duc knows about such things," he said, "and I want him to judge whether I am not just in saying those horns are horns of Pan and not horns of Jupiter Ammon."

All of us in the room closed our mouths, holding our breaths to keep from laughing, almost bursting from it, for if it had been done on purpose, it could not have been more complete, so when Monsieur le Duc was gone, I laughed out loud and had greatest difficulty in convincing Baron von Pufendorf he had blundered. His Highness my Late Papa would often say everybody here below is a demon charged to torment somebody else and this is true.

At last I have won over Monsieur completely, brought him round to laugh with me at his weaknesses, to take what I say pleasantly without being irritated, to have a just confidence in me and always take my part, whereas previously I suffered terribly, he now no longer allows anyone to calumniate and attack me in his presence, so I hope to God our Lord does not take him prematurely or I shall see disappear in one instant the result of all cares and pains I have taken to make myself happy, but happiness does not come cheaply, and to gain all this from Monsieur, I had to please him by being reconciled with Sodomite Lorraine. This is the reason that wretched devil is with us now to hear bells ringing next week.

I was tricked into a reconciliation as if by magic. Monsieur and his boys were in the salon playing cards when Sodomite Lorraine said Monsieur intended to go to Paris without me to hear the bells and I was to go alone to Montargis. At this I became very angry. "I did not think, Madame, you wished to stay in the same place as myself," Monsieur said. "Who made such false reports about me? I have more respect and attachment to you, Monsieur, than those who accuse me falsely," I replied. Monsieur made everyone leave and reproached me for hating Sodomite Lorraine. "It is true I hate him, but only out of attachment to you, Monsieur, and because of evil offices he does me in your esteem. Nevertheless, if it is agreeable to you that I be reconciled with Monsieur de Lorraine, I am ready to be so." This pleased my husband very much, whereupon he sent for Sodomite Lorraine and said to him, "Madame is very willing to be reconciled with you."

Monsieur made us embrace and the affair ended this way. He wishes for his darling to live ever after on good terms with me and I am sure Sodomite Lorraine will make a show of it outwardly, but will continue to play underhand all sorts of tricks, whereas Monsieur is acting in such good faith I believe he may continue to be friendly to me till his last hour.

I would not have minded making a trip to Montargis, but did not want it to appear as if I had done something to deserve being sent from Court, moreover there is also danger I would be forgotten there to die of hunger, for the chateau of Montargis is my dower-house, and now as my dower is nothing, all I have to live upon comes from the king and Monsieur, so I much prefer to be reconciled with Sodomite Lorraine, besides I had no other choice, for I could not go to Orleans as at Orleans there is no house.

I could have gone to Saint-Cloud without making an appearance of being in disgrace as it is not an appanage, for Monsieur bought this property with his own money, but Saint-Cloud is only a house for summer, and as many of my people must lodge in rooms without fireplaces, they cannot pass late autumn or winter there or I would be the cause of their deaths and I am not hard enough for that. Your Highness knows how suffering of others makes me pitiful. There are times I even prefer to deprive myself of necessary attentions rather than require my servants to inconvenience themselves over them, so in consequence they are kind enough in return to refer to me behind my back as 'Good Mistress' and this title I cherish more than all others that burden me.

If Sodomite Lorraine is not more careful, he will die so poor his friends will have to pay for his burial, but of course if he has no friends left, what they will do with what is left of him I do not know. Nor do I care. He has an income from Monsieur of three hundred thousand crowns, but he is a bad manager and his people rob him. As long as they give him a thousand pistoles for gambling and debauchery, he lets them dissipate and pillage his property as they choose.

Your Highness must scold His Highness R_ as regards my secretary who complained of ill treatment while in England, and after relating to me the whole of the matter in great detail, I must take his part. He said to me, "Madame, London was a filthy city. The food was disgusting. The people were ugly and ill-dressed. The money looked unreal. There were too many different coins." "One can say the same of any unfamiliar place," I replied. "This is true," said he. "But Madame cannot imagine their rudeness." "How so," asked I. He said, "Upon arriving at His Highness in Spring Gardens, I showed Madame's letters and said, 'I am to present these to His Highness.' The footman said, 'Is that so? Well, you are either too late or too early for your appointment, for His Highness is not here.' I then said, 'I am sent by Madame.'"

And what does Your Highness think that lazy, good-for-nothing English blockhead of a footman replied? He asked, "Madame who?" Do not your brother's servants know there is only one Madame, and if they do not, do you not think they ought not to know? You must write your younger brother and complain of this insult to My Excellency, for His Highness R_ promised to be kind to my secretary.

As His Highness R_ is not at present in My Excellency's good graces do me a great kindness and ask him to send before second week December a quantity of his Prince Rupert's drops. I wish to give these playthings as small gifts to my friends to amuse them over Christmas holidays. Five or six large chests of them should suffice and I am allowing I have no doubt more than enough time to produce what I require. Be sure to remind your brother to have them well and carefully packed, so there will be as little breakage as possible.

Please also have His Highness R_ send more mezzotints for Monsieur de La Reynie as my good friend seemed quite pleased by those sent previously, and as he is doing a considerable service harboring Die Rotzenhäuserin and His Highness R_'s soon to be new bastard, all concerned ought to be grateful. Monsieur de La Reynie I am certain will be equally grateful for this new thoughtfulness and will just as certainly forward my letter to Your Highness with all due haste and no delay or I shall be sorely disappointed in him and have to keep all those mezzotints to enhance my own collection.

There is the news. Your Highness will forgive me if it is nothing but crap and gossip more suitable for the likes of A_-E_ or L_-H_, but there are some days when there is nothing of importance or interest to write even to you.

My heart is with you always,
Liselotte

Iron Mask: there is almost no way one can come by the truth honestly

Sunday–24 November 1680–Feast of Christ the King
Palais-Royal

Dear English Majesty,

Historians often tell lies. I have constantly before me lies they tell in France concerning His Highness my Grandfather that his wife carried away by ambition never left him a moment's peace till he declared himself King of Bohemia. I say there is no word of truth in it and Her Highness my Grandmother thought of nothing but seeing comedies and ballets and reading romances, but they listen politely and remain unconvinced, for Frenchmen are always willing to believe the worst lies of all who are not French and will hear nothing bad of those who are.

Here is the history of which Your English Majesty inquired that no one will speak of in France except by the backstairs. Late King and Queen Mother hated and despised each other all their lives and were married more than twenty years before His Majesty was born, for he was conceived in one night by sheer accident after Late King had abandoned his wife's bed for more than a decade. Monsieur was conceived under similar circumstances two years later.

Previous Monsieur who had been heir apparent his entire life was vexed at losing the succession and till the day he died, he often exclaimed, "I saw for myself the sons came out of her, but who the devil put them in her?" He was never satisfied they were sons of his brother, for everyone knew Late King disliked doing that business with women.

Monsieur le Duc told me a calumnious tale he was told by his father which explains the king's and Monsieur's conceptions by Queen Mother, for everyone here believes it, but out of fear only speak of it in secret. In late 1630, when Late King was so ill it was thought he would die, Queen Mother took a lover to father an heir, so she would be protected as queen. She chose a lover who had fathered many sons (his identity was never discovered) and he did his job well, for she became pregnant, but then much to her dismay Late King recovered from his illness, and as she could not trick her husband into lying with her, she had an abortion in early 1631. But that is about another pregnancy and not about the birth of the king or Monsieur.

His Majesty's birth was necessary to save Queen Mother's life as the year before he was born she had been deemed guilty of treasonable involvement with Spain and England, so Late King intended to repudiate then execute her, but birth of an heir brought a reprieve. As she had done before, she achieved her pregnancy first and this time she duped Late King into performing his duty afterward, so emboldened by her success at contriving one son, she attempted a second. The true sire of her children has never been discovered.

All this brings me to another curious history of Iron Mask who is called thus, for he wears a steel helmet which completely covers his face, may never take it off even when he sleeps or takes Communion and is permitted to speak with no one but his governor, Monsieur de Saint-Mars. For many years Iron Mask was moved throughout France from prison to prison until he now resides permanently in the fortress-prison of Isle Sainte-Marguerite. Only his governor knows for certain how long Iron Mask has been imprisoned but he declines to say. Except for these inconveniences, Iron Mask is treated with utmost respect, courtesy and deference as one would reserve for Princes of the Blood, for he may be the child Queen Mother was said to have aborted in early 1631 or a later child she refused to destroy. They also say he may be the king's twin, but no one knows for certain who this man is or what he did to deserve his fate.

As Your English Majesty can see, if historians lie in these ways about things which have passed before our noses, what are we to believe as to things far away from us that happened a great many years ago? I think histories (except Holy Scripture) are as false as romances with the only difference being the latter are more amusing.

As for present day there is almost no way one can come by truth honestly. One cannot rely on newspapers and gazettes for truth as they are full of lies. In France people willingly pay to do their enemies harm and all printers eagerly take money for this. It is a simple affair. One merely writes down whatever one desires to be known, wraps the news around a gold coin, sends it to any printer by hand of a third party and one's news will always appear in the next issue.

Chambre Ardente is up to its old tricks, and Monsieur de La Reynie has issued so many arrest warrants since All Saints people say he receives great pleasure and satisfaction from these new persecutions, for Place de Greve was ablaze again and executions were appalling in number and regularity. A deputation of prominent citizens beseeched me to intercede the executions ought to stop as it is a disgrace such things are done during Advent and I said as much to Monsieur de La Reynie which put an end to this wretched business. Parisians are the best people in the world, and if Parlement did not excite them, they would never revolt. Good Parisians (they think kindly and well of me) choose to attribute to me whatever is good and I am much obliged to those poor souls for whatever affection they feel toward me, but it is undeserved.

Two of Official Whore's confidants have been arrested. It is an open secret at Court one of them has several bastards by the king and it seems this distinction of being His Majesty's Occasional Concubine had become too heady for her. News is these two women were involved together in a poisoning plot against Official Whore which I think is quite odd as they are her servants, but in any event one was imprisoned and as for Occasional Concubine she was exiled which is even odder, for they banished her to a charity hospital for the insane.

Monsieur le Duc insists Occasional Concubine is Bastards' Governess's daughter. "Madame, she was doing her mother's bidding in her attempts to poison the king and lay blame on Official Whore," he said. I said, "Bastards' Governess has never had a child of her own." "But Occasional Concubine is her blood kin," replied he. "If Occasional Concubine was sent to the hospital and Bastards' Governess was not moved to pity, it is clear proof there is no blood relation between them, for no mother would permit such a dreadful fate to befall her child as I myself am a mother and know this to be true," I said. Monsieur le Duc is being very obstinate in his misconception and how he came to believe such crap and nonsense I cannot say.

Official Whore's sister and sister-in-law were among peppercorns issued summonses along with mouse droppings, but at the eleventh hour they were snatched from the tribunal's clutches by the king which was no surprise to anyone, for the one's husband and the other herself are held in great esteem and affection by His Majesty and Monsieur.

Even so, the king is cool toward Official Whore of late. There is no open quarrel between them, but he declines to see her except in company of the entire Court, only goes to her apartments escorted and never stays overly long, so no one can remember when they last had a private moment between them. Her star is dipping below the horizon and I doubt it will ever see the midheavens again. Now that the king keeps himself away from her his frequent bouts of dizziness and his vicious headaches have disappeared. She is indeed the king's malady.

Last week a distant cousin of Monsieur de La Reynie's wife was taken before Chambre Ardente and accused of consorting with witches and conspiring to poison her husband, for she wished to be rid of him as he was boring her to death and she feared such a demise would take too long to kill her. Imagine how foolish those inquisitors looked when she came into court with her husband on her left arm and her lover on her right. She brazened her way through and in the end they could find no fault with her, but her defeat came when Maitre de Visscher asked if she had ever seen the Devil, for she pointed to Monsieur de La Reynie and said, "Yes. And he looked like him." He was unamused and evened the score by securing a lettre de cachet against her, wherefore she was quickly on her way to exile at Nerac in the Pyrenees. It is all the talk and causing Monsieur de La Reynie no end of embarrassment.

Please have His Highness R_ send more glass bubbles. Your English Majesty will ask what My Excellency wants with this useless crap. The bubbles amuse my children and the king and Monsieur also. I gave out all six large chests His Highness so very kindly sent me. They would have filched a chest at customs just as they always filch a box of my good German sausages Her Highness S_ von B_-L_ sends to me, but this time they did not, for customs officials are surprisingly clever enough to know useless crap when they see it.

I own no coverlet filled with goose down and never heard of any such thing in my lifetime, but if it is as Your English Majesty says, a new German fashion, then there must be some good sense and logic to it, though all my little dogs sleep on the bed with me which keeps me warm and I cannot imagine anything could be warmer than good little dachshunde, so if Your English Majesty thinks a goose down coverlet is as warm as a good German dog, then please have His Highness R_ send me a dozen. I shall try them.

We pay postage on letters we receive, but as to paying for those we put in the post, this is something new. My Excellency would advise Your English Majesty against such a foolish thing, for your civil servants will have no incentive to deliver letters if they have been paid beforehand for a service they have not yet provided, and as there will be no way of being assured of getting one's letters or of one's letters being delivered, postal service in England will go to the Devil.

Your English Majesty's most humble,
Madame de France

What is black & plagued all over? 1 witch & 13 cats in a sack

Sunday–15 December 1680–Gaudete Sunday
Chateau Fontainebleau

Dear K_ von P_,

My Excellency is sorry you could not read my last letter. I thought you competent of understanding my meaning and able to supply any missing words for yourself, but I am obviously mistaken and repeat much old news, so you will not be left wondering what it was you could not read from those parts torn by one of my dogs as I finished it. I see you dislike dogs, for if you loved them as I do, you would forgive their little faults.

Herr Leibniz once wrote me that animals have immortal souls, so they also have reason. This is very true. Dogs are the best people to be found in France. My little dog, Reine Inconnue, understands as well as a man and never leaves me an instant without weeping and howling as long as I am out of her sight, whereas the same cannot always be said of one's companions, especially if they are French.

Monsieur Descartes claims animals are machines without souls and will come to nothing, but he is after all a Frenchman and the French are heartless, so it follows most logically he would believe a simple innocent creature of God should not have a soul which is something better than the heart he is without. I like Herr Leibniz's philosophy better as it is a nice thought I shall be in the next world with my beloved little animals, my family and friends, moreover if Monsieur Descartes is correct and animals' souls are mortal, seeing as man is also an animal, his soul might be mortal too which means we might all come to nothing together.

Where others failed in divorcing their husbands, La Chatte Comtesse evidently succeeded many years ago and Chambre Ardente issued a warrant for her arrest on hearing this old rumor again, whereupon her mother-in-law gloated and could hardly wait to see

La Chatte Comtesse's head on the executioner's block. La Chatte Comtesse persisted she had not poisoned her husband and refused to go before the tribunal, but His Majesty insisted if she was truly innocent a short stay in Bastille ought not to discommode her too much, nonetheless she was afraid that once in she would never be let out.

Monsieur said the king really wanted her out of France even though he hesitated over her and matters came to a head when Frog La Reynie demanded she be declared contumacious and found guilty, so for two days summonses were heralded beneath her windows at Palais Tuileries, then she had either to present herself before the inquisition or flee.

Monsieur thinks the king gave her time to escape, for His Majesty went to the mother-in-law to make his apology for showing La Chatte Comtesse consideration. Why? Some say he loved her once and thought to marry her which is something he never wished to do with any other mistress. Others say he vacillated as Cardinal Prime Minister was his stepfather, and as this gentleman's niece, La Chatte Comtesse is therefore kith and kin to His Majesty, but everyone knows this hearsay, so fully expected the king to protect her, especially as he did intervene for Official Whore's sister and sister-in-law. Why did not he do the same for La Chatte Comtesse? Why the king's sudden desire to be rid of her? No one can give any reason or answer to My Excellency's good German logic.

What became of her? She stole out of Paris at three o'clock of a morning one fine day. Chambre Ardente convicted her in absentia, sentenced her to perpetual exile, and once judgment and edict were common knowledge, she made for the frontier in earnest moving through the countryside like bubonic plague, for wherever she stopped, evil gossip circulated fueled by a rash of poisoning deaths she left in her wake.

Frog La Reynie and Toad Louvois sent men to harry her out of France into Spanish Netherlands. In Brussels constables and spies caught up with her in a church (all of them together in the vestibule), but being God-fearing men, they balked at forcibly removing a woman from sacred ground, so hats in hands they waited for Mass to end. Frog La Reynie's chief constable entered and asked Toad

Louvois's chief spy, "Why are you here?" Spy answered, "We are here on the same mission. I refuse to molest her during Mass even if she is a devil, but you officials of Chatelet Courts are less particular." Constable was heard to say, "During Communion," then he winked. Spy pointed behind the other's back. "What is in your sack? And why is it whining? Have you a baby in it," he asked.

As La Chatte Comtesse reached the altar to receive Communion the constable opened his sack, let out thirteen black cats and shooed them into the church. Within seconds the congregation was screaming with fear, for everyone thought the cats were demons from Hell come to steal their souls. A cry of "Witch!" went up. Fingers pointed at La Chatte Comtesse and the cry turned to "Kill the witch." She barely managed to escape intact, but having done so, constables and spies joined a crowd gathered to throw stones at her coach as it careened away. Toad Louvois's chief agent was heard to laugh and compliment Frog La Reynie's chief agent, "You constables of police have imagination. I shall credit you this."

Yet, this was not an end to this happy little comedy. They trailed La Chatte Comtesse to Antwerp where she hoodwinked a handsome Italian duc (twenty years younger than she) into becoming her protector and benefactor, so I wonder then she is not practiced at magic arts to accomplish such a miracle, for she is in her forties. News is she has gone to Italy the fatherland of her uncle Cardinal Prime Minister.

To answer those points in your letter, in France it is forbidden to take Communion in one's chamber unless in case of illness. I like to hear sermons in Advent, but after dinner it is impossible, for if I listen to preaching after eating, it does not depend on me not to go to sleep. To sit next to the king during Mass is a great honor, but one I would happily give to someone else, for when it is time for the sermon, His Majesty is constantly poking my ribs with his elbow in order to keep me from falling asleep. It is tiresome to be half asleep and half awake at the same time, so I always get a headache when I sit next to the king at Mass.

I received your letters and answered them, but all my letters are in a packet which is being detained so long I am nearly crazy over it, for unfortunately this is what ministers succeed in far better than governing the kingdom. I am no fool and know all letters entering or leaving France are opened, but it never troubles me and I shall continue to write whatever enters into my head. Frog La Reynie sent word he has nothing to do with postal service which is the exclusive concern of Toad Louvois, but it is the former reptile and not the latter who reads German. Does he think I have forgotten this small detail? Is it not disconcerting enough that he is false? Must he also be a liar and miscreant to blame another dolt for his own incompetence?

I shall do Frog La Reynie justice and say he has capacity, but though he talks well and is good company, he is false, selfish as the Devil and looks like a fox, for his deceitfulness can be read in his eyes and his portrait might be made as a fox crouching on the ground to pounce on a hen. The vogue at Court is to speak naturally and not in a mannered style which is 'to talk like a burgher' as the fashionables call it and among courtiers it seems the more devious the nature the more frankly simple the speech. Toad Louvois was best at it, but now this honor belongs to Frog La Reynie.

Marechal de Villeroy came to Fontainebleau for a visit. As a young man he was quite handsome, but now he is old and also stinky and his entire face is covered with little wrinkles all close together with skin which looks like paper children have played tricks with seeing who can fold it into the tiniest piece. He told me a story about Saint-Francois de Sales who founded the Order of Filles de Sainte-Marie. In their youth Villeroy's father and Francois de Sales were friends, but Old Villeroy could never bring himself to call his friend a saint and would always say, "I was delighted when I heard Monsieur de Sales was a saint. He liked smutty stories and cheated at cards. The best man in the world in other respects but a fool."

This proves most logically how worthless it is to canonize the dead into saints as it is an expensive ceremony and an absolutely useless expense, for when one dies, one becomes either a saint or a devil. I cannot believe it matters to a saint if there is a ceremony certifying he is in Heaven, and if he is a devil in Hell, no canonization is going to get him out, and if those devils who read the post have the wit for understanding, they will know my meaning.

None of this, however, will keep me from expressing my deep and sorrowful grief for my former friend over the loss of his grandson whom I was told died in his sleep on All Saints. Surely, the lad is with angels now and a companion of my poor son. Frog La Reynie must take some small comfort in knowing when he finally joins his grandson, it will be an easy thing to find him, for he will be able to inquire for the boy by name, whereas I shall probably spend a better part of Eternity searching for my poor nameless son, and when he reads this, he may express my sorrow also to Maitre and Madame de Visscher.

I kiss you dearly and most tenderly,
Lotte

The unfortunate incident

Sunday–29 December 1680–Feast of the Holy Family
Chateau Versailles

Dearest Highness-es S_-A_-A_ & H_,

Yesterday was Holy Innocents, so priests wore penitential purple to celebrate Mass, every bell clapper was swaddled to toll a muffled knell, no one wore anything new and no venture of importance was undertaken by anyone, for all these rituals prevent unhappiness and calamity upon one's house and everyone in it, but grief, misfortune and tragedy are to be found everywhere in France and it seems there will be no end to it in spite of this ill-omened day with its traditions and superstitions being gone for another year.

Sodomite Lorraine has an air as if he could eat the images of saints and is blessed with a face fashioned by angels to betray a soul only devils could make, and if one was to ask the Devil his opinion, he would say, "Ah, here is the greatest beauty in the world. See what a soul of pitch he has," so that wretched sodomite has left his soul in the Devil's keeping, while he has taken his miserable hide (and his diamond and pearls) to Brittany. His exile is over 'unfortunate incident' as the courtiers are calling a tragical death which happened on Feast of Saint-Nicolas, and wherever this good and saintly protector of children may have been, he was not at Versailles.

The preferred story is of Sodomite Lorraine and Captain Desgrez on an early morning stroll of the gardens coming upon a drunken page carrying a stick. The page became unruly and hit the sodomite's hand with the stick at which he became angry and hit the page with his sword upon the hind quarters. The page became even more unruly, so the captain drew his sword and killed the boy, whereupon Monsieur ran straightaway to plead mercy for his darling over this awkward business.

But that is a lie and here is the truth. While walking the gardens in a drunken stupor, Sodomite Lorraine and Captain Desgrez came upon one of Monsieur's pages. They seized the boy (pages are never above fourteen years of age) and dragged him into some bushes behind a large drift of snow. He tried to defend himself with a stick, but was quickly overcome by these two grown men, and when they were done raping him many times, they thrust their swords through him in such a way as to create no more holes in his body than God had originally intended. The boy was found with blood pouring out of every orifice, so the doctors could do nothing to help him and poor child bled to death many hours later. I know the heartlessness of the French and yet am always amazed how truly hard these people are.

Monsieur le Duc told me the truth, for that tragical morning he was a wolf (rather a werewolf as he was a wolf who could speak) and had to do his business, so after his valet had leashed him up, they were walking the gardens when they came upon the poor child. Monsieur le Duc went immediately to the king and told everything. His Majesty was so disturbed Sodomite Lorraine was to be imprisoned and Captain Desgrez executed, but the latter vanished as if the Earth had swallowed him whole and the king hesitated over the former as Monsieur drove him to madness with his fuming and fretting and whining, so in the end that wretched sodomite was only banished from Court. He tried to plead his case before the king but was refused permission for an audience and went straightaway into exile.

Monsieur is disconsolate. I said he need not grieve as eventually and unfortunately the king will relent (he always does whenever it concerns his brother), but he gives His Majesty no peace with his incessant weeping, and moreover to break down the king's resolve Monsieur has convinced Monsieur le Duc to yowl like an alley cat in heat the moment tears come to his eyes, so if the king does not relent soon, we shall all go insane or deaf.

Your Highness-es think me an innocent who knows nothing of these things, but I can tell you there are six pleasures to define men in France. First hate all women and love only men (frowned upon but accepted), second love men and women (perfectly acceptable), third love only children (frowned upon and kept secret), fourth love only young men under age of twenty-five (most popular sport), fifth love only themselves with themselves (rare), sixth will love anything, man, woman or beast (I cannot say what they think of this) and not one of these men is worth the Devil.

Die Rotzenhäuserin seems to have some treacherous plan in mind, for she is in league with Frog La Reynie and the pair of them have betrayed me. After His Highness R_'s bastard was born I permitted her to visit Court, even though malicious talk still circulates, for as no one can point to her stomach sticking out a foot in front of her nose, there is no proof and one can pretend what they say is crap and nonsense. I said, "Lenor, you may return to Court now." She said, "What will become of my son?" I said, "Leave your little bastard with Monsieur de La Reynie. You have no money. He is a kind and generous man and will make your bastard a page in his household. From there the bastard will have a good beginning to his future, and when he inherits your title, if he is clever and there is no reason to think he will be otherwise, he will make a good career for himself."

Weeping, she replied, "It is true I have no money, but I also have no future. I am afraid I shall become like Bastards' Governess with her sour and bitter heart. And like her also obliged to rely on pity and kindness of powerful friends and relations. And again like her, without a roof to call my own, my only hope will be to end my days in genteel poverty of a convent." "One cannot be magnificent without money," said I. "This is true," she agreed. And then I continued, "But once money is too important, it makes one calculating and once one is calculating, any and all means are fair in getting of a desired thing. Being without scruples, one becomes false, a liar and a cheat, and being all of these things, one forfeits good faith, sincerity and loyalty."

I am horribly vexed. All this is a result of His Highness R_'s apathy and nullity, for he ought to have been more watchful while she was in his charge. Now, Die Rotzenhäuserin is obsessed with having a roof of her own and remains in the improvident care of Frog La Reynie. Neither does he wish to dispossess her nor does she wish to quit her residency, but it is not a roof she may call her own as he shares it with a wife, and if she contrives to become his mistress, it will still be the wife's roof, so I cannot imagine what is going on in her brainless head. Frog La Reynie is most treacherous and disloyal as it is obvious he had no intention of returning Die Rotzenhäuserin, though what he wants with this useless creature is a mystery to anyone of good or logical sense.

Frog La Reynie and Die Rotzenhäuserin are rotten eggs and rancid butter, and as one is no better than the other they would be more in their place on a gibbet than at Court, for they are not either of them worth the Devil being more treacherous than gallows-wood, and if they have curiosity to read this letter, they will see what eulogy I make upon them and will recognize the truth of our German proverb that listeners never hear any good said of themselves.

Now, I live in solitude in the midst of this great Court where I am whole long days alone retired to my cabinet. I busy myself arranging my collections of coins and medals, playing with my dogs, looking at His Highness R_'s fine mezzotints or my other engravings, reading and writing. Always I find something to do. If anyone pays me a visit, I see them only a few moments to talk of rain and fine weather or news of the day, then afterwards I take refuge in my retreat. All days are not the same and my pursuits may not always bring me pleasure, but they cause me no pain, for one must look for happiness in one's self first before one can find it elsewhere also.

Your Highness-es will be amused to hear your old nemesis has a new brother-in-law. What is amusing about this? It is his footman. Haughtiest Duc does not seem to care if his favorite sister contracted such a misalliance as it is an open secret not only within the family but also in society, for he is so fond of and so friendly with this particular footman cum brother-in-law they even sit down together to play chess. The world is going topsy-turvy when no one knows his proper place and a servant may to marry his master, but at least everyone has good sense and good breeding (even the footman) to pretend it is not so.

I thank Your Highness-es for the medals you sent me, but I would like to receive those made against France and please make them the most insulting. Those struck in early reign of King Wilhelm are most sought after here, and as His Majesty and his ministers have them, you need not hesitate to send them to me on first occasion. I try to collect my medals and coins with judgment and I arrange and keep them with great care. No one can pay court more delicately to me than by bringing a fine specimen. My collection has been gathered from all over the world and is becoming celebrated which pleases me greatly.

One of my favorite pastimes is to arrange my series of coins of Roman emperors (upper and lower empire) before my eyes in their proper order. I then examine them carefully looking at each emperor's features and recalling salient points of his actions and try to fill my head with noble ideas of Roman greatness.

I must go tend to one of my favorite bitches who just had her puppies in my room.

Big kisses,
Liselotte

Bzzz: gossip about Melonhead

Monday–5 February 1680–Feast of Saint Agatha
Chateau Versailles

"Philippe, what's Monsieur le Duc doing?"

Pay attention. An idle request from Monsieur de France requires a command performance from those below, even though you're the one who's always on top. Peer down an immense stretch of corridor with its towering casements which run the entire length of one side. What do you see? A full moon reflects off snow. Glowing shadows cover walls and marble flooring. Tiptoe closer. Take your beloved's hand and drag him along.

"He's buzzing, Monsieur." Lorraine stretched his neck and bobbed his head for a clearer look. "He looks wet and shiny. What do you suppose that is?"

Monsieur called out, "Monsieur le Duc. What are you? A fly?"

"Bzzz. Bzzz." In rerouting his flight pattern, he showed a mean and threatening expression on his simple imbecile's face.

"God in Heaven, he's a wasp." Monsieur pointed toward Monsieur le Duc. "Look at his thing. He's going to sting us. Swat him, Philippe."

Too late.

Monsieur le Duc had varnished his body with a clear substance which deflected moonlight. In the half darkness he glistened like an ice cube. Shadows distorted his approach. He managed to sting Monsieur twice before turning his attack on Lorraine.

Punch him in the stomach or he'll leave little sticky droplets all over you too. Ugh. What's this warm slime he's spit up as he crumples onto the floor? It coats your hands and wrists. It's turning viscous as cold air thickens it into mucous. It's making the folds of lace on your cuffs stick together. Your shoes are covered by an overflow. Is this a shudder of revulsion which has just gone through your body? Does a thick sweet smell wafting up from him redouble your disgust? Your beloved is grinning an idiot's grin. You want desperately to wipe your hands all over Monsieur's clothes. Don't you? Don't. He'll take revenge by cutting your allowance. Hold your hands at full length from your body. At least the mucilage won't drip onto your own clothing.

"Jesus Christ. He's gooey."

"Philippe. Stop making such a fuss. It's only honey. You can wash your hands later."

Poor Monsieur le Duc. All sprawled out on the floor—still buzzing. Who's this opening a door to join your little after-hours party?

"Bloody ghosts. Play dead and wake the living with so many noisemakers."

Liselotte, come join your husband, his lover and your best friend. Wave that annoying finger of yours at Monsieur le Duc.

"Monsieur le Duc it is most unhealthy to buzz around hallways, stark naked, in the dead of a winter night. You will catch a death of cold."

Who's this running toward you? Wave your castigating finger at him.

"Monsieur-le-Valet-who-belongs-to-Monsieur-le-Duc, if your master succumbs to grippe and dies, it will be on your head."

"Monsieur, Madame, Monsieur de Lorraine. Pardon. He got away."

"Bzzz. Madame, I have gossip." Everyone looked down at Monsieur le Duc who was now sitting upright on the floor. "Bzzz. Don't tell anyone. Because nobody knows it. Madame de Maintenon is poisoning Melonhead. Bzzz."

Monsieur, ask the valet. Valets always know everything.

"What is he?"

The Spanish curse: how casually he rubbed snow over his bloody leather gloves

Monday–25 March 1680–Feast of the Annunciation
Hotel Reynie

There is a secret torturers intuit of fragility denied the rest of us: an instinct to nuance their techniques to reach a person's frailty and find that point of humiliation in each of us which surrenders self to tormentor. How do they forge this bond of debasement which one inflicts and the other cannot escape?

Stephane Daimlen-Völs

Jeanne-Jacqueline, you're locked in a dungeon, chained to a wall, tortured into silence and guarded by the greatest seneschal of secrets. No bribe is enough to procure a key. You can't be ransomed.

It's not that Gabriel doesn't notice. He's ashamed too. In spite of all the love and concern crying out to you from his heart, he can't help wondering. Every time he looks at you, he searches for clues which ultimately contradict one another. You act like him, think like him, your temperament and personality are his, but you have her mother's features. You resemble your uncle too closely, Jeanne-Jacqueline. He can't get rid of this hateful thought: an annoying melody playing over and over in his head, until he wants to scream.

When your father looks at his daughter, he sees only she's white as porcelain, and as fragile. All ripeness has been sucked out of her once robust body and rosy flesh. She has a distant and detached gaze. What is she thinking? For the last three months, since Feast of the Holy Innocents, she's withdrawn into a daydream where no one can reach her. Her behavior has become increasingly bizarre in a quiet way. What is your father going to do? How is he going to reach you before you move permanently into another world and deny all access? He hasn't a clue, because he's distanced you in his heart from first to third person—from 'my' to 'his' daughter.

"Jeanne-Jacqueline, why are you constantly washing yourself? Anne-Sophie says the servants are complaining they have to draw so many baths for you. A bath every few weeks is more than adequate, several times a week is excessive, but everyday isn't normal. Your skin will peel away."

"I'm dirty, papa."

She hadn't called him this since she was a baby. Gabriel tried to put his arms around her, but she flinched. "All right, don't get upset again. Don't you have anything you want to tell me?"

She shook her head.

"Are you ill? Do you want a doctor?"

She shook her head. "May I go back to my room?"

"Do you want Anne-Sophie to take you?"

She shook her head. "I can go alone."

Gabriel's heart sank as he watched Jeanne-Jacqueline leave. Anne-Sophie hugged him tightly, but couldn't absorb his pain. He hugged her back and realized how much her body had changed. She had a woman's body. Both his daughters were lost to him.

"Father, she looks awful, she's very ill. You have to get her a doctor."

"I'm not blind. Your mother may be, but I'm not."

"I wasn't suggesting you didn't care."

"Talk to her, find out what's the matter. Hasn't she said anything to you? Why can't she stand for anyone to touch her?"

"Maybe, maman."

Gabriel's body stiffened as he clasped his hands behind his back. His stomach hurt. His fingers were going numb. His head ached. "Neither you nor your sister is any concern of hers anymore. Jeanne-Jacqueline is mine. You're a married woman and your husband's responsibility."

"What a neat package. Like everything else you do. But this house has a pall over it, like Death passing over Egypt. How many plagues do we have to suffer before we all succumb?"

"A neat package especially for you, Madame de Visscher. You have a husband of your own choosing, but I'm the fool who provides the roof over everyone's head."

"My sister's going insane, or dying, or both. Everybody in Paris is scared to death. It's your doing. You're mad for power. The control you have over everything. Life and death even." She saw the hurt in his eyes and wailed, "It's what everybody says. If it's not true, make it different."

"Was Rome so much better?"

"I don't want to bring another child into a world like this."

Michel stood in the hallway and called, "Gabriel, in the garden. Hurry."

Anne-Sophie grabbed her father's hand. "Don't say anything. I haven't told him yet."

At the back of the mansion where vegetable gardens were planted spring and summer, in a patch of snow soaked with blood, a young girl lay supine. Had she watched sunrise turn gray half light to silvery blue sky while her body provided a touch of warmth to this palette of cold colors? She'd been sodomized. Her throat had been slashed. Someone had smeared blood and semen all over her body till her mouth and eyes had frozen into a glazed stare. While everyone's attention was engrossed with this slight of hand, a hulking presence in the background quietly disappeared. Neither Gabriel nor any of the servants milling around noticed the trespasser, though Michel took note of an odd gesture the man made, acknowledged by Armand with a sneer of contemptuous familiarity.

Armand walked up behind Gabriel. "Like the one at Hotel Bordes."

Michel examined the body, then looked Armand in the eyes. "Not at all like that child. Did you find her?"

"Patric. Chased away a mongrel gnawing at her neck. Now you've had a good look, may I have the servants take it away?"

Gabriel said, "Get a priest, get this place blessed, and have her brought to Chatelet. Have the doctors do an autopsy. That should keep you busy for a while."

"All right, Gabriel." Armand rubbed snow over his bloody leather gloves. "It's too bad, isn't it. In Paris, nowadays, a missing child is like the Spanish curse. No one wants it. Everybody knows someone else who has it. And there's no cure."

Gabriel and Michel walked toward the house in silence. Finally, Gabriel wondered out loud, "Why do I put up with him? When this is over, he's going to disappear."

"Why wait? Do it now."

"My daughters love their mother. What can I do? Can't have Marie-Julie hysterical. She'll blurt out something. Cause a scandal. Ruin our lives. What about that poor child back there?"

"Didn't you notice? Clothing was tattered and foul, but her body. Spotlessly clean. Hair glossy and carefully coiffed, even the fingernails scrubbed. Did you smell the perfume?"

"Turn it around. Signs of exquisite care, but wearing rags. She's no street urchin. Someone's going to make a complaint she's missing."

"There's purple sucking bruises around the neck wound. Teeth marks belong to a man, not a dog. Still warm, she was put there. Why here? A warning? From whom?"

Gabriel rode across the pont Notre-Dame to Ile-de-la-Cite and tethered his horse by the south tower of the cathedral. As usual, the tower door was unlocked and it took him just under twenty minutes to climb the spiral staircase, till he was above the clerestory at the tower base. He stopped to catch his breath, then went through another door to an exterior walkway which ran the length of the west facade. His effort was always rewarded. Gabriel put his foot on the low stone railing, and leaning against his thigh, surveyed the spectacular vista of Paris and its faubourgs.

At least twice a week he'd made this pilgrimage since '67. Thirteen years. Was this the year his luck would change? For worse? But the view. Always exciting. Always extraordinary. When hadn't he been here? He couldn't think of a time of day, or time of year, or condition of weather. It was glorious high above the rooftops of Paris where the air was cold, clear and sweet smelling.

Whom was he fooling? There was only a veneer of law and order to which Parisians grudgingly complied. Their compliance hid a baseness beyond words. He loved this city, but hated the people in it. Gabriel thought about how casually Armand had rubbed snow over his bloody leather gloves. How would it look, if he was burning witches at the stake and throwing ordinary citizens into prison, when his own wife and brother-in-law were probably as guilty as any of them?

A murder of crows congregated on the cathedral steps. A good-looking giant with the laughing eyes of Saint Nicholas walked across the parvis toward Notre-Dame. He loitered by Gabriel's horse for a moment as he searched for its owner. Finally, he looked up and saw Gabriel staring off into heaven.

Cuckold's horns & a cockatrice

Thursday–13 June 1680–Feast of Saint Anthony of Padua
Chatelet Courts

Who was King of Snakes in the Garden of Eden? Was he hatched from a yolk-less egg in a Paradise without navels? Was he golden-plumed with poisoning evil reflections in a golden eye? Was he the blood-red sun in the morning to sting the flesh from bones? Could he wilt the Garden with his cock's head and crumble stones beneath his dragon's tail? Is a glance into the mirror of self-awareness venomous enough to kill a monster within you? If you saw your unconscious reflected in front of your eyes, would you die of fright, or is Subconscious cawing at the foot of your death bed the only way you'll ever find everlasting peace?

This boy isn't more than ten or eleven. He's been stripped naked. He stands mute and shivering, while Gabriel and a doctor examine bruises on his severely beaten body. Haven't you any pity in you, Michel? You sit at Gabriel's desk and toy quietly with whatever's within your reach. Anything to avert your eyes. Why can't you look at this boy? Is this what could happen if your own guilty pleasure ever got out of hand? Is it different for you because you're an adult and play your little game with consenting adults? Anne-Sophie was hardly more than a girl when you taught her to give you an erection with a knout. Is it so very different because she's your wife?

"Are those rope burns on his wrists and ankles? And these here on his upper arms?"

The doctor nodded. "They look like rope marks too. He's been burned all over this part. This here. Slashes look like they were made with a razor."

Gabriel took the boy's chin and lifted his head. "What's your name? Who did this?"

The boy's gaze shifted wildly around the room.

"Did they tie you down? What were you doing in the cathedral? How did you get there?"

Michel pressed his hands on the desk to keep them from shaking. "Gabriel, stop it. His wits are gone, you're not going to get anything out of him."

Gabriel let go and the boy's head drooped to one side.

Armand entered the room. "Gabriel, this was left on my desk. It may mean something."

"What the devil is this?" Gabriel threw a drawing at Michel, then clasped his hands behind his back. The pain in his jaw was almost as severe as the throbbing in his stomach. Was that a faint smile in Desgrez's eyes? "You were chasing the boy around Notre-Dame. From whom or what was he seeking sanctuary? Why was he screaming? Did he scream anything intelligible?"

As Armand was about to open his mouth, Michel said, "Cuckold's horns and a cockatrice?"

"What the hell does that mean?" Gabriel heard himself shouting.

Michel turned over the drawing and held it up for Gabriel to see.

The boy became mesmerized. "Cern. Cern. Nunnos. Cer. Nun. Nos."

Armand put his hand on the boy's arm. The boy recognized the signet ring and howled. The doctor grabbed the boy, but he broke loose and ran for the door. Gabriel blocked his path. Before anyone could catch him the boy hurled himself out the window.

War of the Spanish Succession

Bella gerant fortes: tu felix Austria nube;
Nam que Mars aliis, dat tibi regna Venus.

Sunday–1 September 1680–Twelfth Sunday after Pentecost
Hotel Beauvais

Austria's bid to conquer the world via the marriage bed began in 1477 with Maximilian I's marriage to Marie, heiress of Burgundy. Their son, Philipp the Handsome, married Juana the Mad, heiress of Ferdinand and Isabella. Philipp and Juana's older son inherited as Carlos I of Spain and Karl V of the Holy Roman Empire. A younger son became Holy Roman Emperor as Ferdinand I after Carlos/Karl abdicated his thrones in order to enter a monastery and while away his last years as a pious gourmand tinkering with mechanical clocks. Carlos I's older daughter, Maria of Spain, married Ferdinand I's eldest son, Maximilian II. Maximilian II's eldest child, Anna of Austria, married Carlos I's only legitimate son, Felipe II (her fiancé Carlos, Felipe II's eldest son, had died). Felipe II's eighth child and youngest son, Felipe III, married Margarete of Austria, the fourth child and second daughter of Maximilian II's youngest brother, Karl of Austria and Styria (he had married his eldest sister Anna's daughter, Maria of Bavaria). Karl of Austria and Styria's eldest son became Holy Roman Emperor as Ferdinand II. Ferdinand II's second son inherited as Ferdinand III and married Maria Ana of Spain, younger daughter of Felipe III. Felipe III's son, Felipe IV, married Mariana of Austria, eldest daughter of Ferdinand III. Ferdinand III's second son, Leopold I, married Margarita of Spain, younger daughter of Felipe IV.

The result of all this inbreeding was Felipe IV's son (by Ferdinand III's daughter, Mariana of Austria) the sterile, cretinous Carlos II, known among Spanish kings as 'The Desired' and 'The Bewitched.' With Carlos II's death in 1700, AEIOU–Austriae est imperare orbi universo (It is for Austria to rule over all the world.) came to an end, and for his vacant throne all the world went to war in 1701.

In 1367, a century before the Habsburgs began their world conquest via genetic exclusivity, a modest weaver at Graben, Johann Fugger, embarked on a less ambitious strategy to expand his influence over kingdoms of the Earth. Johann had a highly successful business and a son, Johann, also a successful businessman, who married Clara Widolph, thus uniting his father's successful business to her family's successful business, which made the Fuggers successful merchants and citizens of Augsburg. Johann's sons, Jakob and Andreas, were successful businessmen. Andreas was known as 'rich Fugger,' with an even richer son, Lukas. Of Jakob's seven sons, Ulrich, Georg and Jakob made the family business so successful it came to the attention of the Holy Roman Emperor Friedrich III. In 1473, he gave the Fuggers (through Ulrich) the right to bear a coat of arms in exchange for a loan at favorable interest rates.

A coat of arms removes social obstacles which interdict ambitious marriages. The 'von' Fuggers extended their successful marriages into Hungarian copper, Tyrolean silver and the spice, wool and silk trades out of Venice. Through their successful businesses, they became successful bankers to the Habsburgs and financed Maximilian I's successful marriage to Europe's most coveted heiress. They financed Karl's V successful bid as Holy Roman Emperor and a long line of succeeding imperial elections for the Habsburg emperors. When Ulrich's sons, Ulrich and Hieronymus, and Jakob died without heirs, Georg's sons, Raimund and Anton, became the next generation of successful businessmen. They continued financing the Habsburgs (Spanish and Austrian), which made them the most successful merchant bankers in Europe. A social introduction from His Most Catholic Majesty the

King of Spain and His Imperial Majesty the Holy Roman Emperor made the von Fuggers bankers to His Holiness the Pope. Raimund's sons, Sigismund, Johann Jakob and Georg, and Anton's sons, Marcus, Johann and Jakob, were also family successes, as were the next few generations through Johann Jakob's son, Konstantin, Marcus's grandsons, Nicolaus and Franz, Johann's sons, Christoph, Marcus and Jakob, and Christoph's sons, Otto Heinrich and Johann Ernst.

Raimund's fourth son, Ulrich, was the sole failure of the von Fugger dynasty. After serving as banker to Pope Paul III, for reasons incomprehensible to the family which was entirely and devotedly attached to the Roman Catholic Church, Ulrich became Lutheran. All von Fuggers took an instant disliking to him. He escaped their wrath by retiring to the Palatinate, becoming a Greek scholar and an antiquarian, and collecting rare manuscripts for the rest of his life. His son, Andreas, inherited 'rich Fugger's' hatred of poverty and ran away at a young age to his wealthiest Catholic uncle, for Andreas understood, as did all von Fuggers, that when gold begets gold by gold, no matter what the permutation or how incestuous, the result is immutable, and that while all genetic dynasties must eventually perish, **AuEIOU**.

A Lipizzan of the Spanish Riding School carried itself with less panache than Jakob. He paraded his discipline in his unhurried gait, with shoulders squared, head high and eyes focused straight ahead, despite Liselotte's braying to the back of his head.

"Are you from Augsburg too?"

"Yes, Madame."

"Then, you are a Swabian. Swabians are very thrifty people. "Work, work, build a house," as an old Swabian saying goes."

"Yes, Madame."

"Are you Lutheran?"

"No, Madame."

"Then, you are Catholic. I am Lutheran, but in truth, not any longer. For when I came to France, they baptized me, confirmed me and married me Catholic, all at once. What a lot of sacraments in a single day."

"Yes, Madame."

"Have you ever been to the Palatinate?"

"No, Madame."

"Then, most certainly you have not been to Heidelberg. In all the world, there is no air better than air in Heidelberg. And the Necker Valley, sour cherries on the mountainside and good German bread and beer, at five in the morning. Do you not agree?"

"Yes, Madame."

"I am from Heidelberg."

"I know, Madame. Here we are, Madame." Jakob opened the door to a salon.

Andreas von Fugger rose to greet his guest. He ushered Liselotte and her dachshund escort to a wide, elegant sofa. "Madame, many thanks for accepting my invitation."

"A chatty fellow your footman, Herr Graf."

"I hope he wasn't forward, Madame."

"Not at all. Just the proper amount of chattiness and reserve. An excellent footman."

Andreas smiled to himself. If Jakob was present, he'd be upset at being called a footman, but Jakob wasn't present. "Thank you, Madame."

Singlehandedly, Balthasar carried in an elegantly set table which he positioned in front of Liselotte. A regiment of servants followed and arranged for her inspection cauliflower soup, liver dumplings, cold pickled eel, marrow balls in beef stock, rissole of brain, jellied trout with horseradish, cheese delights, miniature sauerkraut puff-pies, stuffed apples, plum dumplings, cherry pancakes and beer. Andreas sat opposite Liselotte, to one side of the table, and watched her drool. With a wave of his hand, he dismissed all the servants except Balthasar. Spy and dachshund remained quietly, protectively by their respective masters and kept wary eyes on each other.

"I took the liberty, Madame. A small reminder of our fatherland. I hope it doesn't trouble Your Highness that I dismissed the servants."

"Bah! There is nothing as tiresome as being surrounded by servants who look at everything one puts in one's mouth. Do you not agree?" Liselotte filled a plate. "So, what do you want, Herr Graf? You did not go to all this trouble from the kindness of your heart."

"How frank. And perceptive. No, indeed, Madame. There's going to be a war."

"That is no news. When has there not been war? The kings of this Earth are forever making war. It makes them feel as if there is something of consequence in their otherwise indolent lives. If they let things be, God and nature would take care of themselves. Eat something, Herr Graf."

"No, thank you, Madame. I'm watching my figure." Andreas poured a beer for Liselotte and wine for himself. "Just a little Rhenish wine for me."

"You are skinny as a pole, Herr Graf."

"Yes, Madame. The issue of this particular war will be Spain. Other nations will make war because they need a fecundating sting on Mars's battlefield, whereas fortunate and fertile Austria marries and rules via Venus's bed. Irrational War and adulterous Love make Harmony."

"A disastrous policy, Herr Graf. The Habsburgs have married their own blood, until it is rotting away, like their Spanish empire is crumbling." Liselotte slurped a mouthful of beer. "All this marrying of nieces will not give Leopold's daughter Spain's throne."

"How astute of you, Madame. Unlike your king who preserved the rights of his queen. A less farsighted man would've insisted on his dowry being paid up."

"But, Herr Graf, all this is a moot question, for heirs of neither sister will ever inherit. When my stepdaughter gives Carlos an heir, Spanish matters will take care of themselves."

"There's a secret treaty. All of Europe is poised to dismember Spain. But France and Austria partitioned her between themselves more than a decade ago. They're content with the arrangement, however, no one else will be." Andreas watched Liselotte digest his thoughts as she chewed on a marrow dumpling. "That Carlos has lived long enough to marry is a miracle. An heir is beyond a miracle. He's incapable of begetting anything on anyone, but not from lack of desire, Madame."

"So, Herr Graf. If France has no intention of honoring her treaty with Austria, then His Majesty my Brother-in-Law married his niece to cretinous King of Spain, so as to influence her feeble-minded husband into naming as his heir a French cousin as opposed to an Austrian one."

"Brava. Just so."

"And, so what? What has any of this to do with My Excellency?" Liselotte put an entire cheese delight into her mouth.

"There'll be a war of devolution. Austria will go to war with France for breaking the treaty, and everyone else over jealousy that France has taken it all for herself. If France keeps the treaty, she and Austria will have to brow beat everyone else into accepting it. If all the other powers accept the partition initially, it won't be long before they're all at each other's throats anyway. War is inevitable. A war, or a series of wars, which would swallow all of Europe."

"But, this war over Spanish succession could be a generation away. Perhaps, several."

"Or tomorrow. All depends on when Carlos dies. In a few months, he'll be nineteen, but his body's like an infirmed, old man's. The Spanish are having a struggle keeping him alive."

Liselotte swallowed her beer. "Well, Herr Graf, you are not telling me all this, as one good German to another, merely for the sake of a little gossip. What is it you want? Be plain about it."

"France would profit from someone of ability representing her in Rome with the Pope."

"Not you, of course. You are the Pope's banker, are you not? Your family's sentiments have been pro-Austrian for several hundred years. Such heartfelt ideals and gratitude do not change because the wind blows from another direction. What man holds your admiration so much so you need to influence me into being your ally?"

"How clever of you, Madame. The son-in-law of your friend, Monsieur de La Reynie. Quite an able young man. He was Benedetto Cardinal Pamphilj's secretary. Has much to recommend him. Intelligent, resourceful. Already has many prestigious connections in Rome, and much experience with Italian and Vatican politics. He's well liked. Respected by everybody. Knows how to play the game well. Could have a decidedly powerful influence for France's interests."

Liselotte was candidly bored.

"He's also well disposed to the German States. Something I influenced in him. He could be helpful to the Palatinate. To your brother and your family. I did Cardinal Pamphilj a favor and took young de Visscher's finances in hand. He's quite rich. Money wouldn't be a problem."

"A cardinal who has had three popes in his family tree within the last hundred years, to say nothing of all those papal secretaries and papal generals and papal this-and-that, ought to be quite rich, Herr Graf. But, that is about papist finances, and not about me."

"No, Madame, I meant Maitre de Visscher is wealthy."

"He has no title."

Andreas was momentarily confused. "A title can be gotten."

"You wish for me, Herr Graf, to ask Monsieur to ask the king for a title for Maitre de Visscher, and then, to go through this same process again, so he becomes ambassador to Rome and the Pope. Have you always lived in Rome, Herr Graf?"

Andreas looked quizzically at Liselotte, while she balanced a brain rissole on top of a sauerkraut puff-pie, then took a bite.

"Are you a sodomite, Herr Graf?"

"I, Madame? No, Madame. I'm a Catholic."

"Monsieur is Catholic, and so is Chevalier de Lorraine, but they are sodomites. His Highness my Late Papa often said all prelates in Rome are sodomites."

"A sentiment of all good Lutherans, no doubt."

"A man who has lived alone too long among prelates in Rome is bound to assume their bad habits. Well, Herr Graf. I shall think on all you have told me. If My Excellency decides to betake myself to be bothered on Maitre de Visscher's behalf, you must understand I would do it only for a dear friend who has always been kind to me."

"Kindness takes many forms, Madame."

"Herr Graf, the most detestable thing in the world is broth. I cannot endure broths. If there is the merest little broth in the dishes I eat, my body swells up, I have colics, and then those royal quacks are forced to bleed me. Then, only blood pudding and ham can settle my stomach."

"How dreadful."

"All food in France is served swimming in broth. They are trying to murder me by poisoning me with broth." Liselotte waved an enthused finger at Andreas's ennui. "Butter and milk in France are in no way as good as in our fatherland, for they have no flavor and taste like water. Cabbages are not good either. Soil in France is not rich but light and sandy, so vegetables have no strength, and cows cannot give good milk. What would give me pleasure is good beer soup, but it cannot be procured here, for beer in France is worthless."

Andreas fought to restrain a panic seizing him. "I see we're going to dine together often."

Liselotte smiled broadly and with menace. "Delicate matters of international consequence take time. It may be years before an auspicious opportunity arises for you to elope with Monsieur de La Reynie's son-in-law."

"More beer, Madame?"

"No, thank you, Herr Graf. There is a fine comedy tonight and I must be off, or I shall miss the beginning of it."

Andreas reached out to kiss Liselotte's hand. "Madame, I'm here incognito, as Kaspar Paumgartner, a wealthy Nuremburg merchant."

Liselotte stood abruptly and unceremoniously waddled toward the door. "Do not concern yourself. All your little secrets are safe."

Balthasar said, "Uh, Madame's forgotten her dog."

"Well, Herr Graf, are you not going to escort My Excellency as etiquette prescribes?"

Andreas tucked the dachshund under one arm and Liselotte's arm in his other. While he accompanied her to the courtyard, Jakob joined Balthasar to scavenge the leftovers. Michel had slipped in the back way and ambushed them.

"What the hell was she doing here?"

Balthasar spit up his food. "Herr Francois-Michel. My god. You startled me."

Jakob was between mouthfuls. "I don't know, Monsieur Francois-Michel. Herr Graf invited Madame for dinner."

Michel looked at the pillaged repast. "Christ, what the hell is this revolting mess?"

Balthasar and Jakob were indignant. "German cuisine."

The mark of Cain

Monday–30 September 1680–Feast of Saint Jerome
Hotel Reynie

A pile of books, lying open on a desk in an apparently empty room, can be a temptation and Patric, Armand Desgrez's valet, wasn't a virtuous man. He despised his enforced vocation of servitude and cherished grand dreams of being a spy in the Ministry of State, dreams which were in no way dimmed by advanced middle age. Had stars rising over the horizon at his birth been aligned differently, Patric could have been a truly great spy. He was deceitful, amoral, corruptible, shameless and had a capacity to effect a convincing imposture of trustworthiness and honesty. The stars, however, had set Patric with the mark of Cain which precluded actualization of his desires. Patric had no understanding of what set him apart from the rest of mankind. There was no blood on his hands. But, the mark of Cain hadn't been on Cain himself. It had been in Cain's fellow man. It was a hiccup which left a taste of distrust in one's mouth and the sight of Cain hateful to the eyes. This same hiccup doomed Patric to serve the vile of the Earth and to be suspected always of malfeasance.

The pile of books in Gabriel's grand-cabinet was irresistible. Patric entered and glanced around. He cleverly avoided disturbing any particulars of the arrangement, and instead, elected to twist his head in every possible direction to get a clear look at strange writing on pages of a leather-bound imperial folio. It gave him the stance and appearance of a chicken in a barnyard, wiggling and bobbing its head to see what the farmer is holding behind his back. By the time Patric decided the illegible writing was code, Michel had crept up like a fox ready to pounce.

Michel said, "What the devil do you want?"

Patric jumped a foot and retreated a few steps the way a chicken does when it finally catches sight of the farmer's ax. "I don't have to answer to you."

Michel picked up a book with both hands and slammed Patric in the face with it. "Didn't like that answer. Try another."

Gabriel entered from his bedroom and gazed coolly, malevolently at Patric. "Don't ever come in here again, or it'll be the end of you."

Patric stood and put his sleeve to his bleeding nose. "Monsieur General, Madame is making her way up from the vestibule. Thought I'd do you a favor and let you know she was here."

"Madame who?"

"Madame," Liselotte boomed as she waddled into the room. With one hand, she clutched the handle of a bucket-shaped basket. "My dear Monsieur de La Reynie. Maitre de Visscher." She turned to Patric. "You. Footman. You may leave us now."

"Pardon, Madame, but I'm no footman. I'm a valet."

"Oh. The man is correct. One must never call a valet a footman. That is like saying a duc and a duck are the same." She waved her finger at Patric. "If a duc does not wish to be mistaken for a duck, he makes sure he is not a sitting target. If a valet does not want to be mistaken for a footman, he should not open doors and announce. Nonetheless. Get your bloody nose out of here."

Gabriel approached her. "May I offer Madame a chair, and may I take her parcel?"

She looked around the room. "How lovely, your grand-cabinet. How clean. How unFrench. So German. As always. Do not act like a frog, Monsieur de La Reynie. Here. It is a gift for you. I made it myself."

Gabriel pulled a long-haired dachshund from the basket.

Michel said, "Madame made it herself?"

"No, you fool. The basket. Ah. Maitre de Visscher. You made a little joke. Very little. My Excellency is amused."

Michel petted the dog's head. "He's like Minette, only fuzzy. Is he christened yet?"

"You should be grateful, Monsieur de La Reynie. Her Highness my Tantchen went to a great deal of trouble on your account. Her Highness had to write to the Elector, but His Highness wrote back Herr Wopke is complaining he is running out of dachshunde and cannot spare anymore. So, I wrote again to Her Highness and said the dog was for you, and so, Her Highness wrote again to Anhalt-Dessau, and so, here is Alphonso. He is hairy unlike Minette is, but you will get used to it. It is not such a tragical thing."

"Alphonso?" Gabriel gave a half smile as he shoved the dog on Michel. "I'm. Honored."

"Maitre de Visscher, where do you think you are going? Who dismissed you?"

"I was on my way to Chatelet Courts. But of course, I'll stay if Madame requires it. They'll just have to hang and burn all the criminals without me today."

She put her hand in his face. "You may go. We shall have no need of your company. What are you waiting for, Maitre de Visscher? You are dismissed."

Gabriel offered her a chair. "May I offer Madame some refreshment?"

"Have you any beer?"

"No, Madame."

"Nothing then." She turned her head. "What a charming room. So, uncluttered. Well, Monsieur de La Reynie," she continued, "I went to Chatelet to see you, but you were not there. You are here. And, this is the reason I am here now. Monsieur de La Reynie. I must to ask you to do My Excellency a great kindness. It is Die Rotzenhäuserin."

"Mademoiselle von Ratsamhausen, your maid-of-honor? The one Madame sent off to England, I believe, in the late summer of last year."

"Is it not nice, do you not think, Monsieur de La Reynie, to be able to read all the gossip in another person's mail with the excuse of doing one's duty to one's country?"

"Madame has Mademoiselle von Ratsamhausen sequestered in a convent at the moment. She's in a delicate condition."

"Delicate? The potrag is pregnant. His Highness my Onkel is six years older than you. His other bastards are grown. Why would he need to burden himself with another bastard now? You are to take Die Rotzenhäuserin into your household."

"What's wrong with the convent?"

"Do not be a fool, Monsieur de La Reynie. I cannot leave a good Lutheran with a gaggle of nuns. Besides they wish to be paid. Do not ever let anyone tell you that nuns will do anything from the charity in their hearts. And, I cannot have Die Rotzenhäuserin with me in her condition. Lenor is a good girl. I am fond of her. You already have a baby in your house. Soon there will be another. What difference could a third make?"

"But, Madame."

"Lenor is very helpful and amusing. She will not cost you much to care for. The little bastard will cost you less. And I have not the means, as I am sure you already know quite well, to feed another mouth who will not be doing something to earn its keep. You should be honored. Die Rotzenhäuserin's little bastard belongs to His Highness Prince Rupert of the Rhine. Besides, Lenor is a baroness in her own right. You did not know this, I am sure, for I have never written it in any of my letters, I think."

"Where do I send to get the mademoiselle, the Baronne von Ratsamhausen?"

"I shall send her to you. I shall write to His Highness my Onkel and tell him of your generosity. I shall have him send you, as a gift, a few of his mezzotints. I have hundreds of them. They are like engravings, but much nicer. His Highness my Onkel invented the process, you know."

"No, I didn't know."

"Well, now you do know. They say some Hollander from Utrecht invented it, but that is a lie. No more delays. I must return to Versailles. There is a fine comedy tonight."

Die Rotzenhäuserin

Wednesday—2 October 1680—Feast of the Guardian Angels
Hotel Reynie

At twenty-nine, Lenor was approaching middle age. Mature men still eyed her, but in the French Court which was over-populated with young flesh, she was too faded for most tastes. Her popularity had a boost when, inexplicably, the king took a brief fancy to her, then Liselotte bundled her off to England before Lenor could capitalize on her good luck. She was on the verge of a complete success with Prince Rupert when Liselotte's good intentions again ruined everything.

Nearly an hour has passed. You haven't much longer to wait, Lenor. Gabriel's making his way down the main staircase. When he enters, put down your reading and look up at him. Do that thing with your eyes. You're almost half his age. You have the look that's all the rage at Court. You're blond, blue-eyed, tall and slender, with an oval face and long beautiful hands. Make him focus on your hands, those very same hands which mesmerized the king because they reminded him so much of his mother's famously fabulously beautiful hands. And, you hide your pregnancy well. One blemish. Those spectacles. Doesn't matter. Don't dwell on it. You wear them with such nonchalance they're nearly invisible. You're serene and confident, but you have something more—you seem unattainable.

Lenor gazed steadily, unforgiving into his eyes, while she pulled from her bible a letter of formal introduction slipped between the pages like a bookmark. "From Madame."

He sat down opposite her and looked at the ink on the paper. "Pardon, Baronne, but it's not a Protestant bible you're reading in my home, is it?"

"Don't worry, Monsieur de La Reynie. This is a Catholic house and I'm a Protestant. The Catholic God won't see me, because I'm Protestant, and the Protestant God can't see me, because the house is Catholic."

Gabriel, her eyes are the blue of cornflowers. And, her mouth. You'd have no trouble sucking on those lips. For hours. Would you, Gabriel.

Seconds slipped a lean knife between Time's ribs.

"It's more clever to say nothing, even when one has much to say, than to say something when one has nothing worth saying. Don't you agree, Monsieur de La Reynie?"

Gabriel watched with startled disbelief, as Lenor leaned over and brushed away some imaginary lint from his jacket. What a severe breach of etiquette and she knew it. Such a casual act. Such familiarity. Something an actress would do, but not a lady. This woman was going to be an easy conquest after all. Too bad. Gabriel returned her intimacy by politely escorting his new 'petite compagne' to his grand-cabinet, and over lunch, making small talk for the next three hours.

Gabriel is engrossed in his new toy, Armand, while you lounge on a chaise in Marie-Julie's bedroom watching her maids fight an heroic battle, pushing and tugging, to stuff her overripe, middle-aged body into a dress easily two sizes too small. This last pregnancy ruined her figure. You prefer women sleek and narrow in the hips, like a well-formed boy, like Jeanne-Jacqueline now that she's lost all her baby fat within the last nine months. In exactly the same amount of time it took your sister to turn into a milch cow, your niece metamorphosed into a race horse. Mother and daughter have exchanged places for you.

Finally, Marie-Julie sat down at her dressing table. Armand pulled up a chair and stroked her hair. "A good thing's come to an end, and I'm not one to overstay my welcome. Besides, I think Gabriel suspects us."

She ordered the maids out of the room and turned a desperate face toward him.

Armand, look at your handsome self in the dressing-table mirror.

"What about me? Don't leave me here. I couldn't stand it."

Yank her by the hair. Hold her down and hit her, again and again. Marie-Julie's wailing pathetically. Admit it, you like the sound of a woman's pain, much more so when there's anguish to intensify a physical hurt. You throb. You go all soft inside. You want to be tender. Sit on the floor, and tenderly, put your arms around her. Let her sob into your embrace. Could love get any better than this? Say a loving word to comfort her.

"Can't drag my perversions around everywhere I go. There you are, stop crying. You really are so unhappy. I'll take you if you bring Jeanne-Jacqueline."

"Jeanne-Jacqueline? Gabriel would never let me take her."

"You have some maternal instincts, don't you? She's your daughter."

"She's his too," she said.

"Is she really? You're sure?"

"He'd never let me take her."

"Either Jeanne-Jacqueline comes too or you stay. It's both or none. So, figure it out."

Cernunnos

Thursday
31 October 1680—All Hallows Eve—Hotel Reynie

In expansion of empires is ultimate triumph to vanquish the gods of the conquered with an adamantine sickle? Does man relegate overthrown deities to those same farthest reaches of the underworld where Hecatoncheires and Cyclopes weep in a realm of man's disappointment in failed divinities? Do gods ever really die or are they like all other matter in the universe, never lost, but transfigured by man's combustive imagination into energy and oxygen of more relevant spirituality?

Who was the horned god Romans mocked with an epithet and whose faded memories Christians transmuted into Satan two millennia ago?

Francois-Michel de Visscher was excited as a schoolboy in Latin class demonstrating his skill at a complicated translation. He laid open a leather-bound imperial folio and carefully turned foxed pages until he came to a section of writing he wanted to show Gabriel.

"*C - e - r - n - u - n - n - o - s.* See, it's Latin, not French. We misunderstood Therese, she pronounced it incorrectly. The boy said it more clearly. That's what got me working on this."

"Horned One? The Devil? Were they talking about the Devil? She said they'd gone down into the basement at La Pomme de Pin, and then seen them coming up from the cathedral crypt."

"What are you talking about? Who," Michel said.

"Is there a passage connecting the two? Does the Devil Incarnate really live 'below' the basement like she said?"

"What basement? Gabriel, talk to me, not to yourself."

"There's something underneath Notre-Dame, I want to know what it is. We'll go after midnight, you and I, alone."

"Alone? Are you crazy? Not tonight, it's All Hallows Eve. What if it's anything like La Voisin's? Go there with a troop of police and arrest everybody you get your hands on. You've got the authority. The king's not going to question it."

There were a lot of poison-happy women, and men, at Court who had immediate access to the king. Gabriel couldn't care less if they all poisoned one another, but with so much poison being flung around, there was a real risk of the king being caught accidentally by a stray dose. Then, there were those persistent assassination attempts. Who wanted the king dead? La Voisin hadn't acted on her own. She had orders. From whom? His intuition told him that all answers and all proof was somewhere below the crypt in Notre-Dame, but those same instincts said he couldn't make this particular investigation official yet, not until he had something concrete.

Gabriel stared into space. "And, what if Montespan is there? Or Chevalier de Lorraine? We can't catch them, you know that. If I'm stupid enough to compromise either of them, I'm going to disappear mysteriously, and so will you, Michel."

"Since when's Lorraine involved in this? Never heard you or anyone mention him till now."

"Actually, he scares me more than Montespan. And that miscreant, Louvois. Don't trust him, never have. Stupid toad. Wouldn't be at all surprised if he's involved with Monsieur's boys. The king's mistresses come and go, their influence over him rising and falling with the predictability of the tide, so eventually, one can always get to him. One way or another. But Monsieur's cabal of boys are dangerous. They form a wall around Monsieur and the king that's impenetrable, and what they don't want known never gets heard."

Michel smiled. If they knew what Gabriel had learned from Liselotte and her letters, they'd silence her permanently, as he knew they had silenced a lot of others, but they thought she was an amusing and ridiculous fool, and Gabriel obviously planned to keep it this way.

"Your translations for Louvois are censored, aren't they?"

"Only knows what I let him. Thank God, he's so stupid he thinks he's smart. He's never had anyone check my translations, and probably never will. So, tonight, just a short reconnaissance. Then, next week I can make some intelligent arrests."

“I’m not going to La Pomme de Pin, not tonight, Gabriel.”

“After midnight, Michel, technically, it’s tomorrow. And, we’ll go through Notre-Dame’s crypt. There’s no way I’m going to La Pomme de Pin either.”

Compline: a prayer for protection during darkness

Thursday—31 October 1680—All Hallows Eve
Bastille

Almost swallowed your tongue, didn’t you, Michel? Was it that dreadful gurgling sound which scared the wits out of you? Death rattles from the depths of lungs and convulses through the entire body before a man’s Shade departs with a peaceful sigh. This witch’s soul flew out the window shaking an angry fist at you and everyone else present. It’s for certain. Didn’t you notice Maurice de La Mer clasping his hands to his temples and howling at the same instant you were choking? Did he also see a damned spirit cursing all of you? Was he wailing from fear of the supernatural or from his knowing Gabriel is going to crucify every last one of you?

Whatever else this witch knew flew out the window with his spirit. Did his dying on the holiest of days for witches assure him of a hallowed place among the goats? Grin at this silly idea, Michel, then think of how you’re going to deal with Gabriel’s ire.

The seventh of canonical hours brought the Divine Office to a close for today. Throughout Paris, when the monodic, a cappella chanting of Compline ended, a zealous tolling of bells began. It filled the air with a vibrating presence, and like an unwelcome in-law, invaded everyone’s privacy. Even in Gabriel’s inner sanctum at Bastille there wasn’t any refuge from it.

“What are you going to do, Gabriel? Since the girl found on your property, it’s eleven with the one found this afternoon.”

The wall directly in front of Gabriel was wallpapered with a map of Paris and its faubourgs. Michel place a mark for this latest victim.

Gabriel mused out loud. "Outside city walls in Poncherons. Where rue des Poncherons intersects rue Hotel Dieu. Last one was at rue Saint-Martin and rue du Grenier Saint-Lazare. One before, was also at intersecting streets. Our 'Gilles de Rais' has graduated from university sites and gardens of private palaces to city gates and road crossings. Only the first two, my home and Pont Notre-Dame, don't seem to fit the pattern."

"There's a pattern?"

"Obviously. Just can't figure out what it is. But, this I'm sure of. They're connected to our witch hunt, and La Voisin."

"No. Not the way they were murdered. Babies at La Voisin's were used for Black Masses. As you say, these are like Gilles de Rais's work. And, what was it Madame said about Montespan?"

"Not about her, Michel. About the governess."

"Makes no sense. It's her control over the king's bastards that endears her to him. Why would she get rid of the very thing which gives her power? Madame must have misunderstood Monsieur le Duc. Or he's wrong. Let's not forget. He is insane."

"Why would Montespan poison her own child? It's unnatural."

"Gabriel, she doesn't care for any of them. They're perfect strangers to her. Except Limping Bastard, and only because the king adores the boy. Melonhead's an embarrassment. The king can't bear to look at him."

"It's no reason to kill the child, Michel. Squirrel him away somewhere, in a remote dungeon. There's precedent for that, but not murder."

"There's precedent for murder too. What's one more sacrifice to the Devil, even if it is her own child. You've executed or imprisoned hundreds to bury her guilt. Doesn't it bother you? The king doesn't even love her anymore."

"I don't know." Gabriel stared at the map. "I don't know. He's a father protecting his children. I can understand it."

"La Voisin's lover." Michel put his cards face down on the table and took a sip of wine. "He's dead."

"Dumb bastard, Maurice, and I warned him. 'I need this one alive.' Where the hell were you? Get your mind off this new mistress of yours, and pay attention to your job."

"I didn't kill him."

"I can't get rid of Maurice, because the La Mers have had their monopoly as chief executioners for two hundred years. But you, you haven't been around that long, and you don't have a monopoly on anything."

"Look, you weren't going to get anything more out of him. He'd been wrung dry."

"You're a stupid asshole." Gabriel threw down his cards. "He knew who hired La Voisin to assassinate the king. Wasn't going to give up information this important for nothing. Longer he held out, better a deal he'd get out of me, and he knew it. All I needed was time."

"Gabriel, stop whining. Forget him, he's gone. Why keep ignoring the obvious?" Michel gathered up the cards and shuffled them. "Montespan was his customer, and he was La Voisin's lover. We know La Voisin went to Saint-Germain in a royal coach. Therefore, Montespan put it at her disposal. This particular official whore, and her clique of girls, has to go. Get the governess to help you." Michel handed the deck to Gabriel. "Get Maintenon to play on the king's religious conscience, which is excessively scrupulous in every respect. Except when it comes to his own sexual excesses. It's time he toed the line with this too. She's devoutly religious and practically the only woman left at Court who's beyond reproach. Just the one to help him."

"She has absolutely no sex appeal."

"Unlike your new mistress." Michel stared back at Gabriel without flinching. "He's ripe for what she's offering. He's forty-two."

"Well, thank you." Gabriel dealt another hand of cards. "Let me tell you about being twenty-nine. You think you'll live forever. That you have your whole life and the world around you completely under control. That being forty is old, and over fifty you don't have sex. Well, when you're finally my age, you'll be glad to learn none of these things is true."

"What's your trumps? Pay attention, Gabriel. What's your trumps?"

Gabriel was completely absorbed by the map again. "It's killing me. What's the pattern?"

Michel suddenly smiled. "That's why they were all found lying within that drawing." He threw down his hand and got up from the table. "What's the saying, the one magicians are taught when they're apprentices?" He walked over to the map, and starting with the mark for the latest victim, connected the dots: rues de Cleri and des Gros Chenet, Porte Saint-Antoine, Pont Notre-Dame, gardens of Hotel de Conti, gardens of Palais Royal, Porte Saint-Martin, rues Saint-Martin and du Grenier Saint-Lazare, Place de Sorbonne, College des Quatre Nations and back to rues des Poncherons and Hotel Dieu. He drew a circle around the figure.

"Jesus Christ. It's why every child was found lying spread-eagle within a circle. Only one who doesn't fit is the girl found at my home."

Michel had drawn a pentagram which covered the entire city of Paris. "Those who know the art, don't betray the master's secrets."

A thousand thousand bells in the night

Thursday–31 October 1680–All Hallows Eve
Hotel Reynie

Armand and Jeanne-Jacqueline passed each other in the night: hound and fox of silent shadows that absorbed into other darkness but avoided merging together. From hallway to hallway near misses continued, until he glimpsed her at the far end of desperation open a door and pass into a room.

Jeanne-Jacqueline tiptoed across the nursery to a sofa. She crouched in a corner of a crawl space behind a wall panel until she faded into a deeper shade of shadow. He hadn't discovered this hiding place yet. For one blessed week she'd been safe from his embrace. He'd hunt her to ground eventually. But maybe, not until tomorrow night or the next.

There was a sound of bare feet moving confidently across the floor. Nothing—not a thousand, not a thousand thousand bells—

could drown out the sound of footsteps in the night. She held her breath. Her heart raced. Her hands were moist with fear. Harsh whispers echoed.

"Jeanne-Jacqueline. I saw you come in here. This game of hide-and-seek we play every night is becoming a bore. I'll find you."

"Armand, what are you doing?"

There was a rustling noise which accompanied other footsteps, a woman's light footsteps, a woman's skirts. Volumes of silk moved through the room, and nothing else. Jeanne-Jacqueline carefully pulled back the panel the width of a peek. Two dark forms entwined, then separated, when another shadow entered. Night and the tolling of bells hushed all voices.

"Your grandson?" A stranger caressed Marie-Julie's cheek. "You're much too young to be a grandmother." The stranger lifted Michel-Nicolas's limp body into his arms. "What's wrong with him? You fool. You didn't kill him, did you? He's no good to me already dead."

Armand said, "No, just drugged. You don't want to get caught wandering the streets in the middle of the night with a screaming brat, do you?"

"You can't take him. Please." Marie-Julie wept.

Patric entered and urged the stranger to leave. Alone once more, Armand choked Marie-Julie into silence. A dim red glow from the fireplace filled the room. Shadows distorted into nightmares as Armand lowered Marie-Julie and possessed her. Jeanne-Jacqueline closed her eyes and put her hands to her mouth to stifle her tears.

Dies Irae

Armand elbowed his way through the crowd in Notre-Dame. Rex Mundi pointed toward the main altar. Where choir and transept walls intersected, a beautiful young woman floated past a door, down a spiral staircase and through a tunnel leading to the cathedral crypt.

Look. Every inch of her body beckons you. Midnight Mass will begin in a moment. What if she goes into labor? Will she be delivered of the Son of Man?

An eternity passed. Rex Mundi led the way into the crypt.

Wait, Armand. Let your eyes adjust to darkness. Here's a candle. Light it. You're alone. Search the walls for the false tomb you know has to be here. Your beloved lies within. Was it her ghost calling to you? But, she looks fresh and alive, as if she's asleep. Pull her corpse from its grave and hold it in your arms. She's beautiful. You're filled with longing, aren't you. Gorge her mouth with passionate kisses.

She opened her eyes, closed them, then responded with equal intensity. Between their kisses, she sighed, "I thought you didn't love me anymore."

"I'll always love you, till I die, only you. Always."

The young woman pulled away from him. Miraculously, they were naked, as she drew him down onto a cold stone floor. She murmured, "I shall enwrap thy soul in the soft and savory sleep of nothingness, wherein it will receive in silence and enjoy it knows not what."

Make love to her, Armand, and she'll sing you refrains from the Song of All Souls'.

"Day of Wrath, day when heavens and Earth shall pass away, both David and the Sibyl prophesied. What terror there will be with the judge's coming to weigh deeds of all. The book is opened, that dead may hear their doom from what is read, a record of conscience. I groan beneath the shame of my ignominy, my guilt reveals stain of sins which still remain. Tearful day, when man to judgement wakes from earth, do you sinner's sentence stay, and grant to all, quiet rest."

Armand looked down at her rotted corpse. "At last, you're at peace and so am I."

Listen, Armand. A familiar voice wails for you.

"Armand. Armand, I thought you loved me."

Through a haze, see candles flicker and feel a cold thumb anoint your forehead with scented oil.

"Make your confession."

Through a haze, see little disks of glass rimmed with gold. Listen carefully to what she says to you.

"Armand, there's an old German proverb which says, 'Where the Devil cannot go himself, he sends a woman.'"

"Denn die Todten reiten schnell."

Friday—1 November 1680—Feast of All Saints
Notre-Dame Cathedral

Even on the sunniest day, when light disperses through leaded glass at its fullest, the nave of Notre-Dame Cathedral is an oppressive twilight. As the spectrum breaks into fireflies of light, angels steal luminescence and hold it tightly. Robbed of its ability to illuminate gloom, lack of light becomes a lack of grace, and in the hours after compline, when darkness dims God's eye, shadows layer over shadows until goodness is obscured.

At night when indigents avail themselves of the Church's tradition to offer the homeless shelter from sunset to sunrise, within Notre-Dame's nave, shadows wander among piles of human refuse huddled in sleep. No better than crows scavenging the dead of a battlefield for an eyeball or any other shiny object, vagrants thieve among their own, just as angels steal grace of day from the church itself which offers sanctuary from brutal darkness, but not from fellow sinners.

A half step closer to heaven, a giant shadow floated noiselessly through the triforium. His shiny eyes peered out of the arcaded gallery to observe the equally mute activities of murderous crows and pernicious men a half step closer to an underworld.

A few minutes past midnight, two archangels maneuvered past the nave altar toward a doorway situated where south choir and east transept walls met. Michel bolted the door from within, while Gabriel lit the candle in a lantern. A spiral staircase worn into concave hollows by the footsteps of a half millennium connected to a narrow, winding tunnel. Candlelight threw long shadows and whispers echoed: spooks following in a passage which died away at the crypt's wrought iron gate. Gabriel held up the lantern and peered through the bars.

Michel jiggled a lock. "This is insane, Gabriel. Are you sure that little prostitute said they were coming up from here? No cathedral was ever built with a secret room underneath its crypt. Gabriel, would you lower that thing? I can't see, keep it still."

They entered at the southeast corner. Niches with their limestone effigies packed the vault. Gabriel balanced the lantern on the stomach of a recumbent bishop stationed a few feet in front of the north wall, then lit two candles. Michel and he ran flames along every mortar line of walls and floor, looking for a faint draft. Candles constantly flickered and died.

Gabriel's determination lasted for hours. Finally, nothing. The place was airtight. An unbearable stuffiness overtook him. Michel stood somewhere behind him; feeble light from his candle threw eerie shadows on the south wall.

"There's nothing here, Michel. I can't believe it, just can't, but there's nothing. We'd better get out. I'm having trouble breathing."

"So, why's the lantern still burning?"

"From air in the passage." Gabriel turned around.

"There isn't any air out there either." Michel held up his extinguished candle, then pointed toward the passage. "Besides, that's south." He pointed toward the lantern. "And, this is the north wall."

Gabriel smiled. "The bishop's breathing on it."

While Gabriel pushed and jabbed at limestones, Michel leaned against the bishop's sarcophagus, looking at his watch. "It's nearly two-thirty. If that prostitute wasn't lying, in a few hours, someone's going to be coming up here from somewhere. Don't want to be here. There's only two of us."

"Just another hour, Michel. If we don't find it, we'll leave."

"Fine. Denn die Todten reiten schnell." Michel hammered a few blows with his fist at some high relief carvings, then looked with irony at the form sculpted into flesh-eating stone. "It's all your fault." He pulled himself up onto the sarcophagus next to the lantern, and sat on the bishop's chest. "I give up, Gabriel. You don't have much longer." He jovially poked the bishop in an eye and the face sank into its skull. There was the whoosh of a seal breaking a vacuum, then a perfectly balanced mechanism swung the entire alcove free of the north wall. Michel shook his head. "Shit. I'm so lucky."

Gabriel entered a cramped space behind the niche. "Come in here, something's wrong. Do you hear it?"

Michel was behind him now. "Don't hear anything."

"Exactly. Living things make sounds." Gabriel moved the lantern up and down.

"What are you looking for?"

"The device that unlocks this from the inside. I don't want to be buried alive in this hole. Well, straight ahead, there's a tunnel."

"Grant, O Lord, to Thy people grace to prevail over powers of darkness. From snares of the Devil, deliver us, Saint-Michel."

"Just don't let Saint-Michel forget to make some chalk marks, so we can find our way back."

Behind the niche in the crypt, a gloomy throat devoured light in one angry gulp. Gabriel held the lantern with the fixed desperation of moths jigging in the halo of a flame. Michel ran chalk along the stone in a continuous line. A wall suddenly veered the tunnel left into another passage with an imperceptible downward incline which seemed to go on forever. In a westward spiral, for several hundred yards, this esophagus sucked them away from shadows toward a gently glowing beacon.

Nearing a journey's end, down a few low, wide steps was a subterranean parvis overgrown with forests of stone. Light from Paschal candles amid rubble revealed walls carved with tortured faces and bodies of damned souls. Clothing and jewels were all over the ground: some thrown down carelessly, some neatly folded. A pile of black robes and masks lay by a pool with running water. Adjacent this pool was an entrance to another tunnel. The grotto curved in a semi-circle, down a few steps and around the corner of a sixth century cathedral to its west facade. All of Saint-Etienne above its typanum was missing. On its demolished remains rested the foundations of Notre-Dame's parvis.

A hundred feet away, embedded in rock directly opposite Saint-Etienne, was a set of bronze doors. Michel pulled them open. The stench which had assaulted them became overpowering. Gabriel looked over his shoulder at gargoyles in the grotto and was convinced they had once been petrified men. Beyond the threshold was an enormous cavern. At its peripheries, where penumbra changed to perfect shadow, ceiling and walls vanished into infinity. Thousands of partially buried braziers dotted the ground, glowing pockmarks, so that the earth seemed illuminated from within. It was forever twilight in this world. Countless piles of small, charred corpses competed for space, and in a breath-taking assault, released an aroma of rotting flesh into the contained atmosphere. In the midst of this, ruins of ancient cities lay curled up, an aborted fetus in a bloody womb.

Michel stared in disbelief as Gabriel vomited without uttering a sound. Silence had a beating heart. Earth devoured sound into an acoustic vacuum and recycled it into an aphonic hum beyond human register, giving it life with weight and mass and physical presence. Noiselessness crashed down in stifling waves. Stillness wrapped itself around living things and suffocated them into a mute timelessness.

Michel steeled himself against unnerving deafness and looked at his watch. The first Mass of the day would begin in half an hour. He wrote on a piece of paper: *5:30. Stay. Keep hidden. Watch. They'll leave for Mass soon.* He shoved the note into Gabriel's hand, but Gabriel waved him away. Michel circled around the cave, well within shadows as he stole through a junkyard of daily life exposed within the vestiges of four or five cities.

Nearing a journey's end, Michel watched several dozen black-robed figures walk eastward toward the bronze doors. He moved past them until he found the heart of the site: an altar stone carved with a horned deity and stained ombre rusty-browns and blacks. The soil underfoot was thick, black and oily from a thousand years of blood and fire sacrifices. How much blood and melted fat had saturated the earth to turn it the consistency of blood pudding? Everywhere in the cavern the soil was the same, force-fed on human life. The fresh remains of a burnt offering, a toddler, lay on the altar stone.

If there was more to see, he was unable to look for it. When he reached the spot where Gabriel had been, he found only the note. Michel found him sitting on the steps of Saint-Etienne.

"Look at you, you're covered with grease and blood. Everything you touch. The soil. They're all gone. Awhile ago."

There was a long pause before Michel could answer. "They'll come looking for us. I bolted the choir door from inside, and we never locked the gate again. All those fucking chalk marks."

A faint echo raced through tunnels. Gabriel looked with horror at the bronze doors, but an instant later found himself inside Saint-Etienne's dark vestibule. Ahead of him, Michel had walked out of darkness into half-shadow and stood dazed by nebulous light in the nave. Distant galaxies twinkled through eons of universal blackness to remind him God was somewhere beyond. The little stars became flickers of torches as he consciously acknowledged cages which had been fitted behind nave piers and an endless string of effaced shadows with glowing red dots for eyes. Mechanical toys and freakish tools filled this deconsecrated sanctuary. Wails and moans of children, women and young men too afraid to scream out their pain filled his head. Michel's penis was erect. Hell would be like this.

A forest of stones, like the one they encountered in the subterranean parvis, choked the cathedral nave. Chapels in the apse glowed of sunrise. Gabriel dragged Michel toward the light. As they circled around the main altar, Michel looked past the choir into the apse. There was the Devil Incarnate of Paris and a handful of men. Blood streamed into little pools wherever it found concavities in the floor. From rivulets and puddles it splattered onto walls and smeared naked flesh with lust for Gilles de Rais's crimes against innocents. Michel's penis became flaccid.

Darkness suddenly yawned at the crypt entrance. Michel tumbled down a short flight of stairs into empty space, then landed face-down into a few inches of water. Gabriel propped him up against the wall of a shallow well. Michel heaved, but nothing came out. As he fell back onto his hunches his voice was a hoarse whisper. "We're going to die here."

Gabriel put his arm around his son-in-law. "I'm not. The tunnel by the pool, maybe it's a way back to La Pomme de Pin. Therese said there was a secret passage and chamber beneath the cellar."

"Maybe it leads nowhere, or to something worse. This was a bad idea."

"Give up, Michel, and you'll die. I won't. We'll go to the north transept doors, it's closer to the pool."

"If it doesn't open?"

"Then, we come back here and wait."

"Gabriel, he's going to find us. You don't know. He's very clever. But, I'll kill myself before I let him put a hand on me. I'm cold. Like you feel when you're going to die. I must be dying."

Gabriel took Michel's head in his hands and kissed him. He'd never touched an angel and couldn't let go, but held his kiss for an extra moment too long when a clear, simple intent becomes an infinite complexity. It left Michel bewildered and himself in denial. His smile softened into a frown. In the cathedral someone was shouting an alarm which echoed throughout Saint-Etienne. "That's a draft. From over there. Let's go."

The bottom of the well sloped down a few yards to an underground stream. Knee-deep in water and with only the current as a guide, Gabriel and Michel groped in darkness. It was cold, as was the water and the air. Along the way, Gabriel pushed aside logs, black and motionless, on which colonies of rats vied for space.

Nearing a journey's end, the two men traveled hundreds of feet, then miles, then the distance to the moon. A sewer opening hung luminous overhead; and Earth, being a mother, despite a stony heart, helped their upward reach from Hades to another goddess's radiant grace. They crawled with rats which crawled over every surface. To one side, where rats were particularly dense, logs had dammed up into a logjam. Here and there, Gabriel could see beneath swarms of wet, furry bodies that the logs had once been human.

Michel was out of breath. "Have to tell you. I saw him. He's here. Desgrez's here."

"Later, let's get out first. Plenty of time later."

The sewer emptied into the Seine beneath Pont Rouge where Ile-de-la-Cite connected to Ile-Saint-Louis. It was daylight. Gabriel hailed a boat and nudged Michel. He gave a deprecating smile and pointed to another being rowed by a titan who had almost reached them.

"I'd feel safer in that one. Your boatman looks a bit puny." Michel sat in the prow.

As Gabriel stepped aboard, he handed the man a gold coin. "What's your name?"

The man grunted and gestured.

Gabriel looked into the giant's benevolent face. He knew this man from half memories of half remembered dreams. "Wonderful. Wasn't Charon mute?"

"Interesting thought. Seine as Styx. But Ile-de-la-Cite is no Elysium."

Gabriel buried his head in his hands and moaned. Michel looked into the giant's eyes. They smiled at each other.

"Too late. Can't take back your coin, Gabriel. But, I think our boatman looks more like Saint Christopher. It's a comfort having a guardian angel. Especially, in a miserable hell like Paris."

Death passing over Egypt

Friday–1 November 1680–Feast of All Saints
Hotel Reynie

What is this cry slicing through crisp, refreshing air with a deafening misery devoid of any physical suffering? Its pain lowers a pall which intensifies an unnameable fear. Maternal tears eclipse sunlight with hatred and clouds sky with a murderous fury. A blood vendetta blows on the wind to every corner of the Earth. Cronus, sucking marrow from the bones of Rhea's offspring in his feeding frenzy, should have understood a mother's killing hunger and unslaked thirst.

A dead fire and cold ashes were the only offerings of the hearth to the morning star shining above the horizon. The hour before dawn crept into Jeanne-Jacqueline's hiding place and threw a quiet twilight onto her fear. She stood in the middle of the room. Everything was still as emptiness. It was freezing. Had it been a dream? Michel-Nicolas's bed was empty. His nurse was asleep in her bed with eyes open, a cold bluish complexion and a blackened tongue.

The sun was approaching noon when Gabriel and Michel first heard Anne-Sophie's song of wrath. Marie-Julie ran toward them, weeping and frantic. As they dismounted, she pummeled Gabriel. "Where were you? You should have been home." Gabriel slapped her, pushed her aside and continued toward the front door. She rushed him from behind and hit him again. "Why weren't you home? Michel-Nicolas's been taken." Gabriel stopped and faced her; she backed up a few steps and shrieked. "The witches have taken my grandson. On the unholiest of nights. They couldn't have taken him if you'd been home."

Somewhere in the distance, Michel heard someone screaming. He felt a soreness in his throat and the sound he'd blocked as being from himself filled his ears. He screamed until he thought his heart would break. If he voiced words, he didn't comprehend them, but Gabriel did. Gabriel raced from the house in terror and anguish.

Jeanne-Jacqueline looked down from a third story window. Her father remounted his horse and rode away, while her brother-in-law ran toward the front door. Her mother followed Michel into the house. Jeanne-Jacqueline pressed her hands and forehead against the windowpane and wept.

Armand walked up behind her and put his hand over her mouth. "Where did you hide last night? I was sure I saw you go into the nursery. Doesn't matter. You may make it up to me now. Everyone in this house is too concerned with his own problems to worry about you and me for the moment." He moved his hand around her throat, kissing her tenderly about the face. Her hands grasped futilely at his arm. Her eyes bulged from his hold. "Come. Show me how much you love me." He pulled her onto the floor and continued choking her, until he was satisfied all her senses were overcome by his lovemaking.

"A Consolation to the Soule, against the dying Life, and living Death of the Body."

Transfixed to the floor, Armand lay in a stable staring at the rafters.

Revelations from never-ending yesterdays and endless tomorrows swirl past you, but not one prophecy is your own. All of the final judgements belong to others.

Arch your neck. Roll your eyes upward. Look into a stall directly behind you and see the hindquarters of a great white Gelding who turns His head to stare down malevolently at you. To the east, a witch holding a torch peers in through an open window. Armand, you're bewitched, not dead. In another stall is a scarlet-colored Beast with seven heads and ten horns. A young woman dressed in purple and scarlet, covered with gold and precious stones and pearls, is on the Beast. She moves from head to head, lifts her skirts and rides on each horn. Armand, turn your head.

"Why do you look away?"

"What you're doing is disgusting."

"If I'm a whore, men made me this way."

She climbed down, lay on top of him and kissed him passionately. The Beast became enraged. The woman stood up and cut her wrists. Drops of blood beaded up and trickled unto the black floor. A pool of it reflected itself into infinity.

"Pray tell, for what does one have blood, except to harden it against cruel treatment, and except to be able to pour it forth?"

Armand lay on his belly on the floor licking up, like a dog, the blood which had fallen from her wounded wrists. He spat it out three times, then stood up and handed the woman a gold coin.

"Here's your blood money."

The woman swallowed the coin. "My love, wolf you are, only be sure that thou eat not the blood: for the blood is the life; and thou mayest not eat the life with the flesh."

Rex Mundi embraced Armand from behind.

Have you learned anything, Armand?

Armand turned to face Him. "I've learned the taste of blood which I hadn't known."

How can you say you've never tasted blood before this? In the womb you have eyes and see not, ears and hear not. There in the womb you are filled for works of darkness, all the while deprived of light. And there in the womb you are taught cruelty, by being fed with blood, and may be damned, though you be never born.

"Is the blood in your mouth for love of the woman also?"

The blood is my own. Mine is the blood of life. Bathe in my tears, suck at my wounds, and lie down in the peace of my grave. Moist with one drop of my blood, thy dry soul. Kiss me on the mouth.

Eblis of smokeless fire & Cerberus chained at the gate

Friday—6 December 1680—Feast of Saint Nicholas
Chatelet Courts

Gabriel, wrestle with your conscience and with angels. Should Michel disappear into Pignerol or Chateau d'If, or should he become ill and die? His health is too good. It might appear suspicious, unlike an accident which can happen to the healthiest. Comfort yourself with your faith in Holy Mother Church and your belief in the Sacrament of Confession for this next mortal sin you'll commit as guardian of Sainte-Genevieve's city.

Listen to the Voice, Gabriel. Don't waste your pity on your son-in-law. Melancholia and black bile hold Michel enthralled. He soothes his grief with a balm of magic he's cast over himself. He mixes his own blood with pigment to make a blacker shade of ink. He signs arrest warrants with virgin quills from a tiding of magpies. He conjures amazing energy and zeal to prosecute every witch brought before Chambre Ardente and relishes attending every execution. Slowly, smoke from the flames consuming witches at Place de Greve seep through his flesh to eat his soul into smokeless fire. Now, when he looks into the mirror each morning, Eblis stares back at him.

Francois-Michel de Visscher counted his sins and felt smokeless fire dry his heart into a stone. He hated himself as much as he wanted revenge and almost as much as he wanted to flee Paris. From hour to hour his desires vacillated. "I've made up my mind, Gabriel."

"You can't leave yet. I've got to find him. I have all this." Gabriel gestured at piles of dossiers holding siege over everything else in the room. "Can't do it alone."

"You don't understand. I can't keep doing this."

"Stop running away every time you have a problem you can't face."

"Paris is hell. You, Gabriel, are nothing but Cerberus chained at the gate."

"If we don't find Desgrez and get rid of him, you and I aren't going anywhere but prison."

"Can't go to prison if I'm in Rome."

Gabriel was icy cold. "If I fall, I'll make sure this scandal follows you to Rome. No one will want to be associated with what you represent. You'll be outcast. A leper. Then, where will you run to? And, if you manage to find somewhere, it won't be with my daughter or my grandsons."

Michel looked at this dragon-tailed dog of a man who had pushed him out of Charon's boat into the Styx. "Well, Gabriel, power and jealous enemies come hand-in-hand. You're pretty much fucked over. And, so am I. I guess I'm staying. Desgrez's our Madame de Montespan."

"Unlike the official whore, his life isn't worth a rat's ass."

Michel played nervously with the lace on his sleeve. "What about Montespan and Lorraine?"

"What else is bothering you?"

"I'm not thinking about anything."

Gabriel, look into the fireplace. Fire can be so purifying and appeasing.

"You're my son. I understand why God asked Abraham to sacrifice Isaac. If He asked me for you, I wouldn't have the strength to do it."

Michel was silent for a long time. He made a deep obeisance, took Gabriel's hands and kissed them, then left the room. It was quiet except for the crackling of fire.

Gabriel, how does one murder one's only son? Could you do it? For Sainte-Genevieve? For the love of your life, for Paris? Now, Michel who had never even suspected knows it too. What a fool you are.

Thlibiae

Friday–6 December 1680–Feast of Saint Nicholas
Chateau Versailles

There's an age when beautiful choir boys with angelic faces and sirens' voices lose their irresistible gift. Within a few years their skin's downy softness, the vestige of their mother's placenta, has a testosterone hardness. It's an age when raging hormones convince libido of manhood's arrival. How ordinary. But there's a delicate moment, a breath's pause before end of boyhood, when Time's ravages can be made to stand still. Once upon a time, men in their longing for God and desire to taste the Divine knew how to make boys into seraphim, to make them a Voice which could lure sailors and commit them to Death and to Hell.

He was a page which meant he was a boy as pages were never older than fourteen. This particular page wasn't yet in his last year of service. He was poised at that special age. He might be cocky among his peers and confrontational when rampaging with a pack of boys, but on his own, face-to-face with a superior authority he was a coward. On this particular morning, this particular boy was afraid of nothing and no one except Monsieur. There was just enough time left in his life for a man to make him angelic.

Monsieur will be furious with you. Do you have a good excuse ready? All those hallways. So many turns and intersections. They go in a million different directions. All those staircases. So many flights and landings. They crisscross everywhere and double back on one another. The backstairs is a maze. Like those topiary labyrinths in the gardens. You got lost? Monsieur won't believe it. The point is you're late. Again.

Look out this window to the other wing where you should have been five minutes ago. Going through the palace will take forever. Cutting across the gardens could save ten or fifteen minutes. Climb out. Jump into a snowbank to break your fall. It's dark. Sunrise isn't for another hour. Only a reflection of whiteness hovers between this Earth and Heaven.

He plowed through snow till he was on a path, and ran. Who were those two men blocking his way, staggering toward him? Drunken courtiers. They'd seen him. One of them was holding out his arms. They didn't look too steady on their feet.

If you run a little faster, you might topple them over. Try. Too bad. You've been caught in an exhilaration of being lifted off your feet. High into the air. Into a strong embrace.

"And, where are you rushing off to at this hour?"

The other man sat down on the path and held his head. "Leave him alone. Let's go."

"Who's keeping you? I'll keep our young friend here company."

The boy kicked and flailed. "Let me go. I'll tell Monsieur you made me late."

"Are you going to entertain Monsieur?"

"You're disgusting. Monsieur's not like that. Leave the boy alone, he's one of Monsieur's pages. That's all he is. Let's go. I'm cold, I'm dizzy and I'm going to vomit if I don't get to bed."

Is flying through the air more intoxicating than being swept off your feet?

An instant later, the page landed face down on another gravel path between two high snow drifts. A man was on top of him, tearing at his clothes.

There's a stick. Just out of reach.

The lower part of his body throbbed with a dull stabbing pain. Tears froze to his face. His fingers were numb. Pain was excruciating.

Why are you screaming? That won't make it feel any better.

The boy prayed. Feet scuffled near his face. The two men struggled viciously.

There's the stick. Just out of your reach.

His fingers wouldn't grip earth through a layer of icy frost coating the gravel. He couldn't pull himself forward. One man fell backward into the snow. Thick stabbing pain started over again. His body was numb with it. He couldn't feel anymore how cold snow was because of it.

Suddenly, all time and the universe was still for a moment. Another pain startled his body. A needle pierced up between his legs into his abdomen. His eardrums burst from a puncturing pain. His ears rang with heat and moisture. He lay in a tepid puddle. Warmth felt so good against chilly air. A warm wet metallic taste filled his mouth. He felt a man turn him over, then straddle his thighs. A gloved hand massaged his cold, limp penis.

Why are you suddenly drowsy? Do you want to go to sleep? Everything's red. It must be sunrise. Monsieur will be angry with you for being late. Again. How are you going to explain you'd gotten so dead tired you had to close your eyes for a Kiss?

The man lying in the snowbank came to and vomited. "Jesus." He screamed with all his heart. "Good Jesus, what have you done? Oh, my God. What have you done, what am I going to do? Jesus."

The other got up and rubbed snow over his bloodied leather gloves.

"You're fucking insane. Fucking insane. My God."

The man swung wildly. The other easily fended him off.

"Grrr. Grrr."

At the sight of two witnesses, one man panicked and ran.

The other man fell to his knees and supplicated. He wept. "Monsieur le Duc. I did nothing. I never touched the boy. I tried to stop him. As God is my judge, I never touched the boy."

Monsieur le Duc sniffed sadly at the body. "Grrr. I'm going to tell the king." Monsieur-le-Valet-who-belongs-to-Monsieur-le-Duc cradled the boy in his arms and followed his master who strained at his leash all the way back to the palace.

The man sat on the icy path and wept hysterically. "I never touched the boy."

At the edge of a wooded area a giant shadow who had observed everything through a spyglass mounted a horse and rode away. In his hurry, he caused an avalanche to fall from surrounding pines. Cries from an unkindness of ravens echoed through sleep in heavenly peace.

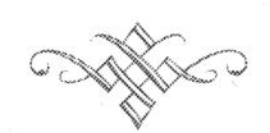

A patron saint for cripples
A diamond & pearls in exile

Saturday–7 December 1680–Feast of Saint Ambrose
Chateau Versailles

Some men are good of their own volition and some men are not. Did men create deities to put the fear of God into man? Is an inherent fear of Ultimate Authority underlying men's respect for those in authority? If men had no fear of authorities over them would they still be impelled toward goodness or is man's natural inclination otherwise? If most men had opportunity to transgress without fear of capture, would most men do so more often than not? Is temptation difficult to resist under these circumstances and when aided by concealment of privacy?

This was the mind set of Francoise's life: she was a shade hidden within shadows. As shadow to whatever man dominated her life at any given moment, while hours moved through days, she loomed large or small or nonexistent. Francoise existed in a half light of men's temptation.

With her sun in Scorpio in the twelfth house, Saturn and Neptune conjunct in Capricorn, Venus in Cancer in opposition to Saturn, and with an afflicted Saturn opposed by Venus, the pattern of her hidden life and abuse was set in motion with her birth in the isolation of a debtor's prison. After her early childhood in an institution which allowed her father's sexual abuse to go unnoticed by prying eyes of a censoring public, the pity of an uncle changed her residency to an obscure, moldering estate in the provinces and a life of solitary confinement where she tended his poultry and him, until he sired a child on her. She escaped her fated move from obscurity to anonymity of a convent by marrying a minor poet and raconteur. It was a marriage contracted in Hell. He was a quarter century older than she and deformed. Whatever other maligned configuration of planets had assembled overhead at her birth, Heaven had cursed her at eighteen to embarked on her life's vocation as a caretaker of cripples.

Francoise's husband may have been a most popular of wits, but he was also the butt of everyone else's: with his legs folded behind his back he was bent into a capital Z. He retaliated by bragging he managed his duties to his wife despite his deformity and her cold, virtuous nature. Everybody laughed: Francoise satisfied her husband perched high up in his chair, regularly and frequently, by kneeling in front him like another capital letter. Why a J and not an L? Because the letters had to face each other. Eight long years Francoise posed as a dutiful and loving wife. Sometimes a woman has to do what she has to do.

A generation had passed since she'd been left a widow. Now, another generation was coming into its own and a lifetime had transpired in which she'd acquired a marquisate and a nursery filled with cripples, though these were royal freaks with the blood of twenty generations of kings flowing through their illegitimate blue veins. As devoted governess of the king's beloved bastards, Francoise had become his confidante and object of desire, but until he'd come to her in the guise of a bedraggled cuckoo, she firmly continued to reject him. Instead, she endeared herself to his children. She played the entrapment game better than any of her rivals. Francoise had learned to adapt and thrive in the anguish of a king's temptation.

Francoise, the boy's whimpering. You're his governess. Sit on the edge of his bed and try to comfort him, even if you're only pretending. He's too frail and in too much pain to notice. Or would you prefer to cradle his younger brother in your arms?

Limping Bastard nestled himself contentedly within her embrace and yawned. He gazed into her eyes with wholehearted trust and devotion. His own mother scorned and neglected him. When she paid attention to him which was seldom, she treated him at best like an animated plaything, one level above a pet, and only conceded him this because unlike an animal he could talk and say things which seemed to amuse her; but, his governess loved him with all her heart. He'd never disappoint her and whatever she said had to be.

"Madame Francoise, what's the matter with him?"

She carried Limping Bastard to another bed, laid him down gently, tucked him lovingly under the covers and bent down until she was close enough to pour honeyed words over his face. "Your brother's ill. If the angels take him, will you accept the will of God?"

"I like my brother, I'd miss him. Will the angels take my sister too?"

"I'm afraid so, my darling. You must learn to accept the will of God. He plans for you to be King of France someday. To be a great king, you must accept everything from Him, even those things you don't like or can't understand."

"But, what of Monseigneur and my brother? They'd be king first."

"God will call them to the foot of a greater throne. I'm afraid you'll have to settle for the throne of France."

Hug and kiss him.

"Will my beloved forget his old governess when he's king?"

"Oh, no."

Now, it's his turn to hug and kiss you.

"I'll make you prime minister."

"Sweetheart, you can't do that. The prime minister must be a man. A woman should never get involved in politics or affairs of the State. As long as you promise to keep me close by your side, and share your burdens of being king with me, I'll be happy."

Lower his head onto the pillow.

"Sleep, my precious. So when you awake, behold, it will have been a dream."

"Good night, darling Madame Francoise."

Limping Bastard is watching you. You're his beautiful swan. Tall and lithe. You glide away disturbing waters of a tranquil pond at daybreak with the rustling of your black silk taffeta. Is there any tenderness left for his older brother? Pay attention to Melonhead for a second. Pick up that pale-green bottle. Force a silver spoon between this embarrassingly hydrocephalic boy's clenched teeth. Give him a second dose.

"Sleep. And may the Dreams take you to the embrace of dreamless sleep."

In moonlight, Francoise, you shimmer pale-green Death, and Hell is following you.

In the small minutes of the small hours of morning, cold air seeped through every pore of Versailles, becoming an ever-present draft, creeping along floors in search of warm-blooded resistance to bring it to life. It whistled past the indifference of the inanimate to heat of a human aura which excited it into a slow cyclone. Then, an insisting parasite, it bore through this atmosphere until it ate into skin and penetrated so deeply into bone it turned one's thoughts heartless as itself.

Except for dying embers in a fireplace the reception salon of the royal nursery is dark with your unhappy thoughts. You huddle in a wing chair by the hearth while unfeeling marble surfaces refrigerate a confined draft until it's almost as cold as the inside of your skull. Listen. It's a door closing. Peek around a side of the wing chair, Lorraine. It's Francoise entering from the nursery. Whistle. Give her a start.

"What are you doing here? Get out before you're discovered."

"Don't get testy now. No one saw me come in, no one will see me leave. That little scene with the little bastard, touching. I'm so touched. Look at me. I'm actually wiping away a tear."

She gave him a bitter look. "I survived my youth lost to a hideous old cripple. I'll survive a despicable blackmailer too. What do you want?"

"Mustn't be ungrateful. Marrying him got you here."

"How wonderful. What an honor to be governess to a small brood of bastards."

"Those are royal hatchlings. You're a heartbeat away from the throne of France."

Francoise hesitated for a moment in which she felt all the regrets of her life. "I'm nothing but an aging caretaker."

"You're still handsome, and very well preserved. Some people are late bloomers."

"You're taking a big risk getting caught in the nursery. What's happened? Someone finally denounced you to La Reynie as the one he really wants?"

"Aren't you going to help me? I'm practically family to you. Speak to the king. Tell him it wasn't my fault. I never touched the boy."

"How unfortunate for you. Exile is so uncomfortable. And expensive. Fend for yourself."

"Mustn't forget everything I've done for you. Behave yourself or you could still end up in a convent. You still need me or you'll never be the official whore."

"Like you? When Monsieur's regent, will you be his official whore? You're an idiot, like most men. A man's love comes and goes with his mood, and so does a woman's influence over him. A child's love you can hold forever. That's lasting influence, real power."

Lorraine looked into a black corner of the room. "See, Andreas, what did I tell you?"

A shadow emerged through penumbra into twilight. Andreas von Fugger smiled benevolently. "Where is he, Francoise? Your uncle's a difficult man to get hold of. Last I heard, he was in England, but I don't think he's still there. I want to talk to him."

A barely perceptible trembling seized her entire body. "I don't know where he is. I didn't even know he'd been to England."

Andreas slapped her. "Don't lie, Francoise. Don't like it when people try to insult my intelligence with ridiculous lies. When he comes to enjoy your company again, tell him I have another assignment for him. An important one." His smile widened into a sneer. "Tell him I have a woman for him. The kind he likes to cut up. That's how important it is. And when he's done the job, there'll be a few more. Whatever he wants. A few children too, if it makes him happy. I like to take good care of the people who work for me."

"Andreas, we ought to go. I have to pack. The king wants me gone before dawn or La Reynie has orders to arrest me."

"Yes, Herr Graf. La Reynie will send poor Philippe to Isle Sainte-Marguerite to keep Iron Mask from getting too lonely. But, Philippe doesn't care for the sunny Mediterranean, do you?"

Andreas raised his hand and silenced her. "Where are they sending you, Philippe?"

"Brittany."

Francoise was full of mock sympathy. "Awful. Cold and damp. And provincial."

"Are there any cities in Brittany?"

Francoise feigned contemplation. "It's so primitive, Herr Graf, I don't think so."

"Well, Philippe, it's a hard lesson. Choose your friends with more discretion in the future."

Monsieur-le-Valet-who-belongs-to-Monsieur-le-Duc burst into the room; Lorraine quickly turned his back to the valet. Francoise became haughty and arrogant. "How dare you."

"Pardon, Madame de Maintenon. I've lost Monsieur le Duc."

"Fool. This is the nursery. He's not here. Go away."

The valet bowed and left immediately, and Lorraine laughed. "Of course, he's here. With all the other cripples."

"Don't forget, Francoise. I expect to hear from Chasteuil. Soon." Andreas looked at a clock on the mantle. "Come along, Philippe. It's past midnight. I want to be back in Paris before sunrise and you have a little homage to pay me first."

Lorraine threw a temper tantrum. "Oh, Andreas. I won't have enough time to pack."

Francoise smiled. "Brittany isn't the sort of place to which one brings a lot of luggage."

Lorraine turned puppy dog eyes on her. "Please. Dear Francoise. Ask the king if I may take my diamond and my pearls with me." He kissed her on the cheek. "I could ignore how frigid you are. Could almost bring myself to have sex with you."

"Your bed's awfully crowded. All those women, and men. And Monsieur."

"You're the closest thing to a man I've come across in a woman. You'd be perfect, Francoise. Both at once."

Andreas was bored. "You may retire now, Francoise. Good night."

Francoise disappeared into her bedroom at the other end of the salon. The lock turned in the door. Andreas assumed a chair by the hearth and Lorraine fell to his knees. In the blackest corner of the room, underneath a large table partially draped with an oriental carpet, Monsieur le Duc crouched, quiet as a church mouse, and nibbled a piece of cheese.

Andreas and Lorraine disappeared via the backstairs, then through a secret passage which led to a wooded area adjacent the palace grounds. Beside Andreas's coach they exchanged a kiss. The coach emerged from the forest onto a road. It drove over snow until that turned to moonlight; at a crossroad, it turned east to face the morning star. On through night, into twilight again toward dawn. Little by little the moon passed through blue shadows until the coach was invisible in its glare.

Lorraine walked out of the woods into moonlight. A short distance away Versailles sparkled with the fire of jeweled fairytales. He had a thought. He had several. How could he ever become the official whore? Why would Monsieur ever become Regent of France? Monseigneur was a married man and would have children of his own soon. Francoise had to clarify that for him immediately, before he faded into exile.

Lorraine, walk along snow-swept paths which will lead you back to the palace and its magic. Moonbeams are glowing pearls. Diamonds are tears. Weep. Cry your heart out. What can they know of diamonds and pearls in Brittany?

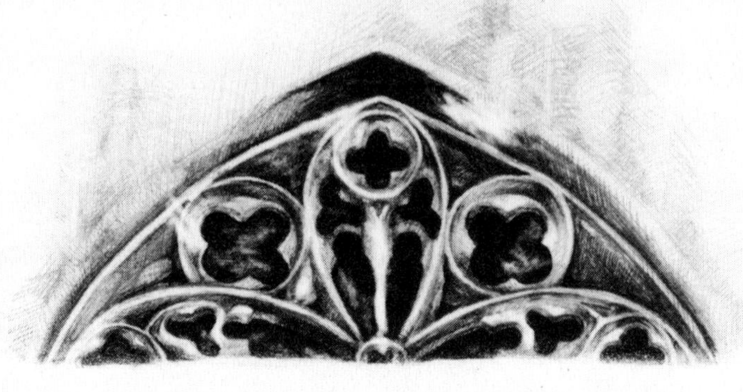

1681

Pretext, pretense, presumption: there would be bliss in being loved by her

Tuesday–25 March 1681–Feast of the Annunciation
Palais-Royal

My precious L_-M_-A_,

Official Whore's eldest child died several weeks ago, but she was not much moved by Melonhead's death even though it is true she locked herself up with him and Bastards' Governess for an entire week it took the boy to die. It is also true she wept, but all of this was only for show as her tears were few and evaporated quickly, for when they said his last Mass over him and it would have been well advised for her to shed tears again, she was hard pressed to make them flow. Neither has she ever given any of her children slightest sign of attachment nor has she ever had any of them in her apartments morning or evening. She treats them as strangers and never calls them 'my son' or 'my daughter' but always Monsieur This or Mademoiselle That, so no foreigner visiting Court would guess they were hers. Now, Limping Bastard is eldest son.

Bastards' Governess put her heart upon her sleeve, behaved as a most tender and loving mother, mourned as if she had lost her own beloved child and made herself so ill all were touched by her suffering most especially the king. Limping Bastard did his best to comfort her but without success. Since Melonhead's death she had herself bled so much to make herself feel better she is pale as a ghost. His Majesty was heard to say of her, "She knows how to love well. There would be bliss in being loved by her." I am alone in my private thoughts of her hypocrisy and in my belief of Official Whore's deportment at least being more sincere though in no slightest way admirable.

When His Majesty was young, women ran after him, whereas he now imagines he has become devout, is almost entirely converted and seems no longer to run after women, but in truth Bastards' Governess watches him so closely he dares not look at a woman. She disgusts him with society in order to govern him under pretense of taking care of his soul and controls him so well he even exiled one of his former minor whores. When Hapless Whore was forbidden to see His Majesty, she had his portrait placed in her coach in order to look at him constantly, but on hearing of it, the king said she made him look ridiculous and sent her an order to go live on her estates.

Bastards' Governess holds the king's heart now and has become all-powerful as he turns every loving glance toward her, so following his lead, all the Court goes flocking after her like stupid geese. She keeps His Majesty a stranger to her bed to make an appearance of virtue and because of it behaves with much arrogance. Tartuffe was written for likes of her as she is the greatest of sanctimonious frauds and her hypocrisy emboldens her to a presumption beyond Official Whore, for that devil rehearses to be a queen.

There is no longer any Court in France and it is fault of Bastards' Governess as there is no distinction of rank or dignity in her rooms, for under pretext of it being a game she has induced Princesses of the Blood and duchesses to wait upon her, even persuading them to hand the dishes, change the plates and pour what she drinks, so everything is topsy-turvy and none of them knows her right place or what she is. I never mix myself up in this, for whenever I must go to see her, I place myself in an armchair close to her niche and never help either at her meals or her toilet, whereupon some persons advised me to do as those princesses and duchesses, but I made answer, "I was never brought up to do servile things, and I am too old to play childish games." From that time no one has said anything more about it.

Bastards' Governess was extremely vexed by this, so expressly to annoy me she imported from Strasbourg two whores who called themselves Comtesses Palatine. Upon hearing of it, Toad Louvois came to taunt me thinking I would weep but not dare resent this affront pointedly aimed at My Excellency because of its source. "Let me settle that," I replied, "I shall manage it, for when I am right, nothing frightens me." Next day I arranged an accidental meeting with one of those whores and treated her in such a manner she took ill and finally died of it. His Majesty contented himself with saying, "It is unsafe to meddle with you in matters of family. Life depends upon it." To which I replied, "I dislike impostors."

I never had French manners and cannot assume them, for I make it a point of honor to be a German woman and to preserve German manners and ways which is little to taste of people here. I feel no regret for what I did. Justice consists of punishing as well as rewarding. It is true it is better to be kind than harsh, but it is certain he who does not make Frenchmen fear him will soon fear them, for they despise those who do not intimidate them.

Monsieur le Duc overheard Official Whore and Bastards' Governess argue viciously about Dumb Beauty's death and it goes back to one of many stories they tell of her secret lying-in and poisoned baby, for in giving birth she was badly managed, so her pretty figure became deformed and she never had an hour's health till she died. They also say Bastards' Governess conceived such a terrible hatred she gave orders for an accoucheur to kill Dumb Beauty in childbed, but when he failed, she poisoned the imbecile by going to see her in perfumed gloves.

Afterward Bastards' Governess said it was Official Whore who wore the gloves but this is untrue. Whore reproached governess for slandering her and asked her to look into her conscience where she knew what she said were falsehoods. Governess said, "I spread this rumor because I believed it." Whore said, "No, you did not believe it, for you knew contrary." Thereupon the governess answered insolently (I admire the patience of the whore), "Did she not die?" "Could she not have died without me? Was she immortal," asked whore. Governess replied, "I was in such despair at her loss, I blamed the person they told me caused it." Whore said to her, "But, madame, you knew of the report rendered to the king. You knew I had done nothing and she was not poisoned by me." "This is true," replied governess, "I shall say no more about it."

His Majesty is kind and just but little educated and suddenly fearful of having just confidence in anyone but his confessor and Bastard's Governess, so with Jesuits and her on one side and ministers (mostly that devil-woman's creatures) on the other, they can make him do exactly as they please. Of late many lettres de cachet sending persons to prison or into exile have followed on secret denunciations, but in truth these evils are not the king's own act as he is imposed upon and misled.

Official Whore never procured these things, for she and her sisters turn people into ridicule and never do anything else. Everyone is a butt of their satire under pretext of amusing the king, and when they have laughed well at anyone, they are satisfied and go no further. For Official Whore's children it is a bad school, but nothing as dangerous as that of Bastards' Governess who goes seriously to work and tells the king every sort of evil under pretense of religion and charity and reforming one's neighbor, so she prevents him from liking to be with anyone other than herself and her creatures who are the sole perfect beings exempt from every fault. All this is not to say I approve of Official Whore in any way, for no sooner had she patched up her differences with Bastards' Governess than those two were queer bedfellows in a scheme against me.

Bastards' Governess was again putting ideas of grandeur into Official Whore's head with plans of marrying Limping Bastard to my daughter (though they are still small children) and in this matter those witches are close as twins in a womb. Monsieur le Duc was being a plant when certain merchants doing business in Official Whore's apartment overheard talk of the proposed misalliance, for both devil-women thought such common persons too dim-witted to understand, but those good merchants spoke up and said, "Mesdames, it will cost your lives if you make such a marriage." Monsieur le Duc then came to life and ran off to tell Monsieur.

This prevented the thing for now as Official Whore was so frightened she begged the king to think no more of it, but she cannot endure any contradiction of her vanity as mother to children of the king and the other is also full of herself as royal governess. Neither comprehends any difference between legitimate and bastard children, so they have made those bastards' nature proud and full of vanity, and in turn those little bastards take flattering things said to them as their right. The bastards of Official Whore come from a malignant race.

As for hunting and great hunts in France, who told you such silly crap and nonsense? His Majesty hunts Monday and Thursday, Wednesday and Friday are Monsieur's days (he does not hunt but rides in his coach to watch his favorites at sport), Thursday and Saturday Monseigneur hunts a wolf, Princes of the Blood hunt on Monday and Friday, Monsieur le Duc hunts or is hunted (his valet decides) on Wednesday and Saturday, Tuesday belongs to anyone who can afford to pay for the privilege to play at being host and no one hunts on Sunday when Almighty God's simpleminded creatures need a rest from being chased about, whereas whores and witches are good sport any day of the week in this country, but do not be misled as all these days and hunters are only for purpose of deciding who pays all expenses so everyone may go hunting all together.

A week ago on Laetare Sunday Monsieur de La Reynie became ill with severe stomach pains, vomiting and diarrhea. He is still wretchedly sick, yet his family is unconcerned as he suffered similarly last year and his doctors, who are every bit as useless as Royal Quack, have diagnosed his malady as 'change of seasons,' but they say someone is trying to poison my friend and I have said as much to Maitre de Visscher.

This is all the news. It concerns nothing but whores these days, so it is not much.

Love and hugs,
Liselotte

A new way of taking revenge

Thursday–15 May 1681–Ascension Thursday
Chateau Saint-Germain

A_-E_ dear,

I cannot endure coffee, chocolate or tea and cannot understand how anyone can like them. A good dish of sauerkraut with smoked sausages is a feast for kings to which nothing is preferable, while in matters of soup I never eat any but milk or wine or cabbage with lard which suits me much better than any delicacy they dote on here. How I would like to eat dishes your cook prepares for you, for they are more to my taste than those my maitre d'hotel serves up to me.

Tragical events are all around us and everywhere. On Feast of Sainte-Genevieve, Monsieur de La Reynie had a most sorrowful story to tell concerning his younger daughter. His profound grief, constant weeping and unceasing supplications for my good offices these many months has moved me to pity, for he is a good father even if he is not most loyal of friends, yet My Excellency is inclined to forgive this little fault as it is clear Die Rotzenhäuserin has iron-fisted control over him and has given up her German ways to become like all other potrags, sluts and witches in this country even to imitating Bastards' Governess.

Monsieur de La Reynie's younger daughter wishes to enter a convent, but she desires to be a Carmelite, so he refuses to pay her dowry to this order and I cannot blame him, for Carmelites lead a miserable life, austere and harsh with a vow of perpetual silence and nothing but prayer and hard labor (scrubbing floors everyday of their lives till their knees bleed) from dawn until midnight, sequestered so as to be dead to the world from moment they take their vows.

I wrote Her Highness A_ de M_ recommending Monsieur de La Reynie as having an intelligent, pious and virtuous daughter of excellent family whose father was prepared to bestow a dowry most generous in extreme, but with so many responsibilities and duties (painting, reading, unifying Christian churches) Her Highness was unable to grant an interview till now, whereupon finding him most agreeable, she accepted his daughter into her convent and out of gratitude my good friend offered a dowry of eight thousand louis d'or, but his ungrateful child is determined to be a Carmelite, so Devil take this obstinate girl and let her scrub floors in a hair shirt for all Eternity.

The queen has caused us much concern lately on account of her health. She had an abscess under her arm which Royal Quack knew should have been drawn out and drained, but instead he ordered Her Majesty to be bled and this caused the abscess to break within, so the whole of it fell upon her heart, whereupon he gave her an emetic nearly choking her to death. Surgeon who bled her said, "Have you reflected? This will kill my mistress." Royal Quack replied, "Do as I order you." Surgeon wept and said, "Do you compel me to be a murderer?" At eleven o'clock he was forced to bleed her, at twelve Royal Quack poisoned her with a great dose of emetic, and at three we thought she would depart for another world.

Her Majesty has since been delicate in health and even sickly. Two Sundays ago Monsieur le Duc and I went to pay our respects and found her in a sad state. She had such frightful pains in her soles and toes tears came into her eyes, even so after three royal quacks consulted together, they decided on bleeding from the foot, but it was difficult to make the queen consent, for suffering in her feet was unbearable and she screamed if the sheets merely touch them.

One quack assured us she would recover after a single bleeding, but as she grew worse they continued to bleed her feet almost daily for a week. Immediately after bleeding, from being red as fire, the queen became pale as death and felt extremely ill, so when they took her out of bed, I cried out they ought to let sweating subside before bleeding, but those quacks were obstinate and scoffed at me. Bastards' Governess said, "Do you think yourself cleverer than these learned doctors who are here?" I replied, "No, madame, but it takes no cleverness to know we ought to follow nature. If nature inclines to sweating, it would be better to follow this indication than to take up a sick person in a perspiration to bleed her." She shrugged her shoulders and smiled ironically.

Monsieur le Duc and I sat on another side of the room and never said another word, but afterward we went and complained to the king who was much moved as he likes the queen for her virtue and sincere attachment to him despite his infidelities. His Majesty immediately changed all doctors and by yesterday the queen was feeling much better, though there are still two great boils on her feet which burn them as if with red-hot irons and she cannot yet walk. It is a singular illness. Twice a week they give her medicine and all other days an enema. Both do her good. Her Majesty often said against Official Whore, "That whore will be the death of me," but I think it more likely Bastards' Governess will kill the queen.

Whenever anyone displeases Bastards' Governess, she pinches her lips, raises the corners of her mouth, drops her under lip and contracts her nostrils which gives a most disagreeable air, so upon hearing of my complaints to the king, fire came to her eyes and her special look of displeasure asserted itself. Many heard her say as a supposed jest, "I have been too far from and too near grandeur to know what it is," but they also say she is sorry for ignoring Monsieur's example, for he always says, "Everything goes well provided Madame knows nothing about it." My son is very clever for his age and made me laugh when he said, "Governess will live wonderfully well into a great old age." I said, "How can you say such a thing with surety?" To which he replied, "Because Almighty God to punish the Devil makes him stay a long time in a villainous body."

Songs are the best way of getting truth, so I am pleased you like my gift. I know people in Paris who have collected many large volumes and take excellent care of them as they are great treasures, for books of songs are difficult to obtain because no one who has one willingly parts with it. When I first came to France, Grande Mademoiselle gave me a splendidly fat book of songs (it had belonged to Previous Monsieur) sung by common people. Most songs in my book are funny and some lewd, from every period and about everything, but all tell their stories as common people believe things happened, and as they never sing praise unless it is deserved, their songs teach history better than history books which are full of flattery, so I hope you receive as many hours of pleasure from the book I sent as I do from mine.

Here is a new way of lawyers taking revenge for a slap in the face. Maitre de Visscher and a wealthy Nuremburg merchant were at a fashionable Paris salon for an evening's entertainment when Official Whore entered into a loud and drunken argument with them, then slapped the lawyer very hard. Without pause and with everyone's attention riveted on him, Maitre de Visscher declared, "No lady would behave thus. This is a man's doing, and I shall confirm it for myself." He then flung Official Whore's skirts over her head, and clutching her tightly in that place where legs join together which no gentleman should ever clutch in public on himself or anyone else, continued, "I shall kiss this hand which struck me if it is a woman, but duel to death with a man. What is it?" Everyone cheered, "A woman." He then let go, bowed deeply and went away.

When His Majesty heard this story, he laughed so hard and so long his royal quacks feared he would have an apoplectic seizure and die, but neither did his brain explode nor did his heart stop beating and on recovering from his laughing fit, he sent Maitre de Visscher a gift of a thousand louis d'or, so Official Whore cannot revenge herself without insulting the king and these days she has no courage for such things.

Much sinister gossip is on the backstairs concerning Monsieur de La Reynie's brother-in-law whose escape they say was aided and abetted by family, and though one must always be obliging to one's blood and loved ones, it sometimes behooves one to abandon this scruple and let justice deal with murderers especially when a certain witch is poisoning one's good reputation with the king.

Here is all the news and there is nothing else to say, so good night to you.

Many tender kisses,
Lotte

"Wake up, sleepy head, rub your eyes, get out of bed."

Tuesday–24 June 1681–Feast of Saint John the Baptist
Chateau Versailles

My beloved Highness A_ de M_,

As brides say it on their wedding night "before I gobble my egg, wind my clocks and go to bed" I shall write a few words, for I am not sleepy and at this hour have no fear of interruption by unwelcome visitors. I am troubled beyond measure Your Highness has received none of my letters written since first of the month, but beyond a doubt will receive this one, for at sunrise I shall go to His Majesty and complain bitterly about those lazy good-for-nothings who handle postal service in this country. But that is about the post and not about my news for today.

Monsieur de La Reyie at last executed La Voisin and a great sigh of rejoicing echoed though all corridors, hallways, niches and backstairs. Every courtier deserted Versailles to witness her last torment at Place de Greve, for all wish to be certain wicked witch is dead, and all Paris joined those from Court in hopes of a fine spectacle entertaining as an opera. None were disappointed, for proud and defiant to the end La Voisin taunted the crowd giving back as good as she got, thus when her executioners tried to light the fire, she kicked away straw to keep faggots from burning, wherefore Monsieur de La Mer finally laid a great pile of wood around her, so no one could see him and a journeyman rip off her head with iron hooks, but Maitre de Visscher would not hear of this act of mercy to spare her suffering violent pains and coerced the executioners instead to cause her prolonged burning from a secret formula for flames which are slow and not very hot. He was heard to say, "A witch is a witch and ought suffer a prelude to Eternal Flames."

When the date of La Voisin's execution was first proclaimed, Bastards' Governess attempted to oust Official Whore from Court by most cleverly goading her into an vicious quarrel with His Majesty concerning a mysterious black strongbox Monsieur de La Reynie put into Toad Louvois's keeping early in December of last year. Official Whore quit Versailles for Paris and paid Monsieur de La Mer to arrange a secret meeting with La Voisin in order to discover if she knew anything of the coffer, but Monsieur le Duc claims it was Maitre de Visscher who accepted the bribe then held Official Whore hostage in Bastille until the king demanded her release. But that is about bribes and Psyche's box and not about a whore's ousting.

Official Whore's grave mistake was departing immediately after her argument with the king, for Limping Bastard (he has studied his lessons well at the hands of Bastards' Governess) so thoroughly detests his own mother he destroyed all her belongings and threw the remains from windows of her apartments, whereupon His Majesty scolded his precocious little bastard most severely yet secretly delights that all the Court understands Official Whore's days of ascendancy are truly at an end. She raced back to Versailles and the king graciously accepted her mild and meek return, but it was too late as deed is done and she has been undone, and if she is stupid enough to do it again and surely she will as she is no genius to learn from her mistakes, it will certainly be the last of her as His Majesty said it would behoove Official Whore to turn religious and enter a convent as her predecessor had good grace and manners to do.

All attention is now on the black coffer. Monsieur de La Reynie's official seals of Paris Ministry of Police guard its secrets so closely neither can Toad Louvois guess its contents nor does he wish to, for several who had misfortune to broach this subject with His Majesty found him visibly distressed by it and themselves suddenly out of favor and exiled to their estates. It is said whoever breaks the lead seals will be put to death secretly, so of course all speculation surmises the box is filled with proof of Official Whore's guilt with La Voisin and many other wicked witches.

Monsieur le Duc says it is true there are proofs against Official Whore yet insists those documents of her worst crimes are fabrications and forgeries made by Bastards' Governess and Sodomite Lorraine, but there are many genuine proofs against La Chatte Comtesse and even more amazingly there are bona fide proofs of Minette's poisoning by Sodomite Lorraine, Bastards' Governess's guilt with La Voisin, an accoucheur's attempted murder of Dumb Beauty and her baby's poisoning, Occasional Concubine's birth and baptismal certificates, etc. etc. etc., for it seems Monsieur le Duc has been squirreling, and having an excess supply of nuts but not knowing where to bury them, threw these treasures into the infamous black box when Monsieur de La Reynie was not looking. "What possessed you to do such a foolish thing," I asked. "They are very important papers. Can you think of a safer place," he asked in return. I said, "But they were perfectly safe all this time." He said, "It was too tiresome constantly changing their hiding place, for all sorts of villains have been looking for them." I asked, "Then, why did you not show them to the king?" To which he replied, "No one likes bad news. I was only trying to be nice and spare His Majesty any hurt feelings. What is wrong with that?" To which I had no further argument.

Tonight I made His Majesty laugh before he retired, for as he had an attack of gas pains I handed him a paper with a remedy on it, and on seeing this, Royal Quack became disconcerted and demanded, "What is in the note you gave the king?" "A remedy for pains," I replied. Bastards' Governess then said, "Only His Majesty's physicians may advise a cure." I said, "It is a sensible medicine and can bring no harm. Let His Majesty judge." He opened my paper, read it, laughed out loud and said, "Madame is right. It is a better cure than either of you ever suggested." Monsieur then took my note from the king's hands and read it out loud.

When bowels are perturbed with distressing winds,
One must not ever hold them in but be relieved of them.
Fart! The best way to free oneself and them. Fart!
Fart! Make them free and be happy too. Fart!

Everyone burst their sides laughing except of course Bastards' Governess and Royal Quack. I remember as a little girl playing this same jest on Her Highness S_ von B_-L_.

It is three-quarters of an hour past midnight and I am sitting in my apartments by the balcony door. The moon is full. There is no whisper of a wind and the sky is clear and full of stars. The air is cool and refreshing. It is very still and peaceful. Sigi lies quietly at my feet. With a thick fog upon the ground the shadows remind me of Dumb Beauty as she looked toward the end when always ill, tall and slender in her silvery white silk dressing gown and frilled mop cap, looking pale about the face, she was like White Woman of Berlin. Poor little silver herring is food for maggots now.

Your Highness must not become accustomed to using of spectacles as they will surely spoil your eyes, so be patient and do not use them and good eyesight will return, for one needs but consider Die Rotzenhäuserin for proof of how spectacles take one's sight away. I see better now than I did in my youth and I have never worn them.

My Excellency is alone in my apartments all day long, yet I am never bored and have lots of books, all my little dogs, my coins and my medals, many engraved stones, in short, enough things to amuse me, but nothing to offend God or world. As for the business causing Your Highness such grief I am sorry to see you are taking everything so to heart. We only come this way once, so why make yourself so unhappy when after all one can always eat, sleep, and drink, sleep, drink and eat.

Sigi's stomach growls and he is passing all sorts of wind and making stinky smells. I must walk him before retiring for tonight or he will present me with a gift I would much prefer to bestow on someone else, so with this happy thought I must leave you now.

All my heart's love,
Lotte

Artificial insemination & a demon bride

Saturday–26 July 1681–Feast of Saints Joachim & Anne
Chateau Saint-Cloud

My beloved Highness R_,

At least Your Highness received the parcels which is something and one ought to be grateful, but My Excellency is most familiar with customs officials and their stupendous greed, so it is unsurprising they did not steal my poor gifts as what I sent was not worth much. You will not like my new portrait as the painter put my fat in all wrong places and it does not look becoming, for in truth my rump is wide, my belly and hips round as a barrel and my shoulders broad, whereas my neck and breasts are flat, so you must readjust this portrait in your imagination to accommodate for differences in my painted imagine.

I do hope you enjoy the other small trifles. Diamonds are rare and costly now, so I sent none, whereas colored jewels especially small ones like those in the packet are plentiful and cheap. I would with all my heart send something better, but these are in keeping with my small purse, for I can stretch my legs only the length of my coverlet as the old German proverb says.

Parisians think themselves better than all others in this country and often imitate Great Huguenot Prince by saying "Paris is worth a Mass" as he did when offered the crown, for they say to hold Paris is to possess the soul of France, while to rule from within the city walls is to hold a seven hundred year legacy of power handed down from Hugh Capet.

Bastards' Governess says Eternal Paris is an eternally young nymph in whom a lover of youth may find delight teaching everything he knows. Nymphal Paris permits he who governs to mold her character in any way he sees fit for her own good, lets him scheme her destiny, dresses and undresses herself in whatever fashion suits his taste, accepts his jealous guard over her against envious suitors and is submissive to him alone, but Paris is a demon bride incapable of mature love.

These days it is Monsieur de La Reynie who chokes Paris in his iron grip, for this city is the burning passion of his life and he behaves in every sense as an obsessed lover having a crisis of age with need of a girlish mistress to adore him unconditionally. Does an aging wife remind him of his foibles whenever he looks into her eyes? Does she know him too well and remember too much? In her too familiarity, does he see reflected back too many of his weaknesses and flaws? Is her contempt his imagining? Will all this be remedied by a considerably younger second wife?

I cannot see how Die Rotzenhäuserin can be my friend's cure as she is not Paris and may be too old for his taste, but better this than a secret vice (a thousand times worse than sodomy) Bastards' Governess told the king Monsieur de La Reynie is said to indulge at La Pomme de Pin on rue de la Juiverie which My Excellency vigorously denied as a vicious libel and so it had better not be true, for Toad Louvois has a very jealous nature, always looking for ways to discredit anyone who has the king's confidence in order to gather all power to himself.

Several days ago Bastards' Governess came to burden me with her company which was most odd, for as everyone seeks her out and she thinks it her right, she waits for visits and never makes them herself. She told a confidence I think she thought would please me, but her story is such to make all hairs stand on one's head.

Queen Mother had a favorite maid-of-honor who was a most remarkable woman as Late King and both Cardinal Prime Ministers held her in greatest esteem also, but more remarkable than Favorite Maid was her husband who was a captain of musketeers, yet still found time to sire eleven children on his wife, and according to Bastards' Governess this man is the king's true father.

In 1637, when Queen Mother was declared treasonous and confined to Louvre, to save herself from repudiation, she found means to conceive an heir through Favorite Maid's husband and it was easily accomplished as he was in command of musketeers guarding Queen Mother, thus could come and go as he pleased. Immediately upon the birth of His Majesty, Favorite Maid's husband was granted royal monopoly on sedan chairs which made him a man of immense wealth overnight, and even after his premature death several years later, Favorite Maid's family's fortunes continued to rise and swell unabated. She was always beyond reproach in the eyes of Queen Mother and Cardinal Prime Minister despite her eldest son's life of horrible debauchery, scandal and crime which became so outrageous his younger brother had him imprisoned forever in the very same hospital where Occasional Concubine resides, and when I think on it, this was very cleverly imagined as in one stroke a younger son rid his family of an evil villain and managed to steal his brother's birthright in the bargain. But that is about Jacob and Esau and not about Iron Mask.

Bastards' Governess continued her story saying there is a man who knows she speaks the truth and can prove it beyond a shadow of doubt, but unfortunately he was imprisoned in late 1650's by Cardinal Prime Minister to keep him silent. If this is Iron Mask's crime, it does not account for the reason to disguise his face, but Bastards' Governess said the mask itself was made by Monsieur de La Mer's father at Cardinal Prime Minister's request, for Iron Mask is a man of great fame and importance whom the world believes to be dead. She then said to me, "If His Majesty is not truly the king, the crown rightfully belongs to Monsieur. Then, Madame, you are true queen of France." I replied, "If I was maid or widow, I would rather marry than become the greatest queen in the world." She asked puzzled, "What has that to do with my proposition?" I then said, "Because I would rather pass my life in celibacy, for marriage is to me an object of horror." She then yelled at me, "Fie. Fie on you for lacking in ambition," and went away angry.

Someday the inventors of these falsehoods will be confounded and will have to ask pardon. Is it not horrible to invent such lies?

What Bastards' Governess cannot know are the stories told by Monsiuer le Duc, besides why would those who are unwilling to believe His Majesty is a son of Late King be any more willing to believe Monsieur is? If that prunefaced devil governess thought I would help her free Iron Mask, she is badly mistaken.

The witch hunt is over. When the Court returns to Versailles, His Majesty will dismiss Chambre Ardente and Monsieur de La Reynie need only to tidy up a bit, so by end of next year all surviving prisoners will be exiled to obscurity in remote dungeons or executed, just a matter of bureaucratic paperwork. There have been over nine hundred interrogations, many hundreds of executions and imprisonments, yet no conclusion, so all wonder where is the link and who is ultimately culpable. In truth, what has changed?

All the courtiers are terrified of Monsieur de La Reynie, scared out of their wits for now and will behave themselves for awhile, yet everyone at Court still wishes to poison somebody and every street corner of Paris still has a demon more than willing to help anyone sell his soul to buy his desires, so My Excellency cannot see how things in this wretched country have been made any better, for children and babies have been slaughtered by tens of thousands in order to make potions, charms, poisons and as sacrifices to the Devil. It has been going on for too many years and there is no reason to suppose it cannot happen again as there is no public outrage to keep these aristocrats in line.

There is also an unnatural silence covering over everything which is truly frightening as an awful lot of men have heard many accusations against Official Whore, enough of whom have no moral obligation to keep silent, but not one word has gone out to the general public about her, yet we all have heard every conceivable manner of disgusting story concerning just about everyone else. Why is this? Who is the eminence grise so clever like magicians upon a stage he disguises truth and makes us see whatever he shows under our noses?

Your Highness is unjust to scold me on account of my children's upbringing as Monsieur is jealous of them, and when he asked me by what precepts I would raise children, I answered, "Always talk reason to them. Show them why such and such a thing is good or bad. Never pass over any foolish caprice. Strive as much as possible that they do not see bad examples. Do not dishearten them with attacks of ill-humor. Praise virtue and inspire horror of vice of every kind." At this Monsieur decided to put governors in charge of them.

In truth, he lets me have more authority over my daughter and stepdaughter than my son, but keeps them from me as much as possible, nonetheless I try to bring them up well and influence them whenever I can, for Monsieur cannot prevent me from telling them plain truths. It is not to be supposed we can bring up children without giving ourselves great trouble. Vigilance and activity are indispensable. Thanks to God, neither my daughter nor stepdaughter shows any inclination toward being a slut, for I have won their respect in all and in this can truly say I recognize my blood, but my son is another matter as he will be his father's son, yet I would be a most unnatural mother if I did not love him from the bottom of my heart.

I am sweating in the worst way and cranky as a bedbug from it. My daughter and my son have gathered all my dachshunde and are playing at herding them from room to room like sheep at pasture. Monsieur le Duc is a wolf. There is so much racket no one could hear a thunderbolt fall, so I must leave you now and go rescue them.

I love you with all my heart,
Liselotte

Secrets & lies & crimes

Saturday—27 September 1681—Feast of Saints Cosmas & Damian
Chateau Versailles

Dearest K_ von P_,

My son studies much, has a good memory and expresses himself well. He is not tall but stout with fat cheeks, his bad sight makes him squint and his eyes protrude, he has a bad walk, yet I do not think he is disagreeable-looking. Close by, he sees very well and can reading the finest writing, but without spectacles at the distance of half the length of a room he recognizes no one. He does not resemble his father, for Monsieur has a long and narrow face, whereas my son's is square, though his walk is like that of Monsieur and he makes the same motions with his hands.

He is in perfect health, but has never been really ill, is very lively and does not keep in one position for a single instant. To tell you the truth, he is very badly brought up, for Monsieur lets him do just what he likes for fear of making him ill. I am convinced he would be less quick-tempered if his tutors corrected him and they do him a great deal of harm by letting him follow his caprices.

Of late Monsieur de La Reynie's behavior is of an avenging angel, for armed with a ream of lettres de cachet signed by His Majesty himself, he disposed of anyone connected with La Pomme de Pin and the Bordes family, whereupon Maitre de Visscher and constables of Chatelet Courts busied themselves with most peculiar behavior, so Bishop of Notre-Dame made complaint to the king concerning troops of constables from Paris Ministry of Police invading the cathedral and committing sacrilege, but as His Majesty would hear none of this prelate's grumbling, the police continued happily about their business.

Monsieur le Duc was playing at church mouse and hiding himself in all those places such simple creatures enjoy, wherefore he followed the constables hard at work on Notre-Dame's foundations and it seems they search for and seal up any openings that may lead to the ruins of Saint-Etienne upon which Notre-Dame rests, for they say this Merovingian cathedral is accursed, so evil and poisonous humors are rising up from it, thus a nook behind a niche in the north wall of Notre-Dame's crypt was filled with rubble and walled over, Pont Rouge which connects Ile-de-la-Cite and Ile-Saint-Louis is destroyed and all trace of any sewers underneath it obliterated, and La Pomme de Pin is razed. This last property was confiscated by royal decree, turned over to municipal jurisdiction, a special ordinance was passed by Parlement of Paris banning for next hundred years any structure requiring a cellar and police stables are to be built on the site.

On account of his mousing about, Monsieur le Duc had a most awful misadventure, became lost in a tunnel behind the north wall in Notre-Dame's crypt and would have been buried alive had his valet not heard his squeals of fear and run to Monsieur de La Reynie for help. Maitre de Visscher had to climb through a hole workmen made in the rubble to rescue my friend who unfortunately conceived a strange delusion of the lawyer being a cat come to devour him, so they played at cat-and-mouse a long time till mouse found his way into Saint-Etienne's vestibule where many hundreds of prisoners in cages wailed most piteously, whereupon cat caught up with mouse and both found their way to safety. When my poor friend told of his experience, he said it was very frightening and stinky underground like rotting of many corpses and ever since he has lost all interest in mousing.

My Excellency and Monsieur le Duc inquired of Monsieur de La Reynie the reason for sealing off all access to the cavern beneath Notre-Dame. "Is it justice to bury alive all those poor devils," I demanded. "There is historical precedent, Madame," he said. "And what is it," asked I. He replied at length, "When Black Death first appeared in the fourteenth century with a potential to kill one-third of all people from India to Sweden, the first three cases to appear in Milan were walled up in their homes with anybody and anything that had misfortune of being in the wrong place. Women, children, servants, animals. It did not matter. Fewer people died of bubonic plague in Milan, because Archbishop Giovanni Visconti had strength, courage and fortitude to sacrifice a few for the greater good." I asked, "Do all those caged in Saint-Etienne suffer from plague?" "Worse than plague. They must be forever silenced or we shall all go to the Devil," he said. I replied, "Prelates have a fine way of justifying a bad conscience. But happy results do not make immoral acts be moral or less immoral. You must wrestle with your conscience and with angels, for no such choice is so clear and simple." "Our Lord created Confession for the forgiveness of mortal sins," he returned, then shrugged his shoulders and walked away.

Captain Desgrez (he disappeared immediately after 'unfortunate incident') is with La Chatte Comtesse in Spanish Netherlands and in his absence causes Monsieur de La Reynie a thousand times more embarrassment than ever he did while in Paris, for they say he is a Satanist and 'Gilles de Rais' who slaughtered many children in the manner of werewolves. People are unwilling to believe the lieutenant general was unaware of it as his brother-in-law lived for twenty years under his very same roof, thus with so much fear engendered by Chambre Ardente, they wish upon my friend the worst evils and accuse him of unconscionable hypocrisy in sending countless souls to hang on the gibbet or burn at the stake for much lesser sins, all the while protecting his own family.

Worse yet are frightening lies whispered throughout Court accusing Monsieur de La Reynie of being an eminence grise in this 'poisons affair,' for as he is the most powerful man in France having unimpeachable authority from the king, they say he uses his prerogatives to divert suspicion of his own culpability with all those poor scapegoats he executes to cover over his own evils.

Bastards' Governess told His Majesty that Maitre de Visscher perpetrates a fraud of his son's death by natural causes, for if truth be discovered, people would know the extreme wickedness of all residing on rue Geoffroy-l'Asnier. The House of La Reynie would fall and neither my friend nor his son-in-law wishes to be another Nicolas Fouquet. It is also said all this sealing up of Notre-Dame's foundations is for purpose of burying all proof of the lieutenant general's crimes and lies and secrets. I keep myself out of it and say nothing as it behooves one to complain of these matters to no one, for there are secret denunciations with poor devils disappearing at night never again to be seen at dawn, and if Bastards' Governess is not more discreet, she may fortunately for us all be next.

Here is an amusing story. Last week Monsieur insisted on hosting a hunt at Saint-Cloud. I warned him against it, for it was unusually rainy all summer and with the first cool weather a horrible damp chill settled into Saint-Cloud, but Monsieur would hear none of it. At the end of a most uncomfortable stay, on the morning we were to depart for Versailles all furniture was sent on ahead as is the custom, whereupon the weather turned suddenly and exceptionally foul, so we were forced to stay another night and depart next day.

This left everyone without a bed except Her Majesty who always insists her bed travels with her and never goes anywhere on its own, so as the queen's bed chamber had the largest fireplace His Majesty decided we would all sleep with her. They put mattresses on the floor and we were all lined up in a row at the foot of Her Majesty's bed. My Excellency, Monsieur, Grande Mademoiselle, Monseigneur, Madame la Dauphine, Bastards' Governess, His Majesty, Official Whore, Monsieur le Duc, and of course Monsieur-le-Valet-who-belongs-to-Monsieur-le-Duc. When the queen saw our sleeping arrangements she cried out, "What? Are you all to sleep together? Is it to be as one big orgy?" To this the king replied, "Leave your bed curtains opened, madame, and you will be able to keep an eye on us all."

There is no more news, so I shall leave you now.

As the French are so fond of saying,
Big kisses,
Lotte

Alley cat, spider, werewolf & mouse: heard a German tiptoe through the back of the house

Friday–3 January 1681–Feast of Saint Genevieve
Chateau Versailles

"What in Heaven's? Why, Monsieur, what are you doing here?"

"I've come for a little visit. And, to hear a funny story, Lotte." Monsieur was teary-eyed. "I have no one else to keep me company."

"Meowww. Owww. Owww. Meowww."

"Monsieur le Duc." Liselotte waved her finger at him. "It is most unbecoming for a Prince of the Blood to yowl like an alley cat. Stop it at once. Be a wolf or a dog or even a big hairy spider, something with more dignity."

Monsieur le Duc sat next to Monsieur and contorted his face into a dozen different expressions. Monsieur and Liselotte sat enthralled.

"Monsieur-le-Valet-who-belongs-to-Monsieur-le-Duc, what is he doing?"

"I don't know, Madame, he's never done this before."

Finally, Monsieur le Duc burst into tears.

Monsieur handed him his handkerchief. "What's the matter, Monsieur le Duc?"

"I don't know what sound a spider makes."

"Bah! Monsieur le Duc. Spiders cannot speak. They are kings of the insect kingdom, and so God in His great wisdom gave them no voice."

Monsieur skewed his mouth. "How does that make God wise, Lotte?"

"Spiders bethink themselves too good to speak to their inferiors, Monsieur, so the Almighty gave the spider's voice to another creature who would put it to better use."

"And, which creature was that, Lotte?"

"I would not know, Monsieur, for I am not God, but an old German nursery rhyme says it was to man God gave the spider's voice." She turned toward her friend. "But as to spiders, Monsieur le Duc, they are always silent, and carry themselves aloof and with a regal air, and smile most graciously at everyone. And, when they condescend to acknowledge inferiors, it is with a nod of the head or a telling expression of the face. Most dignified."

Monsieur said, "But, what if a spider has to ask a question?"

"Spiders never have to ask questions, because they know all things."

"But, what if there's something they don't know? I mean, really, Lotte, they can't possibly know everything. Only God knows everything. That would mean God's a big hairy spider."

"Whatever spiders do not know, God whispers in their ears, so spiders do not have to use a voice they do not have."

"But, Lotte, I don't think spiders have ears. Have you ever seen a spider with ears?" Monsieur looked at Monsieur le Duc. "Have you ever seen ears on a spider?" He said to the valet, "On a spider, ears?" He looked back at Liselotte. "You see, no one's ever seen ears."

"Spiders are deaf mutes. And, this is an end of it."

Monsieur dug into his pockets and produced handsful of chocolates which he gave to everyone. He stuffed a few candies in his mouth. "Tell us a funny story, Lotte. Monsieur le Duc is feeling a bit peevish from his transformation into a big hairy spider. It would make him feel better. Wouldn't it, Monsieur le Duc?"

Monsieur le Duc smiled with affectation and nodded.

"I have a story about Maddening Politeness."

"Good. They're always droll. Aren't they, Monsieur le Duc?" Monsieur pushed a chocolate into Monsieur le Duc's mouth.

A footman entered. "Pardon. Monsieur, Madame, Monsieur le Duc. Monsieur de La Reynie begs an audience."

"Tell that frog to go away. I shall not see him."

"Lotte. He's not your friend anymore?" Monsieur turned to the footman. "Tell Monsieur de La Reynie I'll see him."

Gabriel entered and bowed. "Monsieur." He couldn't continue and started crying. Monsieur le Duc handed him Monsieur's handkerchief.

"Why is everyone weeping today?" Liselotte's finger started waving again. "Monsieur de La Reynie. If misfortune has befallen you, it is because we are usually punished in this world by our own sins. It is God's justice, for you have been most treacherous and disloyal."

"Madame, my younger daughter wants to enter the Carmelites. I'd never be able to see her again. I couldn't stand it. It'd be like burying her alive. I came to beg Madame, most humbly, to speak with the Abbess de Maubuisson."

"How tragical. Tragical."

Monsieur shoved a bon bon into Liselotte's mouth. She gagged. He looked in Monsieur le Duc's direction. "Ugh, just like that pious, silly blonde, Mademoiselle de La Valliere. When Madame de Montespan dethroned her from His Majesty's bed, she took to hard prayer and labor." He fed Monsieur le Duc a chocolate. "Monsieur de La Reynie, your daughter isn't a blonde, is she?"

Madame said, "Monsieur de La Reynie's daughter has hair similar in color to His Majesty, so she is not overly silly or excessively pious. But, she has not hair so dark in color as Mesdames de Montespan and de Maintenon, so she is also neither a whore nor a witch. I shall write to Her Highness Tantchen Louisa-Hollandina for your poor daughter, Monsieur de La Reynie."

"Grrr. Grrr." Everybody looked at Monsieur le Duc.

The valet said, "Monsieur le Duc is becoming *canis lupus*."

"I am no *canis lupus lycaon*. I am *lykos anthropos*, for I may have the appearance of a *lykos*, but I have the intelligence of an *anthropos*." He got up and walked elegantly around the room. "Monsieur de La Reynie, can you tell me why a German, Monsieur de Lorraine and Madame de Maintenon had a midnight tete-a-tete?"

"Pardon, Monsieur le Duc? Is this a riddle?"

The valet interrupted. "Monsieur le Duc was a mouse and had gotten lost. I was looking for him and thought he'd gone into the royal nursery. Madame de Maintenon was with two gentlemen."

"Yes, but quiet as a mouse, so no one knew I was about. They were all in the nursery, together. Madame de Maintenon, Monsieur de Lorraine and a German. Grrr. Being very chatty."

Monsieur swallowed the remains of the chocolate in his mouth. "How do you know one of them was a German? And, what was Philippe doing there?"

"Because he sounded like Madame. After Madame de Maintenon left, the German told Monsieur de Lorraine that Balthasar would remedy everything. Grrr. This was after Monsieur de Lorraine finished his prayers."

"Prayers? What was he praying about with a German? Germans are Lutherans. Philippe's Catholic. What could they have been praying about when they don't even pray to the same God?"

"I don't know. Grrr. But it was very profound, because Monsieur de Lorraine kept choking, and the German was quite delirious, like Sainte-Therese d'Avila, having one of her ecstatic visions."

"Monsieur, you are very red about your face." Liselotte waved her finger at him. "It is most unhealthy to be so red about the face. Calm yourself or your brain will explode. As for Monsieur de Lorraine, I do not think he was praying for he does not know any prayers. Most likely, he was doing that business sodomites so much enjoy."

"Who's Balthasar?"

"I'm surprised at you, Monsieur de La Reynie. Every child knows Balthasar was the Magi with the myrrh. Grrr."

The linage of Chaos: Nyx, Hypnos, Thanatos, Dreams

Sunday–9 February 1681–Sexagesima Sunday Hotel Reynie

Every matrix of chaos evolves change. Immutability ceases and nothing can remain as it was. Dreams release. Sleep restores. Death transforms. In night-darkness of the unconscious, in twilight of the subconscious an otherness originates or develops—temporal to spiritual, past to future, forgetfulness to remembrance—for Death and Sleep are brothers and sons of Night, and Dreams but children of their incestuous bed. To dream is to fondle death with kisses and to die is but to embrace dreamless sleep.

With the fascinated hands of a child below the age of reason, Eleanor Baroness von Ratsamhausen patted a coil of her mother's adult hair in unconscious remembrance of countless dreams at night when she turned away from the carelessness of her father's urgency as he caressed an amputated surrogate, till he could touch flesh and smell a woman's body.

Lenor's mother lay dead in a letter she now held in her hands. Like the hair, it was a betrayal, but the abbess's final denial of her child was in vain. Handwriting in love letters to the baron and this last testament was similar enough to be comforting. Lenor put it into her father's trunk to keep company with his spyglass, his sword, love letters, a three-foot length of blonde hair and a host of other worthless trophies of a failed life which thirty years later would be buried with her.

Now, lost in secret reverie, Lenor transformed the matriarch into a fetish of lost desire through a ritual her father had unknowing taught her in childhood. Her mother was a length of hair, thick as an anchor's rope, and while Lenor's baby slept, her father who had been dead, his memory hauled through stations of her life in a battered trunk, was alive again in genetic memories passed through her to his grandson.

Now, your mother is the baggage of reminiscences.

Lenor maneuvered from one room into another, leaving the past, moving toward an uncertain future. She sat on the floor of Gabriel's grand-cabinet in front of an enormous sea chest just arrived from England. Its lid was propped open. All she could see was a profusion of cotton wadding. She smiled with delight, lost in another secret reverie, until Minette and Alphonso broke into her daydream. Her hand disappeared into the downy mass and retrieved a handful of small elongated glass bubbles. Alphonso sniffed at one she held to his nose. "Watch. Magic."

With brass pincers she nipped off the smallest part of it's tadpole's tail. There was the hollow sound of a popgun; with eruptive force the bubble shattered into fine dust. The dachshunds ran for cover, berserk men routed on a battlefield. Alphonso danced in little circles and barked; Minette hid under a piece of furniture and shook. Lenor re-submerged her arms, groping along the bottom until she found a letter from Prince Rupert, and never heard a sudden stillness in the room.

"Secret papers. A spy for the English?" Gabriel snatched the letter. "Baronne, what are you doing in my grand-cabinet? Alone. Only Maitre and Madame de Visscher are permitted in this room alone. What are those things?"

"A special formula of molten glass dropped into water. In England, they're called 'Prince Rupert's drops.' Because he invented them. His Highness calls them 'larmes Batavique.'" She exploded another vitreous bubble. "Just playthings. His Highness sent a chest full of them to amuse us. Well, the chest is for you. There's a letter for you too."

"And this letter's for?"

"May I have it?"

He knelt down next to her. "Are you still in love with him?"

"I was never in love with him. Whatever gave you such an idea?" She peered at him over her glasses. "Is it time I returned to Madame?"

"But the child."

"Nothing more than a little shrewd business. A man needs convincing he's loved, especially when the woman doesn't love him. That's what children are for. It's how a woman buys her security. And it's the umbilical cord a man can't cut to free himself after a woman's finally tired of all her pretending."

"It's not Prince Rupert's child, is it?"

"The man doesn't exist who can be certain all his children are his own. More men than you can imagine raise another man's child without ever suspecting. Your daughters look just like their mother. Who's their father? Or are you a fool of stupendous ego who believes himself blessed with a wife incapable of infidelity? As for Prince Rupert, he was a generous man in many ways."

"I could be more than generous with you."

"You're very attractive for all the right reasons." She put her hand on his cheek and kissed him. "Behaved yourself with remarkable restraint so far. What a gentleman."

"You haven't made it easy for me to be anything but. I'm tired of being a gentleman."

"Aren't you afraid of me? I'm a treacherous woman."

"My wife's a treacherous woman. I can deal with your kind of sins. They're understandable. You at least are having your baby. Compared to infanticide, your deception's harmless."

"From the moment God put Adam to sleep, there's been no harmless woman. And He gave woman guile to endure the subjugation of men. You want me. Then, you may have me. But it will cost you."

"You need a better attitude." He took her in his arms. "I'll give you anything you want."

Rhea: a royal pardon

Sunday–9 February 1681–Sexagesima Sunday
Hotel Beauvais

Balthasar and an army of well-trained dachshunds played together in a reception salon where Anne-Sophie waited. His attempts to be entertaining with a show of tricks only bored her, but then she noticed Balthasar's groupings of dogs: three groups of seven longhair and two groups of six short-hair. It seemed to annoy him. A mischievous smile filled her eyes. Anne-Sophie had Balthasar keep his playmates in line while she rearranged them: one longhair, one short-hair, two longhair, three short-hair, five longhair, eight short-hair, thirteen longhair.

Andreas entered. "What are you doing, Madame de Visscher?"

"I see Madame thinks highly of you, to have bestowed so many of her little babies. What an amusing way of expressing gratitude for all those German delicacies you've been stuffing her with. Next time she comes, tell her you need another twenty-one bald ones. Or she'll ruin this nice Italian sequence."

"I hate children. I hate dogs. I hate holidays in the countryside."

"And, you hate Paris. If you don't get back to Rome soon, Madame will bury you alive under a pile of German sausage dogs."

"Paris has very little to recommend it. You know my feelings on the matter better than anyone."

"A very different sentiment from my father. He's madly in love with her. Certainly more than he is with his wife whom he's ceased to love altogether. Or even his new mistress who has him so besotted he lives with her openly under his wife's roof." Anne-Sophie sat on the wide, elegant sofa usually occupied by Liselotte. "When I was a little girl, father taught me the man who rules in Paris controls all France. Father has powerful enemies who'd like to see him end his days in disgrace and exile. My father's brother-in-law knows it. He's off somewhere thinking about how he can save himself by helping those enemies. I like Rome, you know. Very much. My children would thrive there. In all that sunshine. But, it can't be until my father's brother-in-law is out of the way. He'll bring father down if he's not caught."

"But, Michel and you'd be in Rome."

"Michel would be with father in Exiles or Chateau d'If. If we made it to Rome, Louvois would send assassins after Michel."

"So what. I'd have the assassins assassinated. Your uncle may never get caught. Rumor is he's in the Spanish Netherlands, but it doesn't mean he's there. And in his position, I'd ally myself with Louvois against your father."

"Everybody in France, except you, Andreas, knows the king hates Louvois. Even Louvois knows it. The king tolerates him because he needs him. For now. Someday, Louvois will fall, and everybody associated with him. It's what father says."

"My dearest, there's more to this than your father's political well-being. I'm fascinated. Do tell me about it."

"Jeanne-Jacqueline's finally told me all her secrets. And from Michel's nightmares, I know what he won't tell either of us. My father's brother-in-law let a man take Michel-Nicolas-Andreas for a Black Mass on All Hallows Eve. My father's wife only made a half-hearted attempt…" She clenched her teeth, swallowed hard and closed her eyes a moment; the tears retreated. "…he has to pay for my son, and for my sister whom he'd been raping for nearly a year. But he's wanted for the page's murder. He can't be punished unless he comes out of hiding. And he won't unless he feels safe."

"I can see you have a plan."

"I need a royal pardon."

"Get it from your father, or Michel."

"Only you have access to the kind which are untraceable. No one can ever know how he got it, or they'll know who killed him."

"Anne-Sophie. Murder is a heavy burden on a conscience."

She looked into Balthasar's eyes. "How many murders have you committed?" He said nothing. "Do you sleep well at night, Balthasar?"

"Sound as the dead, Frau de Visscher."

"You see, Andreas, it's not such a burden. And yes, I have a plan. You and Balthasar are going to help me. We'll discuss the details after you get me the royal pardon."

"What about your father? And Michel?"

"This is our secret. Yours and mine. And Balthasar will be, as always, discreet as a tomb. They needn't know. Michel-Nicolas-Andreas was my son.

"He was Michel's also."

"He was my firstborn. I know you're disappointed that father's asked Monsieur and Monsieur le Duc to be the twin's godfathers. But what will it matter, once we're all in Rome with you again? You'll be the only godfather they'll ever know."

Anne-Sophie stood. Andreas took her hands in his own. There was a wicked smile on the lips which tenderly, reverently kissed both her palms. "Anything to please you, my beloved. My sweetheart."

Balthasar resumed playing with the dogs while he waited for Andreas's return from escorting Anne-Sophie downstairs. He separated them according to his original groupings and regrouped them according to Anne-Sophie's series. He couldn't see what she thought was so clever. His groups made more sense. Of course, there was a problem: they didn't all look the same. All this short-and-long hair disturbed visual symmetry and he was short two dogs to make all his groups equivalent. He could kill three, and then all his groups would have the same amount, but Madame might notice; she knew all the dogs by name. Herr Graf could ask Madame for two more dogs with short hair, but this would make seven per group. Still an uneven number. Balthasar paced the room. He really needed to kill three dogs with long hair.

"Balthasar, stop obsessing about those ridiculous animals and listen to me. We have to retire Chasteuil. What a pity. He's so talented."

"Herr Graf, forgive me. I didn't hear you return. Frau de Visscher is like the rest of her family. She'll make a good successor to Chasteuil."

"Yes, yes. I knew she was a monster from the first moment I laid eyes on her. Charming. She isn't even twenty. She'll do very well among the Italians."

"He isn't done with his work yet. Do you have a preference of method?" Balthasar eyed the dogs. "I prefer the choke. In the style of the ancient Romans. Very slowly."

"Rush him along. I want him done before summer. But nothing so merciful as death."

"Herr Graf. What's an Italian sequence?"

"Don't worry that handsome head of yours over something so complicated. It's an obscure method for counting animals, and a type of mathematics you'll never have need of." Andreas looked at Balthasar looking at the dogs. "Balthasar. Don't. I'll know if any of them is missing. I'll have you ground into bratwurst and feed you to Madame."

Deus, Laudem Meam

"Hold not thy peace, O God of my praise, for my love they are my adversaries, and they have rewarded me evil for good, and hatred for my love.

Let his prayer become sin;

Let his days be few;

Let his children be fatherless, and his wife a widow;

Let his children be continually vagabonds, and beg: let them seek their bread also out of their desolate places;

Let the extortioner catch all that he has;

Let strangers spoil his labor;

Let there be none to extend mercy to him: neither let there be any to favor his fatherless children;

Let his posterity be cut off, and in the generation following, let their name be blotted out; and let not the sin of his mother be blotted out.

As he loves cursing, so let it come to him; as he clothed himself with cursing, so let it come into his bowels like water, and like oil into his bones.

Let this be the reward of my adversaries.

Let my adversaries be clothed with shame.

Let them cover themselves with their own confusion, as with a mantle."

Armand wept to the young woman who sang. "I am gone like the shadow when it declines."

The young woman pointed to Rex Mundi who stood behind Armand. "I give myself to prayer. Set a wicked man over him and let Satan stand at his right hand."

Armand, Rex Mundi stands by your sinister hand. What's He whispering into your ear?

Deus, laudem meam.

Maschalismos

Monday—26 May 1681—Feast of Saint Philip Neri
Isle Sainte-Marguerite

If you killed someone, accidently or otherwise, how would you protect yourself against the anger of the unquiet dead? Would you appease a vengeful spirit by cutting off hands and feet of its worldly remains and hanging these talismans around your neck? Would you then lick up your victim's blood and spit it out three times? What atonement would free you from society's mandated revenge by family? Would you expiate your sin by paying off surviving blood relatives? In the Greek way of death, when the ancients became sick of mutilating corpses to free themselves of obligation to murdered dead, they formulated another ritual cleansing for the aggrieved living—blood money.

Remote. Isolated. Fort Royal stood on a lonely promontory at the farthest distance from the mainland. Between this fortress-prison and a small port which was the island's gateway to Cannes, wide paths criss-crossed through centuries-old forest of Allepo pine and eucalyptus. From the topmost cell of the highest tower the view across Sainte-Marguerite would have been lovely: a ferry's daily arrivals and departures, comings and goings of simple men's lives, the cycle of life in the forest. The only window in the topmost cell of the highest tower faced out to sea. The Iron Mask resided in loneliness. Isolated. Remote.

It happened quickly. Monsieur de Saint-Mars unlocked the cell; the Iron Mask looked up from his meal; Balthasar plunged a dagger into his solar plexus.

Then everything happened in slow motion with a deliberately measured pace constrained by etiquette, a courtly minuet. Four guards escorted their heavily manacled prisoner. His broken knees couldn't support his feet and legs which smeared a bloody trail across the floor. He uttered grunts of a man unaccustomed to being without his tongue.

Balthasar stood rigid with impatience while the prisoner was permanently attached to the wall. Eagerly, he ripped away a hemp sack which had adhered to clotted wounds on the man's head. After a languorous kiss he locked the iron helmet. "I'll miss you. Herr Graf says I may visit every six months to make sure you're alive."

Balthasar then decapitated the corpse and placed its head in the sack which un-stiffened as it absorbed a fresh infusion of blood. The governor of Fort Royal extended a hand for his key to the Iron Mask.

"Monsieur de Saint-Mars, you won't be needing this anymore. Keep your new guest alive at all costs. He mustn't die before I do. I'd hate for an iron helmet to ruin your handsome looks."

Saint-Mars bowed deeply and with reverence.

Andreas acknowledged the obeisance. "Perhaps, before I leave, you may show me a bit more of your devotion." He leaned over the Iron Mask. With his walking stick, he rapped on the helmet. "Your one sin, for which I shall never forgive you, was my godson. Adieu."

"Herr Graf." Balthasar's voice was a whisper.

"Yes. You may stay another ten minutes. Only don't weep. Don't keep me waiting. And wipe that blood off your mouth. It's disgusting."

Saint-Mars couldn't resist the backward glance of Lot's wife as he left the room and was horrified to see Balthasar sodomizing the Iron Mask.

Andreas was bored. "I've never understood their friendship."

An eminence grise revealed

Wednesday–15 October 1681–Feast of Saint Teresa of Avila
Chatelet Courts

Michel snapped his fingers in Gabriel's face. "Gabriel, you've got a faraway look again."

"Montespan still bothers me. She's not the one. I filled that black coffer with all sorts of incriminating evidence against her, and she's not the one. She's a scapegoat. Not that there's any reason to feel sorry for her. What a bitch."

"You give this thing credit for having some purpose. Purges don't have reasons or reason. Forget it. There's justice in it somewhere, but fair or not, Montespan's the one."

"We still have a major problem on our hands, even if the king doesn't think so. Michel, every time a child's missing, won't you wonder?"

"Who cares? What difference does it make? What do I care who the real culprit is? My son's still dead." He fixed an accusing eye on Gabriel. "You won't be Rapporteur-Commissaire anymore. Only the Lieutenant General of Police of Paris. Or isn't it enough power for you?"

"Montespan's greatest sin was spoon-feeding the king a lot of disgusting shit passed off to her as aphrodisiacs."

"What do you expect? She's forty. Old, bloated and desperate. A bad combination. And some of it must have worked. Royal physicians are still complaining he's overtiring himself at night with his sexual exertions. He's not young either."

"You're not listening to me. She and her bastards are safe only as long as the king's alive. If he's dead, she's finished. If the king dies, who's next in line? Who profits from his death?"

"Monseigneur, then Monsieur." Michel was inspired by genius. "Not Limping Bastard."

"That's right, it's the governess."

"Maintenon? But the Princes of the Blood would never let a legitimized bastard ascend the throne. What's all this got to do with the governess?"

"She's the real problem. Took me awhile, but she's the one. I never suspected. Even when she suggested I lock up Occasional Concubine in the hospital. Maintenon arranged for La Voisin to put the girl in Montespan's household. The girl started Montespan on aphrodisiacs. Then it was magic spells, then it escalated into Black Masses. Montespan never had any idea. Fatter she got with each pregnancy, more hysterical she became, trying to fight off rivals for the king's bed. Think about it. If Maintenon had succeeded in lacing one of those aphrodisiacs with poison, Montespan would've gone to the block for the king's murder. But there's still a part of it missing."

"What about that business with the queen's sudden illness at the beginning of the year? You don't think Maintenon's trying to poison her, do you? And, you haven't answered my other question. How could Limping Bastard ever become king?"

"I want a talk with Chevalier de Lorraine. What was he and a German doing in the nursery with Maintenon the same day the page was murdered?" Gabriel's dreamy expression returned. "I'll bet that German was Andreas von Fugger. Now, what the hell is he doing in France?"

Michel was silent a few minutes. "Why are you stalling about Desgrez? Our bargain was when you found him, I could leave. It's almost a year. How much time do you need? If you don't do something soon, I'll leave anyway."

"Even Louvois's spies can't tell me where he is. He's disappeared into thin air. It's like he's covered by a fog. You know he's there somewhere, but you can't get your hands on him, because you can't tell from which direction the sound's coming. Maybe, we'll never find him."

"It's not good enough. You obviously need to be better motivated. So, here's another reason to get rid of him. He was your wife's lover before you and has been all your married life."

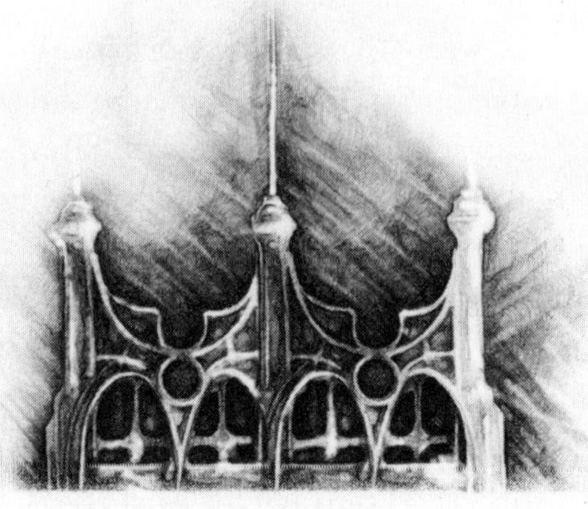

1682

Madame La Solidité

Friday—24 April 1682—Feast of Saint Dismas the Good Thief
Chateau Versailles

Dearest Highness R_ ,

Yesterday Frog La Reynie came to burden My Excellency with his company, all confused, whiny and jealous of the great heights to which his son-in-law has been suddenly catapulted by the king, thereby almost causing Monsieur le Duc and me to miss the great scientific phenomenon of which Your Highness had so kindly written concerning Herr Halley's shooting star.

At express command of His Majesty, Newt Visscher has secretly labored with great diligence on special legislation since last November and that devil lawyer has taken as many months to write his six short paragraphs in order to reap his fabulous rewards. It is a singularly odd law concerning occult sciences and everyone at Court is desperately trying to discern its meaning, but Monsieur le Duc and I conferred at length with his rather clever valet and are well satisfied with our conclusions.

Article I states that persons practicing divination or calling themselves fortunetellers must vacate their homes. Article 2 declares that practices and acts of magic or superstition profaning Holy Writ or Liturgy, or doing or saying things that cannot be explained by natural means are forbidden and will be punished according to their gravity. Article 3 warns that evil-minded persons who augment and compound impiety and sacrilege, under pretext of magic or other deceptions, will be punished by death. Articles 4, 5 and 6 are equally simple and deal with poisons. Manufacture and distribution of anything poisonous is now solely under government control, any livelihood with even remote need to access poisons must be registered with the police, all laboratories or distilleries of anything toxic operated by private citizens are illegal, and medicinal use of poisons or medicine compounded with poisons is forbidden without special authorization from the police.

As Your Highness can see there is no word of witchcraft as it has been demoted to a superstitious practice unpunishable in and of itself with the inherent crime being profanation of the State's religion, for this is His Most Christian Majesty's legal loophole offered as solution to his personal dilemma with Official Whore, so if every effort to conceal her disgraceful behavior fails, her transgressions which are thus decriminalized can be masked simply as blasphemy.

The king fears and detests her, but to shield her reputation so as to keep her sins from being visited upon his children, has need of an imaginative law as clever and graceful as those tricks of magic which conjurers teach to their apprentices. Newt Visscher has given exactly this and in return has been given a marquisite and an ambassadorship so as not to betray the master's secrets.

With a handful of sentences a sly lawyer has singlehandedly put an end to witch hunts and witchcraft trials in France, so it will come as no surprise if within a few years in following the latest fashion of the French as the world is apt to do, all witch hunts cease to be interesting sport everywhere. My Excellency wonders if a time will finally come after a last great hunting party is done when witches will cease to be fair game and witchcraft trials a diversion no longer enjoyed by anyone as everyone will have forgotten its rules of play. Perhaps, the world is but a few generations away from a time when witches will be relegated to those fringes of society inhabited by the likes of actors and circus performers, while magic which man has always taken for granted as an integral part of daily life will disappear to be replaced by reason and so much ordinariness.

It is wonder a few words of no special extraordinariness, expressed as part of a routine of an unknown man's life, has so much power to change men's thinking forever, yet leave the author of such a revolutionary idea anonymous to the ages, but I do not think Newt Visscher will very much care as men are usually much happier with rewards in their own lifetimes seeing as it is impossible for them to enjoy for themselves laurels of posterity, so to be Marquis de Bellevire and Ambassador to Rome and the Pope will have to suffice him.

If My Excellency cannot congratulate him these honors, it is because he has achieved them at expense of my peace of mind and well-being, for Sodomite Lorraine is returned to Court and in favor again, while my children are once more in peril of horrible misalliances being forced upon them. Bastards' Governess is responsible for whispering into the king's ear the notion of that devil lawyer Newt Visscher writing legislation to protect Official Whore's good name, for nothing must reflect badly upon Limping Bastard if he is to become king as all gossip on the backstairs says is plotted on his behalf. Frog La Reynie denied vigorously he had anything to do with Sodomite Lorraine's return to Court, but Monsieur said his darling told him Newt Visscher pleaded mercy with Bastards' Governess on his behalf.

As no one is above being poisoned and dying of it, one can image a world gone topsy-turvy where a bastard inherits the throne of France, for there is none better to accomplish so shocking an affront to majesty than Bastards' Governess. She keeps Sodomite Lorraine under her thumb with threats of perpetual exile in Brittany if he does not work doggedly toward achieving marriages of the king's mouse droppings to my children. She rules over those royal quacks who watch over the queen's health which grows daily more delicate and enfeebled. She eyes the dauphine's first pregnancy with the hunger of a scavenging crow and there is no doubt whatever accoucheur is given charge of her lying-in to bring Monseigneur's firstborn into the world this coming August will manage her as ill and viciously as Dumb Beauty was in her childbed.

His Majesty has re-christened Bastards' Governess as La Solidité and she is true if unacknowledged queen of Versailles, whereas Official Whore lurks with unnerving stubbornness in the background and at the fringes of Court, ever waning in presence and ever waxing in fatness, yet a lost soul unable to let go illusions of glory days and grandeur a longtime disappeared. Her Majesty's now sickly constitution renders her an irrelevant being, and even if the dauphine presents the State with an heir, she is a fat, lazy, stupid milch cow of no consequence except for breeding.

Should the queen die it is now most obvious the king would contract a most grievous misalliance with La Solidité which Court etiquette and propriety would at least require to be kept utterly secret, but this would in no way keep all courtiers from seeking her favor or fawning before her like Turks. And while I think on it that other witch, Die Rotzenhäuserin, may soon find a reward similar to the one sought by La Solidité of the king, for they say Frog La Reynie's wife's health fails her in a manner similar to Her Majesty, so everyone fully expects the lieutenant general will soon be possessed of a new spouse.

Monsieur and My Excellency did great battle concerning who would be my son's next governor, for Sodomite Lorraine had convinced him to appoint one of their boys who is without question the most loathsome sodomite in the kingdom, always strolling through Tuileries gardens to whistle for boys or prowling the parterre of Opera for young men. Monsieur tried to reassure me, saying, "He is repented his sins many years and cured of his vices long ago." "How fortunate for us all. No doubt it is as you say, Monsieur, but it is also neither useful nor necessary to use my son to test this notion," I replied. Straightaway I went to the king who agreed, then commanded Monsieur to appoint a man renowned throughout France for his impeccable conduct and reputation which pleased me greatly, but Sodomite Lorraine is being very sulky about it and Monsieur is taking his part.

Because Your Highness asks it I did speak with La Chatte Comtesse before she departed France forever. All her life she disliked the country and cared for nothing but the life of cities, so she was extremely bored in Savoie with her husband and told me he once said to her, "Good God, madame. If ennui is gnawing you to death, take some amusement. Here are horses and dogs and forests. Will you hunt?" "No," she said, "I dislike hunting." "Will you embroider?" "No, I dislike embroidery." "Will you take a walk or play at some game?" "No, I dislike both." "Then what will you do," he asked. She said, "I cannot say, but I dislike innocent pleasures." She always led an irregular life and penance of exile will probably not change her ways. Why Your Highness wants to know this crap about that slut I cannot imagine, but there it is.

I thank Your Highness with all my heart for the most generous gift of twenty thousand pounds which is not unlike a small inheritance.

I shall use it to pay some minor debts and for modest pensions I give each year to my faithful retainers as I cannot ask Monsieur to help me with this expense, for he laughs at me for giving money to people who use it for their daily bread rather than for idle amusements as his pretty boys do.

A last word concerning La Solidité as it is true we are usually punished in this world by our own sins, for her one rival she managed to be rid of in body seems never will leave us in spirit. Shortly after the king acquired Dumb Beauty she set the fashion of tying up one's hair with ribbons and lace which came about in the most ridiculous manner when she fell from her horse, became totally disheveled and to revive her coiffure, removed her garters from her thighs were they properly belong and used them on her head where they have no business. At that time His Majesty found this act of utter stupidity charming, so all the ladies rushed to parrot the imbecile's adorable ways.

Now all female heads in France are towers of pleated lace, ribbon and hair which reaches a bit higher to the heavens with each passing season, so within a few years with just a bit more height women's faces will appear to protrude from the middle of their bodies. The king grumbles bitterly against this fashion of the hair with its pronounce effect of making the ladies look like turkeys which costs him more in time and worry than all his conquests on the battlefield, but his complaints go unheeded by all who refuse to part with their 'La Fontanges.' This is the king's defeat by coiffure and La Solidité must endure her rival's mocking from every woman's head in the kingdom.

This is the news. My two holy terrors are making such a rumpus I can hardly hear myself think and I am being called, so I must leave now as Monsieur le Duc has come for a visit.

I hug and kiss you with all my heart,
Liselotte

Omens of Death: murder of crows, unkindness of ravens, tiding of magpies

Wednesday–21 January 1682–Feast of Saint Agnes
Hotel Reynie

Crows were originally white birds. In their snowy guise, they were guardians of virtue. It was the fateful assignment to watch over a faithless woman which soured them black. It was being a tattletale that dyed them from pallid to pitch, wound their clock from day's saturation of light into night's absence of color, reversed their time from hoary wisdom to ominous folly. It was the hateful look of a Classical god which forever changed their color in men's iconography to be harbingers of Death.

In man's ancient memory crows were tattlers and messengers were crows. It's the reason messengers who had nothing good to announce were put to death: to honor crows as Death's heralds. Hugin and Munin's everlasting revenge for their fall from grace is that instant of hate we have for those who bring us bad news.

There's that special queasy feeling in your stomach which only Marie-Julie can induce. Soon, it'll become a prolonged, genuine pain you associate only with her. The pain in your stomach is making you dizzy. What good is shaking your head to regain your equilibrium? Your life will wither black at Anne-Sophie's final denouncement.

Marie-Julie's asleep in her bedroom. Rush in. Slap her till she's awake and able to put up a vicious struggle. Then you can beat her with your fists and justify your hands around her throat. Choke incoherent cries from her. What's wrong, Gabriel? Why have you stopped? Because she's cowering and whimpering? Something's gone terribly wrong. What's this childlike begging in her eyes? Do you think perhaps she's paralyzed with fear? Your wife's just like the little prostitute, Therese. Isn't she? Nothing but a pathetic, wounded animal. She's been abused into submission by her brother, and possibly, by her father before him. You never noticed it before? Did she hide it so well from you for the last twenty years? Or do the advantages of your wealth and power just disguise it better? Maybe, you've never seen it, because in your heart, you've never cared about her.

Gabriel let go his rage on inanimate objects around him. He destroyed the room. "Get out before I kill you, you fucking immoral cunt. I've known for two years all your miscarriages were abortions. My own son-in-law told me it's your brother who's been your lover all these years. In my home. I shielded your sins and buried my pain because a scandal would have destroyed my entire family. But my daughter. My daughter. What kind of a man do you think I am? You let him do it. You gave him my daughter."

Gabriel, what's she doing? Why's she clawing at herself? Those eyes belong to a wild, angry animal. Why are you dumb and inert while she cries those menacing howls? Doesn't she know her brother had been raping Jeanne-Jacqueline practically every night for nearly a year? Not possible. But obviously she doesn't. She rages like Medea scorned.

A new fury rose up between them and sucked all the air out of the room, until they were both exhausted and gasping for breath, until quiet had eaten all life out of them, and only anguish was left.

"Why didn't you kill him," she whispered. "My own daughter. Didn't you have the courage? What kind of weakling are you?"

What's this serene mask covering her eyes? Why are you afraid to look at her, Gabriel?

"Get him a royal pardon, so he can come back. Do something useful for a change. He'll come back. Then, I'll kill him."

"So coldly sweet, so deadly fair, we start, for soul is wanting there."

Armand, come. Enter the banquet hall. See a young woman whose excessive sorrow has ruined her beauty. On her lap, on a silver dish—in her loving arms—is an embalmed head bespattered with blood. She sobs disconsolately while kissing the head's tongue passionately with her own. A comet-star reflects off the platter to form a halo around the head and this woman's caresses. Opposite her is a man: naked, except for a black wolf's skin. The wolf's head helmets him; the pelt mantles his shoulders. He holds a beautiful woman in an erotic embrace, and whenever he stops fondling her, the faded beauty sets aside the dish.

Rex Mundi whose face was covered by a dim silver moon put His mouth to Armand's ear.

Once, I was of beautiful face and figure. Once, I was a great king. But nothing in this world is perfect. My curse was a faithless wife. She sought to be rid of me. To supplant me with her lover. Finally, she bewitched me into a wolf, but when she should have said the words, "Be a wolf! With the understanding of a wolf," instead she said the words, "Be a wolf! With the understanding of a man." My wife gave her lover all that rightfully belonged to me. Now, I am revenged. My faithless wife forever adores the remains of her sins. As her grief diminishes her beauty it enhances mine.

Rex Mundi's iron lips kissed him.

Before Decay's effacing fingers have swept the lines where beauty lingers, the branch of the wild rose on his coffin keep that he may not move from it.

Armand turned away—after looking attentively at the satin steel of His face—and whispered softly, "Thy corse shall from its tomb be rent; Then ghastly haunt thy native place, And suck the blood from all thy race; There from thy daughter, sister, wife, At midnight drain the stream of life. Yes, I too can love."

Concatenated sins

Tuesday–3 February 1682–Feast of Saint Blaise
Hotel Reynie

Is gratitude a sign of noble souls? Is this the lesson of Androcles and the lion? Is a thorn in a paw so very different from a fishbone in a boy's throat? Legend says, before Blaise encountered the bone, he healed a cave-full of sick wild animals and rescued a poor woman's pig from a wolf who had it by the throat. Was the Bishop of Sebaste hoping his good deeds wouldn't go unrewarded? He was martyred on 3 February 316. What's the lesson this fable teaches? Can men tame and heal beasts more easily than man's nature? Is the blessing of throats to honor a fish caught in a boy's throat or a pig caught by the throat? When a man has his throat blessed is it to cure him of ailments and thorns he may regurgitate in the name of piety?

It was a tea party: de Visscher, La Reynie and Lorraine around a table set three for tea. There was ink, quill and paper for Michel;

an empty place setting for Gabriel; and Lorraine sipped oolong and dribbled compliments.

"Why, Monsieur de La Reynie, what a lovely room. Well appointed. Very masculine. You're a very, very gracious host. Tea is excellent. Very English. Very fashionable."

"Don't look at me like that."

"Well, they say you like the boys at La Pomme de Pin from time to time. French passive, I think."

In an unguarded moment words fell out of Michel's mouth as he stifled a laugh. "Didn't you already get your throat blessed today, Monsieur de Lorraine?"

Lorraine smiled weakly and sipped his tea.

"Maitre de Visscher will write down everything you say. Coast of Brittany isn't very pleasant this time of year, is it? Cold. Damp. Wind chills you to the bone. Salt in the air's bad for your complexion. Been there over a year. It's a long time. Didn't expect it to be this long, did you?"

"Are you suggesting, Monsieur de La Reynie, Monsieur has a new favorite?"

"You're still the love of Monsieur's life."

"It's that bitch, Liselotte. Like the first one. Meddling wives. Always getting me exiled."

"Actually, Madame tolerates you better than you deserve. It's the other bitch, Madame de Maintenon. Every time the king's on the verge of giving in to Monsieur, Maintenon whispers in his ear. And there's an end to it. You don't return to Court."

"Ungrateful, miserable bitch of a governess. Are you going to help me, Monsieur de La Reynie?"

"I might."

Michel smiled slyly at Lorraine. He munched a pastry, ruminated, finished his tea and motioned for another cup. Gabriel gestured for Lorraine to help himself.

"Maitre de Visscher, please be careful not to put words in my mouth. I'm the one who got her the governess position. Occasional Concubine is her bastard. Some nasty business her uncle sexually abused her when she was young." Lorraine took a sip of tea. "Laying blame on Montespan was easy. She's guilty of all sorts of disgusting behavior anyway. I thought it'd be nice to be the official whore. You know, while Monsieur was regent and Limping Bastard was still a minor."

Michel said, "But, what about the dauphin? And the king?"

"Just like she poisoned Melonhead. Was poisoning him for close to a year before he died. Francoise will get rid of anybody and everybody who's in her way. She'll outlive us all. You'll see. She's been behind every attempted poisoning of the king and the dauphin for years. La Voisin was her cohort."

Gabriel said, "But, why does she want the king dead? Doesn't she want to be the next official whore?"

"Monsieur de La Reynie, it's what I want to be. She wants to be an eminence grise. Has Limping Bastard by the throat. Adores her, he'll do anything she says. She's going to make Limping Bastard king."

"Then, why hasn't she tried to poison Monsieur or Madame? Or you?"

"She's not a firebug. Doesn't burn down buildings just to make herself feel good. There's no reason to poison Lotte. She's never done anything to hurt me. No reason to poison the queen or even Montespan. They're not in the way."

"That's what all this horror has been about? The governess wants power? You want to be the official whore?"

"Well, that's not a very delicate way of putting it."

"What about the queen's sudden illness last year? Is Maintenon trying to poison her?"

"I was in Brittany already. Had nothing to do with it. Things changed unexpectedly after the 'unfortunate incident.' Maybe, the queen's illness came from God."

"Now, what about your other behavior? With Chevalier de Rais at La Pomme de Pin."

"Oh. You know about that. Well, Monsieur de La Reynie, a man should try everything at least once, I say. Don't you think? Who told you about that ugly nasty surgery thing? I only watched. Once. I swear, it's the truth. Why would anybody want to do that?"

"Why would you?"

"I don't."

"Don't lie to me. Seven years in the galleys didn't cure you of the habit."

"I've never been near a galley." Lorraine looked directly at Michel. "Did you tell him all about Chasteuil and Esclavage? Oh, my God."

Michel's expression was stunned and panicked. Gabriel looked at him suspiciously, then accused Lorraine, "You're Esclavage."

"No, I'm not. Who told you such a ridiculous lie? Good, Jesus. Some whore at La Pomme de Pin told you I was that monster Chasteuil's cohort. You believed her? I? Philippe de Guise-Lorraine, Chevalier de Lorraine-Armagnac, son of the most illustrious Comte de Harcourt? Albeit a younger one. Preposterous." Lorraine was indignant. "Well, tell him, Maitre de Visscher. Or shall I?" His pique immediately wheeled around to outflank Gabriel. "Chasteuil's your real father-in-law, Monsieur de La Reynie. Didn't know, did you? Georges Desgrez married Chasteuil's sister, Marie-Julie. Your wife's named for her. She hanged herself, eventually. Courts gave Chasteuil's three brats to their aunt after their mother, Marie-Jacqueline, came to an untimely, and they say, a peculiarly unpleasant end. The niece-sister Chasteuil went to the galleys for murdering was Francoise, the daughter of his other sister-aunt, Jeanne."

A whirling dervish possessed Gabriel's head. His stomach growled an angry pain which spun his thoughts out of control. He couldn't think of any questions.

Michel took command. "How do you know all this?"

"From Balthasar. Francoise, Madame de Maintenon, is Francois Galaup de Chasteuil's cousin-sister by her uncle Armand, attorney-general of Aix-en-Provence, who's Chasteuil and Occasional Concubine's father. This incest business in Monsieur de La Reynie's family is very confusing. His children and grandchildren are consanguineous to the Chasteuils and Francoise in so many ways. It's so difficult keeping it all straight."

Michel clenched his teeth. "How long have you known?"

Lorraine chose another pastry. "Excuse me. Please. Maitre de Visscher. I haven't finished my story. Marie-Jacqueline's corpse was much more bizarre than the one they found in that Carmelite monastery. And then, there was a strange rumor the son used to sleep in the family crypt to keep his mother company. They found her dug up one day, all rotted and moldy looking. The boy was singing Dies Irae to her. At least, it's what they say."

Michel watched the tremor in Gabriel's hands.

Lorraine munched on a pastry like a dumb cow chewing its cud. "Years later, Chasteuil went back and did to his niece what he'd done to Marie-Jacqueline. Would have done the same to his daughter, but they caught him. No one believed his son was involved, he was too young. They said he'd been forced to watch, but he did it too."

"It's all lies."

"Is it? Because you're not capable of it? Or because sex with a hot wash of blood is so repulsive and fascinating to the point of shame you can't admit it. Men are capable of anything under the right circumstances. Even you, Maitre de Visscher." Lorraine turned to Gabriel. "You look perplexed, Monsieur de La Reynie."

Michel continued his interrogation. "You said there were three children. But, there's only Monsieur de La Reynie's brother-in-law and wife."

"The baby, Louis. Balthasar said Chasteuil sold him. To the Vatican. He grew up to become an opera singer. Claudia, Messalina, Luisa, Zambinella. Balthasar wouldn't tell me her name. But she was one of the famous ones."

"Stop your silly jokes. Where's Chasteuil now? Where's Desgrez?"

"How should I know? Balthasar doesn't tell me everything."

Gabriel's trance lifted. "Who's Balthasar?"

Lorraine shrugged his shoulders and swallowed the pastry in his mouth. "Melchior, Caspar and Balthasar. Old, young and middle-aged. Asia, Europe and Africa. Gold, frankincense and myrrh. Royalty, divinity and death. Even I know my Three Wise Men."

Gabriel looked at this man, who sipped his tea and chatted gaily with a nonchalance reserved for afternoon gossip parties, and winced. "The former maitre d'hotel of Saint-Cloud, Morel wasn't Chasteuil?"

"No. Morel had always been himself. Chasteuil arranged for a doctor to poison Morel, then faked his own death by replacing

Morel's identity with his own. Then, Chasteuil poisoned the doctor. Balthasar was in charge of it all. When will you get me back to Court?"

"Why should I?"

Michel said, "Because, Monsieur de Lorraine is the only one who can keep a constant eye on Madame de Maintenon, so she doesn't poison the king or the dauphin."

"I don't need Monsieur de Lorraine for that, I'll tell the king myself."

"Where's your proof, Gabriel? Who'd believe you? The king won't listen to any calumny against her. He's in love with her now. Open your mouth and you'll disappear into some remote fortress-prison like Exiles."

"It's true, Monsieur de La Reynie. Ever since Melonhead's death. She carried on and grieved so much. The king's in love with her maternal instincts. She has him by the throat too, just the way she does Limping Bastard. When will you get me back to Court?"

"You've finished your tea. Sign your statement. Then, you may leave whenever you wish."

While Lorraine read the deposition, Gabriel walked to another part of the room and sat down again. A stiff-backed chair was all Michel and Lorraine saw of him.

"Monsieur de La Reynie, it's not exactly as I said it. Most of it's missing. It's just about Francoise and me. And almost all of it's terribly exaggerated."

Gabriel said, "Just sign it and leave, Monsieur de Lorraine."

Lorraine held out a pastry to Michel. "What did he say?"

Michel threw the pastry on the table and hauled Lorraine from the room.

Francois-Michel de Visscher escorted Philippe Chevalier de Lorraine to the courtyard. Lorraine paused before getting into the coach. Michel stood with his back to the building.

"Your father-in-law has no idea, does he?"

"About Andreas? No. Thank God, he forgot to bring it up. Your recitation unnerved him too much. He knows about Andreas and you visiting Maintenon the day the page was murdered. Monsieur le Duc was spying on all of you and told him."

"Not that. About you and me. And Rome. A good thing while it lasted, the three of us. Andreas was always a little too mature for my taste. But you're still so very beautiful, Michel. I'm going to see him after I leave here. Maybe, you could get away for awhile."

"Don't be obvious, Philippe. Look up to the second floor. He's watching us, isn't he."

"Yes, he is. He'll never find out from me. Andreas would cut my throat if I did anything to hurt you. He'd assassinate the Pope for your sake. Even the great men of this world have their weaknesses. You're his. You could've robbed him blind, and he would've bent over happily for the privilege, but you're basically an honest man. It's why you never amounted to anything, Michel. And, you never will."

"Where's Chasteuil and Desgrez? And, how did you really find out all that stuff?"

"How is it you don't know? Andreas tells you everything. As God is my judge, Balthasar told me about the family. Last year. Except about Francoise. I've always been very nice to Balthasar, so he told me about her just before I left Rome. So, I could make a little pocket money from her for keeping quiet about it. What was the harm? Don't be upset. I had no idea you didn't know."

"Balthasar just happened to tell you the entire Chasteuil-Desgrez family history. When? Same day the page was murdered and you ran to Andreas for help? Why would Andreas have Balthasar do such a stupid thing?"

"What do you mean?"

"Ask Andreas. Good luck with the rest of your life, Philippe."

"Don't say that. Sounds so final."

"Yes, it is."

Tit for tat

Tuesday—3 February 1682—Feast of Saint Blaise
Hotel Beauvais

Balthasar, is that an ecstatic gaze in your eyes? Why is that? Why are you so happy? Is it your six groups of six longhair dachshunds? All your groups are not only equivalent, they're equal. They're not only equal, but six times six is an even number squared which yields an even number. To square a number, the second power of a quantity, second is a form of two, an even number. Squares have four equal sides, and four is an even number. Balance, equalization and visual symmetry. It's all you wanted and it's what your all-powerful master cajoled Madame into doing with the dogs—just to please you. Isn't it a relief you don't have to kill three dogs with the longhair? Especially, as you like them better than the bald ones.

Andreas sat on the wide, elegant sofa in the reception salon, sipping a glass of white wine. Balthasar had so much intellect and common sense, except when it came to odd numbers. "Happy now?"

Balthasar bowed deeply. "Herr Graf, your kindness affects me to my very soul."

Lorraine waltzed in and stood next to Balthasar. He frowned at Lorraine who frowned at Andreas who smiled sarcastically. "Philippe, what are you down at the mouth about now?"

"La Reynie served me English tea. And, he didn't expect me to suck on anything."

"Stuffed yourself silly with pastries too. You're not twenty-eight anymore, my dear. You'll be forty this year. Same age I was when we met. I still have my handsome, hard body. You're getting a bit..." Andreas leaned forward and poked Lorraine's stomach. "...if you're not careful, Philippe, you'll get pudgy. Like Monsieur."

Lorraine was bewildered. "How do you know? I left there only a few minutes ago."

"Sit down. Understand something. I control Francoise who now has the king firmly under her thumb. While you've been out of touch, she's suggested to the king he needs a law written to protect him and his little bastards from Montespan's lapse in judgement over this witchcraft affair. The king's asked La Reynie to have Michel write this law. The reward is a title."

"Is he going to be a marquis?"

"Once you're back at Court, you'll tell Monsieur it's Michel who's brought you out of exile. Monsieur might express some gratitude to the man who's reunited him with his beloved. You'll ask Monsieur to ask the king for the ambassadorship to Rome and the Pope for Michel."

"Why? Ask that bitch, Francoise. What's in it for me?"

"You're really a brainless twit. She has no reason to ask for it. It'd look suspicious. If it comes from you, through Monsieur, the king will think it's just one sodomite boy helping out another. And, as we all know so well, His Most Christian Majesty never says 'no' to his brother, unless Francoise interferes."

"I'm not one of the boys. Michel's going back to Rome anyway. He doesn't need a title and a prestigious career. If everybody in my family died, I'd only be a comte. Michel's going to be a marquis, isn't he?

"Sorry, dear, I forget. You're like Gaius Julius Caesar. Every man's woman, and each woman's man. Can't make up your mind what you are."

"It's just like Michel said. You really didn't help me out over that business with the page."

"Get the story right. Desgrez was never to let you out of his sight until an opportunity arose to ruin you. The page was chance, but his seizing the opportunity wasn't. If it hadn't been the page, it would've been something else. He did an excellent job of things, don't you think?"

"What if I don't want to? What's in it for me?"

"You'll get it done, Monsieur de Lorraine, or exile in Brittany will become fatal. In the manner of the ancient Roman executions." Balthasar waited until Lorraine's fearful expression was to his liking. "And furthermore, Monsieur de Lorraine, since when am I spoken of in front of strangers? I don't exist, monsieur. Or have you forgotten?"

"Philippe. Open your mouth out of turn again, and you'll speak with no language but a cry."

Lorraine skewed his mouth. "I suppose you expect me to open my mouth now."

Andreas was bored. "Go back to Brittany, Philippe. I'm not Saint-Blaise and I'm in no mood. Get someone else to stick it in your mouth and bless your throat today."

fire & ice

Thursday–23 April 1682–Feast of Saint George
Chateau Versailles

Look. Look up to the heavens. Into an infinite, luminous void. Darkness. Midnight blue. A sliver of a silver moon. Stars. Planets. A breeze. Soft white clouds sailing through a clear sky. Sounds of a peaceful night in springtime. A friend beside you. Life can be pleasant, even at the Court of Versailles.

On a spacious terrace adjoining Liselotte's apartments, several dozen German sausage dogs played with abandon: sensing Monsieur le Duc was more dominant than Sigi, they tried to make him lead dog of their pack; did their business even less discreetly than courtiers behind curtains in the palace corridors or on the backstairs; tripped up Monsieur-le-Valet-who-belongs-to-Monsieur-le-Duc as he desperately complied with orders yelled at him over a din of barks and growls; and generally, misbehaved with the innocent charm of Madame's son.

Tap, tap, tap went an impatient foot. One hand slapped a letter into the other to the same beat. "Over there, Monsieur-le-Valet-who-belongs-to-Monsieur-le-Duc." The valet shifted a telescope and its tripod to the other end of the terrace; he waited for a next order to readjust its placement. "What do you think, Monsieur le Duc?"

He smiled lamely.

"Over here. No closer. A bit left. Too far. Back again. Come closer. Closer. No. No. Too close. No. Over there." Her arm made a wide arc; she pointed to the opposite end of the terrace. "Well, what are you waiting for?" She waved her finger at her cohort. "Monsieur le Duc, kindly tell your lazy, good-for-nothing valet to move the telescope."

His expression was the same as before.

"Madame, if I may suggest, Your Royal Highness and Monsieur le Duc are placed in exactly the proper spot, and perhaps, I should bring the telescope to you, rather than you to the telescope."

"Splendid, Monsieur-le-Valet-who-belongs-to-Monsieur-le-Duc. That is a most useful idea. I cannot imagine why Monsieur le Duc did not think of it himself."

"Madame, see why I never go anywhere without Prunelle?"

"You are speaking, Monsieur le Duc. Are you no longer a big hairy spider?"

"No, I'm quite myself. I didn't want to interrupt while you were giving orders to Prunelle."

"I did not know your valet had a name. How curious. But, this is about your valet and not about the shooting star." Liselotte shoved a letter under his nose. "See, Monsieur le Duc, according to His Highness my Onkel, the shooting star will appear for the first time tonight and continue every night for the next seven days."

The valet held up a lantern. Monsieur le Duc squinted and read out loud, "In this same year on 24 April the comet-star was seen not only in England, but or so they say, throughout the entire world, shining for seven days with great brightness."

"The comet, Monsieur le Duc, was an augury of great destiny or an omen of doom. Harold Godwineson asserted it was a sign from God he was the rightful king of England, and would defeat his enemies. William, seventh Duke of Normandy, made the same claims. Unfortunately for Harold, William the Conqueror."

"Monsieur le Duc, Madame has made a small witticism. Brava, Madame." The valet bowed.

"How nice. But, Madame, according to this letter the chronicler was Florence of Worcester, a monk. The year was 1066. Which was."

"Six hundred sixteen years ago."

"Yes, Madame, just what Prunelle's said. We've missed it."

"Monsieur le Duc, read on. A twenty-six year old astronomer, Edmund Halley, estimates this shooting star makes its tour of the heavens about every seventy-six years. He has calculated its perihelion and predicts a next pass will be on Christmas night in 1758. My Excellency, of course, shall be dead. Your Highness might be alive, but you would be—"

The valet said, "One hundred fifteen years. Madame would be but one hundred six years."

"My Excellency does not plan on being alive. If we count backwards from 1758, we get 1682. This is today."

Monsieur le Duc frowned. "But, Madame, the twenty-fourth is tomorrow."

"After midnight it is the twenty-fourth."

"But perhaps, it's tomorrow night, after the sun goes down, but before midnight."

"This is true. But it could also be tonight, after midnight, but before the sun comes up."

"Is it really the same one, Madame? You're sure? Comet-stars are always omens. Nothing good ever comes of them. If it shows up on the twenty-fourth, it'll be creepy, just the way that monk said. Something bad will happen."

"Eight things there be a comet brings, when it on high doth horrid rage: wind, famine, plague and death of kings; war, earthquake, floods and doleful change."

"Yes, Madame, see. Just as Prunelle's said."

"Monsieur le Duc, do not be a superstitious fool. It is but an old German rhyme, and nothing more. Nothing will happen. You must take your example from My Excellency and be of a scientific mind and nature."

"It's a shame. In 1758, it'll make for an entertaining show at Christmas. Probably not as nice as fireworks though. Don't you think so, Prunelle?"

"Most certainly, Monsieur le Duc."

Monsieur le Duc shivered. "Madame, do we have to stand here all night? It's very chilly. Prunelle, why don't you bring some wood out here and build us a nice big fire." He called after his valet who'd disappeared through the doors to a salon. "And bring some chairs, and foot stools, and some warm blankets. And something to eat and some hot chocolate." He turned to Liselotte. "I'm so blessed. My Prunelle's such a good man. What a pleasure."

With her eye glued to the telescope, she scanned the heavens and had only half an ear for him. "Bah! Six pleasures define men in France, Monsieur le Duc. I did not think you one of them." She looked at him and waved her finger. "Because, not one of them is worth the Devil."

Monsieur-le-Valet-who-belongs-to-Monsieur-le-Duc reappeared with provisions and an army of servants for a midnight picnic. He wrapped a sable blanket around his master. Gabriel followed the valet onto the terrace and bowed, elegantly, politely to Liselotte and Monsieur le Duc.

"And speaking of the Devil." She waved her finger in his face. "Monsieur le Duc and I are engaged in a scientific experiment to observe a scientific phenomenon. Go away, Monsieur de La Reynie, for if you stay and are the cause of our missing the shooting star tonight, we shall be most annoyed with you. What do you want?"

"Madame. The strangest thing happened tonight at my audience with the king. And it concerns me greatly on your behalf."

"The strangest things, with the most unpleasant consequences, always seem to happen when you have an audience with the king."

"I'm not responsible for Monsieur de Lorraine's return to Court."

"But your son-in-law is. Monsieur said Monsieur de Lorraine told him Maitre de Visscher pleaded mercy with Bastards' Governess for that worthless, good-for-nothing sodomite. For me, it is the same as if you had betrayed My Excellency yourself."

"Grrr. But this, Madame, is old news about Monsieur de Lorraine's former exile, and not about Monsieur de La Reynie's peculiar audience with His Majesty of this evening."

"Last November, His Majesty commanded Maitre de Visscher to find a way of protecting Madame de Montespan. This evening I handed over the solution. Unsolicited, the king gave me royal warrants bestowing a marquisate and a prestigious ambassadorship."

"So. Your son-in-law drafts a silly law to protect a mean bitch's reputation, and he is rewarded with fabulous gifts, while you who dirtied your hands and burdened your conscience with deaths and imprisonments of so many hundreds of poor souls is not even thanked. If this is your complaint, I do not feel sorry for you. It is true there is no justice in this world."

"No, Madame. It's not my concern. Your Highness is German and must have heard of the von Fuggers of Augsburg. One of them, Andreas Graf von Fugger is the Pope's banker."

"Everyone who counts for anything knows of the von Fuggers. They're the wealthiest family in the world. Even I've heard of them." Monsieur le Duc smiled. "Grrr, Monsieur de La Reynie. You think he was the German with Monsieur de Lorraine and Madame de Maintenon?"

"Yes, Monsieur le Duc. But, Madame, in many of your letters you identify one of Maitre de Visscher's friends as Kaspar Paumgartner. I think he's really Graf von Fugger. How do you know about this friendship with Graf von Fugger?"

"Monsieur de La Reynie, you said I named Kaspar Paumgartner as Maitre de Visscher's friend. And this is the name I wrote. I did not write Andreas Graf von Fugger."

"Madame, when the first Madame was poisoned, Monsieur de Lorraine, my son-in-law and Graf von Fugger lived in Rome. They all knew one another. If I'm correct, then all three are together again in France. Perhaps, they now plot your death."

"I mind my own business and stay out of my husband's bed. I do not filch Monsieur's boys, and more importantly, I do not filch Monsieur's jewels or his dresses or his cosmetics or his perfumes, as Her Highness my Late Cousin was in the bad habit of doing. There is no reason on this Earth to poison me." Liselotte's waved her finger in Gabriel's face. "Well. Monsieur de La Reynie, here is something you should know about. I see you are fully recovered from your own latest bout with poison. Three years in a row now. It is a shame. But, this is about your poisoning and not that of Her Highness my Late Cousin. As for that poisoning, sometimes it is better not to unearth the dead. For if you compromise Monsieur with the plotters, it will make His Majesty most unhappy. And the king will take out his spleen on you, not Monsieur. None of them is poisoning anyone now, are they?" Gabriel shook his head. "Then, the most you can do is pray to the Almighty that He strikes them dead with the French curse."

"The Spanish curse, Madame?"

"You mean to say the French curse, Monsieur de La Reynie."

"No, Madame. Monsieur de La Reynie's right." Monsieur le Duc was delighted with himself. "It's the Spanish curse. Grrr. The Germans and the English call it the French curse. In France it's the Spanish curse. To the Spanish it's the Italian curse. In Italy they call it the German curse. Madame lives in France and ought to call it the Spanish curse. Grrr."

"Spanish curse. Bah! Call it what you like." Liselotte waved her nagging finger at both of them. "But assuredly, a French whore will give it to Monsieur de Lorraine, for that devil leads a most irregular life. And as for the other curse which plagues us all, most especially Monsieur, in whatever country or whatever language, sodomy is the Italian vice. And even the Italians will not argue it false, for they themselves call it so. And this is how Monsieur de Lorraine will give the other curse to those other devils."

Look. Look up to the heavens. All of you. Highest and lowest. Exalted and servants. Men with souls and soulless machines.

Liselotte's finger lost its voice, hooked onto her bottom teeth, immobilized with awe. Sigi and his confreres were mesmerized.

A hazy fireball traveled through the sky, as if the sun had lashed the moon with a silver broom. In its trail, silence glittered onto the Earth. In unison, everyone chorused, "Ahhh...Oooo! Grrr...Woof!"

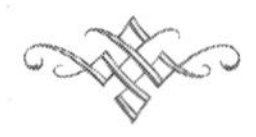

Myrrh: lord of the treasure of death

Saturday–25 April 1682–feast of Saint Mark
Hotel Beauvais

Balthasar was the image of Saint Christopher. With the broad shoulders of Heracles and a delightfully warm smile of Father Christmas, he was a gentle giant who made children laugh and women playful. Men felt safe with him. Whenever he walked into a tavern, drunks sought his company. He bought them drinks and they poured out their woes and their philosophies, and ultimately, their confidences. Sober men sought his company too. He bought them drinks and they also spilled their guts and gushed their secrets. He inspire everyone who met him with the comfort that on a stormy night he could lift them up and ferry them across treacherous flood waters to high ground, just as Saint Christopher had done for a spurious babe in his arms.

Unlike Saint Christopher, Balthasar had intellect and cunning. By profession, he was a spy in the employ of Andreas Graf von Fugger: sometimes on an international scale, trading in State secrets, but most often something more modest, though equally important. He gathered useful information (the kind men are loath to part with willingly and must almost always be pilfered or bought) and he carried out delicate assignments. He was exceptionally good at his trade. He was a chameleon. He was an excellent actor in whatever difficult role Andreas cast him. Heaven had blessed him as the wise man with myrrh and its portents of death. It was men's fear of this gift which made their memories of him dim quickly.

Balthasar, you're Charon without the boat.

Balthasar was a gentleman's gentleman who preferred being in service to gentlemen who preferred gentlemen. As he approached his own half century and a score of years in service to a master blissfully unencumbered by any female presence, he enjoyed a tranquil life among his own kind of maleness. Jakob was Balthasar's preferred partner in all things.

Tonight, spy and valet plotted together in the salle-a-manger. The table was lavishly set. Servants wore festive livery and white leather gloves. Ganymede, slavishly catering to Zeus's every whim, was never more attentive than Jakob was this evening as he supervised two footmen's service to Balthasar and his guest, Jean-Jacques-Armand Desgrez.

From a tureen set in the middle of the table one footman ladled soup into bowls; the other then served this first course. Jakob poured the wine. Every course followed this same ritual: brought to the table and portioned from serving dishes onto plates—in full view. Every course which had been served remained on the table—in full view.

Armand was neither genial nor polite. He imitated all of Balthasar's actions, until the very last mouthful of cheese. He was careful to eat and drink exactly what Balthasar did and never tasted anything until his host had eaten or drunk it first.

Following the entree, as the salad plates were taken away, Balthasar laughed. "Think I'm trying to poison you?"

"Yes. After knowing you all these years. Father always said you were Herr Graf's messenger of death."

"When did you speak with him last? He's disappeared on us. Herr Graf's looking for him."

"It's been over a year since I've heard from him. Francoise hasn't seen him either. It's not like him."

"Your father's never been gone more than a few months without seeing Francoise or you. Where is he?"

"You know I don't know where he is. What's the game?" Armand made a sweeping gesture at the sumptuous meal. "Why all this? Why did Herr Graf go to all the trouble of getting me a royal pardon?"

"Your father's Herr Graf best agent, after me, of course. I hope for his sake he hasn't sought employment elsewhere. Herr Graf wouldn't like it. As you said, Herr Graf went to a great deal of trouble over you, don't be ungrateful. Tell me where he is."

"Don't know. Maybe he's dead. Maybe, you killed him."

"It wouldn't be in Herr Graf's best interests for your father to be dead. It's a bad idea lying to me, Armand. If your father's sworn fealty to another master, it'll be fatal for him and you."

"You've always complained you didn't care for his methods or mine. That what we do is distasteful."

"True. Neither of you has a conscience. You're both amoral."

"And, you're only immoral, so you do have a conscience. How nice for you. But, your conscience lets you sleep as soundly at night as my lack of one does for me. I don't know where he is." The dessert plates where cleared away. Armand stood. "I've no doubt you do. When I finally discover what you've done with him, I'll come for you. Why you've gone through this silly farce for me, I can't guess, but I'm sick of it." Jean-Jacques-Armand Galaup de Chasteuil-Desgrez parted company with Balthasar forever.

Jakob made a nasty face at Armand's afterimage. "Never did like him. The French really are such arrogant assholes." He grimaced at the leftovers. "Why do the French insist on drowning all their food in liquids? There's really nothing worth eating, except the macaroni. And it's Italian."

"I wouldn't were I you. It'll make you sick."

Andreas and Michel suddenly appeared, as if by magic, out of nowhere.

"Don't look so stricken, Jakob." Andreas sat in Armand's chair, toyed with pieces of the table setting and inspected the delicacies. "Bravo, Balthasar. What an excellent liar you are."

Balthasar stood and bowed deeply.

"Shut up, Andreas. I'm in no mood for your inane joviality." Michel looked directly into Balthasar's eyes. "When will you kill him?"

"It's done, Herr Francois-Michel. He'll be in his death agony certainly by morning and dead within a few days, at most." Balthasar was pleased by everyone's confusion. "Arsenic. In small doses. It's in everything. Food, plates and glasses, silver, everything. It's why I insisted Jakob and the footmen wear leather gloves. It's a trick I learned from mountaineers in Tyrol and Salzkammergut. A little bit everyday. Doesn't bother me at all, as long as I don't eat bitter almonds."

Michel warmly embraced him. "Thank you."

Andreas moved his hands away from the table top and placed them in his lap. "Didn't ruin the macaroni too, did you?"

Where the Devil cannot go himself, he sends a woman

Wednesday–29 April 1682–Feast of Saint Catherine of Siena
Hotel Reynie

Seven churches in Asia. Seven spirits before his throne. Seven golden candlesticks. Seven stars in his right hand. Seven lamps of fire burning. A book written within and without sealed with seven seals. A Lamb standing as it were slain having seven horns and seven eyes. Seven thunders uttered their voices. Seven angels who had seven trumpets.

Come and see: behold a white horse, and there went out another horse that was red, and lo a black horse, and behold a pale-green horse: and he that sat upon him, his name was Death, and Hell followed him.

Four beasts had each of them six wings; and round about and within they are full of eyes. Four beasts having harps and golden bowls full of odors. Four beasts gave unto the seven angels seven golden bowls. Seven angels having the seven last plagues. Seven bowls of God's wrath.

Baroness von Ratsamhausen wiped clean the inside of a bowl, then threw aside her leather gloves redolent of ambergris. She sat down at the dinner table and waited. Patric was at her side when her guest arrived.

"I heard on good authority, Captain Desgrez, that you'd been poisoned. But you don't look green around the gills to me."

"Is your skin so white because of all the arsenic in your bath water? Balthasar's not the only one who's an arsenic eater. He forgets how much time he and my father spent together."

"Patric, serve the soup. The one without the arsenic." As the last drop fell from the ladle, Lenor poised her spoon over the dead center of Armand's bowl and skimmed the surface. She sipped the mouthful and smiled shyly at Armand. Circe's soft music sang from her throat. "There. I've tasted it for you. No poison. See. Patric you may serve the wine now. Shall I taste it also for you?"

"I'd prefer some of Gabriel's very expensive armagnac."

"Whatever you want. It's the reason you're here isn't it? Your soup's getting cold."

Armand, taste it. It's delicious. How could anyone resist this creamy suspension of morels with its almond undercurrent? You can't resist it or its smell: gamey and salty-sweet. Like a woman's pussy. It's even pretty to look at. It's white magic shaded a golden ecru from a buttery brown liquid weeping out of these botanic larmes Batavique.

"Let me be perfectly plain. Now that you have your royal pardon, there'll be no getting rid of you. It doesn't suit my plans at all. I'll give you the one thing you want, which you can't have without my help. Jeanne-Jacqueline. She leaves in a few hours for a Carmelite nunnery. In my uncle's safe keeping. He can deliver her there. Or he can deliver her to you."

"And I may go anywhere I want with her?"

"As long as it's not in France."

"It's perfect. Gabriel will never know. I like the idea. Very much. But how are you going to manage it?"

"Herr Graf has agreed to a very fine and very remote villa for you. In Tuscany. Along with his forgiveness, as long as I'm left in control here. Alone. When one thinks of it, life for her with you, really wouldn't be so different from being a Carmelite. All that prayer and hard labor. Have some armagnac. And we'll seal the bargain."

Armand filled Lenor's glass. "You first."

They looked at Patric. "I'll drink it first." He emptied the glass.

Armand, finish your soup. Scrutinize your valet's face. Wait a few minutes. It should be safe now. Savor your armagnac.

Suddenly, his hands became clammy. A cold sweat crept over him. An intense burning swelled in his stomach. His entire body convulsed. Heaving came in waves, but he couldn't vomit. A haze veiled his eyes.

Lenor stood over the writhing body at her feet. Death passing over Egypt spoke. "Patric, move him to the cellar."

"Baronne, how will you get rid of the body without Monsieur General finding out about it?"

"You misunderstand, Patric. Put him in the cellar, because arsenic and bitter almonds are a nasty combination. It's much easier to clean a stone floor."

"Perhaps—"

"Patric. Monsieur de La Reynie and I shall be wed soon." Lenor picked up a large green crystal perfume bottle.

"But Madame de La Reynie isn't dead."

"You aren't needed here any longer. Herr Graf wants you reunited with Chasteuil. A special assignment in the Mediterranean. It'll be you three musketeers all over again. Just like the old days in Algeria. I know my uncle is so much looking forward to it."

"I'd prefer to continue serving Herr Graf in my present employ."

"You haven't a choice. I have to see Herr Graf and my uncle now. And Madame de Visscher. And then, I go to the Chatelet Courts. Meanwhile, clean up this mess. I don't want Monsieur de La Reynie coming home to unsightly filth on the dining room carpet."

Dark night of the soul

"Eli, Eli, lema sabacthani."

The young woman drew back from the writhing body at her feet.

Armand, look at her stone face with its flaming eyes and tangle of serpents dancing voluptuously around her head. Slowly, reluctantly they shrink back into her skull, and the luxurious chestnut curls you love so much fall softly over her rosy flesh. Down past her shoulders, over her breasts, her hair tumbles languidly until it reaches the pelvis which once held your life.

She moved toward his supine form until he could feel the movement of her breath. Sweet it was in one sense, honey-sweet, but with a bitter underlying the sweet, a bitter offensiveness, as one smells in blood.

Armand was afraid to raise his eyelids, but looked out and saw perfectly under the lashes. She went on her knees, and bent over him, fairly gloating. There was a deliberate voluptuousness which was both thrilling and repulsive, and as she arched her neck she actually licked her lips like an animal, till he could see in the moonlight the moisture shining on the scarlet lips and on the red tongue as it lapped the white sharp teeth. He closed his eyes in a languorous ecstasy and waited, waited with beating heart.

Rex Mundi grasped her slender neck and yanked it back, then tenderly He leaned over and gave him a final Kiss. Tears wet Armand's cheeks.

Go to sleep, my son. Hypnos and Thanatos are brothers and sons of Nyx; Chaos the father of an incestuous bed. To dream is to kiss chaos in the night while sleep and death jealously wait their turn.

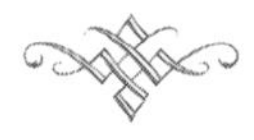

Superstition is not a capital offense, but sodomy is

Wednesday–29 April 1682–Feast of Saint Catherine of Siena
Chatelet Courts

"Monsieur le Marquis de Bellevire. Ambassador to Rome and the Pope." It tasted sweeter than honey on Michel's tongue. "I didn't expect this, Gabriel."

"Do you think men will ever stop taking the Devil and witches seriously? Pass all the laws you like. Say it's nonsense and children's fairytales. But men will always fear being totally alone, and of being touched by the unknown, in the darkness."

"I said, 'thank you,' Gabriel. Didn't expect you to do this for me."

"Didn't. You have well-placed friends. How mysterious."

"But, I thought you." Michel held out the two official documents with royal seals.

"Only acting as messenger of the gods to you."

"Why are you so hateful with me? Have been for months. Stop being coy, that's a game girls play."

Gabriel paced. "I should've had this marriage annulled at the beginning when I could have. You married my daughter out of ambition. Don't give a shit about her at all."

"Well, well, what a surprise. Remember who told you? Has she complained to you? She's my wife. Stay out of it. We'll be leaving soon. If you want us out tomorrow, that's fine too."

"Where will you go? Move my daughter and my grandchildren in with your mistress? Andreas von Fugger?"

"We'll leave today. If Desgrez ever shows up, you deal with him. It's not my problem anymore. We'll be on our way to Rome right after the baby's born."

"Go. But alone. You can't have my daughter or her children. I won't let you."

"You think I'll fill their lives with misery. Like Monsieur does to Madame. Don't make Anne-Sophie choose if you don't want her to disappoint you."

"If she knew what you were, she'd never let you near her children. I'm glad you have your title and your ambassadorship. It'll be easier to get rid of you. I trusted you, loved you like a son. What a fool I was."

A policeman announced Baroness von Ratsamhausen who informed them of Jean-Jacques-Armand Desgrez's arrival at Hotel Reynie.

"I'll get some men. Maitre de Visscher you may do the paperwork for his arrest afterward."

Lenor looked at Michel. "Gabriel, you can't. He has a royal pardon."

"What are you going to do?" Michel spoke more to himself than to Gabriel. "Legally, you can't touch him. If you try, it's the end of you. Leave it alone. It'll take care of itself."

"And, what do you plan on doing?" There was that sadly vulnerable look of his again. That contemplative silence. "You're pathetic and contemptible." Gabriel stormed out.

Michel took Lenor in his arms. "Did you do it right this time?"

"I couldn't live with myself, Michel, if we von Ratsamhausens had twice disappointed you. And Herr Graf. One never disappoints him more than once."

29 April 1682
Feast of Saint Catherine of Siena

Sing me the Dies Irae again, my love

Always, there was Chaos. He spontaneously generated Goddess of All Things. She danced until North Wind, overcome with lust for her nimble feet, metamorphosed into a giant serpent and seduced her. All of creation hatched from the Universal Egg she laid. Or some say, it was black-winged Night—manifest in trinity: Night, Order, Justice—whom Wind inseminated. From her silver egg, nourished in Womb of Darkness, emerged Eros—double-sexed, golden-winged and four-headed—who set the universe in motion. Others claim in the beginning it was abiogenesis of Mother Earth from Chaos. His fond and tender gazes as he watched over her sleep fertilized creation into existence and gave life to their son, Uranus.

Still others tell a dark story. Darkness dawned first from Chaos and from an autoerotic incest came Night, Day, Erebus and Air. From Night and Erebus's incest came Doom, Death, Murder, Sleep, Dreams, Discord, Misery, Nemesis. Incest of Air and Day begat Mother Earth, Sky and Sea. Air's rape of his child, Mother Earth, brought forth Terror, Anger, Strife, Lies, Vengeance, Oblivion, Fear—and Titans who became the first gods.

In the myth of Uranus, he fathered the Titans after Gaia's first attempts at motherhood resulted in Hecatoncheires and Cyclopes. Disowned into Tartarus and the farthest reaches of their father's disappointment in congenitally defective gods, their misery cried out to a mother's resentment which chose her youngest son to commit patricide. While Uranus slept, Cronus grabbed his father's genitals and sliced them off with an adamantine sickle. The blood Uranus spilled on Gaia impregnated her with furious avengers of parricide and perjury. Now, Cronus was sovereign over Earth.

Cronus married his sister and Gaia prophesied one of his sons would strike him dead. Cronus was no fool. He cannibalized his children. He sucked them from Rhea's birth canal as they fought their way out of the safety of her dark womb. Instead of the perilous light of the world, they found another dark passage into their father's ulcerated stomach. Cronus was a potent god. Rhea's belly was always full and so was his, but nothing is more savage than a mother's rage.

It was again the youngest son's lot to take his father's place. Zeus dethroned Cronus with a thunderbolt. Once Zeus was supreme being, he married his sister. Like Mendel's peas, there's no denying an inherited trait.

Stephane Daimlen-Völs

New gods for old. It is the endless cycle of man's longing. As man evolves his gods, one man's religion becomes another man's mythology and another's superstition. Here is Nature's nest of boxes: Heavens contain Earth, Earth, Cities, Cities, Man. All these are concentric: the common center to them all is decay, ruin. It is a fearful state: a concatenation of sins, habitual and customary and concatenated sins. Man and his gods are forever linked immutable.

"Father, come join us." Anne-Sophie was dressed and jeweled for a formal dinner, and looked radiant. "Maman said we should start without her."

"Sorry, I'm not eating with a murderer."

"Gabriel, don't be like that. Join us." Armand held out a folded document. "Want to see it? Signed by the king himself. You're not eating your soup, Anne-Sophie?"

"No, thank you. If I ate anything, I'd vomit. Don't want to ruin dessert."

"More wine, monsieur?" Esclavage poured another glass for Armand.

"Maybe, the wine's bad." Armand tipped over his glass.

"Maybe your luck's still holding." Anne-Sophie stood. "I'm sick of this farce. Adieu."

"Never did like that one." Armand gave Anne-Sophie's memory an evil look. "Let's skip the rest of the meal, Gabriel. But, I'll have some of this very expensive armagnac of yours."

Armand filled Gabriel's glass. "You first."

Both men looked at Esclavage. "I'll drink it first." He emptied the glass.

Marie-Julie walked into the banquet hall. "I'm ready, we may go now."

Armand was genuinely shocked. "Where are you going? I don't want you with me, look at you. You look like a milch cow."

Gabriel stared at him. "Why the devil are you here then? Didn't you come for her?"

"Why would I want your wife? She's too expensive. It was different when you paid her bills, but I can't afford her. I need money." Armand swallowed the armagnac in one gulp.

"You came here to pester me for money?"

"It's one reason." Armand turned to Jeanne-Jacqueline. "Come with me."

"I can't, Uncle Armand, I'm a nun now."

Marie-Julie shrieked with pain. "I'll kill him. My own daughter." She challenged her husband. "Kill him, don't you have the courage to kill him?"

"Not I." Gabriel sneered. "You do it. Go ahead. Do us all a favor."

Armand, look at your hands. Do you feel a cold sweat creeping over you? What's that intense burning in your stomach? Clutching your side won't help. Neither will your pathetic moaning. Your entire body convulses. Heaving comes in waves. But you can't vomit. A haze veils your eyes. Listen to what they're saying about you, Armand.

"When he dies, have this place blessed. Have the entire house blessed. I won't have his soul left behind once he's gone. I want to be completely rid of him."

"But, Gabriel, he needs to disappear. The most expedient is to bury him here in the cellar."

"Do whatever you think best. Only, not in my home. I'll never ask. And, don't ever mention it again. I'll let you get away with this murder, because of my daughter."

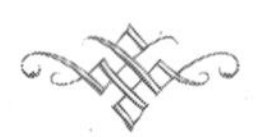

Gabriel made the long journey from the cellars to his daughter's bedroom. He crossed a threshold and silently watched Jeanne-Jacqueline help a maid packing her trunk: each time something luxurious was put in, she removed it and placed it on the bed. Jeanne-Jacqueline was serene.

Gabriel whispered through his tears. "I can't stand the thought of you going."

"But, papa, if you didn't want me to go, why did you pay my dowry? You can't get it back."

"I've changed my mind. You can't go there. I'll pay your dowry to another order's convent. Please. Their life is so brutally harsh and austere. Hard labor and perpetual silence. You'd be dead to the world. I can't bear thinking about it. Please. Don't punish me this way."

"But you said I could. You said I could choose. This is what I want. This would make me happy. Don't you want me to be happy, papa?"

"After you take your vows, I'll never see you again. Don't punish me this way."

Jeanne-Jacqueline hugged Gabriel as tightly was she could. He wept in her arms. "I'm not trying to punish you. You've delayed me leaving nearly a year and a half. If I was angry or hated you, would I have let you?"

"Forgive me."

"You didn't know."

"It was my duty to know. I'll never see you again, if you go there."

"I love you, papa. With all my heart."

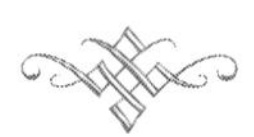

Marie-Julie's dress was the color of verdigris dyed midnight, extravagantly baroque and a beautiful counterpoint to her auburn hair. Gold lace cascading from the sleeves and encircling the neckline delineate the finer points of her life. Fine gold braid and gold-copper ribbon vermiculated among intricate bouquets of delicate flowers embroidered on acres of silk. Her shoes were a perfect match of fabric, laced with gold-copper ribbons to promenade through artificial meadows.

You live in fine details.

Her dress was a lost detail in the grander scheme of her bedroom. She receded into brocade which shrouded the room with a verdure of Allepo pine and eucalyptus. Copper-orange gossamer festooned an artificial sunset which reacted into a poisonous, greenish-blue to lighten the darkness, while a thick, yellow-gold braid cutting through this forest of conflicted desires tied rays of dying sunlight around gardens sewn the colors of semi-precious jewels.

Your life is lost in fine details.

Jeanne-Jacqueline entered her mother's presence. Marie-Julie stoppered a large green crystal perfume bottle and dismissed the maids. She turned to face her daughter who bowed and tried to take her hands to kiss them. She pulled away.

"Maman, I came to say good-bye. I'm leaving in an hour."

Marie-Julie slapped her. "Seductress. Whore. You and your uncle played at Salome and Herod Antipas in my home. Under my nose. Didn't you have enough? You and your sister?"

Jeanne-Jacqueline could only whisper. "Maman. You forget. Salome was Herodias's daughter. It was Herodias who was married to her own uncle, Herod Antipas. And, all of Salome's wickedness, she committed to please her mother's bidding."

Armand, rise up and embrace Rex Mundi.

"I never thought she'd betray me. Did I always misplace my love?"

Why were you angry with her for leaving you? She had no choice. I murdered her for the satisfaction of revenging myself on you. And, for the pleasure. She belonged to me, not to you. It was incest. It was wrong.

"I never thought about her in that way."

All boys feel this way, but they're supposed to outgrow it. Never mind. She poisoned you. And, you deserved it.

"I only ate the soup. My God, the armagnac. Esclavage must be dying too."

Not the armagnac.

"The glass. She poisoned the glass. The way they poisoned the first Madame's cup."

Not that either. A varnish of bitter almonds lacquered over with sugar water. No one saw her but Esclavage.

Rex Mundi took one step to the other side of the room.

See Me as I am.

Jeanne-Jacqueline slipped out of the room, so she could weep alone in the hallway. Sounds of a scuffle and a woman's abruptly stifled cry drew her back to the door of her mother's room. She listened and hesitated, then quietly entered. She closed the door, leaned her back against it and turned the key in the lock.

There was nothing to do but watch. What good would protesting do? It was as good as done. One man, the giant, held her mother's arms behind her back and his hand over her mouth. Her eyes were wild. Like a frightened animal. An accomplice had tied a rope of thick gold braid and satin ribbons around her neck and looped it over a finial in the bed's wooden canopy. He pulled the ribbons taut;

the voice was choked out of her; the giant still held her arms tightly as he pushed her body upward. Then, the men exchanged places. Jeanne-Jacqueline watched her mother's feet search desperately for the floor which was only a finger's width away. Minutes went by. Her feet stopped dancing and came to rest with toes pointed downward.

Embarrassed silence filled the room. The three of them tried to look at one another, but their eyes refused to meet. The giant took a step toward her; with the light touch of a hand, his accomplice stopped him from advancing farther. They all stared at her mother's shoes. What color were they? Dark green. And, the gold-copper ribbons in the shoes matched the trim on her dress. And, the trim matched the ribbons around her neck. The picture was clear. Jeanne-Jacqueline turned away and placed her forehead against the door. The clock ticked. Her heart beat. She turned the key in the lock and left as unassumingly as she'd entered.

Armand, squint if you wish to see an opalescent wraith with four faces, humanized and yet not humane. Rex Mundi is a double Janus of twice two-faced features zooming in and out of focus with eyes always closed in serene sleep. Spectral lights refracting within vapors sparkle through other eyes more numerous than those of Argos, an encrustation of jewels which dazzles at every blink.

"What are you?"

Silent iridescent sparks fly in every direction. He glides closer. He speaks with a quartet of mouths. His words ignite silent embers.

Have you learned anything?

Armand, close your eyes and abandon yourself to an overwhelming embrace and kisses of Rex Mundi who will transport you to ecstasy.

Two black geometric planes intersecting at a dihedral angle stretched into infinity and were pockmarked with an infinite number of glowing doors. Her nakedness more beautiful than he could ever remember, the young woman stood before him, and with a loving glance, pointed to a door.

"Why that one? Why not one of the others?"

"All blessings to you both! And in your delirium your ravings have been dreadful, of wolves and poison and blood, of ghosts and demons, and I fear to say what."

Armand looked at her canine teeth and hesitated. "I couldn't go without you. You were the only one I ever truly loved."

"Sing me the Dies Irae again, my love."

Armand, step over the threshold. Here's a road. Walk moonlight until it turns to dawn. At a crossroad, turn north to face the noonday sun. On through sunlight, into night again toward a comet-star. Little by little it will pass through you until you're invisible in its glare. Finally, you'll be no more, for Sleep has no place it can call its own.

Gabriel found Jeanne-Jacqueline walking in a hallway. He tried to embrace her, but instead, she led him by the hand back into Marie-Julie's room.

"Papa, will you tell she's a suicide? It wouldn't matter to me if she wasn't buried in consecrated ground."

"You hate her more than I."

"She never showed Anne-Sophie or me the slightest affection. We were strangers to her. I almost forgave her. I thought she hated him for what he'd done to me. But, she was just jealous." Jeanne-Jacqueline hesitated, then wept. "Papa, have you ever noticed how much Anne-Sophie resembles Uncle Armand? I never noticed it till today."

Gabriel embraced her as if his heart would break if he her let go. "Jeanne-Jacqueline." His tears fell on her. "You have so many secrets."

"That's why I've chosen a life where it will be easy to keep them."

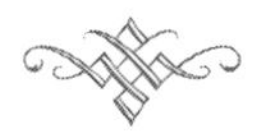

Simony was a sorcerer's prayer

Thursday–6 August 1682–Feast of the Transfiguration
Hotel Reynie

Magus is singular of Three Wise Men. A young man who stands behind a table littered with tools of his hermetic arts—a coin, a cup, a sword—holds a baton of authority wielding destiny. Infinity encircles his head. He's self-mastery and force of will and manipulator of changes unseen. Or these emblems are toys of a juggler and the brim of a foppish hat and a magic wand. He's Trickster: a sleight of hand practitioner. Is he Simon Magus?

Le Bateleur is the first card of the Major Arcana. A footman carried it on a small silver presentation tray.

"It's the gentleman's calling card, Monsieur General."

Gabriel laughed quietly. "Show the gentleman in." The man who stood in the doorway smiling at him was older and thinner than he'd expected and still quite handsome. "Thank you for accepting my invitation. Would you like an armagnac, Herr Graf?"

"Thank you. Didn't expect your daughter to leave. Did you? Especially, after you told her."

"I had no idea she knew or that she didn't care. Or that you and she were such good friends."

"I'll pay you a compliment, Monsieur de La Reynie. Anne-Sophie is the first woman I've ever liked. You raised her well. She understands an important reality of life most women never come to terms with. It's a man's world. Your daughter knows how to use the men around her to get what she wants out of it. She and I shall have great fun together."

"I didn't invite you to talk about my daughter, Herr Graf. I know who murdered my brother-in-law. Who murdered my wife?"

"Gave you a bit of a shock, did she? But she didn't unnerve you too much. You married her anyway, and after an indecently short mourning. As for your wife, well, ask Jeanne-Jacqueline."

"She refuses to tell me. Will only say it was two men. Strangers. I think one was Michel. His motives are compelling enough. Were you the other man?"

"I? I'm a von Fugger. I have servants. You're a gentleman. You should be able to appreciate my position. Certainly, not Michel. I raised him better than that."

"That's not an answer."

"Balthasar. Who's no stranger to either of your daughters. And the other? You know very well whom. Only monsters can kill monsters. But, you need to admit it to yourself, before what's obvious can become apparent. By the way, the armagnac is excellent."

"My daughters are gone. Jeanne-Jacqueline's lost to me forever now. But, I can go to Rome. Next year, or the year after."

Andreas offered his handkerchief to Gabriel. "You have a new wife, Monsieur de La Reynie. Make a new family. Bury the past and forget. Do you really believe you'll ever leave Paris in someone else's keeping to visit Rome? You prefer them pubescent. Paris is good for you. Rome's too old for your taste." He finished the armagnac. "You could write. Reconcile with Michel. Any father would envy Michel's devotion and love for you. Loves you very much."

"If his father had been a good parent, you couldn't have gotten your hands on him."

Andreas was bored. He took back his handkerchief and stuffed it in his pocket. "A sentiment, no doubt, of all men who believe love of the opposite sex is the only natural behavior. Truth is, we're all born what we are. No one makes us what we can't be. Adieu."

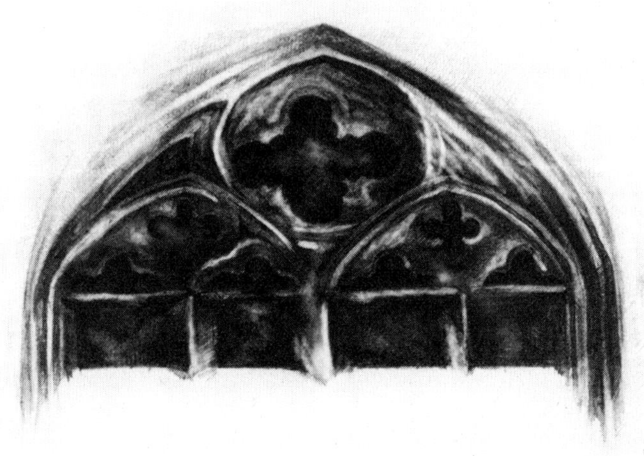

29 November 1722
A Gift for SCF

Arsch lasst nicht von Arsch: nothing new under the sun

Sunday—first Sunday of Advent—29 November 1722
Saint-Cloud

Dear Princeling Friedrich Lewis,

How our wild pigs got so fat this year I cannot imagine as we have had no acorns at all even though the Bois de Boulogne is full of oak trees, and I am certain of this for I examined very carefully a good many of the trees (in fact, I had a good look at quite a lot of them), but did not find a single acorn. But that is not the news.

You will receive but a very short letter, for My Excellency is worse than ever and did not close my eyes all night. Yesterday morning I lost my dear friend, Etienne-Charles, l'Eveque de Vannes. He had no attack. Life just seemed to abandon him. He was a man of great capacity and much merit, and was highly educated though he did not make it apparent. In this he was just the same as his grandfather, the renowned Lieutenant General of Police of Paris, Monsieur de La Reynie. They tell me he chose as his heir the son of his eldest sister.

It is not surprising a person of my seventy years should see so many deaths, young and old, but even so it is always painful to lose a friend, most especially in this detestable country, and in truth in the half century I have lived here, I have found true friendship to be rare as a dodo bird.

I can recall my last encounter with those closest to Monsieur de La Reynie as clearly as the broth in which the French insist on drowning all food. It was at Versailles and the July heat was so vicious the leaves were frying on the trees. Monsieur-le-Valet-who-***belonged***-to-Monsieur-le-Duc circulated air around his master's head with a large, beautiful fan of Brussels lace, while Monsieur le Duc, Siggie and My Excellency watched the maneuverings of courtiers in the salon…

Saturday—feast of Saints Mildred & Silvanus—13 July 1709
Chateau Versailles, France

"I am so sad I could weep. When one is old, so many of one's friends begin to drop dead like flies." Liselotte energetically fanned herself and the dachshund, Siggie. "It is so hot leaves are frying on trees. And yet, it appears the king is cold and suffering from a fit of bizarre behavior."

"How so?"

"Ask your Monsieur-le-Prunelle-who-belongs-to-Your Highness."

Monsieur le Duc twisted in his seat to look at the valet.

"His Majesty has lit a great and blazing conflagration in his grand-cabinet and is burning papers with his Privy Council. Papers from a large black coffer, sealed with the late Monsieur de La Reynie's red seals, from times past, when he was Lieutenant General of Police of Paris. A coffer sealed these last thirty years. Never to be opened, except by His Majesty upon Monsieur de La Reynie's death. A Pandora's jar, a Psyche's box. So they say."

"When Pope Clement VI lived in Avignon, while the Plague was at its height during summer months, his quacks lit great fires in two fireplaces of his bedroom, and had him sit between them all day long. His Holiness sweated a lot, but never caught plague."

"Oh, Madame. Do you think there's plague?"

"Bah! Pshaw. Of course, not. Do they look panicked over the state of their balls?" Liselotte gestured toward a group of courtiers. "When a man contracts plague, Monsieur le Duc, his scrotum turns bloody, then black and stinky with rot, and if he has any sense, he becomes worried over this sad state of affairs. It is the first and sure sign we are beset by plague. As long as they continue to envy and clutch at one another's jewels and not their own, we are safe and in good health."

The valet pointed toward a cardinal and a bishop. Both were strikingly beautiful and bore a strong family resemblance. "Ah. Madame. If Your Highness looks over there."

"Speaking of bloody balls. Do you not find it a scientific curiosity, Monsieur le Duc, no sooner does one speak of a person than he materializes, as if by magic?"

"He's now Francois-Michel Cardinal de Visscher and he's the Pope's secretary. The bishop's one of his sons. They say, these four bachelors are here to claim the late Monsieur de La Reynie's very considerable estate."

"His Highness my Late Papa told me often all prelates in Rome are sodomites, and so it must be very true."

"Oh, Madame, it can't be so. Why he isn't even an Italian. It's the Italian vice. He has eleven surviving children by the late Marquise de Bellevire."

"Gathered like crows on a battlefield, scavenging the corpse for anything which glitters. How considerable is Monsieur de La Reynie's estate?"

"How considerable, Prunelle?"

"Fifty millions. Perhaps more. But at least."

"I should have demanded of His Highness my Late Papa that he buy me a French civil servant for a husband."

"Well, he's still beautiful as an angel. If they're all sodomites in the Vatican, as you say, then it's the reason they must want him walking about in their midst all day long. A little glimpse of Heaven is good for a man's soul."

Michel caught Liselotte's eye and smiled, then motioned for the bishop to follow as he walked toward her. The valet bowed deeply to the prelates. Monsieur le Duc rose, kissed their rings and accepted their blessings over the back on his lowly bowed head. Liselotte clutched Siggie and defiantly refused to budge.

"Madame, may I have the honor of introducing my son, Etienne-Charles?"

"Why, bless me. Monsieur le Duc, do look here. Here is one of your long-lost godsons."

V

Monsieur le Duc crossed his eyes and blinked hard, several times. "When did that happen? I can't recall having a bishop or a sodomite for a godson."

Liselotte looked at Etienne-Charles from head-to-toe, and then from toe-to-head. She addressed Michel with hauteur. "I see, Your Eminence, everyone in your family is a 'religious.'"

"Don't you mean to say a sodomite?"

Liselotte stood and smacked Monsieur le Duc in the face with her fan. "Your Eminence will excuse Monsieur le Duc who is not himself today. He thinks he is a Lutheran. I see His Excellency Your Son the Bishop wears French bishop's robes and not Italian ones."

"His Majesty has been kind enough to confer on Etienne-Charles the Bishopric of Vannes."

"One step away from a cardinal's red hat, and then on to Prime Minister of France. Is this to be your son's calling? Will the tiara keep Your Eminence's head warm in your old age? If so, then you will be the only Pope to openly flaunt his children since. What was the name of that Spaniard turned Italian? Ahhh. Rodrigo Borgia."

"Madame thinks all prelates are sodomites. At least, the ones who live in Rome."

Michel smiled at Monsieur le Duc. "A good Lutheran sentiment, no doubt. I leave tomorrow for Rome, and we'll never see each other again in this life. Perhaps, in the next. Adieu."

"Madame, do you really think Graf von Fugger made Cardinal de Visscher a sodomite?"

"Who told you such crap and nonsense, Monsieur le Duc?"

"Oh. You did. Years ago. I was in one of my fits of not being myself. You don't think I pay attention when I'm not myself, but I listen, and understand every word you say. Always."

"Well, then, Monsieur le Duc, do not be a fool." She waved her finger at him. "The Italian vice is so named for the Italian States. Rome is situated in the Italian States, and so, is predisposed to the Italian vice. Prelates in Rome are predisposed to whatever Rome is predisposed to, which in its turn, is disposed to whatever holds true for the Italian States. Therefore it so follows, and is most logically concluded, by scientific method and observation, prelates in Rome are predisposed to the Italian vice. That is sodomy. To answer your question. No. Graf von Fugger, being a German and neither an Italian nor a prelate, had nothing to do with it. Or with anything else of any consequence in this world."

As for losing spectacular friends Monsieur le Duc came to a sad but spectacular end when one day he suffered from a delusion that had never before afflicted him and thought he was a vampire. On a fine evening this past summer, when a great masque gala was being held in the gardens of Versailles, he tried to swoop down into the crowd to suck the blood from everyone's neck. Monsieur le Duc took a flying leap off the rooftops of the palace and missed. Monsieur-le-Valet-who-***belonged***-to-Monsieur-le-Duc was not there to rescue him for the Almighty had called the valet to a greater service and eternal duties the year before.

If you think there comes a time in everyone's life when there is nothing new under the sun and everything has been done or seen before, I shall tell you a droll story of young Marechal Duc de Richelieu to make a liar of King Solomon, for this young man has a seraglio but very much unlike that of the Turks. All his footmen are women in disguise and he uses them (each and every one in her turn) as valets, so as to have the pleasure of being dressed and undressed by them which is surely something new and unheard of before that only a Frenchman who likes his women as well as he likes his men could invent.

Everything you ask of me, young princeling Friedrich, is ancient history now and were you not a great-grandson of Her Highness my Beloved Tantchen Sophie I should say to you it is unwise to unearth the dead, but as I am old and you are an insistent young man here is an end of it. They say these many years all I wrote concerning that affair of poisons of so long ago is solely of my own thinking, but there was not a courtier in all France who did not think or say or write even worse than My Excellency, as I relied on their gossip, for without it I would have had no stories to tell. The late king never heard any word of it and never knew what people really thought or said about him, for there is nothing like stupendous ego to insulate one from the vicissitudes of public opinion.

I shall tell you about the demise of all those concerned in that scandal in my next letter, for I suffer too much to say more today, and if you could see the state in which I am, you would understand how much I wish it might end, but I must stop now, dear Friedrich.

Tell your mother not to be so impatient as your grandfather is not much younger than My Excellency, so he will not live forever and your father should not have too many more years to wait before he is King of England. The old German proverb is very true that "Arsch lasst nicht von Arsch."

I must go now and remain as always,
Your remotely loving cousin,
Liselotte

This was her last letter. Nine days later, as she lay on her deathbed, she gave this last command to a servant who wished to kiss her hand: "You may kiss me properly. I am going to the land where we are all equal." Liselotte was buried in the French royal necropolis of Saint-Denis where her bones were desecrated and then lost during the Revolution.

Check out these other fine titles by
Durban House at your local book store.

EXCEPTIONAL BOOKS
BY
EXCEPTIONAL WRITERS

Basha
by John Hamilton Lewis

Set in the world of elite professional tennis and rooted in ancient Middle East hatreds of identity and blood loyalties, Basha is charged with the fiercely competitive nature of professional sports and the dangers of terrorism.

Ben Weizman, who has grown up believing his blood parents were killed by Palestinian terrorists. He's handsome, talented and destined to become one of the greats of the game. Nothing seems to be standing in his way: marrying Jenny Corbet, the love of his life, or becoming the number one player in the world. Nothing except the terrible secret his adopted father, Amon Weizman, has kept from him since he was five years old.

Basha, an international terrorist, suddenly appears and powerful members of the Jewish community begin to die. Is the charismatic Ben Weizman on the terrotist's hit list?

The already simmering Middle East begins to boil and CIA Station Chief Grant Corbet is charged with tracking down the highly successful Basha. In a deadly race against time, Grant hunts the illusive killer only to see his worst nightmare realized.

Private Justice
by Richard Sand

After taking brutal revenge for the murder of his twin brother, Lucas Rook leaves the NYPD to work for others who crave justice outside the law when the system fails them. "Mobbed-up" Harry Raimondo's young daughter is murdered, and to find the killer, he needs just the sort of compelling, deep-seated anger which drives Rook.

Rook's dark journey takes him into Inspector Joe Zinn's precinct and on a collison course with Homicide Detective Jimmy Salerno. The Raimondo case was his, and though it has long gone cold, it still haunts him.

Then another little girl turns up dead. And then another. The nightmare is on them fast. The piano player has monstrous hands; the Medical Examiner is a goulish dwarf; an investigator kills himself.

The FBI claims jurisdiction and the police and Rook race to find the killer whose appetite is growing. Betrayal and intrigue is added to the deadly mix as the story careens toward its startling end.

Ruby Tuesday

by Baron Birtcher

Mike Travis sails his yacht to Kona, Hawaii expecting to put LA Homicide behind him: to let the warm emerald sea wash years of blood from his hands. Instead, he finds his family's home ravaged by shotgun blasts, littered with bodies and trashed with drugs. Then things get worse. A rock star involved in a Wall Street deal masterminded by Travis's brother is one of the victims. Another victim is Ruby, Travis's is childhood sweetheart. How was she involved?

Travis begins his own personal search for answers. A rumor of lost studio recordings by one of the world's most infamous bands—tapes that could be worth hundreds of millions—is the only clue he has to follow. But someone is out there ahead of him and more people are dying.

Filled with uncommon atmosphere and style, the story brings together the seamy back streets and dark underbelly of a tropical paradise with the world of music and high finance where wealth and greed are steeped in sex, vengeance and murder.

This hardboiled detective story grabs you by the throat and doesn't let go. A book rich with characters and dialogue so finely drawn they will stay with you long after the last page has been turned.

Deadly Illumination
by Serena Stier

It's summer 1890 in New York City. Florence Tod an ebullient young woman in her mid-twenties—more suffragette than Victorian—must fight the formidable financier, John Pierpont Morgan, to solve a possible murder.

J.P. Morgan's librarian has ingested poison embedded in an illumination of a unique Hildegard van Bingen manuscript. Florence and her cousin, Isabella Stewart Gardner, discover the librarian's body. When Isabella secretly removes a gold tablet from the scene of the crime, she sets off a chain of events that will involve Florence and her in a dangerous conspiracy.

Florence must overcome her fears of the physical world, the tensions of her relationship with Isabella and deal with the attentions of an attractive Pinkerton detective in the course of solving the mystery of the librarian's death.

The many worlds of the turn-of-the-century New York—the ghettos to the gambling dens, the bordellos to the bastions of capitalism—are marvelously recreated in this historical novel of the Gilded Age.

Death of a Healer
by Paul Henry Young

Diehard romanticist and surgeon extraordinaire, Jake Gibson, struggles to preserve his professional oath against the avarice and abuse of power so prevalent in present-day America.

Jake's personal quest is at direct odds with a group of sinister medical and legal practitioners determined to destroy his beloved profession. Events quickly spin out of control when Jake uncovers a nationwide plot by hospital executives to eliminate patient groups in order to improve the bottom line. With the lives of his family on the line, Jake invokes a self-imposed exile as a missionary doctor and rediscovers his lifelong obsession to be a trusted physician.

This compelling tale stunningly exposes the darker side of the medical world in a way nonfiction could never accomplish and clearly places the author into the spoltlight as one of America's premier writers of medical thrillers.

The Serial Killer's Diet Book
by Kenvin Mark Postupack

Fred Orbis is fat—very fat—which is an ideal qualification for his job as editor of *Feast Magaine,* a periodical for gourmands. But Fred daydreams of being an internationally renowned author, existential philosopher, râconteur and lover of beautiful women. In his longing to be thin he will discover the ultimate diet.

Devon DeGroot is one of New York's finest with a bright gold shield. His lastest case is a homicidal maniac who's prowling the streets of Manhattan with meatballs, bologna and egg salad—and taunting him about the body count in *Finnegans Wakean.*

Darby Montana is heiress to the massive Polk's Peanut Roll fortune. As one of the world's richest women she can have anything her heart desires—except for a new set of genes to alter a face and a body so homely not even plastic surgery could help. Then she meets Mr. Monde.

Elizabeth Aphelion is a poet, but her "day job" is cleaning apartments. Her favorite client, Mr. Monde, lives in a modest brownstone on East 54th Street. Elizabeth would sell her soul to quit cleaning toilets and get published.

Mr. Monde is the Devil in the market for a soul or two.

It's a Faustian satire on God and the Devil, Heaven and Hell, beauty, literature and the best-seller list.

What Goes Around
by Don Goldman

Ray Banno was vice president of a large California bank when his boss, Andre Rhodes, framed him for bank fraud.

Ten years later, with a different identity and face, Banno has made a new life for himself as a medical research scientist. He's on the verge of finding a cure for a deadly disease when he's chosen as a juror in the bank fraud trial of Andre Rhodes, and Banno knows the case is so complex he can easily influence the other jurors. Should he take revenge?

Meanwhile, Rhodes is about to gain financial control of Banno's laboratory for the purpose of destroying Banno's work. Treatment, rather than a cure, is much more lucrative—for Rhodes.

Banno's ex-wife, Misty, who is now married to Rhodes, discovers Banno's secret. She has her own agenda and needs Banno's help. The only way she can get it is by blackmail.

It's a maze of deceit, treachery and non-stop action, revolving around money, sex and power.

Mr. Irrelevant
by Jerry Marshall

Sports writer Paul Tenkiller and pro-football player Chesty Hake have been roommates for eight career seasons. Paul's Choctaw background of poverty and his gambling on sports, and Hake's dark memories of his mother being killed are the forces which will make their friendship go horribly wrong.

Chesty Hake, the last man chosen in the draft, has been dubbed Mr. Irrelevant. By every yardstick, he should not be playing pro football. But, because of his heart and high threshold for pain, he perseveres.

Paul Tenkiller has been on a gravy train because of Hake's generosity. Gleaning information vital to gambling on football, his relationship with Hake is at once loyal and deceitful.

Then during his eighth and final season, Hake slides into paranoia and Tenkiller is caught up in the dilemma. But Paul is behind the curve, and events spiral out of his control, until the bloody end comes in murder and betrayal.

Opal Eye Devil
by John Hamilton Lewis

From the teeming wharves of Shanghai to the stately offices of New York and London, schemes are hammered out to bankrupt opponents, wreck inventory, and dynamite oil wells. It is the age of the Robber Baron—a time when powerful men lie, steal, cheat, and even kill in their quest for power.

Sweeping us back to the turn of the twentieth century, John Lewis weaves an extraordinary tale about the brave men and women who risk everything as the discovery of oil rocks the world.

Follow Eric Gradek's rise from Northern Star's dark cargo hold to the pinnacle of high stakes gambling for unrivaled riches.

Aided by his beautiful wife, Katheryn, and the devoted Tong-Po, Eric fights for his dream and for revenge against the man who left him for dead aboard Northern Star.

Roadhouse Blues
by Baron Birtcher

From the sun-drenched sand of Santa Catalina Island to the smoky night clubs and back alleys of West Hollywood, Roadhouse Blues is a taut noir thriller that evokes images both surreal and disturbing.

Newly retired Homicide detective Mike Travis is torn from the comfort of his chartered yacht business into the dark, bizarre underbelly of LA's music scene by a grisly string of murders.

A handsome, drug-addled psychopath has reemerged from an ancient Dionysian cult, leaving a bloody trail of seemingly unrelated victims in his wake. Despite departmental rivalries that threaten to tear the investigation apart, Travis and his former partner reunite in an all-out effort to prevent more innocent blood from spilling into the unforgiving streets of the City of Angels.

Tunnel Runner
by Richard Sand

A fast-paced and deadly espionage thriller, peopled with quirky and most times vicious characters, this is a dark world where murder is committed and no one is brought to account; where loyalties exist side-by-side with lies and extreme violence.

Ashman—"the hunter, the hero, the killer"—is a denizen of that world who awakens to find himself paralyzed in a mental hospital. He escapes and seeks vengeance, confronting his old friends, the Pentagon, the Mafia, and a mysterious general who is covering up the attack on TWA Flight 800.

People begin to die. There are shoot-outs and assassinations. A woman is blown up in her bathtub.

Ashman is cunning and ruthless as he moves through the labyrinth of deceit, violence, and suspicion. He is a tunnel runner, a ferret in the hole, who needs the danger to survive, and hates those who have made him so.

It is this peculiar combination of ruthlessness and vulnerability that redeems Ashman as he goes for those who want him dead. Join him.